The Steel Within

A novel by S. R. Kent

The Steel Within

2nd Edition 2023

CHAPTER 1

The wipers swept back and forth, clearing the drizzling rain from the windshield. Up ahead, the traffic light flipped from green to yellow. Ben slowed, shifting down through the gears, his hands and feet working together in harmony until the BMW crawled to a stop. A white Altima pulled up alongside; behind the wheel was an attractive woman with long auburn hair. He glanced over, his eyes briefly meeting hers; she smiled, obviously drawn by what his wife had referred to as his sly, rugged good looks. He briefly wondered if those rugged looks appeared more rugged than usual. With that solemn thought and a bow of his head, he deliberately began to stare in the other direction. The only thing of interest to him at the moment was the contents of the brown paper bag in the passenger seat beside him. The fifth of Jim Beam he'd purchased from Harlan's liquor store had slid partially out of the bag, as if trying to escape its confines.

The light changed and Ben unconsciously resumed the route back to his home on Forest Drive. He was oblivious to the sounds of the wipers and the particular rhythm they made or even the drum of the tires on the rain-drenched road. The sodium-colored light of the various stores, fast-food joints, and gas stations reflected off the windshield, but his mind registered none of it. Today had been a difficult day, one of the worst he could remember in a while. Not as bad as that Sunday morning in May. Not by a long shot.

Nothing compared to that one.

That was the morning a deputy appeared at his door to give him the kind of news that some never recover. He still didn't know if he would.

Through the rain, he glanced up at the red traffic light, and sighed impatiently. His eyes caught the glint of the gold from the wedding band on his finger. Pulling his hand from the wheel, he began staring at it, turning his hand front to back, as if mesmerized by the ring's reflection. The frown he wore deepened, and he took a deep breath. He thought about taking it off, but the fleeting inclination was quickly banished.

A blare from the car horn behind him startled him back to reality. The light had changed to green. Allowing his thoughts to clear, Ben slipped the car into gear and let off the clutch, much as he had done a million times before, but in his haste, let off too quickly. The car lurched forward and stalled. He was instantly greeted with three more long blasts from the late model, green Oldsmobile behind him.

"I know, I know, for crying out loud!" Ben shouted into the rearview mirror. Just for a moment, it frightened him to realize he didn't recognize the face staring back at him. His features had become harsh and ugly. It took only an extra moment to restart the engine. He revved the accelerator a few times before letting off the clutch and easing it through the intersection. The green Oldsmobile passed him seconds later, the driver laying on the horn one final time while hanging his arm out the window, giving Ben a one-finger wave for good measure.

"Nice. Thank you very much," Ben said, the harsh sarcasm in his voice doing little to calm the sudden storm inside. Then it erupted, an anger, flaming hot, like he'd never felt before. An inconsolable rage, springing to the surface like a powerful geyser. Ben gritted his teeth, gripping the steering wheel so tightly that his knuckles turned white. He pushed the gas pedal to the floor, feeling the nose of the car dip as he sped after the offender. The muted taillights of the green Oldsmobile became visible though the rain-drenched windshield. His thoughts became twisted into a blinding hatred. In his mind, he saw it all clearly. He would force the Oldsmobile off the road, pull the idiot out of his car (Ben hadn't seen the man clearly, but was certain he would be some dim-witted, white-trash, country-music-listening, lunatic with a red and white Budweiser can clutched in his fist) and, as his father would've said, 'Beat the ever-living piss' out of him. Ben envisioned it all, especially what he would say while holding the Oldsmobile guy by his stained t-shirt.

"I just buried my wife and kids not too long ago, so I have very little patience for morons like you," he would say. *"My wife and oldest daughter were lucky, they died instantly. But I got to witness my youngest suffer and die after being burned alive in the crash. She survived for almost four hours. She looked like a burnt roast. Can you believe that? I couldn't even recognize my baby girl anymore, and all I could do was sit there and watch her die. How'd you like to go through something like that? So, whattya think, maybe next time you might consider cutting me a little slack!"*

Then he would pummel the man with a series of

heavy lefts and rights. In his mind, Ben would strike the man so hard his head would rock back and forth violently, like some over-exaggerated fight scene from Rocky. Having little to no experience with boxing, or even fist-fighting for that matter, the movies were pretty much his only means of reference. Finally, he would swing upwards, catch the guy with a solid upper cut, send him flying through the air, and landing on top of the hood of the Olds, sprawled out and unconscious.

It was all so glorious.

Ben pulled even with the green Oldsmobile. He kept a tight grip on the steering wheel, ready to ram him, but spied something that instantly smothered the rage inside of him. Behind the wheel was a nervous-looking young man, a kid really, in his early twenties. In the back, a child strapped into a booster seat. The girl appeared to be no older than his daughter, Tia.

Tia.

A vision of the wreckage filled his mind. He could see what was left of the melted plastic car seat. He saw the charred figure in the hospital, the respirator moving up and down, pumping oxygen into her small body.

And remembered the revulsion he felt.

You wanted her to die. You couldn't stand the sight of that burnt form—your daughter—in that hospital room. You prayed to God she would die. You prayed she would die so you wouldn't have to look at—

"Shut up!" he screamed. A quick sob escaped him as the grief and guilt tried to envelope him. His foot left the accelerator, and the car began to slow. Without thinking, he turned into a parking lot. As he sat slumped in the seat, he felt a terrible agony living, growing, and tearing him apart.

"I can't take anymore!" he cried out. All he wanted, all he prayed for now, was escape. Escape from the excruciating pain that dominated every fiber of his being. In his life before this tragedy, he would have scoffed at the idea that emotional pain could match, or even exceed, any form of physical pain. Now he had no doubt which was worse. It was an unseen wound which cut far deeper than any knife. It touched every sense, dominated every thought, every feeling. And it could not be consoled.

Peering over the steering wheel, he gazed out over the parking lot. There was a U-Haul place with a dozen rental trucks and trailers parked in a row. Next to that was a large, white propane tank, twelve feet tall, which dominated the far end of the lot. It was guarded only by a chain-link fence enclosure. After a moment, he decided he recognized the place; he'd often come here to refill the tank for his grill. He sat upright. The propane tank was about fifty yards away, and he was certain he could get up enough speed to crash through the fence, rupture the tank, and create an explosion.

It's late, there's no one around to get hurt, he thought. *The building would catch hell and would most likely damage a few of the rental trucks. Then again, who cares? What are they going to do, arrest me? It's not like I'll be around to care.*

The idea began to grow. There was a fitting symmetry to it, similar to the manner in which his family had died. Granted, it wasn't a truck hauling gasoline, but the results would be the same. Ben gunned the engine, holding the clutch to the floor. It would be all over in a matter of seconds. No more pain. No more suffering. No more guilt. Then a clear, vivid vision of his late wife, Rebecca—Becca, as he called her—came full into his mind. He saw her face. Her deep blue eyes. Her long brunette hair, and the smile he knew so well. It distracted him for a moment. He pushed the vision away and tried to refocus. And yet, she remained.

You can't do this.

It was his voice.

It was her voice.

The engine continued to roar, but the conflict within him had spread. He wanted relief, and he could have it. It was as simple as allowing his foot to slip from the clutch.

You can't do it, Ben.

This time it was her voice, soft and soothing. He wanted to believe it was her. More than anything, he wanted to believe. Was it possible she was speaking to him from across whatever dimensions that separated the living from the dead?

"Becca!" He said aloud, his face turned towards the roof of the BMW, as if doing so would help his voice find its way to her. "Give me one good reason why." With a pause, he added softly, "God, I miss you so much."

What seemed like an eternity passed, but he never received an answer. Her voice had gone silent. After several long moments he began to calm down. He couldn't do it. For her sake, he couldn't.

"Sorry, Ben, you don't get to take the easy way out," he said with a dry voice. "Guess you're gonna have to find a way to make it through on your own."

The rest of the drive home was a blank, but in a way, he felt as if he'd been pulled back from some sort of edge. It had done little to ease the pain inside of him, but he felt stronger somehow. It was a cliff he hoped he would never have to face again.

Pulling into the driveway, he noted the absence of light at the neighbor's house. Jim and Megan Haslett had been neighbors for five years. Their home was identical to his, except reversed, like two hands held side by side. It was obvious that the two homes were built by the same contractor.

Still feeling a little shaken from his earlier emotional struggle, Ben eased himself out of the car, then leaned back to retrieve the bottle of Jim Beam from the passenger seat. He caught himself glancing at the neighbor's house again. It was odd Megan wasn't there. Jim, you never knew, but Megan was always home by this hour. Then again, things had been a bit erratic over at the Haslett homestead as of late. He was beginning to wonder if there might be a problem. He could care less about Jim. They weren't that close of friends. In fact, he didn't care for him at all. But Megan was different. His wife and daughters had adored her, considered her family, and Ben owed her a debt of gratitude for helping him through the worst part of the funeral arraignments. At that most difficult time, Megan made decisions for him when he was completely unable.

To the right were his other neighbors. Larry and Amy Snider. They were a slightly older couple. They occupied a midsized, bi-level ranch with attached garage. Ben did his best not to notice but could clearly see Larry beneath the hood of his faded blue, ancient-looking, pickup. Even as old as it was, the 1967 GMC pickup Larry had inherited from his father ran like new. It wasn't because Larry was an auto mechanic of any sort, or even into old cars, he just loved to tinker on that truck. Larry was the best kind of friend Ben could ask for, and the only real fault Ben could find with the man was the fact he was a Spartan fan, and that was partly due to the fact that his son was currently enrolled at the university in East Lansing.

As Ben walked back towards his own house, he noticed Larry had taken a break. He was watching Ben steadily while wiping the dirt and grease from his hands with a shop rag. After a moment, Larry gave him an obliging wave. Ben nodded in acknowledgement. After another uneasy moment, Larry stuck his head back under the hood and resumed his tinkering. Ben sighed with relief; as much as he liked Larry, he didn't want any company tonight. He was fairly sure Larry knew that, too.

Once inside, Ben glanced up the stairs. There was a small moment, just an instant, when he actually believed the girls would come bounding down to greet him. An acute pain stabbed his heart as he realized they would never do that again. Their bodies lay buried in a cemetery twenty miles away. He could still see them clearly. Teresa, who looked and sometimes even acted so much like her mother, would've turned ten in September. Tia, only six, had inherited his green eyes and always seemed to know exactly what to say to cheer him up, especially when he got to be 'a bit grumpy,' as she put it.

Dropping his keys in the bowl on the small table next to the door, he stopped. A telephone table was what Becca called it. He smiled, thinking about the argument (if you could call it that) they'd had about the stupid, spindle-legged thing that sat next to the door.

"Why do they call it a Telephone Table when it doesn't

have a telephone on it?" Ben asked.

"Well, for most people, it's where the telephone would be," Becca replied with a half-serious tone and her blue eyes flashing.

"How come we don't put our phone on it, then?" he asked, only in an attempt to get a rise out of her.

"Because, as you know, ours is a cordless and it sits in the living room. Does it really matter if it has a phone on it or not? I mean, it's useful for putting keys and mail and stuff. I like it!" she said with a crooked grin, knowing a smart-ass comment was coming next.

"Then, how come it's not called a 'Keys and Stuff Table' instead? I don't know, I just don't like to be confused like that," he replied with a straight face.

Becca broke into a full grin, grabbed him, and locked her arms around him. "Oh, shut up and stop being so aggravating, will you?" she said, and kissed him hard.

He was standing in the same spot they'd kissed that afternoon. How long ago had that been? A year… maybe two. This place was full of those kinds of memories, small things, some nearly forgotten. They had the ability to pop out of nowhere and cut him.

Turning from that spot, he headed directly for the kitchen. He grabbed a glass tumbler from the cupboard and filled it with ice. His hands were shaking slightly, holding the glass in one hand and the whiskey bottle in the other, as he marched deliberately into the living room. He didn't normally drink whiskey. A few beers were his norm. He hadn't consumed hard liquor since his college days, and even then, he was a lightweight. Tonight, he wasn't about to let any of that stop him. He was desperate to kill the pain, and he would drink the entire bottle if that's what it took.

Ben sat the whiskey on the table next to his recliner and flipped on the stereo. It was tuned to a country music station, no doubt left there by Becca. There was a moment of recognition; the band was one of his wife's favorites, though he couldn't recall the name. He generally abhorred all forms Country music. To him, it sounded like someone trying to pull the tail off of a cat while beating on a washtub. Classic Rock was his favorite, but he found as he got older, he could endure a bit of some of the other stuff, even Jazz and Classical if he were in the right mood. However, Country wasn't something he could handle for very long. Becca loved the stuff and tortured him with it whenever she had the chance. Out of respect for his wife, he would often close his mouth and endure it. Through time, he realized that there were a few tunes he could appreciate. This was one of the very few on that list.

One more day…

One more time…

One more sunset, maybe I'd be satisfied.

But then again—

There it was again. Another memory. Another cut. He felt as if he were trapped in a torture chamber, like something out of a tale by Edgar Allen Poe. It was a slow death of a thousand cuts with every memory containing its own sharp, jagged edge in which to slice him.

He snapped the radio off in disgust, wondering if there would ever be a time when he could listen to the radio without thinking of her. He sank into his recliner and began to stare at the bottle of whiskey as if it were something immoral. He'd convinced himself that buying it was purely for medicinal purposes. A form of liquid Novocain if you like. Shortly after the accident, his sister had convinced him to see a doctor. He was prescribed some heavy-duty anti-depressants, and he still had a whole bottle of them stored in the medicine cabinet, but he despised the pills. He took them the first few weeks following the funeral, then quit them altogether. They made him feel disconnected, as if he were wrapped in cellophane. Not that the whiskey could be dissimilar in nature, but at least he was familiar with the effects of the alcohol, and it wouldn't turn him into a damn zombie at the same time.

I really should eat something. He considered the thought for a moment but shook his head. Ben opened the bottle, pouring the contents over the ice until the glass was three-quarters full. Lifting the glass to his lips, he hesitated, gearing up, before taking a sip. It burned as it went down, but immediately began to warm his insides. He turned the glass in his hand, inspecting the amber liquid that remained, then downed the rest of it.

As Pink Floyd might say, the goal for the night is to be comfortably numb. No more thoughts or memories tonight. And no more nightmares. Please, God, not that nightmare again.

The nightmare was always the same. That morning, a dire warning would be ringing in his ears as he shot out of bed. He would scramble after them, driving his BMW as fast as it would go. Tom Petty would be blaring on the radio, telling him that he was 'Running Down a Dream.' Every time, he would get within sight of the minivan Becca was driving. But time would slow, his BMW would disappear around him until only he remained, flying through the air, with that damn song still playing in his head as he is flung into the fiery explosion along with them. It was only a dream, but it always seemed so real. He told Larry about it once. He believed it might be associated with some kind of latent guilt and Ben's desire to undo the tragedy. Ben didn't know about that. All he knew was he hated feeling helpless, never being able to reach them in time.

Ben leaned back and closed his eyes. Despite his desire to be free of his memories, he found himself drifting back to the day he had met his wife at a party thirteen years ago. Once the memories began, he was powerless to stop them. He poured another drink, filling it to the top, and surrendered to the memories.

Ben wiped the sweat from his eyes and returned to painting the exterior trim on the second story window. It was his final year at Western Michigan University, finishing his Engineering degree. He painted houses during the summer to pick up extra cash. It wasn't his idea of a great job, but the money would help pay for rent and tuition. It wouldn't be so bad except he was working for a meager wage (all under the table), and it was the hottest summer in remembrance, or maybe it just seemed that way. Still, it wasn't all bad. It was a job, and he got to work with Alex, a buddy of his. In reality, Alex didn't do that much actual work. Then again, he didn't necessarily have to.

"Hey, are you almost done?" Alex called up.

"Just about. Why?"

"Because Trapper's throwing a party and I want to head over there."

"Christ, Alex, we can't just up and leave."

Alex smiled. "Sure, we can. It's Friday. Nobody works

late on a Friday. Besides, my dad's the boss, what's he going to do to me?"

"It's not you I'm worried about," Ben mumbled under his breath as he descended the ladder. If there was one thing he knew, it was no use arguing with Alex once he'd set his mind to something. Besides, it was hot, and a cold beer sounded awfully good right about now.

Alex put his arm around him. "Oh, stop worrying so much, will you. Let's go have some fun."

Ben shrugged and relented. "Alright, but I'd need to run back to my place and get cleaned up first."

"We haven't got time, old buddy. Besides, you look fine," Alex said, and then ruffled Ben's hair with his hand and laughed. "You might want to wash your hair later because you've got paint in it. Makes you look like you frosted your hair."

John Trapero, AKA Trapper, had a house near campus. Trapper was notorious for his parties. Normally, they were pretty good, drawing in a good crowd from campus, and even a few that weren't. The funny thing was Trapper didn't attend Western. This party would no doubt be smaller than usual as many of the students were home for the summer.

Ben parked his beat-up, oil guzzling, black Ford Ranger across the street from Trapper's house, telling himself it would be worth it to grab a couple beers and check out the females in attendance, not that today would be the best chance to 'chat one up' as the Brit's might say. He was secure in his looks; he wasn't Hollywood handsome, but certainly had his good points. He had strong features with his light brown hair and green eyes. But today, being sweaty and dirty with paint spattering covering his entire body, today was not the day.

Alex pulled up in his gold firebird, packing directly behind Ben. There were times when Ben felt a little jealous of Alex. It was easy to do, considering Alex got everything he wanted from his parents, while Ben had to scrimp and save just to make it to the end of the week. However, when it came down to it, he felt sorry for Alex because, even with all the riches of his family, he didn't appear to have a clear direction. Ben, at least, knew what he wanted to do with his life. Since he was a child, he'd loved to design and build things. He imagined the grand things which he hoped would change the world. His dream of obtaining a degree was within sight, while Alex was only concerned with the next party.

"Come on, Benji, old pal," Alex said, bounding towards him, grabbing his arm, and pulling him along. "We're gonna have us a good time."

"Don't call me that," Ben said, pulling his arm out of Alex's grip, "You know I hate that."

"Okay, okay... Ben," Alex replied, putting on a mock seriousness which quickly evaporated. "C'mon, you're not going to stay mad at me all night, are you?" Alex asked, spreading his arms, and shrugging his shoulders with a goofy grin covering his face.

Ben couldn't help but laugh. "No, I guess not. Let's go, you bastard."

As they entered Trapper's, the sound of the loud, thumping music flooded their ears, making it difficult to talk without shouting. Dozens of people were already present, spilled out among the living room, dining room and kitchen. Little clumps of them were scattered about, talking, laughing, and drinking. Ben wasn't the least bit surprised, even though it was still quite early.

Alex tapped Ben on the shoulder and pointed to the

stairs. It was easy to figure out that Alex meant. He was going to find Trapper, which wasn't unusual. Probably to smoke a joint. That wasn't Ben's thing, not that he condemned the practice.

Ben nodded and Alex left, moving through the mass of people, and sprinting up the staircase. Ben headed straight for the beer. In the kitchen, he grabbed two, opened one and drained it quickly. It felt cool on his throat and had an immediate effect of making him feel better.

A couple more like that and I won't worry about going home, *he thought.*

Opening his second beer, Ben ambled towards the living room, and began looking for a familiar face among the crowd. After a few minutes, he settled by the arch dividing the living room and the dining room. Almost immediately, he spied a group of girls by the couch. What caught his eye was the one in the middle. She was wearing a flowered patterned summer dress, and had long, dark hair that hung down to the middle of her back. As if feeling his eyes on her, she turned and caught him staring. Thinking quickly, he gave her his best smile, and raised his beer to her. She smiled back and raised her drink to him.

When she smiled, he could have sworn the whole room lit up.

His first instinct was to talk to her. But then he looked down at the paint on his shirt. It quickly deflated him. A sharp realization hit him; she'd probably smiled because he looked at bit comical.

I knew I should've gone home and cleaned up first, *he thought. It was too late to make a good impression. Dispirited, he went outside and plopped down on the front porch step. He sat there, sipping his beer, watching the cars pass. It wasn't entirely clear to him why he hadn't just gone home.*

"Hey, I wondered what happened to you," he heard. "You come out here to be alone?"

Following the sound of the voice, he craned his neck to look behind him. It was the girl with the dark hair. She smiled and he had the same sensation, like as if the world had been in black and white his whole life, and now, it was suddenly in full, bright, blinding colors.

"Oh...um, hello! I just thought—" He took a breath and tried to start over. "Actually, I was a little embarrassed because I came here straight from work, and, as you can see." He held out his shirt and then pointed to his hair.

She stepped down and sat down next to him, looking him over. "Doesn't bother me," she said, staring at him as if she were still appraising him. "At least you're willing to work. Besides, I liked your smile," she paused, and then added, "and your eyes, there's something about your eyes." Then she laughed. "You really have to do something about your hair."

He grinned, ran his hand through his hair, and laughed, too.

"I'm Rebecca, by the way," she said. "And you are?"

"I'm, uh, Ben. Ben Stryker," he stuttered ungracefully. "I'm sorry, Rebecca. I'm not exactly on my A-game tonight."

"You are forgiven. I'm not really a game player anyway. I kind of like it, you know, seeing you with your defenses down," she said with a half-grin, leaning in on him just a bit and bumping his shoulder.

"Ah! So, you think that you can take advantage of me, huh? You women are all the same. Only thinking of one thing," he teased. "I have to warn you, I'm not that easy."

"Oh yeah. I'm pretty sure I can get what I want."

"I'm stronger than you think," he replied with mock

defiance. "Don't think for a minute that you can use your beauty and feminine wiles to lure me in."

"We'll see about that," she said, and laughed a kind of dirty laugh that he liked.

"But I don't even know you," he said, still playing.

There was a seriousness that came over her. "I think you do, Ben Stryker, whether you believe it or not. And somehow, I know you, too," she said softly, and then leaned over and kissed him.

The next morning, he awoke with the light streaming through the window of his little studio apartment. He glanced over; Rebecca was asleep, snuggled close, her hair covering a portion of her face. She was snoring just a little, not a loud snore, but a slight one that he thought was endearing. There was also the realization he was already falling for her.

Be careful not to get too attached just yet, Ben. *His heart cautioned.* When she wakes, she could be up and gone.

He shook the thought away, unwilling to face that reality.

Not yet anyway.

Gently, he moved the hair from her face and put it behind her ear. Rebecca's eyes fluttered. They opened for just a moment, and then closed again. Slowly, she slid her arm around him and squeezed tighter to him.

"Good morning. Didn't mean to wake you," he whispered. "Would you like some coffee?"

"Mm... yeah, okay," Rebecca replied drowsily.

He started to get up; she used her arm to hold him down.

"No, I don't want you to get up," she said, and held him tighter.

"Well, that'll make getting the coffee a little more difficult."

Quite deftly, she jumped on top of him and pinned him down. She was suddenly fully awake and had a firm hold on him.

"Nope, no coffee, just you," she said playfully. The smile on her face made his heart leap. He didn't think he'd ever been this happy, this content, with anyone. She put her face near his with her hair hanging down around both of their faces. She rubbed her nose on his, then kissed him. Still smiling, she looked deep into his eyes. "I really do like your eyes. You have the greenest eyes I've ever seen," she said, holding his gaze. Then she rose up while sitting on him. "I want to know everything there is to know about you. I shan't let you up until you do."

He laughed a bit. "Shan't? Is that even a real word?"

Raising an eyebrow and narrowing her eyes, she cast him a stern look. "Quit stalling. Tell me everything."

"Well, it's a little difficult for me to concentrate with you sitting naked on me like this."

Rebecca looked down for a moment and considered this for a second. "Oh, I think you'll be alright," she said.

"Where do you want me to start?"

"At the beginning, of course."

"In the beginning, God created the heavens and the earth."

She pinched him on the side.

"Ouch! Okay, okay, I give. I was born here in Kalamazoo. My father, Richard Stryker works for Auto-Specialties as a production supervisor of some sort, I'm not even sure. My mother is a teacher at Vicksburg High School. She teaches history." Ben hesitated, giving her a pained look.

"What?" Rebecca asked, catching the strained look on

his face. "You're not embarrassed your mom is a teacher, are you?

"Oh, no, nothing like that. It's just that—" He stopped. "Okay, now, don't laugh. It's just that my mother, well, she's always loved history, and it's had a kind of an effect," he said.

Rebecca shook her head. "I don't understand."

He frowned. "I have a brother and sister, you see. My older brother's name is Thomas Paine Stryker. My younger sister's name is Abigail Adams Stryker."

A sudden realization broached her face. "You mean?"

He nodded.

"So, you're..." A crack of a grin slowly began climbing one side of her mouth. "Benjamin Franklin!"

He was still nodding. She tried to maintain a straight face, but finally it broke.

She was laughing.

They were both laughing.

The next morning, Ben awoke to a dry mouth and terrible headache. His first attempts to get out of the recliner made his head pulsate angrily. He decided to lean back and closed his eyes instead. This seemed to be the least offensive position to keep his head from banging like a drum and his stomach from acting so volatile.

"Lord, what did I do?" he said aloud. Lately, he found himself talking to himself quite a bit. Under normal circumstances it might have concerned him. He glanced over and picked up the whiskey bottle. It was half-empty. Funny thing was, he couldn't remember drinking that much of it. His stomach lurched again, and he fought the urge to vomit. "Next time we eat something first," he said, bending forward, putting his head in his hands, and wondering who "we" he was referring to. The thought quickly disappeared as his stomach gave another lurch. He covered his mouth and ran for the bathroom.

Later, Ben wandered into the kitchen. He automatically went to the fridge and glanced inside. There was an open package of bologna, a half-gallon of milk, a pound of hamburger, a few slices of cheese, and not much more. He wasn't hungry even though he should've been. His stomach roiled at the thought of food. He closed the refrigerator and began to stare out the kitchen window. It had a view which overlooked the lake. Becca loved the view, especially in the morning. One of the main reasons they had bought the place was because of that particular view. She said it was mesmerizing to watch the sparkling reflection of the sun on the rippling water. For several minutes he stood there, hoping somehow it would bring her back to him. As frightening as it was to hear her voice last night, he longed to hear it again, that some kind of connection or thought could give him an answer. Give him some measure of relief.

He felt none.

I need to get out of here. This place isn't doing me any good. He considered his options. *Can't go to work; couldn't concentrate if I wanted to. I could go to Tom's, but he lives in Chicago. Don't really want to go that far. Can rule out Abby while I'm at it; love her to death, and I know she's only an hour away, but I really couldn't take any more of her polite sympathies right now. I just need to get out of this house for a while.*

He thought of Larry. Suddenly, he needed his

friend's company. Larry wouldn't badger him or ask him questions. More than likely, they would limit their conversation to hockey, baseball, or football. He didn't care, just as long as he wasn't alone right now. He ran to the living room and threw back the curtains. He was in time to watch Larry jump in his old GMC truck and leave for work.

A sort of panic was beginning to develop inside of him.

Come on, Ben, get a grip, you can handle this. Just start your day as if it's any other day.

Still rattled, Ben went back into the kitchen to make coffee. He stood over the coffeemaker, gripping the countertop, waiting for it to brew and for the sense of anxiety to pass. After a bit, he chanced a walk outside to get the newspaper. The fresh air helped steady him. The trees were changing, the leaves turning into the wonderful fall colors of red, gold, and brown. Stopping short of the mailbox, he saw Megan's car in the driveway next door. Ben reached in and grabbed the paper, still looking in the direction of Jim and Megan's house. Something strange was going on. Jim's car was gone while Megan's sat alone in the drive. Megan usually left before him in the morning.

Jim Haslett was a trial lawyer. A good one if you listened to him talk. His practice had taken off in the last few years. He once bragged that he was making so much money that he wasn't sure how to spend it all. The odd thing was, in the five years they lived next door, Jim had never left this early in the morning. On the other hand, Megan worked as a secretary (or as she insisted, an executive assistant) and was always gone before eight every morning. He looked down at his watch; it was a quarter to nine.

"Maybe her car wouldn't start?" he said to himself. There was no real reason to believe it, but it made little difference. It really wasn't any of his business. Megan and his wife had been especially close friends. He'd often thought it an unlikely friendship as they were completely different in both looks and personality. Both were striking in their appearance, Becca with dark hair, and Megan with golden blonde. However, Becca was an extrovert, always on the go, and usually let her opinions be known, whereas Megan often remained easy-going, and more of a homebody. Maybe it was their differences that allowed them to become so close. He wasn't sure. When Becca and the girls died, Megan had been there to help him. If it hadn't been for her, well, he was certain that he never would've gotten through the funeral arraignments.

Ben settled into the recliner with his coffee and paper. The coffee helped with his headache, but his stomach felt like someone had punched him several times in the gut. He flipped the paper open. The latest political news from the election filled the front page.

"Uh, way too early for that," he said, skipping directly to the sport section. Before finishing, he heard the doorbell. Ben sat the paper aside and stood; little dark spots appeared before his eyes. He held onto the side of the chair and waited for his head to clear before proceeding to the door.

When he opened it, he found Megan. Her face was wet with tears.

CHAPTER 2

"Hi, Ben," Megan said in a voice not much louder than a whisper. "Can I come in?"

"Oh, uh, sure, sure. Come on in," he said. "I'm sorry, I was just—" *trying to figure out what's wrong,* he finished inside of his head. Megan didn't seem to notice. She stepped inside while Ben closed the door after her.

"Um, Megan. Are you okay?" he asked.

Megan shook her head. "Jim and I are separated," she blurted out. "You wouldn't happen to have anything to drink, would you?"

"I just made a fresh pot of coffee. Do you want some?" Her frown deepened. She shook her head. It dawned on him that she meant a real drink. "I don't think I have any wine or anything like that," he said. "Um... you don't drink whiskey, do you?" He pointed apprehensively to the bottle of Jim Beam on the table. Megan didn't seem the type to have a lot of experience with hard liquor. Mixed drinks maybe, a rum and coke once in a while, but he didn't take her for someone to drink straight whiskey.

"That'll do," she replied. Without hesitation, she tipped back the bottle and took several gulps. She returned the cap and sat down on the couch, still clutching the bottle of Jim Beam.

"Holy—"

"Yeah, I know," she replied sadly. Then her face screwed up with pain and she sobbed, "What am I going to do?" She took another pull off the bottle, and then held it out to Ben.

Ben shook his head. His hand went automatically to his stomach. "I don't think that's such a good idea."

Megan held it out to him again, giving him a look of despondence that told him she didn't want to drink alone.

Sighing heavily, he took the bottle from her. "Oh, what the hell," Ben said while taking a deep breath. He took a small sip. His mouth began to sweat a bit and his stomach took a bit of a turn, but then it settled. After another moment or two, he actually began to feel better. He handed the bottle back to Megan. She stared at it with a faraway look in her eyes. Ben knew she wasn't really looking at the bottle. She wasn't looking at anything. He had done the same thing himself many times in the last few weeks.

"Do you want to talk about it?"

"Not yet," she replied without looking up. "When I —" she stopped short, "—when we've had a few more, I might. Of course, you might want to get another one of these first," she said, holding up the bottle, showing him how little of it was left.

"It's all a lie you know," Megan said, setting the freshly opened fifth of Kentucky bourbon on the floor in front of the couch. She shucked off her shoes and tucked her feet beneath her. "Jim is screwing someone else. I followed him last night. He took the little whore out to dinner, then went back to her place and stayed the night." When she said it, she sounded more defeated than angry.

"I'm sorry, I know that really has to hurt. Do you know her?" Ben asked. His mind reached out and tried to imagine how he would've felt if he had found out Becca was having an affair. It was difficult to do.

Megan sighed just a bit. "Yeah, I do. She works in the Prosecutor's Office, I think. She's a paralegal. I met her once. Jim introduced us—don't that figure." Her eyes were beginning to look a little glassy from the alcohol. "I probably shouldn't have followed them, but at least I know the truth." She picked up the bottle, took another drink then held it out for Ben to take. "Funny thing about the truth… it doesn't make you feel any better."

Ben poured himself a short one. He was out of ice, but that mattered little now.

"The truth is that my husband is a liar and a cheat," she continued. "The truth is I saw this coming and tried to deny it. The truth is that my marriage is over. The truth is that I feel like a part of me is dying." She hesitated before saying, "The truth is, despite everything, I can't convince my heart it's over."

Ben said nothing. There wasn't anything he could say to take away the pain she was going through. Instead, he held up the glass in a salute. "Prost!" he muttered absently.

Megan gave him a quizzical look. "Why do you say that?"

"You mean, Prost? Oh, just an old habit. My grandpa was part German. Growing up, we used to hear him say it. I guess it kind of stuck for some reason," he said chuckling. Megan smiled, but Ben could tell it was a forced smile. "Never mind. I'm sorry you have to go through this right now. I didn't realize you guys were having trouble."

"It's been going on for a little while now," Megan said. "At first, he complained about little things, wanted to blame me for everything. Then he began to grow increasingly distant. Most days, he didn't even want to touch me. I tried to talk to him about it, but he never wanted to. When we did talk, he would get angry. He began staying out late. When he did come home early, he was preoccupied with a case." She trailed off for a moment. "I knew I was losing him but didn't know what to do. I talked to Becky about some of it." Megan stopped. She seemed to be thinking.

"What did she say?" Ben asked.

"That's the funny part. She told me I should prepare for the worst. That if it did happen, I had to start thinking about myself and what is best for me." She looked right at Ben. "Then she told me, 'If the day comes and you need help, talk to Ben. I know he'll be there for you.' She said it as if she knew." Megan stopped, seeing the hurt in Ben's eyes. "I'm sorry, Ben, I didn't mean to— I miss her, too."

"Oh, it's okay. I'm good," he said, although his voice sounded a little dry. "Why don't we have another drink?" Ben poured another for himself, but before he could pass the bottle back, he found Megan's face had become scrunched up in agony. She began to cry in earnest, not just crying but bawling. Setting the bottle down, Ben sat beside her, putting his arm around her. After a few minutes, her crying slowed.

"You know, I am—glad that—you are here," Megan said, speaking between hitches and holding her breath lightly as she spoke, trying to get control. "It's just that —I lost Becky—and now Jim. It's just so hard. I don't know how you do it. Sometimes, I wish I could go back in time, and..." She was crying again. Ben put both arms around her and rocked her back and forth a bit to soothe her.

"I know," he said. "It isn't going to be easy, but we'll make it." He wasn't sure if he believed it, but it was all he had to hang on to. They would make it, somehow. The oddest part was he felt less alone now. In a way, sharing her pain helped take away from his own grief.

Grabbing a blanket from the closet, Ben covered Megan as she slept. She'd passed out on the couch. He had a feeling she was going to sleep for a while. She had gotten little sleep, had drank too much, and was emotionally overwhelmed. He thought about what Jim was doing to her and it made him angry.

What an Ass! He has a beautiful, intelligent wife that loves him, and he throws it all away. If he only knew what I'd give just to have my wife back, even for one second. Ben poured a cup of coffee and sat down at the kitchen table. He wanted to sober up. Besides, something Megan said earlier had stuck in his mind.

She'd said it as if she knew. As if she knew what? That she was going to die? That's crazy. Did she ever say anything like that to me? He tried to remember, but nothing came to him. It was difficult to remember anything clearly in the days leading up to and following the accident. He closed his eyes and tried harder to think.

She left early that Sunday morning to go to her parents

in Battle Creek. Her mother wasn't feeling well, and she was taking the girls with her. I was in bed; she kissed me and told me she loved me before she left. Can't remember why she didn't ask me to go. I was content to sleep in that morning. I was more than happy to keep my lazy ass in bed and sleep away the morning while my wife and children died. Died in those horrible flames. Except Tia. She suffered the most. And you had no answer except to wish she would die quickly so you wouldn't have to watch it anymore. You did it. You as much as killed them—killed your own family—when you allowed them to leave while you slept in that damn bed!

With a sudden burst of anger at himself, he threw the coffee cup at the wall; it shattered explosively against it. Suddenly, he remembered Megan asleep on the couch. He glanced into the living room. She remained sleeping, her knees tucked in front of her. It was easy to figure out why she was sleeping in that position; when the pain of everything you go through is too much, you try and make yourself into a ball. He could definitely understand; curl up and wait for everything to pass. That was the only defense the body had against the agony life handed out.

He picked up the pieces of the coffee cup and dumped them into the trash. Then he grabbed a dish towel and mopped the floor with it.

You know, you could have used the mop. That's if you knew where to find it, and you don't.

The mop? Why was it so difficult to remember where Becca kept it. He peered around the kitchen, and then thought of the basement. The door to the basement was adjacent to the kitchen along the rear hallway. He opened the door and flipped on the light switch. Sure enough, hanging inside the stairwell was the mop along with the broom and dustpan. It wasn't exactly clear to him why it had been so important for him to know where it was, but finding it gave him a small sense of relief. He held onto the door for a moment, looking down into the basement. Slowly, he began to descend the stairs. When he reached the bottom step, he sat, just gazing out at the empty space. When they'd bought the place, he bragged to Becca about how he was going to make it into a family room. That was nine years ago. In that time, he had put up three sections of drywall. The rest were bare walls and concrete, a testament to how little he'd actually accomplished. In truth, with work, family, school, running errands, Girl Scouts, conferences, vacations, and everything else, the basement project just never seemed to get done. Things happened. Life happened. Nine years of it. And now it seemed to have gone by so quickly. In an instant, everything changed, and he wished with all his might that he could have that time back again. It brought to mind an old song from his childhood that his mother had loved.

If I could save time in a bottle, he thought, his mind following the lyrics, *the first thing that I'd like to do—is to save everyday 'til eternity passes away just to spend them with you.*

He stopped and hung his head.

"But you can't," he said flatly. Megan told him she wished she could go back in time. He did too, more than anything, because if he could, he would stop them from ever getting in that minivan.

When Megan awoke, she found Ben asleep in the

recliner. Pulling herself up, she looked at the clock. It was already past five pm. She curled her legs under her and pulled the blanket around her. She wasn't cold, but it felt wonderfully warm and comforting. Her first thought was about Jim and the hurt inside was rekindled.

He doesn't love you anymore. She reminded herself. *He's in love with someone else. You mean nothing to him. After five years, I am just a pain-in-the-ass wife that begged him to keep our marriage together. Begged him to try. I know now that he'd decided long ago that it was over. I'm just finally realizing how over it is, and I'm the last one to know.* Megan tried to stop herself from going on, thinking these hurtful thoughts, but it was inevitable once she started. She could hear Jim's words in her head. *"I do love you, Megan. But I'm not sure I'm 'in love' with you anymore".* Of course, now she knew why. He was 'in love' with someone else. Suddenly, she hated Sabrina. The woman had stolen her husband, the only man she'd ever really loved, the man she had vowed to love and honor, shared her most personal hopes and dreams, and surrendered her heart unconditionally. A bitter hatred began to run through her. Had the woman been standing in front of her at that second, there was no doubt in her mind she would've scratched the eyes right out of her head.

How come I don't hate Jim that much? This is HIS doing. I want to hate him that much.

But she couldn't. Not yet. Her heart was unwilling to push him out completely. The only thing she wanted was for him to walk through the door and say that it was all a mistake, that he still loved her and wanted to make things work. She knew it was wrong to feel that way. Jim had betrayed her. Unfortunately, her heart did not want to hear that. Sometimes the heart clings to what it wants, no matter what the head is telling it.

Megan threw the blanket aside and got up. Her head began to swim just a bit. She regained her balance and went into the kitchen, refilling the coffee maker. Megan wondered how many times she had sat with Becky at this table and talked over a cup of coffee. Becky had been a big sister to her, or at least the closest thing to it. She had been an only child growing up.

The aroma of the coffee filled the kitchen. Megan could hear Ben stirring in the next room as she grabbed two cups from the cupboard. Ben was definitely getting out of the chair now and she could hear him cursing under his breath.

"You still take sugar in your coffee?" she asked as loudly as she could without making her head hurt.

"Yeah, thanks," she heard him reply.

Ben lumbered stiffly into the kitchen and sat down at the table. He was rubbing the back of his neck. Megan sat the coffee in front of him. He glanced noncommittally at it.

"Why were you sleeping in the chair? How come you didn't just go upstairs to bed?" she asked.

Ben opened his mouth, then closed it again. "I don't like sleeping up there. Usually, I bunk out on the couch." He took a small sip, and then sat his cup on the table and stared at it. "I tried, you know, the first few nights after... well, you know." He took a deep breath. "I go in there to get clothes and stuff, but don't like to spend a lot of time up there."

"And the girl's rooms?" Megan asked, not wanting to dig too deep, but still curious.

"Not once," he said.

"Eventually, you're going to have to take care of..." Megan groped for the right word, "things. You know, go through and pack things up. For now, it's all right if you don't want to. It can wait. When the time comes, I'll help you with it." He didn't say anything. She could tell it was still a delicate issue for him, so she tried to change the subject. "How long did I ramble on this morning? I don't quite remember everything I said."

"Oh, you were okay. Could've been a whole lot worse, I'm sure." Ben stopped himself, realizing that probably wasn't the most flattering way of putting it. "I didn't mean for it to sound that way. You know you can tell me anything and I won't—" again he stopped. "Well, you can talk to me anytime you want."

"Thanks, Ben. I'm not sure you could handle all of it."

"In the future, I'd appreciate it if you gave me more of a warning if you want to get trashed first thing in the morning," Ben said grinning.

"I don't normally do that. I guess I don't have to tell you that. It's just, well, there's so much hurt, and so many things." She took a breath, "So many dreams that are dying. I wanted so much to have a family."

"I thought you couldn't have kids?"

"I can," Megan said. "Jim was the one with the one with the problem."

"I'm sorry. Jim said... um... he made it sound as if you were the one." Ben grimaced, knowing he probably unintentionally revealed something rather sensitive. The deep frown on her face confirmed his fears. On the surface, it appeared that she was taking the news rather well, but wondered if it might ultimately cause an eruption of emotions.

"I didn't know he was doing that. Makes me wonder how many other people he told that lie. I guess it doesn't matter anymore. It just kind of pisses me off to think about it." After a few seconds she stood up, her eyes narrowed. Ben realized he was right. It wasn't fine. It was far from fine.

"Do you know, I tried everything I could to convince him to try artificial insemination... or adoption... or anything! And then to find out he's running around telling people it was my fault!" She was shaking with rage, the coffee cup gripped so tightly in her hands it looked as if it might break under the pressure.

"You can go ahead and throw it. I already broke one this morning."

Megan looked at the cup for a moment, then sat it back down on the table. The rage inside her appeared to shrink. She sat down. It was several moments before she spoke. "Did you have any idea how envious I was of you and Becky? You know how much I loved those girls. How much I loved having Teresa and Tia over to spend the night, thinking about the day my own little girl would grow up next door," she laughed, "being best friends," she said almost as an afterthought. "But now it's all gone. We both have lost so much." Megan grew angry at this thought. "Sometimes I just want to scream, why me?"

"I know," Ben said finally. "Life throws you for a gigantic loop, and you're left to deal with it. I think about how many car accidents there are every day." He shrugged. "Why did it have to be them? I know it's selfish, but I think, why couldn't it have been someone else's family? Why couldn't it be someone else that suffers this way? Why did it have to be Becca and the kids? I would've rather—" he stopped short. It would've sounded a little to cliché to say he would've rather died, even though it was true.

"Rather what?" Megan asked.

"Nothing, forget it," Ben said, waving his hand dismissively. He got up, poured some more coffee, and then motioned to Megan if she wanted some.

Megan shook her head. "No, thanks."

"You know," Ben said, sitting down again. "You're still quite young. What are you, twenty-four?"

"I happen to be twenty-five, if you must know," Megan said, trying to smile. It was the first one he'd seen from her in a while.

"All I meant was, you're still young and attractive," Ben continued. "There's still time for you to find someone and have what you want. I know it's probably hard to hear right now, seeing how you're just coming out of... well, you know what I mean."

Again, Megan frowned. "I do know what you mean, and I don't mean to sound harsh, but I don't want someone else. Not yet. It's difficult enough for me to think about the future, much less starting a new relationship. Everything seems so dark and empty, like going into a tunnel where you can only see a little bit of the light at the other end. I didn't... I still don't... want this divorce, even though I know it'll happen. Everything seems like such a blinding emotional pain."

"I'm sorry, Megan. I'm really good at sticking my foot in my mouth sometimes."

"No, that's alright. I'm glad to have someone to talk to about it." Megan glanced down at her hands, deep in thought. "Do you know what I'm afraid of? That I'll never love anyone that deeply ever again. That someday, I'll end up with somebody simply because I don't want to be alone. That seems so sad, don't you think? Do you worry about that, Ben?

He looked at her thoughtfully for a moment. "No, I don't. What does frighten me—what scares the crap out of me—is that once all the pain is gone, once there's nothing left, I'll never feel anything ever again."

CHAPTER 3

Ben awoke the next morning on the couch, yawning and stretching. He really did like the couch. It was what he thought of as a sleeping couch. It was large, fluffy, and comfortable. Becca had fought him on it. She had wanted the smaller one with matching chair.

"What good is a couch if you can't sleep on it?" he had complained. Becca tried to reason with him, but knowing her husband, she had relented. The memory made his heart ache with grief and longing.

Damn, I miss her.

He forced these feelings out of his mind. Pulling the curtain back, he noticed that Megan's car was gone.

I imagine she's gone to confront Jim. God, I hope that she gets through it alright.

He knew it was going to be difficult for her; it always is when your head and your heart are fighting for what it wants. Ultimately, Ben knew that her heart was going to lose, and thought that she knew that, too. The basic problem being, no matter how much you love someone, you can't make them love you back. The only option left is to let them go.

He went to the kitchen and started the coffeemaker going. On the stove were the leftovers from the previous night. Hamburger Helper and Tater Tots. It wasn't exactly a gourmet meal as the noodles came out a bit crunchy and the Tater Tots a little undercooked, but as far as he was concerned it hit the spot. Megan ate only a meager amount, claiming her stomach was still in knots. He seriously hoped it wasn't his cooking. She'd left after dinner, her demeanor still sullen. Ben honestly didn't believe he'd been much of a help to her, but some things just can't be fixed.

Upstairs, Ben opened the bedroom door and looked in; the air had a stale smell to it. He hated going in there. Taking a deep breath, he went inside and pulled some clothes from the dresser. His intention was to get in and out as quickly as possible, but the conversation he had with Megan had taken root in his mind. Eventually, he would have to pack things up. Turning slowly, he sat down at the end of the bed. His wife's jewelry box was standing open on the dresser. On the nightstand, a tall bottle of perfume stood among an assortment of hair-ties, make-up, and hairspray. Around the house, Becca was an organizational wizard; everything had a place and she liked to keep things that way. The bedroom was another matter. It was the one place she liked to be comfortable. It was here that he felt the closest to her. The place they had spent many a night lying in bed, talking about their future, talking about the girls, talking about the things that mattered the most to them. It was the place that they'd been the most intimate, physically and emotionally.

Suddenly, Ben started to feel that panicky feeling again. The pain that was always so close to the surface came rushing at him. He pushed back against it, like a man trying to stop an on-coming car with just his hands. Grabbing his clothes, he ran from the room, slamming the door behind him, as if doing so would keep the pain inside that room. He stood in the hallway holding the clothes against his chest, breathing deeply.

That was a bright idea. Tell you what, let's just go into the girls' room next and see how you do there, huh?

"How about a shower instead," he said aloud, regaining his composure. He took one last look at the door before heading to the bathroom.

Ben went into the kitchen and pulled a notepad from one of the drawers. The thing probably belonged to one of the girls. He flipped through the pages to see if there was anything written inside. He wasn't sure he could take that right now. Thankfully it was blank. After a moment of thought, he began to draw. The idea of going back in time had been stuck in his mind ever since Megan mentioned it. As an engineer, he liked to translate ideas into practicality. Usually, the first step was to use sketches to formulate those ideas, and then from sketches to models, and so on. Only this time, he was a little out of his league. How do you put on paper something that abstract? Theoretical Physics wasn't in his realm of experience. He'd had a semester of it at Western, and he tried to remember exactly what his college physics professor had said. It was something to the effect of time and space being like a sheet, that gravity and other forces could bend and alter it. He tried to picture the classroom. Professor Phelps, with his dark beard and the over-large glasses, looked like a throwback from the seventies.

"If time and space where like this rug," Professor Phelps said, and put what looked like an ordinary cloth rug on the table at the front of the classroom, "and you could push one end of it." The rug bunched up forming fold after fold. "And then you were to move across the top of it, you could travel either forwards or backwards in time. The problem is finding a way to push the carpet into folds. Oh, and move across it at the same time."

After that, Professor Collins went into more theory, but even then, the idea of the rug had stuck in his mind.

Ripping the first page from the notebook, he began to sketch a platform. It was quite good; he had a hand for drawing which was almost necessary for engineering drawings.

What if I made it so the platform created the folds? You could pass over it as it's created. Okay, Smart-ass, how does the platform create the folds?

Ben pushed the notebook away from him, a bit disgusted. "Who am I kidding? I have no idea."

Larry Snider flipped through the channel guide looking for the football game. He checked every sports channel, and every local station he could find. There was nothing. He swore and threw the remote control at the couch out of frustration.

Larry turned forty-nine over the summer. His thinning red hair was showing streaks of grey. He didn't really care that fifty was just around the corner. To him, it was just another year older. He'd worked as an electrician and been employed by the same construction company he'd worked for most of his adult life. He and his wife had lived in this same house since they were married. Every remodeling job ever done had been done by his own two hands, and he knew every leak and creak in the place.

He huffed, sat down, and stared at the blank television screen. There was a deep scowl set upon his face. His wife walked in, wiping her hands on a dishtowel.

"What's the matter, Dear?" she asked. Amy Snider was a kind woman who was a little on the heavy side. They had a nineteen-year-old son, Derrick, who'd left for college earlier that spring. It had been a bit of an adjustment getting used to having only each other for company.

"Oh, the State game isn't on television. You can watch the damn Wolverines all you want, but the networks treat State like a red-headed stepchild."

Amy put down the dishtowel and sat on his lap. They'd been married for more than twenty-five years. And despite the fact that they yelled, argued, bitched, and complained about each other, they loved each other very much. Not that Larry would ever actually come out and say it aloud.

"Why don't you go to the bar? They might have the game on down there," she said putting her arms around his neck and hugging him gently.

Larry wrapped his arm around her waist, still brooding. "No, they wouldn't have the game either," he sighed.

"Well, why not go see Ben? I know you've been thinking about it. It would be good for you to hang out with him. I do worry about him," she said, then kissed her husband on the cheek before going back into the kitchen. Larry didn't even bother to ask her how she knew he was thinking about looking in on Ben. He hadn't said anything to her about it. Of course, there were times when he honestly believed she knew him better than he did himself.

"Oh, I need you to take out the trash while you are at it," she told him as he strode across the room.

"Christ Almighty, I just took it out last night."

"I know, but I cleaned out the refrigerator this morning. You know my sister is coming over today. I wanted to clean things up a little before she got here."

Larry stomped over to the garbage can and looked in. "It isn't even full."

"It will stink," Amy said, putting her hands on her hips. "Will you please just take it out?"

"Yeah, yeah, I'm doing it," Larry said, throwing the lid to one side, roughly pulling out the bag, and walking towards the door.

"You are going to replace the garbage bag, aren't you?"

"You're really pushing it," Larry said through gritted teeth as he left.

"I know," she said softly, watching him through the window, "that's my job."

Megan played with the straw from her iced tea as she waited for Jim to arrive. She'd asked him to meet at this restaurant, a little family-owned place they were familiar with. The restaurant was cramped with only a half-dozen tables, but they served genuinely good food, and the coffee was the best around.

When the door swung open next, her husband entered the place. He was wearing his usual suit and tie combination. Upon seeing Megan, he smiled and sat down across from her. Megan instantly became even more anxious. She could hear the thumping of her heart inside of her chest. This conversation would most likely be the final nail for her marriage.

"Hey, how are you?" he asked with a casual air. He went on without noticing her dour expression. "So, what's this about? You said on the phone you wanted to talk?" His attitude appeared quite content, almost happy.

He should, he got laid last night. She tried to block this thought and focus on why she was here. "Yeah, I do," she said, deciding it was best just to be blunt. "I just want to know the truth. Do you want a divorce?"

Jim seemed a little taken back by this question. "Wow, okay. I guess you really did want to talk, didn't you?" he replied, and laughed a little. He stopped, realizing she wasn't in the mood for any kind of humor.

"Well?"

"Megan, you know we've had some rough times in the past and have grown apart the last few years. I'd love to just wave a magic wand and make all of our problems disappear, but I can't." Jim stopped; Megan could tell he was trying to think quickly. "I just need some time to figure out what went wrong, and maybe—later—we can fix things. I don't know."

Megan's features remained stony. "I'm sorry, what? Are you telling me you don't want a divorce?"

"There's no reason to rush headlong into it until we've figured out our problems and fix them," he said, gently putting his hand on hers and patting it. His patronizing tone made her even angrier.

"Oh, I think I know the problem," Megan spat while

pulling her hand away from his.

"What are you talking about?"

"Don't play stupid. And don't pretend I am."

Jim shook his head slightly, as if baffled by her statement. "What are you talking about... other women? I told you when I moved out, I'm not interested in getting involved with someone else until we find out if we can fix our problems." His voice made it sound as if he had been insulted. Then, on a dime, he softened his attitude again. "We need to concentrate on fixing our relationship. That's all I want. I just need time to figure out what I'm doing wrong, too."

Megan was amazed. It was no wonder he was such a good lawyer. If she hadn't known the truth, she might've even been swayed by his smooth eloquence. Her heart suddenly went cold with the thought of how much of it was a lie. She gathered her thoughts quickly while fighting to control the hurt, angry monster inside of her. She stood up. "You're such a coward, you lying bastard."

"C'mon, Megan. For heaven sakes, sit down, will you," Jim said firmly, trying his best to keep her from making a scene. Megan did sit, but the fury was still there, in the pit of her stomach.

"I'm not your fool. Not anymore," she said in low a menacing voice. "Maybe we should ask Sabrina what she thinks."

"Don't be petulant, Megan," Jim said, quickly turning his head to see if anyone was listening. "You can't prove anything."

"Is that what this is about?" she said incredulously. "For a moment there I thought that you might be trying to keep me on a string just in case these other women didn't work out."

"It's not that," he said, trying to regain his composure. It was evident he disliked being on the defensive. "You know that I care about you. It's just—"

"All I want is the house and my car," Megan said cutting him off bluntly. Her heart had, it seemed, finally yielded. Her heart and head were in agreement. It was over. "I don't care about anything else. You can have it all as far as I'm concerned."

"Megan," Jim said, cutting off what he was going to say when the waitress approached.

"Can I get you anything?" she asked, holding out a coffee decanter.

Jim seemed disturbed by the interruption. "No, no, thank you, we're fine." With the waitress gone, Jim continued on without missing a beat. "Yes, okay, you're right. I've been seeing someone. It wasn't something I planned, it just sort of happened. I know it wasn't exactly right, but I wasn't sure how long it would be before we put things back together," he said as if he didn't consider it a big deal. When he saw Megan's eyes, he realized his miscalculation, but instead of backtracking or apologizing, he held onto his pride and pressed on. "Besides, I have needs just like every other man. Nobody likes to be alone. I mean, really, it's not like I love her."

"Who do you love, Jim? That's what I'd like to know. I've loved you for so long, only now am I starting to realize you are nothing like what I thought you were. You used to be a good man." Megan hesitated, her heart breaking into many pieces. "How many have there been? Just tell me that much. How many women? At the end of our road, tell me the truth. How much of our marriage has been a lie?"

Jim turned his head so as not to look at her.

"That many," Megan said, shaking her head in disgust. "Just like your lie about having kids. You blamed me for that. I can't believe you told people it was my fault. Is your ego that big? Listen Jim, for my sake and yours, let's end this thing now. File the divorce papers and have it done with. Like I said, all I want is my car, and I'd like to stay in the house. I'll take over the mortgage. I think I can afford it, even on my salary." She stared at him expectantly for a moment. "I know you can live with that."

At first, it appeared as if Jim wanted to say something, but ultimately left speechless. The conversation was coming to an end with nothing left but silence between them. There was Megan on one side of the table, her breath held in painful anticipation, and Jim on the other, looking down at his hands. Unable to find his voice, he nodded.

"Good," Megan said finally. "I hope you find what you want. I have to thank you, though. You really have opened my eyes. For the longest time I held onto the hope of saving our marriage. Now, I can't wait for it to be over."

Megan left the restaurant feeling both free and heartbroken at the same time.

Ben was in the backyard patio when he heard Larry coming through the side gate. It was an unusually warm day for this time of year, perfect for the outdoors.

"Want a beer?" Ben asked, not even bothering to look in his direction.

Larry sat down in the chair next to him at the patio table. “Hmm, let’s see… Does a large furry mammal with sharp teeth and large claws defecate in the in a forested area?”

“You are either employing a new bent to a common rhetorical device, or you are literally asking me if a bear craps in the woods,” Ben said lightly, and then laughed. “If it’s the latter, I believe they do, but never thought to get close enough to ask one where they do their business.”

“Probably a wise idea,” Larry replied grinning.

Ben went inside and grabbed two beers from the fridge. He came back and handed one to Larry.

“I thought you would be watching the MSU game. Didn’t it start at noon?” Ben asked.

“Yeah, but it’s against some small school. South Louisiana Tech, or something like that, I can’t remember. You didn’t think they were going to carry that on television, did you?”

“Actually, I hadn’t thought that much about it,” Ben replied. “You know, Michigan game will be on at three. You can watch them if you like?”

“Bah!” Larry answered. Ben couldn’t help but laugh. “You mean you aren’t going to watch your beloved Wolverines today?” Larry asked.

Ben shook his head. “No. I’m just not in the mood for football.”

“Plus, the fact that they stink this year,” Larry threw in for good measure.

Ben gave him a halfhearted smile. “Yeah, well, that, too.”

That wasn’t the reason and Larry knew it.

“I’ve got tickets for the Red Wings next month. Do

you want to go?" Larry asked. "It's against the Maple Leafs."

"Thought you were going to take Amy?"

"I was but figured you would enjoy it a whole lot more. Besides, I wouldn't have to hear her complain about the restrooms if I took you instead."

Ben thought about it for a moment. "I appreciate it, but I don't think I'd be a whole lot of fun right now."

Larry chuckled. "You think it's going to be fun taking the old ball and chain with me? Thanks a lot, Buddy."

Ben knew Larry talked a lot of crap when it came to his wife, but it was mostly for show. Larry had once admitted (while mildly intoxicated) that, although she could be a pain, he really did love Amy, and she was the one person he depended on the most. He also admitted he was amazed that she had stuck with him as long as she had. Of course, Ben, being the good friend that he was, never threw it in his face.

"I'm sorry. Normally I'd love to go, but it just doesn't seem as important to me right now."

"Oh hell, I was just trying to get your mind off of things is all," Larry said. "You know as well as I do, you're the only person my wife would ever give up her seat to."

Ben smiled. "Yeah, she does try to spoil me, doesn't she?"

"Tries to mother you is what she does," said Larry quickly. "Probably a little too much at times, but you're like family to us."

"Yeah, and I'm not sure what I'd have done without you guys in the last few months." Ben paused, "You guys and Megan."

Larry saw something in his expression. "What's

going on with her? It's that idiot husband of hers, isn't it?"

Ben froze, holding his beer halfway to his mouth. He wasn't certain if it was his place to say anything.

"Come on, what's wrong? I know them two have been having troubles for a while now," Larry said.

"They are separated," Ben said at last. "And it looks like they're heading towards divorce."

Larry thought about it for a bit, and then nodded. "Good. I never liked that idiot to start with. Megan is way too special of a girl to waste her time with a no-good, scumbag like that anyway. That sleazy bastard as much as admitted he was cheating on her, do you remember? If it hadn't been for the family thing going on, I probably would've whooped his ass right then and there."

"When was that," Ben asked.

A shadow passed over Larry's face before he spoke. "It was a while back. You might not remember."

Ben accepted his clarification, as weak as it was. "Hey, Larry. Don't say anything about the divorce stuff, okay?"

"Who the hell do you think you're talking to? You know me," Larry said indignantly.

"I know. It's just that Megan has had enough hell to go through right now. I don't want to add to it. If it was me..."

"I know, if it was you, nothing would've ever been said. Ben, you're one of the best friends I have, but you keep way too much bottled up inside." Larry hesitated. It was evident he was weighing whether or not to proceed with what he wanted to say. "I say this now because it's just you and me out here. You're harboring so much grief, and yet you never let anyone see it. It tears me up to see it. You put on a brave face to the rest of the world and hide your true emotions."

"You see a lot, don't you, Larry?"

"Too much sometimes," Larry added reluctantly. "Like a man who tries to drink away the memory of his wife and two daughters. A man who hides inside his house and treats it like it's haunted at the same time. A man who wishes he was as dead as the family he had to bury."

"Can we not talk about that right now?" Ben asked sternly. Larry was way too close to the truth, and he didn't want to look at it. He took a swig of beer and then stared at the label.

"I'm sorry, Ben. You know, for the most part, I don't press you on these matters, but there will come a time you'll have to face it. I'm hoping you can do it sooner rather than later."

Ben slammed his beer on the patio table. "I have faced it, alright. They're gone, I get it, alright!"

"Oh, you know they're gone, there's no doubt to that. The problem is that you haven't let them go. You torture yourself over how they died, that somehow, it's your fault. That, had you done something differently, none of it would've happened. Even now, you are bottling things up inside, refusing to let it out. The truth is that it did happen and there's not a damn thing you could've done to stop it. It does you no good to walk around every day believing it's your fault they're dead. You didn't kill them, Ben. It was an unfortunate accident, nothing more."

The words unhinged Ben. He picked up the patio table and tossed it into the yard, all the time hurling a stream of obscenities at Larry for exposing the deep lesions that tormented him, for opening wide the wounds he carried with him every day. Ben's eyes were wild, and for a moment Larry was afraid things might end up coming to blows. But instead, Ben returned to his seat, leaned forward, and put his head into his hands. It was evident Ben was fighting to control the rage, bitterness, and confusion locked inside of him. Emotions so powerful, it was twisting him in knots, making him sick.

"What do you think, Larry? Ben took in breath, and then added harshly, "How was that for letting it out?"

Larry went to put his hand on Ben's shoulder. Ben immediately knocked it away. Larry nodded to himself, as if acknowledging something he expected. He dropped his hand to his side.

"I'm sorry, Ben. I don't know how else to get you to see. What happened was an accident, there was nothing you could do. Now, you have to be the one to decide if you want to keep this pain inside or let it go. Anyway, if you need me, I'm always just next door."

Larry left, going back out the side gate. Ben was still fuming on the inside.

Why did he have to do that? He thought feverishly. *I was dealing with this just fine until he stirred everything up.* After a moment, his thoughts continued in a different direction. *Of course, you've thought of driving your car into that propane tank. You can't go upstairs because you can't cope with—well—with everything there. You can't face the fact that you slept while they died.* There was a pause in his thinking as the part he had the most difficulty facing, the part that registered most remorse, rose to the surface.

You can't face the fact that you wished your daughter would die.

With a sudden, sickening convulsion, Ben lurched forward on his hands and knees and hurled.

When Larry returned home, Amy was busy sweeping the kitchen floor.

"I thought you were going over to see Ben?" she asked. Then she saw the deep frown on her husband's face and knew something was wrong. She set the broom against the wall and when to him. "What happened?"

Larry kept his head down, staring at his feet. "I think I pushed him a little too hard. Told him he's closing himself off from the world and blaming himself for the accident." Larry sighed. "I know he hates me right now for doing it and can't say I blame him."

Amy looked up at her husband, taking his hand into hers. "You did what you had to. I know it was a difficult thing to do. I think that's why you kept putting it off." Amy smiled at him. "Ben knows you were only doing it because you care. He'll get over it quick enough, I promise."

"You think so? You should've seen him. Angriest I've ever seen him. He even threw in the old F-bomb to boot." Larry squeezed her hand gently. "I really do hope you're right."

Amy hugged him, putting her face into his chest. After a moment, she let go of him, went over, and picked up the phone.

"What are you doing?" Larry asked quickly, thinking she may be calling Ben. That was the last thing he wanted right now.

"Calling my sister, Mary," she said, putting her hand over the receiver out of habit. "We really don't need visitors coming over today. I'll make an excuse. We can make it for another day. Then you and I will go over to the sporting goods store so you can look around for a new fishing pole or whatever. Then we'll go out for dinner and a movie. What do you say?"

He still appeared a bit glum. "Can I get a new tackle box?" he asked. "My old one is busted."

Amy smiled. "Yes, you can get a tackle box."

Megan pulled into the driveway, the radio playing. She didn't know the name of the song or even who sang it, but Megan definitely knew how she felt at this moment. The words supplied her with equal amounts of satisfaction and pain.

Curtain's finally closing
That was quite a show
Very entertaining

She cut the engine and sat there, her hands gripping the steering wheel. "You really did put on quite a show —very entertaining," she repeated. "At least it would've been if it hadn't been my heart he was ripping out at the same time."

After a few moments, she pulled the keys from the ignition and got out of the car. She had the strangest feeling of disconnection. There was no doubt about now. Her marriage, the life she had for the last five years now was over. Dead and gone forever, amen.

Once inside, she kicked off her shoes and plopped

down on the couch. Then she reached over and pulled the blanket around her, folding her legs under her at the same time.

Is this what it is going to be like from now on? An empty house and an empty heart.

Something else crossed her mind.

Ben has been dealing with it for a while now. And it was worse for him, never having a chance to say goodbye. The finality came in one swift strike. It was no wonder he never wants to talk about it.

The doorbell rang. Megan shuffled across the floor and looked out to see who was there. Standing on the front step, looking rather uncomfortable, was Ben. She opened the door for him.

"Hey," Ben said, still looking rather nervous. "Um... how's it going?"

"You want to come in?" Megan asked in kind of a monotone.

"Oh... um, okay," he said, stepping inside. "I didn't want to bother you or anything."

Megan shuffled back over to the couch and plopped back down. "No, you're not bothering me," she said, but had a faraway look in her eyes.

"So, I take it you talked to Jim today," Ben said, sitting down on the love seat across from her.

"Yep. Picked a real winner there, didn't I?" she said sarcastically, and then shook her head in vague disgust. "He's been cheating on me for a while now, I'm sure of it. He tried to lie to me at first. Isn't that a surprise?" She paused. "Anyway, we are filing for divorce. I know it's the right thing to do, but it still sucks."

Ben wanted to say something, but 'sorry' sounded weak, and 'it's for the best' wasn't going to get it, so he said nothing.

"So, now that it's over," Megan continued, "I thought I'd come back here and zone out for a bit."

"Do you want to get out of here? Go do something? I don't want to sit in that house, and I wondered if you wanted a distraction as well."

Slowly, she moved her head to look at him. She knew he was only trying to help. "No, Ben. Right now, I don't know what I want or what I'm going to do. Tomorrow may be different."

"Yeah, hey, that's fine," he said. "I can see that you want to be alone. I'll see my way out."

Megan sighed. "I'm sorry Ben..." The words hung there as if she wanted to say more, but her voice just kind of trailed off and the blank stare was back.

"Don't worry about it. I completely understand, believe me. If there's anyone who understands, it's me."

Back at home, Ben sat down at the kitchen table. He really did want to get away for a while. To have some kind of diversion, but he didn't want to go alone. Larry's visit had made him uncomfortable inside his own head. The things he said kept ricocheting inside his skull, making it worse. He spotted the notepad lying on the table and pulled it towards him. Halfheartedly, he began to think about it, his hand moving, sketching lightly.

Time travel. It was the stuff of science fiction and difficult to take seriously, but he needed a distraction.

Alright, what kind of conditions would you need? Gravity is one way of affecting time and space, but there's no way to create extreme gravity, and then turn it off again to make the ripple effect.

Ben set the pencil down and concentrated on the platform for a second. *What about a magnetic field? Or how about making it some kind of alternating magnetic field? Maybe that would have some kind of effect on gravity. Okay, how would you do that?*

Then another idea hit him. Ben started to sketch furiously.

The platform will create a magnetic field. He drew a bar across the front of the platform then two arms to the end of it attached to the center of the platform, like a large swing that would circle the platform. *The bar will be oppositely charged, swinging downwards, and then uncharged as it sweeps beneath the platform. In theory, it would make the folds in time and pull them under the platform.*

He almost laughed. It looked a bit like an oversized mousetrap.

"It could work. I think. Maybe?" he said. He sat back in his chair. "Question is, do magnetic fields have any effect on time?" He chuckled at the absurdity of his own question, the basis of which the whole design would be based. "Probably not."

The little voice of doubt crept into his head. *Are you really going to waste your time and energy on this thing? You don't even an inkling it'll even work.*

Ben tilted his head side to side just a bit, considering it. "Yeah, I think I will," he said, not caring if the damn thing ever worked. It would be something he could design and build. It would give him something to focus on, occupy his mind, and get him moving forward instead of drowning in grief.

Finally, he said, "Oh, what the hell. Seriously, what can it hurt?"

CHAPTER 4

The leaves had fallen making the trees appear barren. Winter was bearing down, closing in, bringing with it the gray clouds and a feeling of obscurity. The cold had brought with it a light snow which melted as soon as it hit the ground.

Megan sat on the love seat with her body half turned, looking out the picture window. She watched as the snow fell. Watching it swirl and move with the wind. It reminded her of when she was a girl and the excitement of the first snowfall. Things were much easier when you were a child. Little things could make you happy, while disappointments were quickly forgotten. She wished she could be more like that now. It had been more than a month since she had confronted Jim about the divorce. Jim had indeed filed, and it looked as if he was going to give her what she wanted. Everything would be final by the end of December. Several weeks back, Jim had come by the house to pick up his clothes and a few of his personal belongings, and for her to sign the divorce papers. It was a somber encounter, very little was said during that time. He'd told her she could keep the furnishings and everything else. She wasn't certain if he did it out of guilt or that he just didn't want any of it. Either way, it didn't matter. He also mentioned that he was staying with a friend. The friend turned out to be Sabrina, but she had heard that from someone else. Megan didn't challenge him about it, thinking that he couldn't help but to lie to her. Old habits and all.

She turned and stared blankly at the dark screen of the television. Did she really want to watch that thing?

Not really.

What about shopping? I could use a new wardrobe. Maybe even get my hair done—the whole nine yards. While I'm at it, I'll take Ben along.

Megan smiled at the thought. It was good to have him around. They were able to talk freely worrying what the other person would think. She had no desire to start dating and Ben didn't either, so it was easy for them to hang out together as friends. Plus, as Becky's husband, she really didn't think of him that way.

She wondered if he would even be interested in going along. Shopping wasn't exactly a guy thing.

"Oh, he'll go. I'll make him go, poor boy," she said with a smirk.

Ben shuffled from foot to foot trying to be patient. It was the third store and about twenty different outfits. He never in his life believed a woman could try on so many clothes without buying any of them.

"When you said you wanted to go to the mall, I thought you meant just to look around," he said over the dressing room door.

"I told you on the way down here I wanted to look for a new wardrobe," Megan called back. "Besides, I'm a woman. You know what happens when a woman goes shopping."

"Yeah, you'd think I would have been smart enough to know," Ben tried to say under his breath.

"What was that?"

"Nothing, I didn't say anything," Ben said but thought he could hear her giggle.

Megan opened the door to the dressing room, turned, and put all the clothes on the return rack.

"You aren't going to buy any of them?" he asked, his eyes wide with bewilderment.

"Nope."

"This is the third store you've done this. Why in God's name did you spend so much time going through picking out clothes just to put them back?"

"Becca didn't take you shopping very often, did she?" Megan said a little patronizingly, but only to irritate him.

"Well, matter of fact, no."

"Uh-huh, I didn't think so. Well, you see Ben, sometime we women—and of course, you know we're all the same—like to shop for clothes, try them on, and feel the satisfaction of putting them back because we don't like them, thus reinforcing the idea that we have good taste in fashion."

"Next time, I get to decide where we go and what we do," Ben said. "I thought that maybe you wanted to do some Christmas shopping."

Megan thought about it for a second. "No, I really only have my mom and dad to shop for this year. That won't take long."

"You forgot your most favorite neighbor in the whole world! You're supposed to get him something extra nice this year," Ben chipped in.

"You're right," Megan said playing along. "I wonder what I should get for Larry this year."

"Now you are just being mean," he said, and Megan laughed. Ben just chuckled. "So, is there anything else here you wanted to look at?"

Megan sighed. "No, not now. I do want to get some new clothes eventually. You know, for the new me," she said. "But once again, I don't seem to know who I am or what I want just yet." She seemed a little saddened by this thought.

Ben put his arm around her. "It will come. Just have patience."

"I hope so," she said, and gave him a half-smile. "You seem to be doing a lot better lately."

Ben dropped his arm. "Yeah, I guess I am. I'll be going back to work on Monday. Actually, Larry came over to see me a while back and, well, let's just say he kind of smacked me across the head with a two-by-four. Not literally, of course," he said, and then hesitated. "And, I have kind of a... project... I guess you would call it. It keeps me occupied."

"What is it?"

"Oh, nothing I really want to talk about just yet. It's still an idea right now. I promise I'll show it to you if it ever gets finished."

"Okay. You can be quite secretive when you want to be, can't you?" Megan said, raising her eyebrows at him, and then laughing.

"That reminds me, if we get the chance, I'd like to go by home improvement store to look for some stuff," Ben added.

"I think we can do that. Besides I might get the chance to see what your secret is," she said slyly. "That's something else you probably should already know about us women. We love to hear secrets."

When Ben entered his office, he had the feeling of greeting an old friend. It was on the east side of the building where the windows always got the morning light. Outside, he could see the KFC and Walmart, as well as the continual flow of traffic on Westnedge Avenue. His desk sat near the front of his office. Occasionally, he would leave the door open so he could look down the hallway. For now, he left it closed. He wanted a bit of privacy.

He sat down and flipped though some of the old drafts that were on top of his desk. After this long, he was certain they were outdated. He stashed them in the drawer and leaned back in his chair.

Very shortly, there came a knock on the door.

"Come in," Ben said, not looking at the door. He'd been expecting this and dreading it at the same time.

"Good to have you back, Ben," said a deep, familiar voice. It was Joe Murphy, his boss. Joe was easy to dislike. He was tall and built like a linebacker. He'd actually been a football player in college, a Defensive End at Western, at least until he was injured. Unfortunately, he was also a control freak, a backstabber, and a complete fake.

And he never forgot a grudge.

"You know, Ben. I really feel bad about—you know—your wife and kids." There was a kind of false sincerity in his voice. Joe shrugged and blew air out of his mouth as if to show empathy for Ben's situation. Ben, knowing this show was for him, simply nodded. Joe moved on quickly, as if he had gotten past the part he dreaded.

"Listen, Ben, I'm going to put you on Engineering Plans Review for the time being, let you get back into the flow of things slowly."

"WHAT?" Ben said, unable to control his tone. "I'm a full Associate here. I haven't done reviews since my first year out of college."

"You may be an Associate, but I'm the Executive Manager," Joe said with a puffed-up, condescending tone he used on everyone. "I've talked to Mr. Pearson and Mr. Walker about your situation, and we agree that it's for the best right now. We're just trying to protect you and the company right now. We can't very well have you working in mechanical design and have something go wrong because your mind wasn't on your work, can we?"

Ben felt his anger rising. Through gritted teeth he asked, "And if I go to Walker and Pearson about this?"

"Go ahead. I doubt you'll get very far. You may have been here a long time, but I'm the one who has the last say in this department."

Ben's shoulders slumped a little unconsciously. Joseph Murphy was married to George Pearson's daughter, Hannah. Everyone knew George Pearson was getting ready to retire and Joe was poised to step into his position as a full partner at the firm. This, despite the fact he wasn't an engineer, had never finished his degree, and was generally considered the worst manager ever.

Ben glowered at him but remained silent. Joe took this as a sign that he wasn't going to fight him on the matter. Ben tried to remind himself that a bully, like Joe, thrived on attention, especially negative attention. The last few years, Ben had found silence to be best means to fight this particular bully. However, at this moment, he found silence a difficult thing to maintain.

"It's good to see that you can be reasonable. I'll send up those review files in a bit." Joe turned before leaving and pointed his finger at him like a gun. "It's good to have you back, Ben," he said, and walked away without closing the door.

Ben finally had enough. "Yeah, nice to see you too… Jackass!" Ben said in a clear, loud voice. He was certain Joe heard him as he walked away. For added emphasis, Ben slammed the door.

I think I'm pretty close to the end of working for Walker & Pearson. Or should I say, soon-to-be, Walker and Murphy. God help us. Good thing you don't absolutely have to have this job.

As he flipped on the computer and waited for it to run through its startup, someone else appeared at the door.

"Hey, Buddy." It was Cliff Anderson, friend, associate, and compatriots in their dislike for Joe Murphy. "Good Lord, I heard what you said all the way down the hall."

"I know. I let him get to me this time. I really should know better, but he came in here with all that phony sympathy crap, and then tells me I'll be working Plans Review instead of Design."

"You had to know he was going to try something. He's always hated you, thinks you're a favorite of Walker's."

"Yeah, I know," Ben said, then waved his hand as if he didn't want to think about it. "I don't care what he does as long as he stays away from me."

"Hey, I've got to go, but it really is good to have you back." Cliff pulled his head back out from the door and closed it.

Ben forgot how much he missed being around Cliff. He was always one to bring a little flavor into one's day. It would've been easy to guess that in school, Cliff was the class clown.

The computer screen flashed on, and Ben opened the CAD program, making a new project file for his initial design for The Machine. That's the way he thought of it, that's what he called it. The Machine. Never, ever, The Time Machine. If anyone ever caught wind of what he was doing, what he was thinking, they would lock him away for sure. A little padded room, complete with a jacket with long sleeves that went all the way around. One of the main reasons he asked to come back was to work on his project. At home, he had limited access to computer design. The program here could generate a 3D model of a design. It would describe any mechanical problems, alert him to structural design errors, and even give him a list of materials needed. His attempts to build a small working model at home had only yielded minimal success. He knew he needed a more advanced design. Ben had created a miniature model of his mousetrap design at home, working with just stuff he found at the hardware store. He'd put together a small shop in the basement and attempted to make the platform by gluing the magnets together. This did not work because they had a polarizing effect and would either stick together or be repulsed. So, he spaced them apart and glued Popsicle sticks to the bottom, attaching them like a raft. Then he obtained a small battery-operated motor for the swing arm and wired it to a 9-volt battery. The last item he had to get was upstairs in Tia's room. He opened the door and scanned the shelves, spotting a small plastic doll only three inches high.

"Sorry, Tia," he said, grabbing the doll from the shelf and going back downstairs. He placed it on the platform, put the wires in place, and then hooked up the battery. The little swing arm started to move around the platform but didn't have enough power to properly operate the way he wanted.

Thinking that more power was the answer, he switched to a small electric motor he'd scavenged off an old weed-eater. Problem was, it had no cord. So, he ran back upstairs and cut the cord off the lamp with a kitchen knife, getting a quick shock because in his haste, he'd forgotten to unplug it first. After that, he ransacked the kitchen, looking for an extension cord before finally finding one in the last drawer he searched. Ben then rewired the whole operation to the lamp cord. The lamp cord had an on-off switch wired into it, which was the reason he'd picked that particular cord. He flipped the switch. The swing arm whirled around at a break-neck speed, electricity jumped in every which way between the platform, the swing arm, and the little doll, which was currently catching about 110 volts. Ben could also just make out a faint blue static field encircle the platform. After only ten or fifteen seconds, it began to smoke and the motor for the swing arm blew.

He switched it off, waving the smoke away trying to see what kind of damage was done. The Popsicle sticks on the bottom of the platform were black and smoldering. The little motor had unwillingly sacrificed itself; the thing would never run again. The worst of it was the doll. It had singed hair and scorch marks covering it. Ben picked up the doll and looked it over. The plastic feet had melted.

"I hope this wasn't one of her favorites," he said, setting the doll aside and staring at the burnt model. "Okay, looks like we have bit of a design problem. I'm not up for getting electrocuted."

There was something, I'm sure of it. Maybe I'm on the right track but wrong design. He picked up the model and examined it. *The right track? You don't actually believe that frying a little plastic doll on that contraption is your idea of time travel, do you?* Ben chuckled to himself. *No, but it is kind of fun having a project to work on again, even if it is a bit insane.*

He was brought back to the present when the door opened once again. Joe's secretary, Jennifer Reynolds, entered his office carrying a stack of folders, nearly overwhelming her. Jenny, as almost everyone in the office knew her, had short brown hair, brown eyes, and a slight build. She reminded Ben of Sally Fields, only with thick glasses. She was a good person, but invariably timid.

"Hi, Ben. I brought you the files Mr. Murphy wanted you to have," she said.

"Oh, yeah. Thanks, Jenny," Ben replied, jumping up to take them from her, "Wow, there must be quite a backup in Plans Review."

Jenny lowered her voice, "Actually, Mr. Murphy was supposed to have assigned these weeks ago, but left them sitting. He was reprimanded by Mr. Walker about it."

"And that's how I ended up with the job."

Jenny nodded meekly. Ben sat the files on the corner of his desk.

"It figures."

"I wanted to tell you again how very sorry I am

about Rebecca and the girls," Jenny said, her eyes shiny with tears. Of all the people Ben worked with, Becca liked Jenny the best. "Anyway, I'm glad you're back. I've missed you," she said, pushing her glasses up the bridge of her nose, and then going over and giving him a quick hug.

"Thank you, Jenny," he told her. She smiled shyly before leaving.

Ben picked up the top folder and began flipping through it. "So, you wanted me to get back into things slowly, huh Joe?" he said, tossing the folder back on top of the stack. "I guess the machine will have to wait."

Around noon, Cliff banged quickly on Ben's door and walked in without waiting for an answer. He looked over Ben's shoulder at the computer screen.

"What the hell is that thing?" Cliff asked.

"Oh, just something I was tinkering with. Hasn't looked good so far," Ben said, and quickly shut down the program. He spun in the seat to face Cliff.

"You want to grab some lunch? It's my treat," Cliff said.

Ben shook his head. "I'm not hungry." He really wanted to work on his machine.

"Pah! Who cares if you eat? I'll buy you a beer instead," Cliff said.

For a moment or two, Ben found himself going back and forth, considering it. "Okay, I'll go. But you're buying me lunch."

"Sure. Fine. Whatever," Cliff said, acting as if Ben had taken advantage of him. "Now I'm buying you lunch and beer. Sheesh! Next, you'll be telling me you want to go to Hooters, too."

Ben raised his eyebrow; he knew Hooters was Cliff's favorite place to go. And it wasn't for the food.

"Okay, okay, we'll go to Hooters if it makes you happy."

"Oh goody," Cliff said, and then began to do a childish little dance.

"If you're going to act like that, I'm not taking you."

Cliff stuck out his lip and clapped his hands together in mock admonishment. "I'll be good, I promise."

Ben couldn't help but laugh.

"Come on, Old Man," Cliff said, pulling Ben out of the chair and patting him on the back as they walked.

They sat at a table nearest the serving area where the Hooter girls went to get their orders. Ben didn't even ask why Cliff had chosen this particular table when it was so clearly apparent why. Cliff was twice divorced, and on the lookout for wife number three. Ben was finding it difficult to carry on a conversation with Cliff continually turning his head to watch the girls.

"Cliff," Ben said, trying to get his attention.

"Yeah?" Cliff answered without turning to look at Ben.

"Are you going to eat?"

"Oh… Yeah, I guess so," Cliff said, and picked up his sandwich. He chewed his food quickly then swallowed while scanning the entire place. He caught Ben's eyes and saw his exasperated expression.

"Sorry, Ben."

"It's alright," Ben said, chuckling a bit. "I should've remembered your propensity for girl watching."

Cliff looked seriously at Ben for a moment. "You know, I'm not like you, Ben. I've always had trouble keeping good relationships. That's why it's so hard for you right now. You're one of those commitment people. It's hard for you to get over something like that. But I also know you'll come through this because you're, I don't know," he groped for the right word. "Strong."

"What the hell are you talking about?"

Cliff laughed. "I didn't mean like muscles or whatever. I mean, like, strong inside. I know you can't see it, but other people do."

"Yeah, well, I don't feel very strong, inside or outside, right now."

A waitress with long, curly brown hair stopped at their table. She had gentle dark brown eyes to match her hair. "Can I get you gentlemen anything else? Another beer maybe?" she asked, while picking up the empty glasses in front of them.

"Yes," Cliff said smiling, "Another beer for each of us. And one more thing, if you don't mind?"

"What's that?" she asked.

"Your name. My friend here has been asking about you ever since we got here."

Ben resisted the temptation to remind Cliff that her nametag clearly stated her name, Amber.

She smiled and blushed just a little, then held out her hand and shook Ben's. "I'm Amber, nice to meet you."

"Uh... I'm Ben. It's very nice to meet you, Amber," Ben said playing along, but the young woman continued to hold his gaze, smiling. Feeling a little uncomfortable, Ben tried to divert her attention away from him. "This is Cliff. Cliff Anderson. My somewhat facetious co-worker and supposed friend."

Amber grinned and shook Cliff's hand. "Nice to meet you, too," she said graciously, but her gaze quickly returned to Ben.

"Well, Ben. I'll get that beer for you," Amber said.

As she walked away, Ben hit Cliff hard on the arm.

"Ouch!"

"What the hell were you trying to do?" Ben asked, trying to keep his voice low.

"That hurt," Cliff said, rubbing his shoulder. Then he chuckled. "Hey, I think she really likes you."

"I didn't come here to get a date."

"I know that. Actually, I didn't expect it to work quite that well. Never works for me."

"What am I going to do now?" Ben asked, looking anxious.

"Calm down, will you? You just got flirted with just a little. It's not like you have to marry the girl."

"I will if I end up hanging around with you all the time."

Cliff laughed. "Yeah, that's a distinct possibility."

They quieted as Amber returned with the drinks.

"Here you go," she said warmly, setting a beer in front of Cliff. Amber then moved over to Ben, pressing her body against his as she leaned in to set the beer in front of him. The temperature inside his suit jumped about thirty degrees as he felt the warmth of her body and the sweet smell of her perfume. He noticed that she had placed an extra napkin next to his beer.

"I hope you enjoy your beer, Ben. And you, too—"

"Cliff," he said, knowing she had already forgotten.

Amber smiled again. "Yes, of course. I remember now. I'm sorry... Cliff," she said deliberately.

She walked away, but halfway across the room, she glanced back at Ben.

Ben picked up the napkin. On the back of it, she

had printed her phone number. "She left me her phone number."

"Why does that surprise you?"

"I'm at least twelve years older than her."

"Doesn't seem to bother her any," Cliff said as he lifted his head to scan the room for her.

"She doesn't know anything about me."

"That's probably why she left the phone number... to get to know you better."

Ben shook his head. "You're enjoying this, aren't you?"

"You bet," Cliff said laughing. "Still, I should probably be a little upset. She didn't even give me a second look." Cliff checked his watch. "We better get going."

Cliff picked up the check; Ben held his arm down. "I can get that," Ben said, trying to take it from him.

"Oh no, I promised, and I stick to my promises," Cliff said.

"Alright, I'll get the next one."

"I'll agree to that. Can we go to the Roadhouse? I'll order a huge Porterhouse, at least two pounds."

Ben laughed. "Sure, why not?"

Cliff quickly paid the check and came back.

"Better take that along," Cliff said, pointing to the napkin. "Don't want to make the lady feel bad, do you?"

Ben stuffed the napkin in his pocket, but before they got to the door, Amber rushed over and gave him a quick hug. She whispered in his ear, "Call me," then let go. She waved at both of them as they left. "Bye, Cliff. Goodbye, Ben."

Cliff snickered at him. "Well, at least she remembered my name this time."

They climbed in Ben's car; Cliff was grinning like a

Cheshire cat.

"What?" Ben asked.

"How do you feel?"

He considered it for a moment. "Strangely enough, pretty good," Ben admitted. He really had no desire to get into a relationship with the young woman. Still, it made him feel good inside.

"Good. You know that kind of proves my earlier point in a way."

"What do you mean?"

"Well, people see something in you, Ben. She sure did."

"I'll admit, it's a boost to my ego, but I have a long way to go before I'm whole again, and I know it," Ben said.

"Yeah, well, one day at a time, good buddy, one day at a time. By the way, if you aren't going to use that number, would you mind giving it to me?"

The file was open in front of him, but he hadn't gotten very far. Ben knew, despite the manner he'd gotten the review files, people were depending on him to get the job done. Unfortunately, he was having a hard time concentrating.

Ben closed the file and sat back for a moment. A soft knock on the door drew his attention away from his thoughts. When the door opened, an elderly gentleman, Paul Walker, entered.

"Hello, Ben," Mr. Walker said.

"Mr. Walker. Come in, come in," Ben said, standing.

Mr. Walker walked slowly across the room and sat down across him. He was a frail man, but in physical appearance only. The thinning white hair and his slow movement misrepresented the man inside. His bright blue eyes were sharp, seeing everything. And if you ever ran afoul of his temper, you knew he was still as formidable as ever.

"How are you holding up, Ben?" he asked, looking straight at him as if to gauge his reply. It was a bit like a poker player trying to get a read on an opponent.

Ben sat, slowly and hesitantly, trying to weigh the truth against a lie. He decided it was best not to lie. "It's been hell. I have days when I don't know how I'm going to make it. But I think I've been doing better lately."

Mr. Walker gave a faint nod, his eyes never left Ben. "You know, I can still remember the day I hired you. You were fresh out of college, and eager as hell," he said with a slight laugh. "Eager to learn, and ready to take on anything we could hand you. I have watched you grow from that young man into probably the best engineer we have. I've also watched as you matured into a father, family man, and the good and moral person that you are now. In a way, you're the son I never had. It grieves me greatly to know the kind of pain you're in."

Ben was a little astonished at what he was hearing. He always knew that Mr. Walker liked him. Early on, he had been a mentor, and it had meant a lot to Ben. Through the years, Ben knew if he had a problem, he could go to Mr. Walker. But he never would've guessed how much Mr. Walker actually thought of him.

"I know I've never told you these things," Mr. Walker continued. "I keep a lot of things to myself. I guess that is just my nature. Not to different from your own, I suspect. I do want you to know this, Ben. The firm is here for you. And I'm here for you if there is anything you need."

"Thank you, Mr. Walker. I have to admit, I don't know what to say."

"Well, you don't have to say anything. If you ever feel the need to leave in the middle of the day, then go. If you need more time off, you have it. If Murphy gives you any of his crap, tell him... well, I guess you haven't got any trouble telling him, do you?"

Ben grinned, almost embarrassed. "You heard about that?"

Mr. Walker shook his head. "Nope, didn't hear about it. I heard it myself. I was just down the hall. Had a good laugh, too."

"Sorry about that."

"Don't be. He's a jackass and everybody here knows it. You're just one of the few who will say it out loud. God help us if George goes ahead with his plans to make Joe Murphy partner when he retires. Anyway, if he tries to gull you into doing extra work, or tries to pull rank, just tell him to come see me. I'll take care of it."

"Thank you, Mr. Walker," Ben said, knowing he'd never do it. The little battles that went on in the trenches weren't the stuff to take to him.

Mr. Walker got up and walked slowly to the door. He glanced at the files on Ben's desk and stopped.

"Those aren't the Plan Review files, are they?"

"Ah... yes, they are. Joe Murphy told me he talked to you and Mr. Pearson about doing Plans Review for a while."

Mr. Walker's eyes were blazing as he heard this. He was about as furious as Ben had ever seen him.

"Excuse me, Ben. I need to use your phone for just a minute," he said, tight-lipped.

"Yes, of course," Ben stepped out of his way.

Mr. Walker used the desk for support as he moved around it to get to the phone. "Jennifer, have Mr. Murphy come to my office immediately," he paused listening, and then he looked at his watch. "It's a quarter past two. Exactly how long does Mr. Murphy take for lunch these days? No, it isn't your fault, Jennifer. Just do me a favor, get him on his cell phone. Tell him he had better find his way back here, pronto. Also, I'm sending Ben over with the Plan Review files. No, that's all right. Ben can take them. The stack is almost as large as you are. Thank you, Jennifer."

He hung up the phone.

"You know, Mr. Walker, I can take care of these—"

Mr. Walker cut across him instantly. "I know you could. That isn't the problem. We have junior associates hired to do this kind of work. Plus, I'm not going to put you under that kind of pressure. They are already overdue. You knew that too, didn't you? On top of that, we—Mr. Pearson and I—specifically told Murphy that you were to take it easy, take things slowly, and only work on projects that you felt like you wanted to do. Hell, I even told him I didn't care if you sat around playing solitaire all day long. Instead, he dumped a load of work on you that he was supposed to have taken care of weeks ago." He paused and added, "You will take these down to Jennifer, won't you?"

"Yes, Sir."

"Good, Good. Thank you, Ben," he said. He walked slowly to the door, taking small, deliberate steps. When he got to the door, he stopped and looked at Ben. "Take care of yourself, alright?"

"I will try, Mr. Walker."

On the way home, Ben tried to filter all that happened that day, including lunch. While deep in this process, his cell phone rang. He pulled it off the clip and looked at the caller ID. It was Megan.

"Well, hello," he said brightly.

"How did the first day back go?" she asked, sounding almost excited for him.

"It was eventful to say the least."

"What happened?"

"Well, to make a long story short, my boss tried to screw me over and he ended up behind the woodshed for it. I got hit on during lunch, even got a phone number out of it. And the owner of the firm told me that I was like a son to him."

"That is quite a day."

"I was pretty astonished when Mr. Walker told me what he did. I'm touched that he thinks so much of me."

"I'm sure that was nice to hear coming from him."

"It was."

"I want to hear about you getting hit on during lunch. Who was she?"

"Oh, it was Cliff's fault. He thought it would be funny to introduce me to one of the waitresses at—" Ben hesitated, "—the restaurant we went to, and she ended up leaving me her phone number."

"Okay, Ben. What are you leaving out?"

"What are you talking about?"

"I can tell by your voice. There's more to the story."

"No, you can't," Ben said, trying to sound convincing.

"Fine. If you don't want to tell me, then don't."

"I'll tell you, but you have to promise not to laugh."

"I promise not laugh." Megan said, trying to sound solemn.

"We were at Hooters."

"You got hit on by a Hooters girl?" He could tell she had pulled the phone away from her ear and could hear her laughing.

"Didn't you swear you weren't going to laugh?"

"I did, I did. I'm sorry, Ben. How old was she?

"I don't know, maybe twenty-one or twenty-two."

There was more laughing coming from the phone.

"You're kidding?" Megan said.

"Nope."

"What did she look like?"

"Brown hair, brown eyes... she was very pretty."

"Really? I'm impressed, Mr. Stryker. Are you going to call her?"

"No, I am not."

"Well, at least the girl has good taste."

"Thank you, Megan. That's probably the nicest thing you have said to me today."

"The day isn't over with yet. Well, I have to let you go. I have to admit that story made my day. I'll talk to you later. Bye, Ben."

"Bye, Megan."

It was actually kind of a nice thing to happen to him, and he had to admit made him feel good.

What do you think Becca would have thought about it?

Ben tried to push the thought away. *You know damn well, if I had a choice between Becca and that girl, I'd take Becca every time.*

The guilty voice hammered him again. *She was very young and beautiful. Are you sure you wouldn't like to call her and find out what she's like. Becca can't see you.*

She's gone. Gone because you wouldn't get out of that bed. Becca, Teresa, Tia—all dead because of you. Go ahead. Call her! What difference does it make to them anymore? Who knows, you might even get lucky.

He pulled the car into the next parking lot he could find and shut off the engine. He held his hands to the sides of his head, as if to keep it from coming apart.

"Stop!" he screamed in anguish.

Then the dam broke, and Ben was crying in great wails of agony. All the feelings of guilt and pain which had dominated him for so long were coming out in a river of emotion that he was unable to hold back any longer. There, behind the wheel of his car, Ben let go of much of the guilt he'd carried so long. He cried for Becca. Cried for Teresa and for Tia. But mostly he cried for himself.

CHAPTER 5

The next morning Ben woke up with a hangover that could kill a bear. He swung his legs off the couch and knocked over the bottle of whiskey he'd been working on last night. Luckily, the top was still on it. An old saying came to mind.

Using an old remedy for a familiar problem.

He ran his hand through his hair. *The problem is, the remedy is constantly giving me a hangover, and isn't helping that much anymore.*

The odd part of it all was he felt somewhat cleaned out on the inside.

Ben picked up the bottle and stood it upright, then pushed himself off the couch. His head hurt, but not as bad as the night he had drank without eating first. He had at least learned his lesson from that. Still, he was a little unsteady and his mouth was dry. He went into the kitchen, held his mouth under the faucet and drank. Then he stuck his head beneath the flowing water and let it wash over his head and neck.

"Ah, that's better." He shook his head like a dog after a bath, sending water flying everywhere. He looked up at the clock; he had less than an hour before work.

Just call in, they will understand. Something inside of

him resisted that idea. *No. Better get in the shower and get around. I don't want people thinking I couldn't make it a week—even a short week like this one. Thanksgiving is Thursday. I only have today and tomorrow to go.*

Ben pulled his clothes out of the closet. He had moved them all down to the living room after the last fiasco. With the clothes still in his arms, he sat down on the couch. He'd meant to get into the shower, but his thoughts were distracting him.

I thought I'd gotten past the worst of the pain and guilt. Why does it keep resurfacing and hitting me so hard. You know you can't keep this up. You've got to come to terms with the truth.

You didn't kill your family.

It was an accident.

You didn't want Tia to die. You just didn't want her to suffer.

You didn't bring this on yourself.

You did nothing wrong.

It was an accident, plain and simple.

Even had you gotten out of bed, you probably couldn't have stopped it.

But the guilty voice inside him took did want to surrender.

You could've stopped it, and you KNOW IT!

"Quit it, that kind of thinking doesn't help me," Ben said aloud, trying to end the conflict within him.

He looked at the clock and realized that he had been sitting there for almost ten minutes.

"I better get around," he said. "You can do this," he said determinately, then marched off to the bathroom.

Hannah Murphy woke slowly. Joey, her seven-year-old son, was standing at the foot of the bed. He had sandy brown hair and hazel, blue-green, eyes like his mother's.

"Momma?" he said with his eyes wide on her.

She started to get up, but pain shot through her head and jaw. She did her best to stifle a painful cry. Joey saw his mother's distress.

"Momma, are you alright?"

She sat up in the bed and tried to smile for her son. It took everything she had to hide the pain and discomfort she felt.

"Come here, Honey," she said. Joey moved to her side. Hannah took his hands in hers. "Are you hungry?"

Joey nodded slowly, still frowning.

"Go downstairs and I'll be down in just a couple minutes. I'll make you some pancakes." She tried to smile convincingly; it hurt her face to do it. The voice inside of her head warned her not to let on or it may frighten her son.

"Why is your face red?"

"Oh—" Hannah gently placed her hand on her face both to sooth herself and to hide that side of it from Joey. "I tripped last night and hit the edge of the chair. I'll be okay. It probably looks worse than what it really is," she said, hoping it was true.

Hannah ran her hand through her son's hair, and then picked him up and gave him a hug. "Mm... I love you!" She sat him back down.

"Love you, too, Momma," Joey said, seemingly satisfied that his mother was okay. He ran out of the bedroom and went downstairs.

Hannah went into the bathroom to inspect the damage. It wasn't as bad as she had feared. The right side of her face remained red from where Joe had hit her. It would probably be gone by the afternoon; she could cover it with make-up until then. Her jaw was throbbing and painful. It occurred to her that if Joe had hit her any harder, she probably would've been eating through a straw for the next couple months. She tried to open her mouth and stretch her jaw to see how bad it was.

"Ouch!" She quickly closed her mouth and used her hand to soothe her aching jaw. Then she reached back and touched the back of her head where she had hit the wall. It was tender, but would be fine, just as long as she didn't mess with it. One thought that kept going through her mind.

How did I end up here, and how much longer will it be before he ends up seriously hurting me… or worse, Joey?

There were a lot of things she could endure, but the realization that Joey was in danger awoke something inside of her. She had to leave. They had to leave. And they had to do it now.

Hannah had married Joe eight years ago. She met him at college. Joe was the starting inside linebacker for Western but had blown out his knee and couldn't play anymore. At the time, she considered Joe to be handsome and he never lacked self-confidence. She was thrilled when he had taken an interest in her. For much of her life, she always thought of herself as pretty, but always a bit shy. So, when Joe had pursued her—gone out of his way to be with her—she had fallen very quickly. After only a few months of dating, Hannah got pregnant with Joey. Despite the circumstances, she believed it to be a blessing because she loved children. Had things worked out differently, she would've finished her degree in order to become an elementary school teacher.

Surprisingly, Joe had acknowledged his responsibility, and even asked her to marry him. The manner in which he asked wasn't the most romantic. He acted almost indifferent about it, and then handed her the ring with it still in the box. Hannah accepted, not because she thought Joe loved her, but because she hoped he would grow to love her—and the baby. The arrangement made her parents feel better about the unplanned pregnancy. In her mind, marriage could always meld people into a family, full of love, and acceptance. Her parents' own marriage was the example she used. They were always so in tune with each other, knew each other so well, that they rarely argued. It didn't take long for Hannah to realize just how naïve she had been.

Immediately after they were married, Joe started pressuring her father to hire him in the firm. He told her that they would need a steady income, and at the time it seemed like a good idea. Her father agreed to take him on, but he was to start at the bottom. Anything more than that would make it look like he was showing favoritism. Joe agreed to take the job and the modest salary, but privately fumed that his father-in-law would make him, the sole provider for his daughters' family, do menial jobs that were beneath him.

It wasn't long after that Joe's temper started to surface, and she got a good look at the man she had married. Early on, Joe didn't hit her, but he never hesitated to demean her, calling her stupid or lazy. The house had to be spotless. Some nights, he would throw her cooking, plate and all, against the wall, and then tell her what a lousy cook she was. Later, he would apologize and try to make it up to her by buying her flowers or taking her out for an evening. Hannah had taken it because she had loved him. He always seemed sincere, and she tried to convince herself that he was under a lot of pressure. So, she had accepted things the way they were.

Eighteen months into their marriage, he hit her.

At the time, Hannah hadn't told Joe that she was pregnant with their second child. She was going to tell him that night, but Joe had stayed out late at the bar. When he came home at two in the morning, he found her waiting for him. She worried something had happened to him. Plus, she was anxious to tell him about the baby.

"I was out, alright. Now quit your bitching," he told her while standing in the kitchen. He was swaying lightly, the smell of tequila on his breath.

"Joe, I have something to tell—" She never got the chance to finish. Joe moved so quickly she didn't have the chance to react.

"Shut up!" He roared and hit her, open handed, across the head. Hannah fell to the floor, weeping.

"Joe, please don't," she sobbed.

He kicked her several times. "I told you to shut your mouth!"

Her head was ringing, her body wracked with a burning pain inside. Her first thought was of the baby. Hannah remained curled up on the floor with her knees pulled into her chest. Joe stepped over her, leaving her on the floor. Before leaving, he turned and said in a sober voice, "Now see what you made me do? Why couldn't you just keep your face shut?"

Even up to the present, Hannah never told him that he had caused her to lose that baby, never even told him that she had been pregnant. The next day, Joe was repentant. He claimed the alcohol was to blame and that he would give it up for good. Joe did stop, and even the berating came to a halt. There were times he even tried to act like a good father by helping with Joey—although it appeared as if Joey, even at a very young age, wanted very little do to with his father.

Hannah kept the secret of that night. She did her best to forgive him and was happy that the incident seemed to be a wakeup call. Joe was doing all the things that he had to in order to turn his life around.

Around this time, he also began putting pressure on his father-in-law to give him more responsibility and a better salary. Joe's main line of attack was to argue how difficult it was to adequately provide for his family with such a low income and position. Joe had even recruited Hannah to talk to her father about it. George Pearson had finally relented, raised his pay, and slowly began to groom him to take over as Operational Manager.

Over the next few years, Joe kept his word. He stayed sober and did his best to deny his true nature. There were times when he would slip, use a harsh word on her, but he refrained from using his hands on her. Then, very slowly, Joe began to fall back into his old patterns. Once promoted to Manager, the drinking started again. And the abuse. This time it was more subtle—at least until last night.

Joe came home later than usual. When he walked

through the door, Hannah knew instinctively it wasn't going to be good. The heady smell of alcohol couldn't be missed.

"Joey, run upstairs and watch television in your bedroom, will you?" Hannah had told her son.

"Yes, Momma," Joey said. He slowly left the room while staring apprehensively back at his mother.

"What did you do that for?" Joe asked her.

"I made some spaghetti if you want some," Hanna said, pushing his question aside, and going to the stove.

"Are you going to answer my question?" he asked. "Or are you too much of a coward like your father and going to ignore me?"

"What are you talking about?" she asked, trying to keep the fear out of her voice. It took all of her courage to keep from running upstairs and locking herself in the bedroom with Joey.

"After everything that I've done for that stupid company of his—after all the crap I've put up with—they treat me like I'm a little kid."

Hannah said nothing. Joe was dangerous right now, and she knew it.

"They want to coddle that moron, Stryker—your father and that idiot, Walker—sitting there, rubbing my nose in it."

She didn't know how wise it was but decided to try and talk him down a little. It had worked in the past, but he'd usually been sober. "I can't believe they would try and rub your nose in anything, Joe," Hannah said, taking a step closer to him with her hands out and turned upward to show empathy. "They're just trying to protect him right now. I'm sure it has nothing to do with you and how you run things."

"Yeah, well, that idiot Walker used it to his advantage that's for sure. 'I told you to leave him alone… you knew better… blah-blah-blah!'"

"Joe, the man just lost his family. How would you feel —"

Again, it happened so quickly she hadn't seen it coming. Joe hit her squarely on the jaw. The blow knocked her backwards, flying almost comically through the air. Her head hit the wall hard enough to leave a dent in the drywall. That was the last she could remember. She slumped to the floor sitting cockeyed behind the end table.

"Nobody tells on me and gets away with it. And nobody tells me how to run my office—that includes your idiot father and that pea-wit partner of his!"

It took a few seconds to register the fact that Hannah wasn't getting up. Joe went over and pulled her upright.

"What have I done?" He corrected himself. "Look what you've gone and made me do?" He said angrily at her unconscious form. Joe reached down and checked her for a pulse; she was still alive. Her eyes started fluttering and she opened them. At the same time, there came a noise from the top of the stairs.

"Momma?" asked a small voice at the top of the stairs.

"It's alright, Joey. Go back to bed," Joe said sternly to his son.

Hannah gave Joe a frightful look, as if to say, 'don't let him see this'.

Joe listened carefully; Joey hadn't moved. After a minute, he could hear the shuffle of the boy's small feet and then heard the bedroom door close.

"Come on," Joe said, holding out his hand. She pulled

back instinctively. "I'm not gonna hit you, alright."

Joe picked her up, cradled her in his arms, and carried her to the bedroom. She hadn't said a word to him and that appeared to suit him just fine. He put her on the bed and then left the room, but she knew nothing would ever be the same again. The incident had smashed any illusions she had and finally awakened her to the danger she and her son faced. As she lay there with her eyes closed and her head throbbing, consciousness began to slip from her. Whatever plans she needed to make would have to wait.

Megan sat at her desk, the computer monitor staring back at her. The spreadsheet she was working on was open, waiting for the input, but her mind was elsewhere.

"Megan!"

She jumped, her hands hitting the computer keyboard. Looking up, she found her boss, Sarah Elliott, staring at her from across the desk.

"Sorry, Mrs. Elliott."

"Well?"

"Um… I'm sorry, did you say something?"

Mrs. Elliott appeared annoyed that she had to repeat herself. "Where are the daily reports? Did you finish them or not?"

"Oh, yes, they're done. I have them here." Megan pulled them from the filing cabinet. "Here they are," she said, holding them out to Mrs. Elliott.

Mrs. Elliott looked down her nose at her. She made no move to take them. "I don't want them. I simply wanted to make sure they were finished. Wanda will be by to pick them up, as usual," she said, and left just as abruptly as she arrived.

She didn't care about those damn reports. She just wanted to stick her nose in my business, see if I was doing my job. She probably saw me sitting here, not doing anything, and jumped to a conclusion.

Megan was angry but tried to keep it in context. *No use thinking about it. Damn insufferable know-it-all.*

She went back to the spreadsheet, trying to find where she had left off before drifting off into Never Land. The problem continued to be that her mind was filled with conflicting thoughts. Her mother had been pressuring her to reconcile with Jim. Megan had tried to explain that Jim was currently living with another woman and the divorce would be final in a matter of days. Her mother dismissed all of her arguments.

"Meg, Honey. I don't know why you don't just try harder to get him back. Jim is a man. He'll get tired of this other woman soon, and when that happens, he'll come home," her mother had told her confidently.

"Whether he gets tired of her or not makes no difference to me. He made his decision. I'm not a damn rug he can walk over, then wipe his feet on," Megan said.

Her mother had frowned. "I know you love him. Sometimes women have to put up with things that are, well, you know… distasteful. Just put off the divorce for a few months until things clear up."

Megan gritted her teeth. She was beginning to be sorry she'd gone to visit her parents.

"Mother, you know I love you, and I appreciate your trying to help, but I will not do that. This isn't the Thirteenth Century where the woman has to cow to everything the man says and does."

"I'll say one last thing, and I hope you can appreciate what I'm saying. Jim is an attorney and makes very good money. How are you going to find someone that could take care of you as well as he can? Also, you know how difficult it can be for divorced women to find a man. I fear that you'll end up alone if you don't fix things now."

"I know that you grew up in a different time, Mother, but honestly, I don't need a man to take care of me. I have a job and do rather well by myself. As far as finding another man, well, that's my last concern right now. I don't want to end up alone. Nobody wants that. But I refuse to sacrifice who I am simply to keep from being alone."

Her mother hugged her briefly. "I'm sorry, Meg. I just worry so. I don't want you to be unhappy. It seems like you are throwing away so much."

"Well, you don't have to worry. The decision is made and it's the right one. I know that in my heart. Jim isn't the same man I married. Or maybe, never was the man I thought he was. Either way, my course has been set. I must go through this." Megan tried to smile for her mother. "You're right about one thing. There's still a part of me that loves him. That is why it is so difficult to do what is right."

Megan looked up from her computer realizing she had been lost, deep in thought once again. She looked around to make sure no one was paying attention and was relieved to find they weren't.

She dived back into the spreadsheet for the third time. *Alright, get back to work, Megan.*

At the same time Megan was having difficulty focusing, Ben was also at his desk, working on what he thought of as the mousetrap design for his machine. Every variation he put into the computer presented him with problems.

A sobering thought crossed his mind. *There may not be an answer.*

Sitting back, he gave serious thought about giving up on the idea. There were plenty of projects for the company to keep him busy. Still, the idea pestered him. He didn't like to give up that easily.

He gave a sideways glance at a miniature globe sitting at the corner of his desk. Becca had given it to him on his first day of work. It was made of brass, about ten inches tall, with raised edges to contrast the continents against the oceans. The only thing it was good for was a paperweight, but something in its shape latched onto his mind. Ben pulled the little globe towards him and spun it on its axis.

What if you made it round? A chamber with metal frame.

Before Ben could return to his computer, the door to his office flew open. In walked Joe Murphy, a wry smile on his face. This should've been the first warning to Ben, but he chose to ignore it.

"Hello, Ben," Joe said, speaking as if they were the best of friends.

Ben had become exasperated by Joe's theatrics. "As much as I enjoy your visits, I'd appreciate it if you were to knock first," Ben said flatly.

"I'm sure you would."

Joe strolled over and sat himself easily across from Ben.

"What do you want?" Ben asked, now getting annoyed.

"Thought we might sit and chat for a minute. You can spare a minute of your busy day now, can't you?" Joe said, still grinning.

Ben decided it was best to be direct. He'd had enough of Joe to last him a lifetime. "Either get to the point or get out."

"Alright, I suppose we could dispense with the niceties." Joe dropped his grin and his eyes narrowed. He leaned forward in the chair just slightly. "If you run to Walker and pull your whiney, spoiled brat routine again, I'm going to shove a baseball bat so far up your ass you'll know how a Popsicle feels. Now, was that direct enough for you?"

"Is that a threat?"

Joe's grin was back. "Take it for whatever you want."

"Let's get something straight, okay? I never went to Mr. Walker or anyone else. You sent the files down here for me to do. Mr. Walker stopped by, saw them on my desk, and knew what you had done. You left the plans unassigned, letting them stack up, so don't get pissed at me because you weren't doing your job. Do you know the sad part of it? I was going to do them, believe it or not. I was going to do them because I care about this firm. I know people depend on the job getting done. Unlike you, who's only care is to see how you can use your influence to extend your power around this place."

Joe turned red-faced. He jumped up out of the chair and was halfway across Ben's desk in one motion. "Listen here, you little cockroach, I'm going to stomp your pompous ass into the ground!"

Ben leaned forward out of his chair and looked him straight in the eye. "Any time you want to go outside and take care of this is fine with me. Come on... Come on! Let's go right now. I don't need this job. If I lose it pounding the crap out a self-righteous, narcissistic, piece of crap like you, then it'll be worth it." Ben's adrenaline was pumping, ready to go, but as he feared, a bully like Joe Murphy only makes a move when he is certain he can win.

Joe gritted his teeth but remained on his side of the desk.

"What's the matter, Joe? Are you such a pussy you're afraid to take on a real man?" Ben said.

Joe's eyes narrowed to slits, and his lips were pursed. Ben got a good look at the insanity going on behind those eyes. A thought ran through his head very quickly.

Throwing that in might not have been a good idea. He may be a coward, but he's also damn close to losing his mind.

But there was to be no outburst. Joe left without a further word. Ben took a deep breath, letting it out slowly. "Well, I think that was enough excitement for one day."

Hannah threw Joey's clothes in a suitcase, but each time she heard something, she jumped. If Joe came home for any reason and saw what she was doing, there would be hell to pay. The little sandy haired boy entered the room and sat down on the bed watching his mother.

"Did you pack up your video games and stuff?" she asked while closing the suitcase and zipping it shut.

"Yes," Joey replied, waiting a moment before asking his mother a question. "Where are we going, Momma?"

"I thought we'd go spend some time with your grandparents."

"You mean Grandma and Grandpa Pearson?"

Hannah smiled at Joey and put her hand under his chin. "Yes, Honey."

"Good. I like Grandma and Grandpa Pearson."

She closed the dresser drawers, picked up the suitcase, and then held her hand out to Joey, wanting him to come with her.

"Momma?" he said, holding back for a moment.

"Yes, Honey?"

"Are we leaving because of Dad?"

Hannah looked seriously at him for a moment. She sat the suitcase down and sat next to him. For only being seven years old, he was smart. Hannah wondered how much he really knew.

"Why would you ask that?"

"Because Dad likes to yell and call you names. I don't like it."

"I know, Honey."

"Did he hit you last night?" Joey asked, looking directly at her.

Hannah considered lying, but there was a part of her that knew he had already figured things out for himself.

"Yes, and I'm sorry I lied to you about it this morning. Sometimes I do things because I want to protect you."

"It's okay, Momma. Is it okay that I'm glad we are leaving Dad?"

Hanna nodded. "It is. But now that you know, I think we should hurry before he comes home."

"Yes, Momma," Joey replied.

Hannah put the suitcases in the car, buckled Joey in his car seat, and turned to take one last look at the house. Once she left all of it would come into the open. She'd have to explain why she stayed as long as she had. She'd have to file for divorce. Joey would never see his father again. Of that, she would make sure. Would Joey hate her for that someday? She didn't know. Once they left, there would be no going back. Of course, she and Joey would be safe.

Once they left.

With that thought, Hannah got in the car and drove away.

Ben's mind was deep in his work when his cell phone rang. He didn't bother to check the caller ID, and just answered it. As he figured, it was Megan.

"Hey, how's your day going so far?" she asked.

"Could be better, I suppose."

"Oh, yeah. Do tell."

"My boss threatened to beat me up."

"Um, okay. How did you manage that?"

"It was a misunderstanding. He didn't care to see it that way. I told him we could step outside and settle it anytime he wanted. Of course, he didn't."

"You should be careful, Ben. From what you told me, sounds like he's a bit unstable right now."

"You're telling me? I'm pretty sure the guy is Coo-Coo for Coco Puffs."

"You really need to be careful," Megan hesitated, and then added with a chuckle. "I wish my boss would ask me to fight. She's a gray-haired old biddy. I'm pretty sure

I could take her."

Ben laughed. "Has she been that bad?"

"Yeah, well, I've had a hard time concentrating. She hasn't made it any easier."

"Did you go out for lunch?" Ben asked.

"No, I've been working straight through trying to keep from falling behind. What about you?"

"Nah, been working on my project. Thought I would keep at it."

"Oh yeah, your secret. When are you going to show it to me?"

"I'm not sure. I don't think it'll even work."

"Okay, okay, I get it. I can wait. I should warn you; I am a very patient person."

"I promise to show it to you as soon as I prove to myself what a genius I really am."

"So, I can cut the waiting time down just by telling you that you're a genius? That's good to know," Megan said laughing.

"Talk to you later. Bye, Megan."

Ben made a rough sketch of his design by making a circle and adding the framework, the electro-magnet, aligned horizontally, and then a chamber inside that appeared as a ball of sorts. He added the swing arm, only curved this time, mounted on the inside of the base, so it could go all the way around.

Ben began to laugh. It reminded him of a hamster ball of some sort. He liked it, but it was only a start. There were still problems to work out. Actually, there were more questions than answers as of yet, but something deep down was again telling him he was on the right track.

"Okay, let's get this party started," Ben said, and began to put the new design into the computer.

Joe Murphy went home early, stopping by the florist shop to pick up a dozen white roses for his wife. They were her favorite, although, he couldn't say why. He hadn't bothered to ask, and he really didn't care. Before he even opened the door, he began to get a bad feeling.

"Hannah!" he called out.

Nothing…

He put the flowers on the kitchen table and went into the living room. It was empty. The bad feeling got stronger.

I knew I should've taken the day off.

He went upstairs, peeking into each of the rooms, even checking her closet. Nothing seemed out of place, but then again, he really didn't pay attention to Hannah's selection of clothes. He went into Joey's room and opened the top dresser drawer. It was empty. He opened all the drawers, pulling them out and tossing them across the room. They were all empty. Joe swore loudly and pounded the top of the dresser with both his fists. In a rush, he vaulted down the stairs and grabbed the phone. He quickly dialed her parents' phone number.

"Hello, Beverly? This is Joe. Hannah isn't there, is she?" Joe listened silently as Beverly's voice came over the line.

"Beverly, you have to believe me, I would never do anything like that." His heart sank; Hannah had given him up completely—something he'd never thought she would do.

"Yeah, yeah, yeah... whatever," Joe said, knowing the conversation was over. He slammed the phone down. A defenseless glass sitting a bit too close was thrown against the wall. It shattered, leaving debris scattered across the kitchen floor. There was little doubt that his marriage, his career, and just about everything else, had just been thrown into the toilet.

The phone rang again, and he was hopeful of an appeal. Hannah was weak, depended on him for everything. He thought he'd broken her spirit long ago. However, he now wondered if he might have underestimated her a bit. Even a cowering dog will bite when cornered. "Hello," he said quickly into the receiver, hoping it was Hannah. Instead, he found Mr. Pearson on the other end. Joe tried quickly to gather his thoughts. "No, Sir. You know I would never do that sort of thing. I think Hannah may be a little confused, is all. We've just been having a difficult time lately." He listened to his father-in-law, and his heart sank further. "I understand. Yes, I know—if I could just speak to Hannah. Of course, I understand completely. I'm suspended until..."

Joseph Murphy understood, alright. They had suspended him, but only until they could fire him directly. Walker hated him, always had, and wouldn't hesitate to join his father-in-law in giving him the boot. Paul Walker and Ben Stryker would probably dance around his office in a sort of victory dance. Joe pictured the scene inside of his head and something inside of him snapped. He slammed the phone down; the plastic casing cracked under the force.

Joseph Michael Murphy had finally dropped off that

cliff. He'd lost everything. The guardrails he used to keep his life in check—his job, his wife, his family—had all been removed. Everything was in a freefall. He stared blankly, thinking about the one person who had started this whole chain of events.

Ben Stryker.

Ben stopped off at the local pizza place on the way home and picked up a large pizza with everything. Then, he went to the party store next door for a six-pack of beer. The incident with Joe Murphy was still on his mind. Ben didn't like the look in Joe's eyes as he left.

That boy isn't playing with a full deck, and you just had to go and push him, didn't you? It wouldn't take much before he completely crashed. Went nuts. If that did happen, do you know the first person he would come looking for? That's right, Ben… ding—ding—ding… Yours truly!

Ben shook his head. *No, he's just a blow-hard and a bully. I pretty much proved that today. The Joe Murphy's of this world screw up, and then blame everyone else for the crap they do. In the end, he'll resume his power-hungry ways, get what he wants, and go back to being the miserable person he already is.*

This eased his mind just a bit, but that small voice had to throw in one last comment. *Just be careful you don't underestimate him. He hates your guts.*

Once inside the house, Ben threw the pizza on the table and opened a beer.

"Ah, nothing better," he said after taking a long slug.

The doorbell rang. Ben put his beer on the table and went to the door. Larry stood outside the bottom step. "Hey, come on in," Ben said, swinging the door open.

"You want a slice of pizza? It's still hot."

"Really? Did you get it from Marconis?" Larry asked greedily as he followed Ben into the kitchen.

"But of course," Ben said, holding the box out to him. Larry seemed enthralled at first, but then looked anxious.

"You won't tell Amy about this, will you?" Larry asked while pulling a piece from the box. "She'll have my head if she found out I was eating pizza."

"Yeah, I was figuring on running right over there to tell on you."

Larry tried to laugh despite the chewing. He swallowed hard. "You would, too."

"It'd be worth it just to watch you get your ass chewed. Amy still got you on that low-fat garden diet?"

Larry head bobbed up and down. Ben grabbed another beer and handed it to Larry.

"Oh, this is so good. I really do miss pizza," Larry said, wiping the grease from his chin with the back of his hand.

"Why has she got you on a diet anyway?"

Larry frowned. "Actually, Amy is the one who wanted to lose some weight. I told her… well, I liked her no matter how she looked. Then I joked that she was losing weight so she could go find herself a boyfriend. She didn't take that to well. But she figured it would be easier if we both were on a diet. So…" Larry shrugged.

"What are you going to do about Thursday?"

"Amy has granted permission for both of us to be off the diet for one day. Oh, that reminds me, the reason I'm here. You are coming over for Thanksgiving dinner, right? Amy told me she would box your ears if you didn't show."

"I don't know, Larry. I'd thought that I would just stay here, make a turkey pot pie."

Larry cut over him. "Good Lord, Ben. You can't leave me over there by myself. I've got to have someone hang out with. You could at least stay long enough to watch the Lions game with me."

"Can't say I'd have much of an appetite if I watched them play," Ben said.

Larry laughed. "Yeah, I can understand that? Oh, come on Ben. Do it for me."

"Alright, I suppose. If only to bail you out," Ben said, "but you owe me, big-time."

"Sure, why not? It's better to owe you than to never pay you at all," Larry joked. Ben smiled, but only briefly. "Besides, Megan is going to be there. I'm sure she'd be glad to have you there. Amy talked to her earlier, made sure she said she would come." Larry reached out and motioned for another piece. "Amy is going to wonder why I'm not very hungry for dinner. Thankfully, it isn't hard to choke down a handful of lettuce."

Ben grabbed a slice for himself and then handed the box to Larry.

"I'm glad to see that you and Megan have been hanging out together. With everything you two have been through," Larry said.

Ben took a swig of beer and nodded in agreement. "Yeah, she's had a tough time of it. Helping her kind of helps me in a way. When she tells me something she's going through, it's easier for me to open up and say things that I normally wouldn't. I guess you know that. At first, I was a little worried about what people might think about why we were spending so much time together."

"Not the people who know you. Good Lord, I as much as told you that you had better figure out a way of dealing with things. I'm only glad that you've found a way of doing just that. Not that I'm glad Megan has to deal with such a hardship. But it has been a blessing in disguise for you." Larry was silent for a moment, and then added, "I can see that you've been doing much better lately, and I'm thankful for that, too. There for a while, I was seriously worried about you."

"There are still times when I'm not sure. It all becomes like a battering ram in my brain and drives me mad. What you told me helped me see I wasn't dealing with things the way I should. I'm indebted to you for it." Ben chuckled. "I know it didn't seem that way at the time."

"Yeah, didn't make me feel too good, either, but I had to try. You know me, hate to stick my nose in other people's business. At least, not until I absolutely have to."

"Well, having Megan around to talk to has made things easier. And I also have a new project to keep me occupied. Which reminds me, how much do you think it would cost for your company to put a small concrete building in my back yard?"

"How big do you want it?"

"I don't know, maybe fifty by twenty. I'll need a poured concrete floor, heating/cooling system, electrical service, and all the permits that go with it."

Larry thought about it. "I'm not sure, will have to get back to you with a number. But if you are nice to me, I might be able to get them to drop their bid a little," Larry said. "This is for your project, then?"

Ben nodded. "However, money really isn't an issue."

"Hell, money is always an issue. Just ask anyone who needs it."

"I think I have plenty of it."

"What do you mean? You didn't go and win the lottery, did you?" Larry asked, and then chuckled.

Ben didn't laugh; instead, he kept a somber look on his face. When he finally spoke, it was in a soft tone. "You know Becca was a CPA. She took care of all the finances, and she was good at it. Between her job and mine, we were never hurting for money. She always paid off the credit cards at the beginning of each month. Hell, the house was paid off two years ago. Becca always dickered for the best deal for the cars we bought." Ben grinned at the thought. "She made me stay home when she went to talk to the dealer because she said I was a push-over. Anyway, by the time all was said and done, she'd stashed away over a hundred and eighty thousand dollars. When she, when Becca and the girls died, she had a two hundred-thousand-dollar life insurance policy through her work, and ten thousand on each of the girls. There was another hundred and fifty thousand in her 401k that they just recently sent me. And..." Ben sighed, "...a five hundred-thousand-dollar accidental death insurance policy on each member of the family. She bought the policies about a year before she died. The funny thing is, she never told me about it, Megan found the paperwork during the funeral stuff." He paused for a moment. "I know for a fact, Becca thought that accidental death insurance wasn't worth the money you paid for it."

Larry face held a bewildered expression. The pizza box slid off his lap, onto the floor. "Holy cow. You realize that's over two million dollars."

"Yeah, I do. As you can guess, I'm not hurting for money. Matter of fact, seems like the only thing I do have is money."

CHAPTER 6

Ben held the ball, concentrating on his delivery. He took four steps and rolled it, spinning down the alley. It slowly hooked left, into the gutter, missing every pin. "Now, would you look at that?" Ben said, pointing at the pins. "Whose idea was it to go bowling?"

"I believe it was yours, Hotshot," Megan replied. "Why is it so hard for you to hit those little pins down there? You know, if you were to roll it down the middle, you just might hit a few."

"Oh, we are being funny now, are we? Just because you're beating me, you think it's funny."

"It's not my fault you want to do that hooky thing and can't hit any of the pins."

"I haven't bowled since high school. I'm just a little rusty, is all."

"Really? Is that all it is? Rusty?" she said mocking him.

"Oh, shut up," Ben told her gruffly, then shook his head and smiled at her. "It's your turn."

Megan paraded up to the end of the lane, took a couple steps, and let go of the ball. It rolled slowly down the lane and hit the headpin. The pins cascaded into each other, knocking them all down.

"Did you see that? I got a strike!" She was jumping up and down.

"You really got to rub it in, don't you?" Ben said, hanging his head.

"Oh, I'm sorry, Ben. I don't mean to," she said, going over and roughing his hair playfully.

"Yes, you did," he smirked.

"Yeah, you're right," she said, "but you were right about one thing. This is fun."

"Well, I just figured it would be a good distraction for the both of us. I wanted to get out, and you—"

"Needed to forget about the divorce," she finished for him.

"I'm sorry, Megan. I didn't mean... well, you know."

Megan waved her hand dismissively. "It's alright. I'm okay with it. Actually, it's a relief to have it over with. Heck of a Christmas present though, coming a week before," she said a bit sadly.

Ben turned towards the lane and grimaced. *Why'd you have to go and say that? Idiot!* He thought.

Taking her advice, Ben threw his ball down the middle of the lane. It hit the headpin dead on, taking out all of them except the back corner pins. "Damn, a seven-ten split."

"It was better. You got most of them this time."

Ben laughed. "How about we finish this game and grab some dinner over at the Roadhouse?"

"Hm... bowling and dinner. I suppose I can't say no. It is after all the first date I've been on since becoming a single woman again."

Ben threw the ball at the seven pin as hard as he could. The ball glanced off of it and sent it flying into the ten pin, knocking it down. He pumped his fist in triumph. "Yes!" Then he did a little dance as he walked off the end of the lane.

Megan laughed and clapped as he did.

"I told you we'd have a good time," Ben said, still doing his little dance.

"That you did. But as you might recall, I'm still beating you by quite a bit."

Ben stopped. "You couldn't just let me have the moment, could you?"

"Nope," she said and began laughing again.

At the restaurant, they sat at the bar so Ben could watch the hockey game on the big screen. Between bites, Ben would glance up at the game.

"How's your steak?" Megan asked.

"It's good," Ben said, dipping a piece into steak sauce. "How's your—uh, you know—rabbit food?" he asked, pointing to her salad with his fork.

Megan rolled her eyes. "It's not rabbit food, it's a salad. And it is particularly good, thank you."

"You know, you could've gotten a steak." He leaned in closer to her and lowered his voice. "I wouldn't have told anyone I saw you eating real food."

"You may not be aware, but salad is real food. Besides, I didn't want a steak. I wanted a salad," she replied in a quiet voice to mimic his.

Ben cut his eyes back to the screen. His expression soured instantly. "How in the world do you give up a goal like that?" he said to the television. Out of frustration, he began to roughly cut another piece of his steak.

"How can you watch a stupid game like hockey?"

Ben nearly choked. “You take that back. Hockey is not stupid.”

Megan continued as if she had not heard him. “All they do is run around hitting that little puck around.”

“If you watched it once and a while, I could tell you what is going on,” Ben said.

Megan ignored this too.

“And that big guy in front of the net, if you got rid of him, they would score a whole lot more. It would make things a lot more exciting.”

“You can’t get rid of the goalie. They would just run up the score. It would be unbelievable.”

“Why? In basketball they score a whole bunch and people still like it. And even I can understand basketball,” Megan said with a smirk.

“Bah! Now you are just messing with me.”

“I guess I am,” she said. “How are things going at work?”

“It's been great,” Ben said, picking through his sautéed onions to get to the mushrooms. “The place has never run smoother since they fired Joe Murphy.”

“Oh, your boss… that’s right.” She paused. “You don’t even feel a little bad about him getting fired?”

Ben hesitated about five seconds with his head up. “Hmm… let me think,” he said, tapping his fingers sarcastically. Finally, he shook his head. “Nope, not a bit.”

“What about his family? I mean, he doesn’t have a job anymore, can’t take care of them. Don’t you feel bad about that?”

“Oh, I thought you knew.” Ben wiped his mouth with a napkin and pushed the plate away from him. “Not sure if you remember, but you met them once. Anyway, Joe is married to Hannah, George Pearson's daughter, one of the owners, which is why he moved up so quickly despite his wonderful management techniques. And yes, I'm being sarcastic. Come to find out, he'd become quite abusive. Not that it surprises many who know Joe Murphy. Hannah finally had enough and went to her father about it. When George learned what was going on, he didn't hesitate to fire him."

"Oh my," Megan exclaimed lightly, thinking about her own failed marriage. She may have had a rough ride, but at least not that bad.

"Yeah, I do feel bad for her—and the little boy, Joey. She was always nice enough. It kind of explains her attitude though, she never seemed to say very much. I thought it might be because he was the jealous type."

"How old is the little boy?" Megan asked.

"Joey? Not sure. About Tia's age. Now that I think about it, they were born about the same time. Anyway, he was always a good kid, very polite, from what I remember. They are staying with her parents for now."

"That's good. At least they're taken care of," Megan said.

Ben was looking up at the television screen, but his mind was still on the subject. "I wonder how safe they are. Joe Murphy isn't one to forgive easily. May even want a little revenge."

"On more than just them if what you tell me is right. He may come after you, Ben."

"Oh, he hates me, I won't deny that." Ben shrugged. "But he's nothing more than an overgrown bully. If he comes after me, I have no qualms about taking him on. I made that pretty clear at our last encounter."

Megan looked anxiously at him. "Ben, promise me

you'll be careful. I don't like it. I don't like it one bit."

"No need to worry," he said, then shot a glance up at the television. His face lit up, and he raised his arms. "Score! Did you see that? They won," he said, looking at her with a wide grin, and then back to the television.

Megan put her hand to her chin, resting her elbow on the edge of the bar, just shaking her head at him.

Hannah's eyes were constantly moving, scanning the waves of moving people. "Mother, did we have to come to the mall three days before Christmas? Seriously, I don't think you couldn't have picked a worse day," Hannah exclaimed as a small crowd of teenagers bustled by them. She held tightly onto Joey's hand, still keeping watch.

"I only have a few more gifts to pick up. It'll be alright," Beverly told her.

"I just don't like to be, you know, out in the open like this." Hannah lowered her voice. "What if Joe—"

Beverly cut her off, "Joey is right here. He can hear you, and he's a lot smarter than you give him credit for sometimes."

Hannah looked down at her son and smiled. "I know he's smart. I just..."

"Worry. Yes, I know." Her mother finished for her.

Joey knew his mother was nervous about being at the mall. He reached out to touch his mother, not with his hands, but with his mind and with his feelings. He immediately picked up on the prickly feeling of anxiety and fear. Fear of his father showing up and trying to take him away. He didn't know if it would work, but sent out his own feelings, trying to calm the fear inside of her. After a second or two, his mother did seem to relax a little. Joey wasn't certain if he'd done it or not. He knew so little of his gift—if that's what you would call it. Sometimes he thought of it as a curse, especially when he found someone to be particularly ugly on the inside. Someone like his father.

He hadn't had it long. About six months ago he began to sense other people's emotions. It was more than just empathy. It was a bit like looking inside of them and feeling what that person was feeling. If a person were bitter or angry, he could recognize them by a hot, burning sensation. If they were in a good mood, they had a nice warm feeling to them. Later, he began to understand that the gift ran deeper than that. Different qualities in people had different feelings attached to them. For some reason, Joey had no difficulty deciphering them.

At first, he didn't think it was real. Then he tried it on his mother. The reading he got made sense: She was a protective, loving person, who was intelligent, but not always self-confident. Beneath that was the fear, like that of a live wire. Images of his father flashed in his mind as he did this. Not mind reading exactly, but shadowy pictures linked to the feeling.

Joey had tried it on his father as well. It felt like hot tar. It was anger, selfishness, and jealousy. The feelings were detestable to him, as if someone had covered him with something hot and slimy. He had used it on his father only one other time—the night he hurt his mother. From the top of the stairs, Joey had reached out and known what he had done. He had felt both of them, his father's rage, and his mother's anguish. The only reason he hadn't come down from those stairs that night was he was aware of his mother's desperate desire for him not to.

Of course, Joey hadn't told his mother what he could do. She had problems enough. Besides, he was worried what she might think of him if he did tell her. He decided he would only use it when it was necessary. Something inside him told him it wasn't a toy, wasn't something to be taken out and played with whenever he wanted. He didn't know where this caution came from but heeded it anyway. One thing was certain—it didn't come from him. The question was, if not him, then who? Joey had tried to stretch his feelings, using the gift, to find out where it came from. He didn't know if it would work. There was no one to grab hold of, as he would think of it, but he did get a sense of something. A faint image painted itself inside of his mind; it was of a girl, about his age, with dark hair. A girl, he was certain, he had met before.

Ben pulled into the driveway and cut the engine. It was a warm evening considering it was towards the end of December. There were patches of grass visible on the lawn where the snow had melted. Neither Ben nor Megan made a move to get out right away. It was as if each were waiting for the other to speak. It was Megan who finally broke the uncomfortable silence.

"Thank you, Ben. I really did have a good time. It was nice of you to take me out to get my mind off of things," she said.

"Oh, you thought I was doing it for you. I just wanted to get out of the house for a while and needed a playmate."

"Well then, thank you for inviting me to be your

playmate? That didn't sound right, did it? Makes me feel like I should be wearing a playboy bunny outfit," Megan said laughing.

Ben grinned. Suddenly, the image of Megan in a playboy bunny outfit jumped into his mind. *Get your mind out of the gutter.* His thoughts went immediately back to it. *Got to admit, she would look hot.* He tried to erase the erotic image of Megan from his memory as he got out of the car. It was the first time he'd even considered what she might look like under those clothes. He expected to feel shameful or even guilty about even thinking about it, but for some reason he felt none of it. Instead, he found himself more conscious of her figure and her physical beauty.

"We should do this again sometime," Megan said casually. "Only next time, I get to pick the restaurant."

Ben shot her a serious look. "I don't have to eat rabbit food, do I?"

Megan smiled. Ben became acutely aware of her deep blue eyes and delightful smile. It was as if he was seeing her for the first time. Really seeing her.

"No, Ben, you can have anything your heart desires," she said.

"Alright. Goodnight, Megan," he said.

"Goodnight, I'll talk to you tomorrow," she said while crossing the yard and unlocking the front door. She waved to him before going inside.

Ben unlocked his door and went inside. He began to grope in the darkness for the light switch. From the corner of his eye, he caught a shadow of movement from inside the living room. He froze. Adrenaline began pumping through his body. He began in earnest to find the light switch, moving his hand back and forth to find a damn switch he'd flipped on and off maybe a thousand times before.

"Joe, is that you? Are you in there?" Ben said, trying to sound intimidating. "I don't know what you're after, but you'd better leave now before I call the police."

If he has a gun, it would be best to leave the light off.

Ben dropped his hand off the wall. Ironically, it hit the light switch as it came down. The sudden flood of light made him jump. He scanned the living room, searching the dark areas. He fully expected to find Joe Murphy standing in the corner, gun in hand. Instead, the room appeared empty. He searched the entire room, going around the couch and behind the recliner. Then a light breeze pushed the curtain. Ben cursed his overactive imagination while slamming the window shut. He'd opened it himself earlier in the day to air out the place. With his heart still beating hard, he plopped down in the recliner and gave a heavy sigh of relief.

Let's not do that again. Nearly gave me a heart attack over a damn curtain.

The next morning, Ben sat at his desk, double-checking the financial figures. Since Joe's firing, he'd assumed the majority of the managerial duties. Mr. Walker and Mr. Pearson didn't like the idea, but Ben reasoned with them. He was one of the few people capable of doing the job adequately and would fill in until they found a replacement. They had relented, but with the stipulation that if it got to be too much, he was to let them know right away.

In truth, he enjoyed staying busy. The majority of the manager's job was to keep track of the budget and to delegate assignments. Since he knew everyone who worked there, he needed only to match the job with the person he thought could best handle it. The only bad part was he had less time to work on his project.

Since inheriting the position, he'd noticed something curious. He wasn't a wizard at bookkeeping the way Becca had been, but he knew enough to realize something was amiss. The company finances appeared to be out of whack. A hefty sum of money was missing, and he kept finding duplicate billings for the same item purchased. Last year, the company had bought a printer for large-scale blueprints. It was a nice machine, he'd used it many times, but it wasn't cheap. However, the inventory listed two printers. Ben knew only of one.

So, where is the other one? He thought. *Joe Murphy made the purchase, meaning there's a good chance the second one a mirage. The money funneled to another account, one with his name on it. I wonder how many more of these double billings I'll find.*

There was a gentle knock on the door. Ben glanced up from his paperwork. "Mr. Walker, come on in. I just finished up the future projects list. I was going to bring them up for you and Mr. Pearson to look at," Ben told him. He thought about saying something to Mr. Walker about the budget but decided to wait until he was certain.

"Good work, Ben. We hadn't planned on finishing that until the end of January." Mr. Walker hesitated. Ben noticed he was holding a single folder in his hands. "Of course, that wasn't the reason I came here. I wanted to ask you about something." Mr. Walker held the folder out to Ben. "The Poor Richard account. Have you heard of it?"

"Um... yeah, sure. I've been working with them," Ben said, taking the folder, and flipping through it casually to make it look as if it wasn't a big deal. "They were asking for specification for something or another. I'd have to look at it to know for sure."

"Really?" Mr. Walker said, looking at Ben as if he was x-raying him. "It's funny—the company doesn't give an address or phone number. Just a Post Office box. When I checked the shipping records, it had an attachment saying that you were to give instructions on shipping. Can you tell me what is going on here?"

Ben opened and closed his mouth a few times.

"Is it a coincidence that the name of the company is Poor Richards? As I recall, that was the pseudonym for Benjamin Franklin. A name I believe you have in common with the founding father."

Ben surrendered. "I'm sorry, Mr. Walker. It's my own personal project. Poor Richards is my company if you could call it that. I'm its only employee."

"Why didn't you just tell us what you were doing? A bit silly to charge your company for work you were doing, don't you think?"

"Well, I figured it was only right. I mean, you pay me to do work for the firm—not for me to play with a pet project. I just figured it was the right thing to do."

Mr. Walker laughed, shaking his head. "Ben, you're a good man. I'm happy that you found something that interests you, albeit a personal one."

"So, you aren't angry then?"

Mr. Walker shook his head. "No. But from now on, don't bill your company for the work you do. You'll have to pay for the materials and such," he said, then hesitated for a moment and asked, "If you don't mind my asking, what is it?"

"I can't really… I don't…" Ben tried to start over. "It's kind of hard to explain. For now, I'd kinda like to keep it to myself."

"Alright, I can live with that," Mr. Walker said kindly. "You have permission to work freely on it. And if there ever comes a time you can, or want, to explain what you are doing, I'd be happy to hear about it." He got up, leaning hard on the edge of the chair as he did.

"Thank you, Mr. Walker."

Mr. Walker walked to the door, looked back at Ben, and shook his head. "You're a piece of work, Ben, you know that?" he said as he left.

Ben blew out in a sigh of relief. *There isn't getting anything past that old man.* Then he looked down at the budget. *At least I hope so. God knows how much Joe took this company for if no one knew about it.*

CHAPTER 7

The snow fell hard on Christmas morning. Ben stood alone at the foot of the graves, oblivious to the snow, the cold, and the sounds around him. All, except the names on the headstones before him. Memorial cemetery was in Battle Creek, a twenty-minute ride from home. Rebecca had grown up in Battle Creek. Her mother and father still lived in the same house, just a few blocks away on Highland Avenue. The last time he was here was on Teresa's birthday, a little over a month after they perished in that car accident. He nearly lost his mind that day. The grief had been too much for him. He thought about how he'd never get to see either of his daughters grow up, get married, and start families of their own. How he would never know what kind of people they would become. They would forever remain children in his memory.

"Merry Christmas, Teresa. Merry Christmas, Tia." He sighed heavily. "And to you my dearest Becca, Merry Christmas. I miss you all so very much." His voice cracked on the last part. There was never a time when he felt as alone as he did right now. There was a part of him that believed that if the ground were to open, and the graves were to swallow him, he would welcome it gladly. But that was not going to happen. They were gone and he was here. He had to go on without them. The realization broke something free inside of him, like a hand balled into a fist, and then slowly releases its grip. He was finally beginning to let go, of finally letting go of the grief. Finally on the path to the end of his grief.

Ben trudged back to the car, the snow crunching beneath his feet. He knew it would be difficult coming here today. Megan had volunteered to come with him, but he felt he should come alone, at least today. He'd promised her they would come back another time, but he wanted to be here with them on Christmas morning because the day was special to them, especially Rebecca. Christmas was his wife's favorite holiday, and she absolutely went all out for it. Every year, the decorations went up, inside and outside of the house. The plans she would make for the holiday went from the end of Thanksgiving all the way to Christmas day. The meal on Christmas day was always the most lavish —bigger than even Thanksgiving. To her, Christmas was more than just a holiday. It was a celebration of the people she loved the most. She also insisted on a real tree. Ben tried to get an artificial Christmas tree only one time. He had actually bought one and brought it home. It was an experience he wasn't likely to forget.

"Benjamin Stryker, what in the world is that thing?" Becca said pointing to the box.

"Mommy, we've got a Christmas tree," Tia said.

"That's not a real Christmas tree," Teresa chipped in.

"I just thought that this would be easier, and a lot safer, than a real tree," he said, beginning to understand how badly he screwed up. He tried to recover by using reason

and logic on his wife. "This one is flame resistant and much safer to have in the home. Plus, this model is one of the fullest, prettiest, most expensive they have," he explained.

"I like it, Daddy," Tia added.

"Thank you, Tia," he said, pulling Tia closer to him and putting his arm around her. He knew he needed an ally at this point. "See, Tia likes it."

Becca stood there silently; her arms crossed in front of her. This was never a good sign. When she was angry, she didn't yell. She got quiet. It was like a ticking time bomb. Ben braced himself for the explosion he knew was coming. Finally, she broke the silence. "When I sent you to get a Christmas tree, you knew what I wanted. I will not have this abomination in my house," she said, kicking the box with the side of her foot. "If we were so poor that we couldn't afford presents, decorations, or even a fancy Christmas dinner, I'd still have you march out into the woods, chop down a tree, and bring it home. So, I suggest you throw that thing back into the car, take it back to whatever store you got it from, and get me a real Christmas tree."

"What if—"

"No!"

He finally conceded, knowing there was no use in arguing with her. He went to his wife, held her hand, and looked into her eyes. "If it means that much to you, I'll get rid of it," he said.

"Ben, I'm sorry. I don't mean to overreact," Becca said.

"I'm just curious why it is so important to have a real tree."

"Because they've already tried to make Christmas into such a fake holiday. Things like this," she pushed the box with her toe, "only add to it. Christmas should be a day

that is real, full of the love that we share. Not some damn commercial you'd see on television."

Ben raised his hands. "Alright, I'll take it back."

"Mommy, what's an ablomininination? Tia asked, looking up at her mother.

Becca smiled, knelt down, and hugged her daughter. "It just means it doesn't belong here, that's all."

"Is Daddy in trouble?" Teresa asked.

"Yes... every day since the day he met me," Becca said grinning.

Ben opened the car door while looking back over at the gravesites. He had invited family and friends for Christmas dinner. He wanted to keep alive the feelings and traditions Becca had brought to this day. He'd even got a real tree and put it in the front window as she had every year. Eventually, he would forget some of the things about his wife and daughters. Memories would fade, but this one he would hold dear.

He climbed into the car, took one long, last look before driving off.

An unshaven Joe Murphy sat on the couch with a bottle of Cuervo Gold in his lap. The house stank from the neglect. Empty pizza boxes littered the kitchen counter, unwashed clothes lying about, and an overflowing trashcan. Joe stared blankly at the television screen. It's A Wonderful Life was playing, but he wasn't really watching it. To Joe, it was simply a distraction for his drinking.

"Merry Christmas, Joe," he said before taking a long

drink, then setting the bottle back on his lap. "Merry Christmas to everyone—you bastards!" he yelled this time, and then laughed. It echoed throughout the empty house. He held up the bottle, swished the liquor around inside of it, and then took another swig.

"I wonder how my darling wife and son are enjoying Christmas this year. I wonder if I should pay them a visit at her Mommy and Daddy's house. They'd love that, wouldn't they?" The idea made him laugh, and then stopped abruptly. A scowl covered his face. "Oh, Hannah has a wonderful present coming to her this year. It may be a little late, but she will definitely get a great big surprise from me."

The hatred inside of Joe was growing like a cancer, infecting every part of him. He had developed such a bitter loathing for Hannah, for her mother and father, for that idiot Paul Walker, and for Ben Stryker.

Especially Ben Stryker.

It was Ben and his holier-than-thou attitude who had defied him, mocked him, and set into motion the events that caused him to lose everything. Joe had consulted a lawyer about the divorce, custody, and his job. It hadn't been good. A full week had passed since Joe met with the guy, Mr. Bishop, at a cafeteria near the courthouse. While waiting for the lawyer to arrive, Joe found himself fighting to control that anger. It had become a hungry monster, feeding on his hate, trying to escape. It wanted to strike out at anyone and everything. At a quarter to one, Mr. Bishop finally arrived. Bishop was a man of medium height with graying hair, watery eyes, and pasty complexion. In some ways, he reminded Joe of a picture he'd seen of President John Adams. Mr. Bishop spotted Joe easily and settled in the seat across from him.

"Mr. Murphy, it's good to see you," Mr. Bishop had said, extending his hand. They shook, but only briefly. Joe wasn't in the mood for the normal niceties and decided to get right to the point.

"So, what's the verdict?"

Mr. Bishop laughed. "Verdict? Yes, I suppose that's an apt way of putting it," he said smiling, and then realized his client wasn't smiling. He sighed and opened his briefcase. "Well, I think we can get you at least half of the assets. From what her lawyer has told me, she doesn't want the house, but she would like half of the money once it's sold. Or you could buy out her half, whatever is easiest."

"She wants half. It's my house," he said angrily while the monster inside of him tried to get loose.

"Mr. Murphy, in this state, a spouse is entitled to half of the assets acquired during the marriage. That would include the house," Mr. Bishop stated. "Is there anything else? Do you own any stocks?"

Joe shook his head.

"Bonds?"

"Nope."

"Savings?"

"None, whatsoever," he said. There was the two hundred-thousand-dollars he'd stashed away—money he had siphoned off of the company books—but he wasn't about to tell Bishop or anyone else about that. It was all in cash, sitting in a safety deposit box in Florida.

"So, you have no assets other than the home, the two cars, and the furnishings. Is that correct?" Mr. Bishop asked.

"Yeah, I guess so."

"Well, that should be relatively easy then. She has listed her car and some of her personal items that she wants to keep. Is there any equity in the home?"

"In this market, are you kidding me? It's not even worth what I owe."

"Oh, I see. I'll talk to Mr. Goldman, her lawyer, about that and see what can be done."

"What about custody? I told you I wanted custody of Joey. She walked out on me and just took him. Isn't right to take a man's kid away without having any say in it," Joe said, pounding his fist on the table. The coffee cup in front of Joe rattled but stayed upright without spilling.

Mr. Bishop looked a little uncomfortable about this part. "Yes… well, Mr. Murphy, it seems she has evidence of physical abuse and verbal threats. Your parental rights have been rescinded, that includes visitation rights. The judge has also granted a restraining order, which I am guessing, you have received?"

"Yeah, I did. Still doesn't make it right."

"May I be blunt?" Mr. Bishop said. "You're fortunate you're not in prison. The police have documented reports of you threatening the lives of your wife and her parents. You made threats that you'd take the minor child by force, that you'd burn their house to the ground." Mr. Bishop shook his head. "Mr. Murphy, you'll be lucky to get visitation in a couple of years, and that's not even a guarantee. At a minimum, you would have to attend some sort of counselling, maybe Anger Management, not to mention putting an end to your hostile behavior and establish, at least, a somewhat civil relationship with the mother of the child."

Joe gritted his teeth. "You mean, I'm just supposed to swallow this crap and try and smile while I do it?"

"I don't know what else to tell you. Until we are able to convince the courts that you're not a threat to the minor child or the family, that's the way it is."

"What about my job? You can at least give me some good news there, can't you?"

Mr. Bishop shook his head again. "I'm afraid that you were considered part of management, and as such, they have the right to change, move, or fire any member of its executive team. They need no other reason or excuse to do so. Minus a contract, Executives can be hired and fired at the will of the owners or its board... and you had no such contract."

"So, you can do nothing? Miserable little Cockroach, you took my money and did nothing!" he shouted. The monster was loose, and there was no stopping it now. Mr. Bishop was scooting in his chair, backing away from him, his briefcase still open on the table. Joe threw it at the little man, papers flying everywhere. "Did you honestly believe you could rip me off and just walk away?" His voice sounded low and calm, but inside of him was a raging inferno of hatred and disgust.

"Mr. Murphy, I'm warning you, leave me alone or—"

"Or what? You're going to cry?" Joe grabbed him by the neck with one hand. Mr. Bishop looked a bit comical, sitting with his rear-end half out of the chair with his legs splayed out in front of him, holding onto Joe's arm.

"I could snap your neck like a chicken's right now. Do you know what?" Joe moved his face into his. "It'd be worth it."

One of the patrons, a young man who had been sitting with his girlfriend, tried to intervene. He grabbed Joe by shoulders and managed to pull him away from Mr. Bishop. Joe never hesitated. In one fluid motion, he let go of Mr. Bishop, and rounded on the guy with his fist clenched. The young man flew backwards, hit the edge of a table, and slumped onto the floor. Joe laughed, staring at the unconscious young man.

"Well, that just goes to prove, no good deed ever goes unpunished." Joe laughed again. "I always liked that saying."

Walking deliberately toward the door, Joe paused before exiting. "I don't believe I'll need your representation any longer, Mr. Bishop. I just want you to know, as a lawyer, you really do suck."

Joe took another swig of tequila. He had different plans now. If the court system wasn't going to help him, then he didn't need them. He was actually a little surprised that Bishop or the other idiot hadn't filed assault charges. His initial plan had been simply to walk away and cancel the check he had given the attorney if the news was bad. He was smart enough to know that his chances of getting custody were slim, and even slimmer of getting his job back. He'd hired Mr. Bishop because he had a reputation for getting things done. Joe had hoped that Bishop could manipulate Hannah's lawyer into granting partial custody or even visitation for the kid, and pressure the firm into handing him some kind of severance package. The divorce was an afterthought. He really didn't care about actually seeing the snot-nosed brat. Joey had always been a momma's boy. There were times the little nosepicker had the audacity to glare at him after an altercation with Hannah. Back then, he could easily fight the urge not to smack him and wipe that stupid look off his face. If it were to happen now, the little snot-rag would have to turn sideways to look straight. No, he didn't want the kid because they were so very close. He simply wanted to take him to hurt Hannah. And now, with a restraining order in place, it would be even more difficult. Still, Joe kept surveillance on the boy, trying to figure out a way to get him alone. He planned on taking Joey last, some weekend he had visitation, but with these complications, he would have to move that up. The last target on his list was Stryker. He wanted to make it slow and painful. He wanted Stryker to beg for mercy. That option may have to change, too. He would have to wait and see.

Joe uncapped the bottle and took another drink. He swallowed it slowly, still thinking about Ben's fate.

"Oh, I think I can arrange something nice for Ben Stryker, I'm sure."

The Pearson home was in Parchment which sat on the northern edge of Kalamazoo. Though Parchment was still an incorporated village, the larger city had nearly swallowed it up. The house was built sometime in the early nineteen-hundreds, about the same time the paper mill opened. It was a modest, two-story home with a garden in the backyard (maintained mostly by Mrs. Pearson), and flower beds on each side of the house. It sat on a side street, just a few blocks from Main Street. There was a detached garage that sat to the right of the house, connected only by a low picket fence and a gate that led to the back yard. The only entrance into the house was also on the right side and led directly into the kitchen. George Pearson could've very easily afforded a newer home, even a mansion if he wished, but he considered this home. He grew up here and didn't feel it necessary to have anything larger or more extravagant. Inside, the kitchen countertop ran along the wall and curved around, separating the kitchen from the living room. The living room was the largest room of the house. It had a picture window facing the road. Bookshelves covered what used to be the front door, which had closed up long ago by George's father. This time of year, the Christmas tree dominated the front picture window. Along the opposite wall was a narrow stairway. It ran straight up, with no landing and no lighting, making it look like a dark shadow along the wall. There were three bedrooms up there. Hannah and Joey occupied two of them. George had always intended to fix the stairway, make it wider, but never seemed to find the time or inclination to follow through. From there, the living room opened into two small hallways with one leading to the master bedroom and the other to the bathroom.

Hannah stood behind the couch as she watched Joey open his Christmas presents. George Pearson was in his favorite chair, watching his grandson's eyes light up as he opened each one. Beverly came out of the kitchen, a coffee in hand and stood next to Hannah. She put her arm around her daughter.

"Merry Christmas, Hannah," her mother told her, squeezing her gently.

"Thanks, Mom. Merry Christmas," she said. "And thank you for the gifts. I don't know how to repay you and Dad for everything you've done. You know I don't have—" Hannah stopped herself. "I'm just glad we're here with you."

"There's no need to worry. We were more than happy to get him his presents. Look at him, he seems so happy."

"Yeah, well living with Joe wasn't exactly the best of time for him. I just feel so guilty that I stayed in that situation for such a long time," Hannah said. Her eyes became glossy, she tried to hide her face from her mother.

"There's no need to think about that, now," Beverly told her daughter. "You will start your life over again with Joey. It doesn't matter how or when you finally discovered it was necessary to leave. The fact is you did. We love you, Honey. Nothing else matters." She smoothed the hair out of her daughter's face which was now wet with tears.

Joey ran over to his mother holding a bright yellow toy dump truck, a look of joy in his eyes.

"Momma, look at what Grandpa got me." Joey stopped when he saw his mother had been crying. "Momma, are you alright?" he asked, dropping the toy truck.

Hannah sniffed, wiped her eyes, and smiled as widely as she could. "I'm fine. I'm happy that you are having such a great Christmas this year."

Joey was still suspicious. "Are you sure? Dad hasn't tried to bother you again, has he?"

"No, he hasn't."

"Good," Joey said sternly. "I saw him at the school on Friday. He was hiding in his car. I don't think he wanted me to see him."

Hannah threw her mother a startled look. She took Joey's hand, walked him to the couch, and sat down with him. "Joey, you do understand that it's especially important that you never go up to him. You know that, right?"

"I do, Momma."

"If your father ever approaches you, tries to get you to go with him, I want you run away. Go tell a teacher, a policeman, or any adult, because it would be bad if he were to take you. Do you understand, Joey? Your father may want to take you just to hurt me, and it would be..." she wanted to emphasize the danger, but not scare him too badly, "...frightening for you. He's not the same person anymore. It would be very bad if he got you alone."

"I understand, Momma," Joey said. "Dad has always been a bad person on the inside. I have seen it. Sometimes I wondered if it was wrong to wish he weren't my dad."

Hannah sat speechless, impressed with her son's understanding of his father, and how really intuitive he was.

"You really are a smart boy, aren't you?" Beverly said.

"Yes, you are," Hannah added, and smiled at him. "Now go help your grandpa open the present we got for him, okay?"

Joey did as he was asked while Hannah pulled her mother into the kitchen.

"If that lunatic is watching the school, he means to try something. I know him that well." Hannah exclaimed in a hushed voice to her mother.

Beverly took Hannah's hand. "Not to worry. We'll just have to be more careful, especially when we're dropping off and picking up Joey from school. Joe hasn't tried anything because he knows he can't get near Joey right now. The school and the teachers know the situation."

None of this was making Hannah feel any better. She'd experienced the kind of spite Joe was capable of and knew the lengths he would go to get at her. Despite all her hopes, this wouldn't be the end of it. Joe would remain firmly planted in her fears as long as possible. "I know, but was it too much to hope that he would just go away?"

Her mother hugged her. "No, it isn't. We just have to be patient and watchful for a while. Joe will get tired of this game and move on."

"I pray you're right, Mom. I don't know what I'd do if that evil monster got a hold of Joey."

Standing at the head of the table, Ben tapped the glass with a fork to get everyone's attention. After a moment, everyone in the room quieted and their attention turned to him.

"Most of you know, I'm not much of a public speaker, so I'll do my best to keep this short," he said. There were a few chuckles from among his audience, and at least one good-natured snort of derision. The loudest, he was certain, came from his brother, Tom. Ben nodded and smiled. "Yeah, yeah… very funny. Anyway, I'd like to propose a toast. To all of you whom I consider my family. I'd like to thank you for sharing this day with me. And even though the turkey was dry, and the stuffing a bit runny, I hope you have enjoyed being here. Becca told me once that Christmas was a day that was to be real, celebrated with the people we loved the most. I never fully appreciated what she meant by that until now." He paused; his head dipped just a little. "You never know how much time you have left with the one's you love." Ben shook his head as if to clear the last from his thoughts. "Anyway, I intend to continue the tradition she started. You are all cordially invited back here next year for some more dry turkey, my company, and my gratitude for being the most important people in my life."

They lifted their glasses and drank.

"Do you think that we could get Amy or Megan to cook the turkey next year?" Larry asked. Everyone in the room broke out in laughter.

"Go ahead, joke about my cooking, but it's getting better," Ben said.

"Yeah, it is. We haven't had to take anyone to the hospital yet," Megan threw in.

"That's right, go ahead and make fun," Ben said. Susan, Ben's four-year-old niece, tugged on his pant leg. He looked down at her; she was the perfect likeness to her mother, Abby, at that age. Ben bent down and scooped her up. "Well, hello, Suzy."

"Uncle Ben, I liked your turkey."

"Thank you, Suzy. I'm glad you liked it," Ben replied, then said to everyone listening, "You see, she likes my cooking. What do you think of that?"

"Suzy, tell your Uncle Ben what you thought of his stuffing," Abby told her daughter.

Suzy scrunched up her face stuck out her tongue, making her opinion of it quite evident.

Ben couldn't help but laugh. "It was a bit nasty, wasn't it?"

Never thinking it possible, Ben felt his heart swell, feeling as full tonight as it was empty this morning. Having the house full again warmed him. He wouldn't have doubted that Becca had channeled her spirit, here —on her day—to give her husband a chance to feel joy, even if only for a little while.

Ben led Larry, Cliff, Tom, and Abby's husband, Frank, into the kitchen. He opened the cabinet and pulled out a bottle of expensive looking bottle of bourbon. "This is the smoothest whiskey known to man. Or at least me. Anyone up for a snort?" Ben asked.

"Sure, we're staying the night," Frank said.

"Nobody is going anywhere tonight," Ben said, pouring the round.

"I think Amy and I could make it home if we had to," Larry joked.

Megan walked in on them. "What's going on here?"

"Just pouring a few shots of this fine, imported whiskey. You don't want one, do you?" Ben asked.

"Are you kidding? I would've figured you'd poured one for me already," she said smugly.

"Oh, really?" Frank said.

"Oh, believe me, when she's in the right frame of mind, she can put me to shame," Ben said.

"That isn't hard to do," Tom said laughing.

"Just my kind of woman," Cliff added. "You aren't married, are you?"

Ben gave Cliff a stern look. Cliff shrugged his shoulders. "What? I was only asking?"

"It's alright, Ben. I'm a big girl, I can take care of myself," Megan told him, and then turned to Cliff. "No, I'm not married. Not anymore. And no, I'm not interested, thank you."

Cliff was still looking back and forth from Ben to Megan. "Oh, I get it. Never mind."

"Cliff, remind me to beat the crap out of you later,

okay." Ben told him.

Abby entered the kitchen followed by Amy.

"What do we have here?" Amy asked. Her tone implied disappointment.

"This is his doing," Larry said, quickly pointing to Ben.

Amy punched her husband in the arm. "You probably instigated it."

Ben grabbed two more glasses and added them to the mix. "Now that you are here, you have to have one with us."

The drinks were passed around, and they stood there waiting for Ben. He held up his shot glass and they followed suit. "To those we have lost," he paused, "and to those we love the most... Prost!"

"Prost? What does that mean?" Amy asked.

"Don't ask. Believe me, don't ask," Megan told her. Ben sneered at Megan playfully.

"Wait a minute. Isn't that what Grandpa used to say?" Abby said, and they all began to laugh.

Later, Larry and Ben stood at the patio door, looking out into the backyard. The snow was still falling lightly as the sky dimmed toward evening. A cement slab poured for the floor of his building was covered by a foot of snow. The rest of the construction had to wait for better weather, which wouldn't be until spring.

"You know, I got a bonus for getting the contract for your little project there," Larry said. "I hope that doesn't bother you."

"No, not a bit. I'm glad you got it. I would've given you the money myself for putting it together for me."

"Wasn't that hard to do," Larry replied. "I told them what you wanted, and they took care of the permits and such. Don't be getting any ideas in your head that you need to be paying me anything. Excel Contracting pays me pretty well, and with the bonus they gave me, I think I'm more than compensated."

"Well, it's appreciated," Ben said. He took a swig of beer while gazing out into the yard. He wished his project were at least a little further along. If it had walls and a roof, he could at least get started.

"Are you still doing everything through that company you created? What was it called, Poor Richards?"

"Yep," Ben answered blankly.

"Why'd you go and name it something like that? It's a bit odd, don't you think?"

Ben grinned; Larry didn't know his full name. "Just thought it appropriate is all," Ben said.

Megan and Abby approached. "What are you building out there, Ben?" Abby asked.

"Oh, he won't tell," Megan said. "I've tried everything I know to get it out of him, but he won't tell."

"It's for a project that I'm working on. If I were to tell you what it was for, you'd have me put in a padded cell. But I'm committed—" he smiled at his own play on words, "—to see it through."

"Oh, Ben, I hope you're not throwing your money away on some cockamamie idea you've cooked up," Abby said.

Tom had joined their little group. "What? Ben with a cockamamie idea. That's hard to believe," Tom said sarcastically.

"What's that supposed to mean?" Ben asked.

"You remember when we were kids, and you decided to build an electric car. We nailed together some crates, slapped on some wheels." Tom was laughing by this point in the story. "Ben hooked up a pulley to Dad's grinder, and used a long extension cord to see if it would run."

"I'd forgotten all about that," Abby said, giggling.

"Yeah, it went like a bat out of hell for about thirty seconds, and then the whole thing fell apart," Ben said. "Didn't even get all the way to the end of the extension cord. Dad was pissed when he found out I burned up the motor in his grinder. As I recall, we both got a whooping for that." He sighed. "No, this is a little bigger than that, but probably no less crazy."

At one in the morning, Ben couldn't sleep. His mind was still running. Larry and Amy had gone home around midnight. Tom and his wife were upstairs in the master bedroom. Abby and Frank were in Teresa's old room. And his nieces and nephews were next door with Amy and Larry.

Megan was asleep on the couch.

Trying to be quiet, Ben extended his recliner and pulled a blanket over him. His eyes were still on her. She had done so much for him, and it didn't take a genius to figure out that there was something special about her.

She really is quite beautiful. He acknowledged this thought.

Megan began to snore just a bit. It reminded him of Becca.

It's no wonder they were such good friends. I never would've thought it before, but they really are alike in so many ways.

A familiar voice joined his thoughts, one that wasn't

his own. *I wouldn't mind if you were to fall for her. She could help you find the happiness you deserve.*

Ben sat up quickly, taking a sharp breath. The voice he heard had been his wife's. He hadn't heard it since that night in the car. This time, the alcohol made him uncertain if it was real. In some odd way, it made him feel guilty. He tried to explain just in case it was Becca listening in on his thoughts.

We're just friends. I care about her, I really do. But I don't want to go there. She's been hurt. My job is to protect her.

In a soft tone, her voice was there again, easing his mind. *It's alright, go to sleep, Ben. Time takes care of all, I promise.*

In his stupor, Ben felt satisfied that he wasn't in any kind of trouble. He pulled the blanket up to his chin and fell asleep.

Megan woke early that next morning. When she saw Ben sleeping in the recliner, she had to smile. Her feelings for him ran stronger than she wanted to admit.

You may have feelings for him, but he hasn't gotten over Becky. Not yet. The best thing you could do is keep him at arm's length and go on with your life. The ink on your divorce isn't even dry.

Megan shook her head.

There's nothing wrong with helping him through this time. Nothing wrong with helping each other get through.

Ben shifted uneasily in the chair. She could tell he was uncomfortable because he normally slept on the couch. There had been a part of her that hoped he would've slept next to her on the couch. Not for sex, it wasn't about sex. Just to have him near, someone she trusted. But that wasn't going to happen. Even if he wanted to, he wouldn't have done it. Her mind took over from her heart. *He lost his wife—your best friend. If you want to go on, then do it with someone else.*

Megan rose, stretching and yawning. She glanced over at Ben again. *God, I really wish I hadn't gotten to know him so well.*

She approached and shook him gently. "Ben, wake up," she said softly. It took Ben a few seconds to register her. His eyes opened slowly. He rubbed them with the back of his hands.

"Good morning," she said standing over him, looking down into his face.

Ben closed his eyes. "Morning, Beautiful," he said. His eyes suddenly flashed wide as if he hadn't meant to say it. Megan decided to act as if she hadn't heard him. She tried to convince herself it was only a slip. It was dangerous to allow her feelings to go any deeper. It was better to put up a wall against them. They could never be more than friends.

"We need to get up, get some breakfast going," she said pretending to sound sleepy, and then yawning again to make it more convincing.

"Yeah, you're right. Did you make coffee?"

"I'll brew some if you get up," she said.

"Megan... what I said... the comment I made a second ago. I didn't mean anything by it. Hope it didn't bother you."

"What comment?" she asked. "You mean about the coffee? Why would that bother me?" Her tone was bland, hoping he would believe she hadn't heard him.

"No, not the coffee. I'm sorry, it was nothing, forget

it."

"I just want to know if you're going to get up," she said, slapping him on the arm.

"Okay, okay. I'm up, I'm up."

"Good, you can cook the bacon," Megan said, glancing over her shoulder at him. "You can cook bacon, right?"

Ben smiled. "I think so. As long it isn't turkey or stuffing, I think we'll be safe."

CHAPTER 8

The cars on Westnedge Avenue crept along on the sloshy, slick road. The exhaust came out in a ghostly white fog. It had snowed the day before, then rained, and turned cold again this morning. The result was cold, sloppy, and slick conditions. Joe glanced over at his dashboard clock; it was a quarter past eight.

"Oh God, I hate this frigging place," he said, watching as the frost began to build up on the inside of the windshield. He started the engine of his Chevy Blazer and turned up the heat. His eyes kept watch on the entrance to the parking lot. His vehicle was parked outside of the office building of Walker and Pearson. Walker and Pearson occupied the east wing of the complex while the west side contained a mix of smaller businesses. The parking lot out front was large and shared it with a strip mall at the south end. He knew with a fair amount of certainty that Ben would be coming from the south. Several cars did turn into the parking lot, but none of them the blue BMW he was anxiously waiting for. He knew Ben usually arrived early, between eight-thirty and eight-forty. Joe was counting on it. Joe zipped up his jacket in anticipation and pulled the baseball bat closer to him. He would have only one chance at this and not very much time to take care of business. The parking lot was slippery, which meant he would have to be cautious. The last thing he wanted was to slip and fall, but more than that, he wanted to avoid being seen.

More minutes passed; Joe began to grow uneasy. "Where are you, Ben? I've got a present for you," he said in a kind of singsong tone. His voice turned suddenly bitter, as if it were two people talking. "You're starting to piss me off, Stryker," he spat hatefully, glancing over at the dash clock again. Just then, Joe caught sight of the blue BMW. He ducked down as the dark blue sedan passed in front of him, and then watched as it moved cautiously through the lot. The BMW finally parked at the south end, three rows over. Joe jumped out of the Blazer while firmly gripping the bat in both hands. He moved quickly, almost at a trot, between the rows of cars, angling to a point where Ben would have to pass. Finally, he positioned himself on the side of a tan colored Dodge Durango. He peeked around the back of the vehicle; Ben was approaching, walking deliberately, bundling up as he walked. Scanning the lot one last time, Joe readied himself, cocking the bat over his shoulder.

Oh, this is going to be good. I'm going to enjoy breaking open that thick skull of his. Come here, Stryker. Come and get it!

After folding his long coat around him, Ben locked the car with his key remote. The wintery wind struck him, and he grabbed the front of his coat, closing it about his neck. From the corner of his eye, he saw a figure moving between the vehicles. He stopped.

Something was wrong, he could sense it. The wind blew again, icy cold, stinging his face and hands. He remembered the curtain in the living room, how his imagination had convinced him into thinking someone was in the house.

Stop it. Just get inside and warm up. It's just someone trying to get out of the cold.

Ben started again, the freezing wind now blowing against his back. As he passed a large SUV, Joe appeared. He had a baseball bat, perched high and extended back, as if he intended to hit a home run. Ben had no time to react. Joe swung hard and stuck Ben squarely on his right arm. The blow sent him to the ground. Ben had heard the sickening sound of crunching bone and knew it was broken. Aside from the pain, which was considerable, the limb has become a heavy, useless appendage. He pushed himself up to his knees with his left arm. The pain was making it difficult for him to think and to act. "Joe, what the hell are you doing?" Ben gasped. It was nonsense to ask such a thing when it was clear what he meant to do. Joe simply ignored the question.

"Hello, Ben. So nice to see you again," Joe said with a grin so wide it looked unnatural. "You don't seem happy to see me. For shame. And I thought we were friends." Joe laughed and swung again, this time aiming for his head. Ben tried to block the blow with his left arm. The bat glanced off his wrist, just missing his head.

He means to kill you. You'd better think fast.

Ben swung his leg out wide and knocked Joe's feet out from underneath him. The slick pavement helped propel Joe's feet upwards and he landed on his back. Slowly, Ben got back on his feet only to have Joe swing the bat from his knees, hitting him in the left leg. Ben went down again, and his knee felt strangely unhinged. With it came a sharp, agonizing pain.

Joe was back on his feet. "I was hoping you'd cry out or something. You're starting to disappoint me."

Ben struggled to rise, even though the pain was blinding. With all the strength left in his body, he launched himself at his attacker. Taken by surprise, Joe backed away and swung the bat almost defensively to fend him off. It struck Ben high above the temple. Ben fell instantly to the slushy pavement. Bright red blood ran from his head, staining the wet snow.

Joe heard a commotion, and someone shouted, "Hey, what's going on there?"

With little time to decide, Joe raised the bat, wanting to finish the job, but could see more people running toward them. His nerve broke as he dropped the bat and ran for the Blazer. He tore out of the parking lot, hoping no one had the chance to clearly identify him.

Cliff was the first to Ben, finding him lying face down and bleeding profusely from the head. He rolled Ben over onto his back, then pulled off his coat and put it beneath Ben's head. "Somebody call an ambulance!" he shouted in a panic. The cell phone in Ben's coat pocket began to ring, surprising Cliff just a little. He stuck his hand in the pocket and retrieved the cell phone. His fingers were almost numb, but he barely noticed. He ignored the call and quickly dialed 911.

"Joey, Dear, don't get too close to the road," his teacher, Mrs. Bergstrom, called out to him. Joey stood near the curb, bundled up in his snowsuit with hat and gloves. The attire was bulky, making it difficult for him to move. Joey stayed at the edge of a group of kids waiting for their parents to arrive. It wasn't snowing, but the wind made it colder, and his toes were starting to freeze, even with his new boots. But it wasn't the cold that was bothering him. Something was wrong. His mother was late, and she was never late. His mind buzzed with a warning something bad was about to happen.

She's just running late because of the slippery roads, Joey told himself.

Joey took a few steps back towards his teacher, but as he did, a familiar silver Blazer zipped past him, hit the curb, and slid to a stop. Joey glanced over his shoulder and instantly recognized his father's vehicle. His breath caught as he turned to run, the heavy winter clothing slowing him down. Within moments, he felt himself being picked up and carried.

"STOP! Somebody stop him, he's got Joey!"

His teacher's warning came too late. Joe had swung him around like a sack of flour before tossing him into the back seat. Joey bounced off the seat and landed on the floor. His father got behind the wheel just as Joey pushed himself up. He could see his mother's Buick getting larger in the windshield; there was a determined look on her face. She meant to ram them. Joey braced himself just as the Blazer rocked with the collision. Because of the slippery roads, the Blazer merely slid, jolted backwards in the crash. His father began cursing while cutting hard around the Buick. Joey got up from the floor and looked out the back window. His mother was following them, sliding on the slick roads, and trying frantically to keep up. Joey reached out and tried to touch his mother with his mind.

She's almost electric with panic.

He wanted to try and calm her as he'd done before at the mall but knew that was impossible right now. He was close to panicking himself.

"Not going to say hello to your father? Give me a big sloppy kiss. Tell me that you missed me or something stupid like that?" Joe laughed making Joey's skin crawl.

Joey kept quiet, trying to think. If he didn't do something, he might never see his mother again. He reached out to meet his father's mind, bracing himself for whatever nastiness might be there. He had to pull back right away. It felt like hot lava—a murderous hatred. And there was something else. There was sort of laughing going on inside of his head… laughing when there was nothing funny to laugh at.

Joe put the Blaser in four-wheel drive and was able to maneuver through traffic despite the slushy road conditions. Joey looked back again; his mother was falling behind, getting lost in traffic. He felt around on the floor and in the seats for anything that might help him escape. The best he could do was an old hand towel and a couple of stale French fries. In no time, they were on the Interstate. Joe settled back and they appeared to be slowing a little.

Joey tried to think. *He must've completely lost her, which is why he's relaxed. I've got to think of something.*

"Dad, I need to go pee," he whined, trying to sound convincing.

Joe glanced back at him and grunted. "Go ahead. Pee in your suit for all I care, we aren't stopping."

Ten minutes went by, then twenty. His father began to appear irritated, but Joey wasn't sure why. Then the vehicle began to slow.

"I'm going to pull over to a gas station. The radiator was damaged when she rammed me. The engine temperature is way too hot. I'll have to stop somewhere to fix it. Don't move and don't make a sound. I want you to just sit back there and keep quiet. You got it!" Joe barked at him.

"Yes, Dad," Joey replied.

Joe exited the interstate and pulled into a Marathon station. When he opened the hood, hot white steam blew out of the radiator, nearly scalding him. Joey perked up, if he were to ever get to safety, to get back to his mother, this would be his only chance to do so. He stripped out of the snow suit and readied himself. From the thin view under the hood, he watched as his father went inside the Marathon station. Joey's eyes searched for some form of sanctuary, somewhere he would be safe from his father. At last, he spotted a building about fifty yards away that reminded him of the fire station in Parchment. It had the large garage doors, and he could almost make out the glint of red paint of fire trucks inside. He settled on it; it wasn't the police, but it would have to do. Now all he had to do was get there. He opened the door a crack, pushing it wide enough for him to slip through. He got out and slowly began to back away from the Blazer. Without his snowsuit, the wintery cold made him shiver. After a dozen or so steps, he turned and began to sprint. The fire station remained another twenty yards away when he heard his father shouting after him.

"Hey, you little brat, where in the hell do you think you're going? When I catch..."

Joey couldn't hear the rest, and he didn't dare look

back.

If he catches me before I get inside, it's all over.

When he reached the door, he shot through it and found himself in a large bay filled with fire trucks.

"Help me! Is there anybody here? Please, I need help!"

All at once, three men in uniform rushed out into the bay. The first man he took note of was a stocky built Black man wearing a white shirt. There was a gold badge over his breast pocket. The other two men were in dark blue uniforms. Immediately, Joey assumed that the man with the white shirt and gold badge was in charge somehow. He quickly reached out with his mind, knowing he didn't have much time. The man had a warm feeling to him, his sense of duty was strong, but he also had intelligence and good humor. Immediately, he understood that he was the man to talk to. "Please, Sir, will you help me?"

Before he could receive and answer, the door behind him flew open and his father stood there, appearing wild-eyed. As soon as Joe saw the firefighters, he tried to soften his appearance.

"Joey, come here," Joe said sternly. "I'm sorry if he's bothered you gentlemen. That's my son. He ran off and just doesn't want to go home because he knows he's in trouble. I'm not sure what he told you, but he's a rather good liar." Joe strode across the bay floor and tried to seize Joey by the arm. The big man in the white uniform and gold badge latched onto Joe's arm while gently pushing Joey behind him. One of the firefighters pulled Joey back even further from the scene while the others moved in next to the white-shirted man, forming a barrier.

Joe appeared upset by this move. "I told you, I'm

his father. Go on, Joey, tell them who I am. You should know, it isn't the first time he's done this."

Joey kept his mouth shut, pleading to them with his eyes. The big man looked unconvinced by his father's explanation.

"I'm Chief Tompkins. I'm not sure exactly what is going on here, but it's obvious the kid is scared to death of you. I think it would be best if we kept the boy here until the police arrive. We can sort things out after that."

Five more firefighters came rushing out onto the bay floor, watching their chief during the confrontation.

"That's my son!" Joe shouted. Using both arms, he shoved the chief, trying to go around him. Chief Tompkins grabbed Joe's wrist in a powerful grip and pushed him to the floor. Joe landed hard on his backside, a look of humiliation on his face.

"I told you—the boy stays here until we sort this out," Chief Tomkins stated.

Joe regained his feet and then raised his hands as if he'd given up on the matter. Then he quickly balled his fist and swung hard at the chief. Chief Tompkins wasn't fooled, he blocked the punch and countered with his own, smashing his fist into the side of Joe's face. Joe flew backwards, hitting his head on the side of the fire truck.

"You want to try that again?"

The expression on Joe's face seemed to indicate he was thinking about it, but instead he ran for the door.

"Somebody grab him," the chief said, but it was too late. Joe was out the door and gone before anyone could get to him. Three firefighters went in pursuit, chasing him as far as the Marathon station.

"Can you believe that SOB? Taking a swing at me?" he

said, and then turned to Joey. “Are you alright, kid? You aren’t hurt or anything, are you?”

“No, Sir.”

“What’s your name?”

“Joey... Joey Murphy.”

“Tell me one thing, will you. That was your father, wasn’t it?

Joey nodded hesitantly. “Yes, Sir. He was trying to take me from my mom.”

“Well, Son, coming here was one smart thing to do.”

“Thank you, Sir,” Joey said.

Chief Tompkins shook his head. “Polite, too. Are you sure you’re related to that nutcase?”

Joey frowned, and then nodded solemnly.

“I’m sorry, I know he’s still your father,” the chief said.

“It’s okay. I know he’s...” Joey didn’t quite know how to finish.

“Crazy?” he said, raising his eyebrows.

“Yeah, something like that,” Joey said, still frowning.

Chief Tompkins decided it was best to change the subject. “Alright, enough of that. Can you tell me what kind of vehicle he’s traveling in so we can have the police go after him? I’m sure he’s in a world of trouble by now.”

Joey gave him a description of the Blazer, including the fact it had been damaged and may not be running right.

“Good. Thank you, Joey,” he turned immediately to one of his men and asked to relay all the information to the police, including a description of Joe Murphy. The chief put out his large hand to Joey. “Well, for the time being, you’ll be our guest here, Joey. Why don’t we go into the dayroom and sit down for a little bit?”

Joey took the chief's hand and was guided into a room beyond the truck bay. It was a large area with a kitchen on the left, a television, couch, and a few recliners to the right. Joey quickly surmised that the dayroom was kind of like the living place for the firefighters. The chief motioned to one of his men. "Get a coke for Joey here," he said. The firefighter nodded and left in a hurry. They sat down on the couch and the chief eyed Joey carefully, as if appraising him. "You're one brave boy, Joey. If you think you could, I'd like you to tell me everything that happened. Can you do that?"

"Yes, Sir," Joey said, and then took a breath, "but, do you think I could call my mom first? She'll be worried about me."

Chief Tompkins' face lit up in a wide grin. "Yes, of course. Guess I should've thought of that already. Come on, let's go call your mom, give her the good news."

Cliff was still at the hospital when the cell phone in his pocket rang. He'd forgotten about it until now. It was Ben's.

"Hello!"

"Hello?" said the female voice on the other end in a confused reply. "Where's Ben?"

"I'm sorry, this is Cliff. I grabbed Ben's phone earlier to call the ambulance. He's in the hospital." Cliff said, still not knowing the identity of the caller.

"Cliff? This is Megan. Do you remember me? What happened? How is he?"

"Yeah, I remember you. Ben is in surgery right now. I know he's alive, but not much more than that."

"How did this happen?"

"I'm not sure, but I'm certain was Joe Murphy. He must've been waiting for Ben in the parking lot. Messed him up pretty good. I found a baseball bat nearby. Ben was on the ground, unconscious and..." Cliff hesitated, no knowing if he should expand on what he saw.

"And what!" she demanded.

"Well, he was bleeding quite a bit from the head."

"Where are you? What hospital?"

"Bronson Central."

"I'll be there right away. Cliff? Is he going to be okay? Tell me he's going to be alright, please."

Cliff thought about what he had seen and didn't want to lie, "I don't know, it looked pretty bad."

There was silence; Megan seemed to be nowhere on the line.

"Megan?"

"I'm still here," she said. The panic he'd heard in her voice had been replaced with a tone of determination. "If you have Ben's phone you should call his family—and Larry Snider. They should be in his phone. Just tell them what you told me."

"Okay, I will."

"Thanks, Cliff. I'll be there shortly."

Cliff hung up and began searching the directory of Ben's phone.

Joe was upset that things had gone bad so quickly. It had seemed like he had everything just as he wanted it, and then watched as it all unraveled in front of him.

That snot-nosed brat played you. The voice mocked him, it was his father's voice that he heard. *He waited for his chance and ran off while you were busy screwing around. You're such a moron. He's a little kid, for crying out loud, can't you do anything right?*

Joe tried desperately to quiet the voice inside of his head. *Shut up, shut up! I just ran into a few problems is all, it isn't my fault.*

He turned the Blazer into a Walmart parking lot. It was six blocks from the city bus station. The engine was spewing steam and wouldn't have gone much further. He drove to an area that had the heaviest concentration of cars and parked. It would take the police a while to find the vehicle—not that it would matter by that point.

What are you going to do now? Never were too bright. They're gonna catch you, you know that don't you? It was his father's voice again, condemning him, belittling him.

"Shut up, Old Man," he said aloud.

As he walked, several people glanced over at him as he was talking to himself, though no one said anything.

Just shut up, I have to take care of things.

His father's voice grew quiet inside of his head for the moment. Joe walked briskly, looking for the bus station. If at all possible, he wanted to catch the next bus south, head to Berrien Springs, Benton Harbor, or even Niles. Initially, he had planned on going north, and then loop back around to the south where he'd rented a place for the winter. His plan had included having the Blazer with him, hidden in the garage. But that was impossible now. The place was located in a small community outside of Dowagiac called Sister Lakes. He'd rented a cabin on one of the lakes, usually occupied by tenants vacationing from Chicago during the summer. During the winter, hardly anyone wants to live by a frozen lake, so it was cheap. Joe had paid cash, six months, all in advance. The landlord was happy just to have it rented for the winter and didn't ask questions.

The bus station was a block away now. Joe continued to walk at a quick pace with his head down while keeping an eye out for the police. At the same time, he was doing everything he could to keep the voices inside his head under control. Once at the ticket counter, he kept his eyes and his head down.

"One ticket for Benton Harbor," he said.

The ticket person didn't even look up, gave him the ticket, and told him the bus would be leaving in twenty minutes. For the duration of his wait, Joe moved about the bus station. There were a few derelicts and homeless people about, some asking for money. Joe did his best to avoid them.

Do they think I've got money to waste on them? They're just going to use the money on liquor or drugs. Suddenly his mouth was dry. He could use a drink himself. Joe shook it off, once he was safe in the cabin, he could drink himself into oblivion if he wanted. His father's voice entered his mind again.

What are you going to do then, Joe? You didn't get the boy... didn't kill Stryker. He's still alive. Probably going to testify that you tried to kill him. How long can you hold up in that cabin? Until May, if you are lucky. Then it's prison time for you. You're going to love that.

"Shut up! Joe screamed while holding the sides of his head. People looked at him for a moment then turned away again. They were used to crazies hanging out at the bus station. What was one more?

A middle-aged doctor with graying hair entered the

waiting room and asked for anyone from the Stryker family. Tom, Abby, Megan, and Larry huddled around the doctor. Amy, Cliff, Paul Walker, and George Pearson were there, but stayed back from the rest of the group while they talked to the doctor.

"How is he?" Abby asked immediately.

"I'm afraid we won't know for a while," the doctor told them. "The blow to the head caused some minor swelling to the brain and he's yet to regain consciousness. We have no way of knowing how long it will be before he comes out of it. There doesn't appear to be any permanent damage, but again, we won't know anything for certain until later."

"Why were you in surgery so long?" Megan asked. "Cliff said he was bleeding."

"The scalp wound did cause some bleeding, but that wasn't the most significant injury. It was his knee we operated on this evening," the doctor explained. "It suffered considerable damage. I had to call in one of our best orthopedic surgeons to lead the operation. It's going take some time for it to heal, and even then, we might have to go back in if it doesn't heal right." The doctor shook his head. "He also suffered a couple broken bones, but they will heal. For now, I'm concerned that he hasn't regained consciousness. Normally, we would administer drugs to keep him in a comatose state, and then wean him off of them. It's easier for the brain to heal this way. In this case, the injury to the brain itself was negligible and the swelling minimal. He's even breathing on his own. I can explain it." He paused. "However, head injuries of this type can be unpredictable. I'll just feel better when he wakes up. The next twenty-four hours will give us a better idea of his condition."

"Should we be worried? What if he doesn't wake soon?" Megan asked.

The doctor dropped his eyes to the clipboard. "While it is uncommon, there's no reason be alarmed. There are still a lot of things we haven't tried yet."

Megan's heart dropped; the doctor's evasive manner meant Ben's condition was a lot more serious than he presented it. It didn't take a genius to figure that out.

"When will we be able to see him?" Abby asked.

"He's in recovery now and should be moved shortly. You can see him then. I'll ask the nurse to let you know the moment he's moved," the doctor said. "We'll know more when he's conscious. Until then, all we can do is wait."

After the doctor left, little was said among the group until Larry piped up. "Oh, hell, you know Ben's gonna be okay. He's too stubborn to lie around long," he said, trying to sound optimistic, though he didn't feel that way.

Megan let go of Abby, wiped her face, and hugged Larry for it. "He is pretty stubborn, isn't he?" she said hopefully.

"I think we used to call it pig-headed," Tom chipped in.

"That's what we called you," Abby said, moving over and holding her brother's hand.

"Oh, yeah, I guess it was. At least we know where he gets it from," Tom said. He turned to the rest of the group. "Look, we might as well go down to the cafeteria, get some food. It could be a while."

Everyone began moving towards the door. Everyone except Abby and Megan.

"I'm not very hungry," Abby said. Megan shook her head, acknowledging she wasn't hungry either. Abby squeezed Megan's hand. "Megan and I will stay here and wait. You go ahead. I wouldn't mind if you brought back some coffee, though."

"Alright, Abby," Tom said.

After everyone else was gone, Abby and Megan sat on the couch.

"Ben means a lot to you, doesn't he?" Abby asked. It was more of a statement than an actual question. Megan nodded, and then her face scrunched up with pain. She began to cry again. Abby pulled her into a hug and held her gently. "He'll be okay, Megan, I promise."

CHAPTER 9

When Ben opened his eyes, he found himself sitting in his own recliner. At least it looked and felt like his recliner. He had no memory of how he got here. The living room seemed a little more brilliantly lit than normal, but nothing was out of the ordinary.

Except something was out of sorts. The smell was all wrong. It had the heady smell of bleach and antiseptic. He went to the window and pulled back the curtain. It looked as it always did, but again, there was something wrong. That's when he realized there were no cars, no people, no kids, no dogs. Nothing. No movement whatsoever. Something else dawned on him, there was no snow on the ground. It was the wrong season. It had the appearance of a spring day. He rushed to the front door and flung it open. Large grey blocks, like that of cement blocks, filled the doorway, blocking the way.

Where am I? What is this place?

He checked the patio door. Again, the view was that of a spring day, but when he opened the sliding door the gray concrete blocks appeared again. Looking closer, the blocks appeared as if they had wavy grooves imprinted on them. The closest he could associate it with were pictures he'd seen of brain matter, but he couldn't understand what it was doing here.

What the hell is going on?

Just in case, he checked the rest of the house, trying windows and doors. Still no way out.

Okay, it looks as if I'm staying.

Suddenly, a brilliant light began to fill the kitchen. He shielded his eyes with his hand, but it was just too bright. Then, a peaceful feeling began to emanate from it, like a warm bath of delight. His first instinct was to walk into it. That was until he saw a dark shape approaching from the midst of the light. Finally, a figure stepped out from the light.

It was Becca.

Megan felt a hand on her shoulder as she slowly resurfaced from her nap. She had fallen asleep in the chair next to Ben's bed. She'd been dreaming of Becky. Parts of the dream still lingered. It was like a scene from the past. They were sitting around the kitchen table, talking, and laughing about anything and everything. Her heart hurt for it, and she missed Becky so much more because of it.

"Megan?"

It was Larry, lightly shaking her.

Megan blinked and said nothing. Her frown deepened.

"Good morning," Larry said, looking at her with concern. Megan tried to straighten up. There was a crick in her neck from sleeping awkwardly in the chair. She rubbed her neck, and then looked at Ben, hoping for some kind of sign of consciousness.

"No change?" Larry asked.

Megan shook her head. "No. Not yet."

A heavy bandage covered Ben's head and his eyes were black and blue. His right arm was in a cast, as well as his left wrist. Another cast covered his left leg. Megan began fussing with the blanket covering him.

"Don't you have to work today?" Larry asked.

Megan shook her head. She had called and told them there was a family emergency. In a sense, it was true. To her, Ben was family.

"Why don't you go home and get some rest. I'll stay here with him."

Megan didn't response. She continued her hopeful stare, waiting for Ben to wake.

"Megan?"

"I dreamt of Becky," she said calmly as if she hadn't heard him. "Do you know how much I miss her? How much I wish she were here right now to tell me things were going to be alright?" Megan kept her gaze on Ben, but her eyes narrowed, and her voice turned severe. "He doesn't deserve this. He's suffered enough. We've all suffered enough." Her hands balled into fists. "I don't understand. Why in God's name would anyone want to hurt him like this? It just doesn't make sense."

Larry put his hand on her shoulder. "I don't know, Megan. Probably because we don't know what God's plans are. Sometimes I think he tests us to see how much we can take, to see what we are made of inside, not because he's cruel, but because we become stronger from it." Larry paused, knowing he was delving into a subject that she might not want to hear. "If it's God's will that he should go on to be with his family, then we shouldn't be angry about it. Ben wouldn't be. You're angry because you're afraid he'll be taken from you when you need him the most. There's nothing wrong with that. Ben is one of the best friends I have. Don't you think I want him here just a badly?"

There was nothing but pure anger now showing on Megan's face. "I don't know if I believe in God anymore," she said with a fury rising inside her. "You want to preach to me about how God is testing us to make us stronger. Well, that's bullshit! No God I believe in would allow so much pain on one person. And yes, I want him here. You can call me selfish if you want, but I want him here." Megan covered her face with her hands. She didn't want to cry, she wanted to be angry. Anger was the only weapon she had against the anguish she felt at the moment.

"No, you aren't selfish. It's always difficult when you care about someone so much it's hard to let them go. And you've had to do that a lot lately, I know," he said. "Now, go home and get some rest. I'll call you the second he wakes."

"I'm staying here," Megan said with her chin held out defiantly.

Larry sighed. "Okay, suit yourself." He sat down in a plastic chair near the window. "I'll wait here with you."

"Hello, Sweetheart," Becca said. She appeared to be the same age, wearing the same flowered summer dress as the first time they'd met. Ben stood there, rooted to the spot. His mind had locked up, unable to conceive how any of this was happening. Then joy, as he hadn't known for an exceptionally long time, flooded his heart. He didn't care how it happened, only that she was here with him now. He pulled her into an embrace, lifting her off the floor.

"Oh God, Becca, I can't tell you how much I've missed you," he told her, frightened that if he let go, she might disappear. He sat her down and kissed her passionately. Then he held her in his arms, gazing directly into her eyes, and she into his. It was a look that only two souls so intricately connected could comprehend and interpret. It's a secret and searching look of familiarity and of love. But there was something else in her eyes, something he recognized almost immediately:

She was here for a reason.

"I've missed you, too, Ben. More than I can tell you." She paused, as if not wanting to continue. "But my time here will not be long. I cannot stay."

"Why not?"

She shook her head. "I just can't."

"Will you be back?"

"I really don't know. I think part of it depends on you."

Ben's brow deepened in a confused look. "What do you mean?"

"What do you remember? What's the last thing you remember before coming here?"

He thought about it for a moment. "I remember it was cold. That must have been yesterday morning. I was going to work and—" he stopped, "—Joe Murphy was there. Am I dead? Is that what it is?"

Becca shook her head.

"If I am not dead, then why is this happening? What is this, some sort of purgatory? Am I being punished?"

Becca smiled at him. "No, not quite. And we both know you don't believe in that kind of stuff. You're in the hospital, and you're in a coma. This place is something you created in your subconscious. You did a fairly good job, too, I must add," she said, walking a short distance from him, but still holding onto his hand. "I really do miss this house. We had so much happiness here." Becca sighed, and then turned back to him, trying to hold her smile.

"It isn't the same without you and the girls. It's been so difficult..."

She put a finger to his lips. "Shh! Let's not think about it, okay. Just enjoy the moment. Oh, speaking of the girls." Becca motioned towards the kitchen. Two small figures appeared out of the light. Ben's heart leaped as Teresa and Tia ran to him. He knelt down and hugged them both, unaware he was crying. Then he turned his head, looking back and forth at both of them, taking in everything he could.

"We missed you so much, Daddy," Teresa said, hugging her father's neck.

"Oh, I missed you, too," Ben said, wiping his face with the back of his hand.

"Daddy, you don't have to feel bad about us. We're okay. It wasn't your fault," Tia said looking at him with her big green eyes.

Ben stroked her hair, his eyes never leaving either of them. "I know, but it's been difficult to stop thinking that I should've done something to stop it."

Becca knelt down and joined them in their little group, making a circle. "There was nothing you could've done. It was our time. Don't tie yourself up in knots thinking it's your fault or feeling that you could have stopped it somehow. And the guilt you hold in your heart over Tia's death is not right."

Tia held her father's hand and looked directly at him.

"I didn't hurt any, Daddy. But I could feel your hurts. They were bigger than anything I ever had. You have to let go of the hurt, Daddy. I don't want you to feel that way," she said.

"I'm trying," he told her.

"It's time to go, girls," Becca said. "We have to say goodbye for now."

The girls took turns hugging and kissing their father goodbye.

"Goodbye Tia, Goodbye Teresa. I love you." Ben's voice was starting to crack as he said it.

"I want you girls to go on ahead. I'll be with you shortly." Becca told them. Teresa and Tia held hands and walked slowly back towards the kitchen, disappearing into the light.

"I want to go with you," Ben said, searching her eyes for any hope that it was possible. "I don't care about anything else."

"I know you do, Ben. If I thought it was the right thing to do, I wouldn't hesitate—but you can't. You have to go on. There are things that you still must do. It won't be easy, but I promise, life will go on and you'll find your way once again."

He said nothing. If he couldn't go with them, he was going to soak up as much of her as he could in the brief time they had left.

"I must go now," she said. "You will remember parts of this, but you won't know for sure what was real. Ben, you must find your way out of here. There's someone coming to help you. Follow him. He's a good boy and can get you back. Also, take caution with the machine you are building. Time has a funny way of protecting itself and it doesn't like to be messed with. One more thing, beware of Joe Murphy, he's not finished yet, and he's much more dangerous than you realize. You and everyone you care about are in danger as long as he lives. Keep a close eye on Hannah and Joey, protect them the best you can. And lastly, tell Megan we love her and to be strong. She means the world to me—and to you, I know." Becca caressed his face as she said this. "There's no reason to feel guilty about that either. Sometimes, happiness comes from sorrow. If you let it."

Becca kissed him one last time and turned towards the light. "I love you, Benjamin Franklin Stryker. Always have, always will." Then she was gone. The light from the kitchen disappeared as well.

"Love you," Ben whispered. He went back to his recliner. It took him a second to realize it wasn't his living room anymore. It was someone else's. And the Christmas tree was still up.

Joey watched his mother and grandparents as they chatted over coffee in the kitchen. He wasn't certain about what they spoke of but figured it had something to do with his father. He moved closer to the counter that separated the living room and kitchen and listened.

"Do you think they would be upset if I went up there?" he heard his mother ask.

Mr. Pearson shook his head. "I don't think so. They don't blame you for any of this. How could they?"

Hannah seemed to struggle with this.

"Hannah, Dear, if it's important to you, then I can't see any harm in it. Your father will go with you. Let them know how you feel. It isn't your fault, they know that."

"In some ways, it is. I knew what kind of person he was. I knew what he was capable of. If I had warned Ben, this never would've happened. How can I ever apologize for that?"

Joey decided he should talk to his mother about going to the hospital. His intuition was acting on him, telling him it was important for him to go. When Joey walked into the kitchen, they stopped talking immediately.

"Good morning," Hannah said, hugging her son, and then ruffling his hair affectionately as she usually did.

"Momma?"

"Yes, Honey?"

"Can I go with you to the hospital?"

Hannah seemed a little puzzled. "Were you listening? Did you hear what we were talking about?"

Joey nodded.

Hannah looked at her mother and father. They both had the same surprised expression on their face.

"Okay, we'll go." She turned to her father. "Will you go with us?"

"Of course," George said, grabbing his coat.

They arrived at Bronson Central in the early afternoon and rode the elevator up to the third floor. They traversed the wide hallway with George Pearson in the lead. Hannah and Joey stayed several steps behind. Joey noticed that several people had congregated outside the room. His grandfather stopped and talked with two men. Joey would find out later their names: Tom Stryker and Larry Snider. Hannah pulled Joey to the side and waited. A woman with blonde, shoulder-length hair came out of the room. She appeared tired and careworn at the moment. She saw Joey and his mother standing in the hallway, seemed to pause for a moment, and then walked towards them.

"Hi, I'm Megan. I'm a friend of Ben's," she said.

"I'm Hannah. Joe is… or at least, was, my husband. I'm guessing you knew that," his mother said hesitantly. "This is my son, Joey." She paused again, as if unsure how to apologize for her estranged husband's actions. "I'm so sorry, I wish that I'd done more to warn him."

Megan took both of Hannah's hands into her own. Ben had mentioned they had met once before, and she just about commented on it, but seeing how it appeared neither of them remembered, it felt appropriate to say nothing. "Ben knew of the danger. He said as much. Actually, he was more worried about you and Joey here, than he was himself."

Hannah stroked Joey's hair. "Yeah, when Joe kidnapped him, I thought for sure I'd never see him again. It was only good fortune—and Joey's quick thinking—that he survived."

While the adults continued to talk in the hallway, Joey was getting anxious to get to what he needed to do. Even at that, he wasn't certain what was driving him to do so. While his mother was occupied in conversation, he slipped into Ben's room. It was empty except for Ben. He was relieved for that much, as he wasn't sure how to explain what we wanted to do. Bandages covered much of the man, but he tried not let it bother him too much. It was his father's work. He'd beaten this man, tried to break him, both body and spirit, as he did with most everyone.

Joey pushed these things from his mind. He had to work fast; something was telling him he didn't have a lot of time. Joey pushed the chair up to edge of the bed, climbed into it, and leaned over. He reached out with his feelings and immediately got an immutable sense of the injured man. The strongest feeling he got was something almost indefinable. The colors of his mind, the part that interpreted these things, suggested it was a blend of intelligence, courage, and compassion. But even that did not explain it. It was a powerful strength of character. A kind of steel. Steel that, even though dented and battered by grief, had held steadfast. In fact, the pain had acted as a forge, making it stronger.

Joey closed his eyes and extended all of his power into trying to contact Ben's mind. He created a room that he was familiar with—Grandpa and Grandma Pearson's living room. He held onto the image and placed the room in the center of his mind, stretching out to Ben at the same time. He didn't know how he knew it would work, he'd never tried anything like this before, but somehow, he knew it would. When the room came into focus, he found himself on the couch. Ben was on the recliner. The bandages were no longer covering his head. The room looked the same as it had on Christmas morning with the tree and the presents under it, probably because it was the clearest memory Joey had to work with.

"Where am I?" Ben asked. His conversation with Becca had already started slipping away from him, as if it had taken place years ago. It was like having a shattered memory with bits and pieces sticking in his mind like fragments of glass.

"We're in my grandpa's house. But really, it's all made up," Joey said.

Ben stared at him. "I know you."

Joey nodded. "I'm here to help."

Ben looked around the living room. "And this isn't real?"

"No, it isn't. You were hurt by—" Joey hesitated, uncertain how he would react, "by my father."

"You mean, Joe. You're his son?" Ben leaned back, still staring at him. "That's right, you're Joey. I remember you."

Joey nodded again. "You're hurt, and need to find your way out," he said. "I think I can help you."

"Why would I want to leave? Becca, Tia, and Teresa are here. I haven't been this happy in a long time," Ben said, looking over his shoulder to where his kitchen would've been.

"I know you don't understand, but we don't have much time. You have to follow me." Joey stretched out his hand to Ben.

Ben looked hesitant about it. "Can I come back?"

Joey shook his head, his hand still extended.

"And none of this is real?"

Again, Joey shook his head.

Ben considered this, and then asked, "Why are you doing this?"

"I can't tell you, because I'm not sure," Joey answered honestly. "It's just important, that's all I know."

"And if I don't go with you—if I stay here—what will happen?" Ben asked.

"You'll be trapped here, but your body will be back there. You might find your way back. You might not."

Ben recognized that Joey wasn't lying. That meant he was left with only one question. Should he stay, or should he go? The urgency the little boy stressed meant he didn't have a lot of time to decide. He could vaguely remember Becca foretelling him that someone was coming. She had told him to go with him. "Okay," Ben said. "I'll go with you. Show me the way."

Joey let him to the front door. When they opened it, they found darkness beyond the threshold. "Keep holding on to my hand, okay?" Joey said anxiously, "I don't know what's going to happen."

"I will," Ben replied.

Together, they crossed into the unknown darkness.

There was an abrupt sensation of being pulled and then suddenly dropped. Ben blinked several times before realizing he was lying on a hospital bed, his head wrapped in bandages. He could see little on one side because his left eye was swollen shut, but he saw Joey's face was not far from his, leaning over him. Joey's eyes were still closed.

"Joey."

Joey opened his eyes all at once. "We made it. I wasn't sure it was going to work."

"Yes, we made it. You did it," Ben said. "Thanks, Kiddo."

Joey grinned.

All at once, the pain caused by his injuries caught up with Ben. He sucked in his breath as if he'd been punched in the gut.

The snow was coming down in thick, heavy snowflakes. The wind was strong enough to blow it around, making for poor visibility. An old brown Ford Bronco II, rusted and dented, pulled into the parking lot, coming to a stop at the local grocery store. The passenger, a pimple faced teenager got out and pulled the seat forward. Joe climbed out of the back. The pimply teen said something to him as he walked away. Joe ignored it. The teen got back into the Bronco, and it was off again, into the blinding snow.

Joe looked up at the sign hanging over the top of the grocery store.

Harding's Friendly Market

"Friendly, huh? We'll see about that," he said aloud while looking around. "So, this is Sister Lakes?"

From what he could see, there wasn't much. The grocery store of course, a restaurant, a coin operated laundry mat, and a bank. They all shared one parking lot. Another road, the one his cabin was on, formed a T off the main road, and ran down towards the lakes. On the opposite corner of the road was a Marathon gas station. It had only two gas pumps and was already closed for the day. He checked his watch. "It's only a little after six, and they are closed already," he said, then looked back at the grocery store. The lights were on and there was at least one person inside that he could see. "Well, at least they're open."

There was an audible crunch of snow under foot as he walked. At the door, he shook off the snow and went inside. He was grateful for the heat as his fingers and toes had already begun to lose feeling. But there was really only one thing on his mind. A drink. He needed a drink badly. He had already determined that if there wasn't a liquor store in this town it was going to be an extremely long winter. There was another, larger town, six miles north, but making that journey tonight would be impossible.

The store had only four aisles and a large cooler that ran the length of the wall. Joe grabbed a few frozen TV dinners, a couple packages of sandwich meat, sliced cheese, and a loaf of bread. When he got to the front of the store, he threw it all on the checkout counter. At the cash register was an older woman. She had silver colored hair and wore black horn-rimmed glasses that made her look a bit like a schoolteacher out of the 1950's. There was a smile on her face as he approached the checkout.

"How are you today?" she asked genially.

"I'm fine, thank you," Joe said, using his fake smile and fake sincerity, doing his best to play the part. He didn't want to draw attention to himself since he'd have to come back to this place regularly. It was best just to play nice-nice, even if it made him sick to his stomach to do it. The woman's smile faltered when she did get a good look at him. However, the woman rang up the items up without a word.

"Will there be anything else?" she asked finally trying to be polite. Joe could tell her eyes were scrutinizing him.

"Um, yes. Do you sell alcohol here as well? I mean, other than beer," he asked in his friendliest tone of voice.

"We do, but we keep it behind the front counter. It keeps the younger folks from trying to buy it," she said flatly. There was no disapproval in her voice, but there was something. "What did you want?"

"Well, if you have it, um, three bottles of Cuervo Gold," he said, trying to make it sound casual.

"Denny?" the woman yelled towards the back of the store. "Denny, can you come up here?"

A young man in his early twenties with shoulder length brown hair and a stocking cap ran up the aisle towards them. "Did you need something, Mrs. Harris?" he asked, rounding to the front aisle.

"Denny, be a good boy and grab three bottles of Cuervo Gold for me, will you?"

"Sure, no problem," Denny said brightly, and headed off in the direction of the front counter.

"So, are you just passing through?" Mrs. Harris asked him, mostly to cut the awkward silence between them.

"Um... no, I rented a place out on Cable Lake," Joe replied. It was more information than he wanted to give but could think of no way around the question. To be vague at this point would only further raise the old woman's suspicions.

"Well then, we should be seeing you here quite a bit this winter, I expect."

"Yes, I expect you will."

Denny came back a few minutes later with the bottles in hand. "Here you go," he said, setting them on the counter. "I had to look for the third one. We are out after this, Mrs. Harris. I'll make sure they restock it when they come in Monday."

"Thank you, Denny," she said as she rang up the tequila and bagged it for him. "That will be ninety-six, thirty-two, altogether."

Joe handed her a hundred-dollar bill. She glanced at the bill to check it, and then went to give him the change. He waved his hand and picked up the bags. "That's okay, keep it," Joe said, walking out of the store and back into the falling snow.

Mrs. Harris watched as the stranger tracked through the snow. He didn't have a car. That was odd enough, especially for this rural countryside. More than that was the look in his eyes. The stranger had been smiling, but his eyes. His eyes never smiled. There was something deeper going on behind them. And yet, they were familiar to her in some way. She thought about it for a moment, but it didn't take her long to remember. When she was young woman, many years ago, she worked at the State Hospital in Kalamazoo. A mental asylum. It was a sad, harrowing place. It closed in the early eighties, the patients were sent to group homes or smaller mental institutions, but she never forgot the place. Most patients had a look of innocence or of confusion in their eyes. A few, just a few, had a far more distinctive look. Those eyes still haunted her, and she knew now why the stranger had upset her. The look in the stranger's eyes had been the same as those patients she knew to be criminally insane.

Denny caught Mrs. Harris watching the stranger. She hadn't noticed him yet.

"You know that's not very polite?" Denny said, startling her.

She nearly jumped out of her shoes. "Denny, I told you not to sneak up on me like that," she said holding her hand over her heart.

"I just couldn't resist."

Turning back towards the window, she again tried to watch the stranger as he disappeared into the night. "I know it isn't polite, but there was something about him that bothered me."

"He seemed nice enough to me," Denny said, looking over her shoulder.

Mrs. Harris turned back again, and then tried to brighten a little. "Oh, never mind me. I'm just an old woman. I'm probably seeing something that isn't there. Now, isn't it time for you to go home, it's after six. You need to be home, studying for your classes. How are you going to get your degree by fussing around this place all night long?"

"Yes, Mrs. Harris. I am going," Denny said, trying to sound apologetic and then laughed, "Goodnight."

"Goodnight, Denny, and be careful driving home. Your aunt would shoot me if anything happened to you because I kept you out late in this weather."

"What the hell was up with that old biddy?" Joe said aloud, but inside he knew she hadn't fallen for his act. She was suspicious of him.

"She had better just keep her nose to herself. Otherwise, I might have to cut it right off her face," he said, and then laughed. He continued to trudge down the road trying to walk quickly without falling, and his breath visible every time he exhaled.

"I need a car. This stuff is just too miserable to walk in."

The road curved a little, following the edge of the lake. His cabin sat on the corner just past 95th street. It was a fairly decent size considering it was only a cabin. There was just one main room with a kitchen area. Joe had invested in a microwave and a large screen television for the place. He reasoned that some type of entertainment would be necessary being cooped up in this place all winter.

The cabin sat about a hundred and fifty feet from the road, and you could see the smallest of the sister lakes on that side. On the backside, the yard ran out about thirty yards then quickly sloped down toward Cable Lake. There was a fine view of it through the large window in the back. But he hadn't rented it for the view. He got it because the landlord didn't ask questions, and because it was secluded. There wasn't another house for a quarter mile in any direction.

When he reached the front door, he sat the bags on the step and pulled out his keys. He fumbled with them trying to flip through to find the one he wanted. His fingers were frozen, which didn't help. When he finally got the door open, he hastily went inside. He rummaged through the bags for a bottle of tequila, then immediately tipped it back. The warmth of the alcohol spread through him. He wiped his mouth with his sleeve and glanced around the place. With another long swig, he sat down and took a deep breath. He had made it. He didn't have the brat with him, but at least he was safe for now. That was a score he could settle another time.

CHAPTER 10

Ben gritted his teeth; the pain was beginning to overwhelm him. "Joey," he said, grabbing the boy's arm. He hadn't intended it to be a strong grip, but at the moment it was difficult for him to control himself.

"Yes, Mr. Stryker?" Joey said, sounding alarmed.

Ben was doing all he could to control the pain. "Go get someone, a nurse or something, okay."

"Yes, Sir." Joey jumped down from the chair and started to run out of the room.

"Joey!" Ben called out urgently. Joey stopped and looked back at him. "I think—we should—talk—later," he said, taking small breaths, trying to control the pain.

Joey nodded, and then ran from the room.

"Momma," Joey said, trying to get his mother's attention. Hannah was busy talking with Larry Snider; Megan was leaning against the wall near them. Joey tugged on his mother's arm insistently while pointing to Ben's room.

"What is it, Joey?" Hannah finally asked, feeling a little exasperated he would interrupt her.

"Mr. Stryker. He wants a nurse. He said he's hurting

really bad," Joey told her. Hannah looked at Larry and Megan with a stunned look.

"Are you sure, Joey? He's awake?" Megan asked before Hannah could say anything.

Joey nodded his head.

Megan ran past them and into the room with Larry close behind. "Ben, Ben," she exclaimed loudly, shaking him. "Damn you, Ben, if you're awake, look at me!"

Ben opened his eyes while trying to control the pain that was surging through his body.

"Hi, Megan," he said. "Do you think you could get the nurse for me?"

Megan threw herself across him, hugging him, and crying at the same time.

"Megan, uh... that hurts."

She got off of him, tears were streaming down cheeks, but she was smiling, "I was so worried about you."

"You know me," Ben said. "I'm like a bad penny—keep coming back."

The nurse, a slight Black woman of about forty-five, wearing hospital garb, came into the room. She acted casually while giving Ben the once over. Then she looked down her nose at him. "So, Mr. Stryker, you've decided to return to the land of the living, then?" she said.

"Yeah, thought it might be a good idea," Ben said, trying to keep his voice under control. "The problem is my head hurts so much it feels like it's going to explode. And my leg—I'm pretty sure somebody put a handful of glass in my knee."

"Alright, Mr. Stryker, I'll see what I can do for you. By the way, I'm Gloria, your nurse. It's nice to finally have a patient that'll talk back to me," she said chuckling, and then left the room.

Megan moved back to the side of the bed; Larry went to the other.

"Nice to have you back, Buddy," Larry said.

Ben grimaced again from the pain. "Yeah, it's good to be back, other than feeling like ten miles of bad road. What happened to Joe? Did they catch him?"

"No," Megan said. "He's disappeared."

The nurse came back in with the gray-haired doctor they had met the night before.

"Hello, Ben," he said. "I'm Dr. Hastings. I understand you're in a little bit of pain?"

"Quite a bit, actually," Ben said in a strained voice.

"We'll get you something for that in just a second. I just want to check a few things before we do, okay?"

"Sure. Just do it quick."

Dr. Hastings proceeded to check his eyes with a pen light, flashing it in each of his eyes to check pupil dilation and movement. While he was doing that, Gloria pulled Megan and Larry aside.

"Could you step outside for now? It may be a little while," Gloria said, putting her hands on the small of their backs and guiding them towards the door.

"Oh yes, of course. Sorry," Larry said. They walked out into the hallway and waited near the door.

"Larry," Megan whispered, "I want to apologize for biting your head off earlier. I know you were just trying to help."

"Apology accepted," he said. Megan hugged him, just as much out of pure relief as anything else. Whether they realized it or not, they'd been forged into their own little family with Ben at the center of it. They leaned on each other, now more than ever.

"So, how is he doing?" a familiar voice asked.

Megan turned to find her ex-husband, Jim, standing there.

The hospital cafeteria was only lightly occupied. Megan sat, stirring her coffee with a red plastic straw. It had long since been stirred, but moving the straw around inside the cup gave her hands something to do while they talked. It was a habit she'd unwittingly developed. Jim sat on the other side of the table, his right hand holding the handle of his coffee cup.

"You really look good," Jim said. "Did you cut your hair?"

Megan's hand went instinctively to her hair. "Yeah, just a trim," she said a little shyly, not meaning for it to sound that way, and hating herself for acting so meek. She abruptly pulled her hand away from her hair.

"And new clothes, too. It's a good look for you. I almost didn't recognize you," he said, and then laughed just a bit. "I'd forgotten just how beautiful you are."

"Thank you," Megan said, and began stirring her coffee again.

"So, how've you been?" Jim asked, raising his cup to drink.

"I've been good… other than worrying about Ben. He's had it so rough, and now to have this happen," her voice trailed off. The stirring became quicker. When she realized it, she stopped and put the straw down. Jim didn't seem to notice.

Jim raised his eyebrows and nodded in empathy. "Yeah, I know. Poor Ben. He's had it pretty rough, hasn't he?"

There was a moment she wanted to say something, to expand on the kind of relationship they had formed over the last few months. Instead, she nodded weakly.

"I'm curious. Are you and Ben together?" He seemed almost embarrassed to ask.

"No, not like that. We're friends, nothing more. Becca was my best friend. You know that. No, we've just have been through quite a bit. We hang out sometimes. And we talk a lot, mostly. Just talk."

A part of her heart screamed over the denial.

His reaction was that of a small smile.

"Well, it's good that you have someone to talk to."

Again, Megan only nodded while she sipped her coffee.

"What was the deal with the guy who beat him up anyway? Is he some kind of nut job?"

"He was Ben's former boss. In some twisted way, he blames Ben for getting fired. He also tried to kidnap his son, Joey," she said. "You wouldn't believe it. The kid jumped out of the car at a gas station and ran into the local fire department." Megan shook her head and laughed a little. "At his age, I probably would've been so scared wouldn't have known what to do, much less what he did."

"Sounds like a bright kid. Brave, too."

Megan nodded again. For the life of her, she couldn't figure out why she was sitting here with her ex-husband. Part of her was telling her she needed to cut this conversation short and go back up to be with Ben. The other part missed Jim and wanted to stay. So far, that part was winning.

"I've thought about you a lot lately," Jim said. "Do you

ever think about us?"

"I used to," she admitted, frowning a bit. "I used to think about all the times that we had together, think about the love we had. But then, I wondered what it was that I did that made things change, what I did wrong. I blamed myself for so many things, thinking that I was worthless, that if I had done things differently you wouldn't have left me for someone else."

"Megan," Jim reached across the table and took her hand, "you didn't do anything wrong. It was entirely my fault. I just got comfortable with the relationship we had, I thought that what we had was common. Little did I realize that the kind of love that we shared is rare, and that I was a fool for letting you go," Jim sighed. "You're an exceptional woman, Megan. I knew that when I married you but forgot. I can only hope that you can forgive me someday for being such an idiot."

"I hope so, too," she said flatly, not being completely sold. "What happened to you and Sabrina?"

"We broke things off a while back. I've got an apartment uptown now, living by myself. Things just never worked between us. I think she sensed that I was never fully over you," Jim said sadly, looking down at his cup.

Megan didn't know what to say. Her heart was fighting viciously with itself. There would never be a time she could trust this man, but she was finding it difficult to detach herself from him completely.

"I wondered, if you're not seeing anyone, maybe you'd like to go out sometime and see a movie, or just do something. We could start out as friends, and see what happens? I don't want to put any pressure on you. I just thought… well, you know."

"I don't know, Ben," she said, and then quickly rectified herself, "I mean, Jim."

Jim allowed himself another small grin. He knew if she hadn't said no, then he at least had a chance, even if she had said Ben's name instead of his.

"Just think about it, okay?"

"I will. I'll think about it," she said sounding unnerved. "I really have to get back upstairs."

"I have to get going myself. Tell Ben I send my best." They got up from the table; Jim gave her a hug. Megan accepted the embrace, warning her heart against it and enjoying it at the same time. Jim gave her hand a gentle squeeze before walking towards the cafeteria exit. He turned back one last time. "Think about it. I'll call you later," he said before leaving.

Megan sat back down, feeling miserable with herself. *Why didn't you tell that lying, cheating, little prick to go take a flying leap?* She put both elbows on the table and put her head in her hands. *Because a small part of you still loves him—that's why.* Her mind wheeled around again, bringing up a subject she didn't often like to ponder. *What about Ben? You love him, even if you don't want to admit it. Jim is a scurvy little spider compared to him.*

Megan sighed; she already knew the answer. As much as she cared for Ben, he wasn't ready.

She took the last drink of her coffee and started to get up. Thoughts continued to bang away at her. *Look, I haven't agreed to anything. Jim might be a low-life little creep, but maybe he has learned something, and he still cares about me. Maybe my mother was right, I don't know. But it isn't going to hurt anything to start out as friends and see how things go.*

Once Megan reached the elevator, she pushed the button to go up and began rummaging through her purse, not exactly looking for anything. She simply wanted to take her mind off Jim, but while she did, an old saying that her father often used kept running through her mind.

Those who forget the past are doomed to repeat it.

Nervous excitement was boiling up inside Joe as he grabbed a soda from the fridge. For a moment he almost forgot about it while searching for the remote control for the television to turn the volume down. He put the soda on the floor beside the chair. The excitement he felt reached its peak as he pulled out his cell phone and flipped through the Kalamazoo phone book. There was a pause as he found the number he wanted. Getting into character, he dialed while running his lines through his head. He had deliberately sobered up in order to think clearly.

"Yes, hello, I wonder if you could be so kind as to connect me to admissions, please," he said politely. As he waited, Joe reached down blindly to find the soda can and knocked it over with the side of his hand, spilling it everywhere. He swore and jumped to his feet, throwing the offending can against the wall, splattering the wall with the remainder of its contents. Just then, someone on the other end picked up. There was an instant change to his tone as he returned to character.

"Um, yes... I just wanted to know if my good friend, Ben Stryker, had been admitted to your hospital. I was told he was in some kind of accident or something." There was another pause as the woman at the hospital checked. He waited patiently, keeping his mouth shut.

"What's that? There's no record of Ben Stryker being admitted. I see... yes, of course. I will try Bronson Central to see if he is there. Thank you."

He hung up. If he wasn't at Northside, then he felt there was a good chance that he had killed him. Joe sat back down, scanned through the page again, and found the number to Bronson Central. Again, he tried to clear his mind and dialed the number. He started pacing as it rang.

"Hello, yes could I please be connected with admissions? Oh, you can? Stryker, Ben Stryker is the name." Again, he waited; this time filled with the expectation that she was going to come back on the line and say Stryker had died on the operating table or something along those lines. Then, she would add some crybaby crap about how deeply sorry she was.

She came back on the line a moment later.

"Oh, I see. He's in room 318. What's his condition?" Joe was punching himself in the leg with the opposite hand as she told him the news. "Well, that is excellent news. I'll have to visit him. Thank you ever so much." He hung up the phone and then plopped back down into the brown recliner. With his right hand, he fished beneath the chair and pulled out a bottle of tequila; his face was sneering, twisted with hate.

"Damn, I should've finished the job when I had the chance."

The hallway outside Ben's room was empty. Megan could hear Ben's voice as she entered the room. Larry, standing by the window, was laughing. Megan walked to the foot of his bed, feeling a little bewildered.

"How are you feeling?" she asked.

"Believe it or not, I feel great," he said enthusiastically. "I don't know what they put in that IV, but it is some good stuff. God, you look beautiful. Isn't she beautiful, Larry?" Ben asked Larry in a bemused sort of way. "And smart, too. Smarter than me. I don't know if she's smarter than you. You're pretty smart. She's a bigger smart aleck."

Megan looked at Larry questioningly. Ben was feeling a little too good.

Larry caught her look and chuckled. "He's baked."

Megan looked back at Ben. He nodded. "Yep!" he said grinning widely.

"Is he going to be alright?" she asked, moving to Ben's side.

"Yeah, the doctor said he didn't want him going to sleep and they wanted to make sure he wasn't, you know... uncomfortable. So, they gave him a healthy dose," Larry said.

"Oh, I wanted to tell you something," Ben said, looking at Megan. He touched her arm. "I saw Becca and the girls when I was—well, you know. Anyway, she wanted me to tell you that they love you and miss you. Becca said that you mean the world to her and—" a solemn look passed his face as he tried to remember the rest of it, "that you need to be strong. There was something else, but I can't remember it exactly. Something about sorrow sometimes comes—no, that isn't it. Sometimes love comes from sorrow. I think that was it. I don't know. I'll have to think about it."

Megan smiled at the thought that he believed he'd seen Becca and the girls. More than likely, it was just his subconscious working overtime while in the coma. But she was struck by one comment. She had heard something similar from Becca one other time; it was also the last time she saw Becca. *Happiness sometimes comes from sorrow*—that's what she'd said. But it was love she meant. At that time, she assumed Becca had been talking about her relationship with Jim—that things would get better. Now, she wasn't certain. Was Becca sending her a message about Jim… or Ben? The idea spun inside her brain, but only caused more confusion for her heart. She pushed all of it aside for now.

"I miss them, too, Ben," Megan told him.

Ben's smile faltered. "I wanted to go with them, but she said I couldn't." He reached for Megan's hand. "Why does life have to be so hard sometimes?"

"I don't know," Megan said softly, "but we are here for you."

This thought brightened him again, making him forget his earlier sadness—this effect largely aided by the drugs. "Yep. Sorry, looks like you guys are stuck with me," he said.

Larry and Megan walked to the elevator; she pushed the button to go down. There was a heavy silence between them. Both knew what the other was thinking, but neither wanted to be the first to broach the subject of Jim Haslett. Finally, Larry broke the silent truce between them.

"Ben is going to be okay. It may be a long recovery, but he'll come through it."

"I hope so," Megan said. The doors opened and they

walked into the elevator; they were alone inside of it; soft elevator music playing on the speaker overhead.

Larry hesitated with the next question. “What did Jim want?”

There it was, out in the open. Megan wanted to keep the conversation vague, if at all possible; she was acutely aware of exactly how much Larry disliked her ex-husband.

“He was just curious how Ben was doing… and he asked about me, that’s all.”

“Good,” Larry said quickly. “For a moment there, I was afraid he might try and weasel his way back into your life.”

“He might have mentioned that he would like, um… would like to be friends,” she blurted out.

“Jim wants to be your friend?”

“Yes, friends. What’s so crazy about that?”

Larry shot her a disgusted look. Megan moved quickly to defend herself. “Look, Larry, there’s nothing wrong with starting out slow, and seeing where things go. It isn't like I’m jumping back into the sack with him or anything. I think he may have changed. I don't know. Oh—don't give me that look,” she said, turning away from him.

A moment passed; the elevator continued its descent before Larry spoke, “Okay, I promise to leave you alone about this. I think it’s a mistake, but it’s your life and you have to make the decisions that make you happy. I’m just trying to protect you is all.”

“I know you are,” she said, glancing back over at him. “But seriously, I’m not going to jump into anything, okay? You don't have to worry your head over it. I’ve got it under control.”

The doors to the elevator opened; Larry paused, put his hand on Megan's shoulder, and pointed at her with his other hand. "You do what you have to do," he said, "but I reserve the right to tell you 'I told you so' when the time comes."

"It's a deal," Megan said.

"It's your move," Ben said gleefully.

"I know it is," Larry said, sounding irritated. Ben had been in the hospital almost two weeks by this point. Larry had come in early after work, and they had taken up a game of chess to occupy their time. At the moment, Larry was losing, and Ben wasn't going to pass up the chance to jab him about it.

"I'm just pointing it out, in case you didn't know," Ben added.

Larry looked up from the board at Ben and narrowed his eyes. "If you're not careful, you're going to need another surgery to remove certain chess pieces from your rectum."

"Okay, okay. I'm sorry. But I can't help but rub it in a little. I don't think I've ever been this close to beating you before."

"You've beaten me before and you know it. I'm just surprised you don't remember what a terrible loser I am," Larry said, still concentrating on the board. He moved his Rook to protect his King. Ben moved his Bishop diagonally across the board taking Larry's Queen. Larry had some choice words for him, most of them profane.

The door swung open, and Megan came into the room. She went over and stood at the foot of his bed. She was wearing a blue dress, earrings, and make-up. Her hair was soft and hung down to her shoulders in long curls. Ben looked up from the chessboard and whistled. “Wow, look at you. You didn’t get all spiffed up for me, did you?”

“No. I’m going out tonight,” Megan said quickly, unwilling to go into detail.

Ben expression changed instantly. “You’ve got a date?”

“Kind of,” Megan said, “it's not like a date-date.” She tried to make it sound as if it weren’t a big deal, but turned a little when she said it, so she didn't have to look at Ben.

In a sudden rush, Ben felt as if he was falling. His ears were filled with the sound of soft static and a flush of warmth accompanied it. There wasn’t a good reason for him to be so opposed to the idea of her going out with someone. He should’ve been happy for her. That’s what friends do, isn’t it? So why did the idea upset him so much? Automatically, Ben put on a full grin to cover his feelings. “Well, that’s great. I’m glad to hear you found a new playmate,” he said, trying to hold the smile the best he could, “seeing how your old one is broken now.”

“Oh hush, we can still go shopping and stuff. I know how much you like that. And once you heal up, I’ll take you bowling. Then again, I’d hate to embarrass you,” she said. “Maybe you can find something else you can beat me at.”

“Just don't play chess,” Larry said flatly. “He’s whipping me good right now.”

“Who… um… who is it?” Ben asked, but the answer came through the door that very moment. Jim entered the room, dressed in one of his finest suits. He looked around meekly, and then went over and stood next to Megan. He placed his hand on the small of her back.

"Hey, Ben, how are you feeling?"

"Oh, ah—yeah. It's good to see you, Jim. I'm doing better. The knee gives me a little bit of trouble, but they tell me I'm recovering." Ben was stunned by the turn of events and gave Larry a quick sideways look as if to ask if he knew about this. Larry shrugged noncommittally as if it were none of his business.

Jim smiled politely. "Good. That's really good. I'm glad," he said impassively, then turned his attention to Megan. "Are you ready to go? The movie starts in a half an hour."

"Really? I only just got here and wanted to visit with Ben for a bit."

"We could catch a later movie if you want," Jim told her.

Ben, still trying to regain his bearings piped in, "Hey, no, that's okay. If you have plans, then you should go."

"Are you sure?" Megan asked.

"Oh sure, I'm not going anywhere," Ben said with a dismissive wave. "You guys go on. Have a good time."

Megan seemed conflicted about it, but finally conceded. "Okay, but tomorrow I'll be back to take you on at a game of chess. Maybe you can actually beat me at that. You know, unlike bowling," she said smiling.

"Sounds good to me," Ben said, returning a smile, trying to sell it the best he could. It wasn't easy. Inside, his guts were churning. The last thing he wanted was for her to return to the man who'd hurt her the most. If she weren't careful, he would hurt her again. Of that, he was almost certain. But when it came down to it, he found he couldn't stand in her way of trying to be happy. She had to make her own choices.

“Bye, guys. I’ll talk to you later,” Megan said. Jim gave a short wave to them, and then took Megan's hand as they started for the door.

“Bye, Megan… Jim,” Ben said. Larry, still absorbed in the chess match, didn’t even bother to acknowledge they were leaving.

After they left, Ben turned to Larry.

“You knew about this?”

Larry said nothing but nodded.

Ben looked back towards the door again. “She’s seeing Jim. Why didn't you say something? Why didn't she say something?”

“Maybe she didn't want you to know for other reasons,” Larry said, moving his rook across the chess board.

“What do you mean by that?” Ben asked.

Larry looked at him, opened his mouth to say something, and then closed it. Then something in his expression changed. “Oh, forget it, knucklehead. If you’re not smart enough to figure it out, I sure as hell ain’t gonna tell you.” He paused. “It's your move by the way.”

Without really looking at the board, Ben arbitrarily moved one of his pieces. Larry moved quickly after that.

“There isn't anything else going on that you haven't told me, is there?” Ben asked, once again looking in the direction of the door.

“Just one thing,” Larry said, pointing at the board, “you're in checkmate.”

CHAPTER 11

Ben sat back in the hospital bed with his hands laced behind his head. He was trying to be patient, but it was difficult to do because the doctor had agreed to release him that afternoon. After being cooped up in a hospital room for a month, his patience was all but gone. The surgery to his knee had been extensive but was healing. Dr. Hastings told him there was a chance that he might end up with a slight limp. Ben thought that he could live with that as long as he could still walk. They had removed the cast on his arm and wrist yesterday; he was relieved to have them gone.

The door opened slowly, and he heard a woman's voice.

"Hello? Can we come in?"

"Yeah, I'm decent. Come on in," Ben said.

Hannah walked in with Joey in tow.

"I'm sorry to bother you, Ben. Joey insisted on coming today," Hannah said, looking down at her son, frowning. "If we are bothering you—"

Ben jumped in quickly, "No, it's no bother. I was hoping you would stop by." He shifted a little, setting himself up in bed. "I wanted to talk to you about Joe." Ben could see her look down a little in shame.

"I'm sorry, I should've warned you. I knew he was insane and that he'd go after you. At the time, I was so wrapped up in other things."

"I appreciate it, but I don't blame you, Hannah. I had my suspicions Joe would try to pull something, but I let my guard down and paid the price for it. Even if you had warned me, it probably would've happened anyway. Megan tried—" He stopped himself. "That's not the issue right now. The problem is that Joe is still out there somewhere, and you and Joey are still in danger."

"What can we do, though? The police were unable to find him. I live every day wondering if he is going to show up again," Hannah exclaimed.

"I made a... well... I guess you could call it a promise, that I'd do my best to help protect you and Joey." The statement was an earnest one, but when he searched his memory, he couldn't remember ever making such a promise. He disregarded that thinking. It made little difference if he made the promise or not, it was his intent to protect them to the best of his ability. "The best thing we could do right now is stay in touch with each other and keep a careful watch. I don't think he's going to be in a hurry to come around just yet. He's wanted by the police, and they are watching for him. But I think eventually he'll try something. We should be prepared."

Hannah nodded in agreement.

Ben continued, "I just wanted you to know that I'll do all I can to help you."

"Thank you," Hannah said.

"I wanted to ask something else. Would you mind if I talked to Joey alone for just a few minutes? We have something to discuss. It's, you know, man to man type stuff," Ben said, and winked at Joey. Joey cracked a grin.

"Yes, that would be fine," Hannah said. "I'll be outside."

After his mother left, Joey pushed the chair up to the bed like the last time and stood in it with a knowing look on his face.

"You know what I want to talk to you about?"

Joey nodded.

"How much of what happened was real?" Ben asked him.

"Only a little. The stuff we talked about was real, but the house... I made that up."

Ben was a little shocked but hid it well.

"How were Becca and the girls able to talk to me? You know they are dead."

"I don't know, Mr. Stryker," Joey said, "It feels like a doorway that opens. But I really don't know for sure."

"I see," Ben said, considering the things Joey had told him. "By the way, you can call me Ben."

"Yes, Sir," Joey said in an automatic response, and then grinned, realizing his mistake, "I mean, Ben."

"What other things can you do, Joey?"

At first, it appeared as if Joey wasn't going to answer, but they shared a secret. "I can see what people are feeling, and I can see what kind of person they are on the inside."

"Have you told your mother about this?"

Joey's eyes got wide, and he slowly shook his head.

"And you don't want to tell her either, do you?"

Joey shook his head again.

"Okay, we'll keep it between us," Ben said. He thought for a minute, and then asked Joey another question. "Joey, do you think that you'd be able to feel it if your father came back around. If he was, you know, close by?"

"I don't know. Maybe, if I practiced," he said, shrugging slightly.

"I want you to practice on me, then. When you get home later, let's say seven o'clock, reach out and see if you can find me, you know, with your gift. Then call me at this number." Ben scribbled his number on a scrap of paper. "Will your mother let you make a phone call?"

Joey nodded this time.

Ben handed him the piece of paper. "Okay, I'll try to relax or something at that time. It might make it easier for you." Ben looked seriously at Joey, "You know why it's important, don't you?"

"Yes, if we know where my father is, we can keep Momma safe from him," he said. There was a sadness in his voice that went beyond his years.

"That's right," Ben said, "and to keep you safe as well."

Out in the hallway, Megan saw Hannah as she approached the room. "Hey, how are you doing?" Megan asked.

Hannah smiled. "Doing good... well, considering things."

"Joe hasn't come back around, has he?" Megan asked.

"No, but I live in fear of him. We were just talking to Ben. I think he's decided to take on the role of protector for us. I have to admit, I'm willing to take any help at this point. Ben really is something else. I don't think I've ever met anyone like him before."

And you never will, Megan thought.

"Yeah, he's one of a kind," she said instead.

"He's in there talking to Joey right now. I think he's trying to tell him to be brave and to take care of me," Hannah said. "I wish I had someone to tell me to be brave. Seems so hard to do right now."

"Sounds like what you could use is a way of taking your mind off of things for a while," Megan told her.

"Yeah, I really could. I keep wondering how much good I'll be to Joey if I keep letting this fear eat away at me. I could really go for a vacation. Go somewhere warm." She laughed. "Or a job. I really need to start looking for something. I hate living off my parents. There has to be a time when I finally stand on my own."

"Do you have any secretarial skills?"

"I did at one time. I worked part time at the firm while going to college, but that was years ago."

"I'll tell you what, my office has an opening right now. It's an entry level position, but I could put in a word for you if you want."

"I don't know what to say. It'd be great if you could do that for me," Hannah said with a bit of excitement in her voice.

"We'd be working together. I think it would be nice," Megan said. "Come on, we'll go tell Ben and Joey the news."

When they walked in, Joey was standing in the chair next to the bed, talking with Ben in whispers. They looked up and stopped talking at once. Ben smiled and waved them in. "Come in, come in," he said. "Where's Larry? Wasn't he supposed to come with you?"

"He was, but when I asked him about it, he said—" Megan puffed up her shoulders and put on a sour face to imitate Larry, "there ain't no way he's getting out of there by three. If they said three, it means five or six." Then she laughed. "He should be here in a little bit," she said in her normal voice.

Larry walked in the middle of Megan's little scene. Amy was beside him. "Someone talking bad about me?" he asked.

"Not talking bad, just poking fun," Megan said, grinning at him.

"Sure, sure, always got to be picking on me," Larry replied stoically.

Megan turned back to Ben. "Oh, I wanted to tell you. I think I can get Hannah a job over at my company. They have a position open, and I know the woman who does the hiring. She's bound for the nine to five life I get to endure."

Suddenly, Hannah's face fell. "Oh dear. I completely forgot about Joey. What am I going to do about him in the afternoons if I go back to work? I can't leave him in a daycare after what happened."

"He can stay with me, I don't mind. I'm going to be off work until my leg heals up anyway," Ben said, looking over at Joey. "What do you think, Kid?"

Joey nodded, smiling a little.

"I can help out, too," Amy added. "Once Ben goes back to work, he can stay with me. It'd be nice to have a little boy around again, since mine is all grown up," she said, looking delighted.

"See. Problem solved," Ben said.

"Well, if you don't mind having him around. He's a good boy and doesn't get into a lot of trouble."

"No, really, I think it's a grand idea," Ben said.

Nurse Gloria entered the room holding Ben's discharge papers. She ignored everyone, rolled the hospital tray over in front of Ben, and laid the paperwork on top of it. "The quicker you put your John Hancock on these, the quicker we can get rid of you, Mr. Stryker," she said, looking down her nose at him, "not that you haven't been a pain-in-the-ass and I'm ready to see you leave or anything."

"Oh, come on, Gloria. You know you're going to miss me." Ben teased.

"Uh-huh! Gonna miss you like I would miss having hemorrhoids."

"That much," Ben said, and a smile crossed Gloria's face. She grabbed the papers he'd finished signing and put them in order.

"I might miss you just a little," she said. "I think you'll do fine, Ben Stryker." She strode away without looking back.

Ben clapped his hands together. "Okay. Larry, grab a wheelchair and let's blow this Popsicle stand. In celebration of my release from this prison, and the hospital food I've had to endure, I'm taking you all out to dinner."

Megan unlocked the front door to Ben's house, pulling the key free of the lock before handing it back to him. Ben used his crutches to get inside and went to his favorite chair. He pulled the crutches out from under him and sat down.

"Ah, it's good to be home," he said, patting the arms of the recliner.

Megan sat on the couch.

"Thanks for bringing me home," Ben said.

Megan waved her hand. "Not a problem. I figured

I'd done my good deed for the day if I helped a cripple home."

"You know what would be really good?" Ben said, and mimicked tipping a shot of whiskey back.

"No, Ben," Megan replied quickly. "You've been on pain medication."

"I didn't take them today. I knew I was coming home, and I was fairly certain I could talk you into going to get me something to drink." Megan pondered the wisdom of it, but it was Friday night, and she didn't have to work in the morning. "Come on, Megan. Pretty, pretty please! I promise I'll give you some. Well, one."

"If I'm the one going to get it, I'm damn well having more than one," she replied.

"Okay... two."

"You're nothing but trouble, you know that?" she said, shaking her head at him.

"Yep," he replied, undaunted by her remark. Megan could only laugh.

She got up and trudged to the door. "I'll be back shortly, Your Highness. Anything else you want while I'm out?"

"Nope," Ben changed his tone from playful to serious. "I really do appreciate this, Megan."

For a long moment, she stared at him, only smiling, and then sensed her awkwardness of just standing there. "You're welcome. I'll be back in a little bit," she said before leaving.

Ben looked up at the clock; it was nearly seven. He remembered the promise he made to Joey. He tilted back in the recliner and cleared his mind. There was no way of knowing if would help Joey or not, but he would try, at least until Megan came back with the booze.

When Joey and his mother returned home, they found George and Beverly sitting in the living room watching television. Hannah let go of Joey's hand as they walked in. It was as if being in this house, the house she grew up in, was a safe zone for her and she could relax. Hannah immediately went to her parents and began talking about the job that Megan had mentioned. She spoke in high, excited tones. Joey smiled; it was wonderful that his mother would find something to make her so happy when the last few years of her life had been so miserable. When Joey heard Megan and his mother talking about the job, he sensed her excitement and felt a little anxious for her. Even though she seemed nice enough, he didn't know Megan that well. She could be exaggerating, or even outright lying about getting her the job. If she was, his mother was in for a gigantic let-down. So, he'd reached out to find out what kind of person Megan was on the inside. He was a bit surprised by what he found. She was intelligent, that much he had figured out without help, but she was also emotionally strong. She hadn't always been that way. Something happened to her, and she was becoming more than what she was. Her sharp wit and her modesty also stood out. She lacked the vanity most attractive women possessed. She was sincere, but she also kept a wall to protect her heart. She hid what she felt, but inside, her emotions radiated out toward Ben in waves.

She loves him, but she cannot tell him, had passed through Joey's mind. He also realized something else: Ben loved her, too, even if he didn't realize how much.

Joey glanced up at the clock; it was already five past seven. He needed to be alone to try the experiment with

Ben.

"Momma, I want to go upstairs to my room."

"Okay, Honey. Are you tired? Want to lie down?"

Joey nodded.

Hannah kissed her son on the forehead. "Love you," she said.

"Love you, too, Momma. Goodnight, Grandma, Grandpa."

Joey gave them hugs before going upstairs. When he got halfway up the stairs, he could hear them talking again.

"Hannah, if you wanted a job, I could have gotten you one at the firm," he heard his grandfather saying. Joey ignored the rest, ran into his bedroom, and shut the door. He jumped on his bed and closed his eyes. He concentrated on Ben's strongest characteristic—the steel he'd found inside of him—then pulled himself toward that, not knowing what direction to do so. He thought he felt something but found no connection to Ben. For a moment, he considered giving up.

And then it dawned on him.

Joey closed his eyes again and thought of the living room downstairs. He focused on that room, creating it in his mind, this time leaving out the Christmas tree and decorations. Then he stretched out his mind to find his friend.

Minutes had passed, but still there was nothing. Ben opened one eye and looked at the clock; it was ten past seven. He closed his eyes and tried to focus again. Without meaning to, his mind began to wander, first on Megan, who would be back soon. She was seeing her ex,

Jim. He needed to let her be happy and not get in the way of that. Then he began to think of Joe, who could be anywhere, planning anything. Behind his closed eyes, a room started to come into focus. At first, it appeared as a blurry whiteness. Ben opened his eyes, and it was gone. He closed them again and it was there again, becoming clearer. Soon, Ben recognized the place. It was the same room they had been in the last time. The kid appeared on one of the chairs, his hands folded as if waiting for him.

Ben did all he could to keep his eyes shut. He was surprised how hard it was to keep them closed while consciously trying to keep them shut. Now that they'd established contact, he wondered if they could communicate.

"Joey, can you hear me?" Ben asked.

Joey nodded in the room behind his eyes.

"Can you say something?"

"Hi?" Joey said meekly.

Ben laughed. "Hi, Joey," he said, and then paused, trying to think. "Is there any way for you to know where I am?"

Joey shook his head. "No. I know you're not far away, but not where you are."

"Well, that's something at least," Ben said.

"What do you want me to do now?" Joey asked.

Ben thought about it for a second. "How hard was it for you to find me?"

"It was easy once I figured out that I should make this room for us to meet in."

"Could you do this with your father?" Ben asked anxiously.

Joey hesitated. "I suppose so."

"Okay. You did really well for tonight, Joey."

"Do you still want me to call you?" Joey asked.

Ben shrugged. "I don't think it's necessary, do you?"

"No, I guess not."

"Bye, Joey. Nice work."

"Bye, Mr. Stryker... I mean, Ben."

The room disappeared behind his eyes. "That kid is something else," Ben said, just as Megan walked in holding a bottle of Crown Royal. She gave him a funny look.

"Who were you talking too?" she asked.

"Um... just myself," he replied quickly. "Who else am I going to talk to?"

Megan had purchased a fifth but thought it would be wise if they limited their drinking. It wasn't that she didn't trust Ben. She just didn't trust herself not to go and say or do something stupid. However, by eleven, they were already three quarters of the way through the bottle. They were both feeling the effects of the alcohol, probably because neither of them had any since Christmas.

"You know what?" Ben said, "This is some really good stuff."

"Yep," Megan answered. She poured the last two shots from the bottle and handed one to Ben.

"Why have we been drinking that cheap stuff all this time?" he asked, and then tipped his back.

"Because that's what you buy," Megan answered.

"Oh, yeah," he said.

"From now on, I'll buy the good stuff for you," Megan said, and then started laughing. Ben grinned.

"You're an idiot," Ben joked.

"I am not," Megan said, sounding offended but was

still grinning.

"Are, too!"

"How?"

Ben hadn't intended to get into a discussion about the subject of her ex-husband, but now that it started, there was no way to stop. "You're going out with Jim, your smooth-talking ex, are you not?"

"Yeah, I guess I am." Megan sighed, and then laughed just a little. "Maybe I am kind of an idiot."

"Yes, you are," Ben said with a bit of irritation in his voice. "How in the world could you even think of allowing that dirt-bag back into your life? Especially after everything he did to you. You do remember he left you for that one woman? What was her name? Sabrina? Do you remember how he hurt you? I sure do." Ben shook his head. "What? Once wasn't enough? You gotta go back for seconds?" Ben closed his mouth, realizing he'd gone too far. He'd vowed to keep his mouth shut on the subject, and then broke that vow.

"Well, I appreciate your opinion, but idiot or not, it's still my life. At least I'm willing to take a chance to do whatever it takes to be happy," Megan said spitefully. "Maybe you should consider doing the same."

Ben hung his head. "I'm sorry. I shouldn't have said that. I have no right. If anyone is an idiot, it's me."

"You're a lot of things, Ben, but you're no idiot."

Ben turned away, his voice small, "At least you didn't kill your family."

Megan's first instinct was to rebut his statement, to tell him there was no way possible he was responsible. But she could tell the alcohol was having an effect on him and realized he was revealing a deep-seated guilt he'd carried for a while now. "I didn't know you felt that way," she said. "How come you never told me this before?"

"I was ashamed." His eyes were glossy with tears. "And Tia..."

"What about Tia?"

Ben closed his eyes. The bitter tears were forced from his eyes. "At the hospital, I prayed she would hurry up and die. Can you believe that? What kind of monster prays for his daughter to die?" He bent forward, tears rolling down his cheek and falling onto the floor.

Megan went to him, knelt down, and gently wrapped her arms around him in a soft embrace. Then she wiped the tears from his face, and then kissed him tenderly on the mouth. She held the kiss longer than intended. Finally, she drew away from him. "You're not a monster," was all she said.

"Thank you," Ben replied. He was grateful that she'd known that allowing him to say the words out loud, to admit his guilt without having to explain, was what he needed most.

"You're welcome," she said, and then got to her feet. She still had a hold of his hand. "Come over and lay on the couch. I know it's where you sleep."

Ben tried to get up but had difficulty because of his bad leg. Megan helped him over to the couch. He stretched out, but before he could get comfortable, Megan gestured for him to move over some. Then she lay down beside him.

"Ben," she said softly, her face and body turned away from his, "if you don't mind, I thought I would stay here with you... alright?"

Ben grabbed the blanket off the back of the couch and spread it out over both of them. "Anything you want, Megan," he whispered.

Megan grabbed his arm and pulled it around her. She wanted to feel guilty about it, she wanted to feel bad, but couldn't. They settled into sleep, sharing their warmth, and slept more soundly than they had in a long time.

Joe Murphy rolled out of the bed at about nine in the morning and put his feet on the floor; it was freezing cold. He blinked several times trying to get his eyes working properly, and then realized that he could see his breath.

"It's frigging freezing in here."

He quickly wrapped the blanket around him and went to check the thermostat; it read thirty-five degrees. He glanced out the back window and saw the propane tank sitting in the back yard, covered with snow.

He heard his father's voice in his head. *You forgot to have the tank refilled. What kind of moron are you?*

Joe's shoulders slumped. His father, Patrick Murphy, had berated him since he was a child. Now the old man lived alone in the house where he'd grown up. His mother died ten years ago, but the rotten old bastard was still hanging in there, alive and kicking, both inside their old house and inside his head.

Joe kicked the empty tequila bottles out his way as he stumbled back to the bed.

What kind of idiot son did I raise? You really are stupid, you know.

Joe threw the blanket on the floor and grabbed his pants, then rummaged around the floor to find a sweatshirt. He found a green one, held it up to his nose, and sniffed. His face twisted in revulsion at the smell. He tossed the shirt back on the floor and felt around for another, finding one that wasn't quite as bad. After getting dressed, Joe put on his heavy winter jacket and zipped it all the way up, stemming the cold for the time being. The cabin had been badly neglected. There were dirty clothes everywhere; the trash bin was overflowing, half-eaten TV dinners sat on the counter, and empty beer and tequila bottles littered the floor. There was broken glass from an empty bottle he had thrown against the wall. But what really turned his stomach was the unappealing stench the place had developed. Thankfully, the extreme cold had the effect of curtailing the unpleasant smell and brought it to a manageable level.

Joe found a half-full bottle of tequila and took a swig.

So, are you going to sit here and freeze to death? God knows you're dumb enough to do it.

"Shut up, Old Man," Joe told the voice.

He had three thousand in cash left on him. That would last him a little while, but he would have to leave this place eventually and go south to get the money he had stashed. For now, he needed to get the tank filled to heat this place. He pulled the yellow pages out from under the chair and flipped through the pages, but when he went to turn on the cell phone, he found the battery was dead.

What kind of idiot—

"I said SHUT UP!" Joe screamed. "I'm going to kill you if you don't just shut UP!"

He took another long swig of tequila.

"You always hated me, didn't you? I was never good

enough. Nothing I did was ever right." Pulling a hunting knife from its leather sheath, he stared at the blade as it flashed in the light. "One of these days, Old Man, I'm going to shut you up—but good."

Megan opened her eyes and lifted her head just a bit. She must have turned over during the night because she was facing Ben and had her head in the crook of his shoulder. Ben had shifted just a bit too because he was sleeping more or less on his back now.

She watched him as he slept, wanting to caress his face, but worried it would wake him. Instead, she got up slowly, pulling the blanket back over him. He didn't stir. Then, she pulled her hair back and gently kissed him on the mouth. She watched for a moment to see if he had awakened and was relieved to find he was still asleep. Finally, she picked up her shoes, and quietly crept out of the house.

As soon as Ben heard the door close, he opened his eyes; he'd been awake the entire time. He sat up and put his hand to his lips as if touching the remnants of the kiss they shared. "What the hell are you doing?" he said, shaking his head and trying to make sense of the confusion going on inside of him.

CHAPTER 12

Ben stood by the rear patio doors. He was watching the workers finish the roof of his new building. The glass for the skylight would be the last to go in. It had been nearly a month since he'd returned home. Since the night Megan stayed the night. To Ben, it seemed much longer.

He gripped the cane and limped back into the living room. He sat in his recliner and leaned the cane against the end table. The cane was easier to use than the crutches, but it wore on him more quickly. It would take time for him to adjust.

His mind went back to that night with Megan, to the morning after when they had kissed. They hadn't spoken since, and it bothered him. He tried calling a few times, but only got her voice mail. He took that as a sign. Jim was still in her life. He'd seen them through the kitchen window leaving her house a few times. While his mind was still occupied with Megan, he heard a brief knock at the front door before it swung open. Larry trudged in with Joey behind him.

"Well, your guest is here," Larry said, holding out Joey's arm as if to present him to Ben.

"Thanks for picking him up, Larry," Ben said. He

turned to Joey. “How was school?”

Joey shrugged. “It was okay,” the boy replied while stripping off his coat. However, something in the tone of his voice suggested it wasn’t okay.

“I forgot. School isn't supposed to be that much fun, is it?” Ben said, hoping that might open Joey up a little. However, Joey remained silent and sullen.

“I'm going to go help them with the roof,” Larry said. He looked to Ben and gave a subtle nod towards Joey. Something was bothering the kid.

“Okay, I’ll talk to you later,” Ben said absently to Larry.

“Ben, Momma wanted me to call her when I got here so she knows I’m alright,” Joey said.

“No problem,” Ben said. He gave the phone to Joey. “Do you know the number?”

“Yes. I can see the numbers in my head,” Joey said and began to dial. “Hello, Momma? I’m at Ben's house. I’m okay,” Joey said into the phone.

“What? Oh, uh, yeah, I mean, Mr. Stryker. Okay, love you, Momma. Bye.”

Joey handed the phone back to Ben.

Ben wondered if, on top of everything else, Joey had an eidetic, or as it is better known, a photographic memory. Could it be part of the telekinetic powers he had? He would’ve liked to ask Joey about it but decided to keep the question to himself for the time being. Joey appeared to be struggling with other things right now. “As I understand it, your mother started her first day of work today. How do you feel about that?” Ben asked.

Joey shrugged again, almost listlessly, while staring blankly out the living room window.

“What's the matter, Joey? I know something is

bothering you."

Joey frowned deepened.

"Come over here and tell me what's going on."

Ben limped over to the couch; Joey sat down beside him.

"Tell me what happened."

Joey didn't answer right away. For a minute, Ben wasn't sure if he was going to.

"I don't like this… thing… I have," Joey said finally.

It never crossed Ben's mind how difficult it might be for a little kid like Joey to handle the enormity of it all. To be saddled with the burden of such a gift.

"Today, in gym class, Freddy Marsh said I was a freak," Joey continued.

"Why did he call you that?"

"Because I don't act like the rest of the kids."

Again, Ben understood what he meant. Joey carried himself differently from your average seven-year-old. Probably because he was mature for his age. He had to be. Of course, there was also the gift that he couldn't explain. That alone would tend to make anyone feel isolated.

Joey looked up at him. "I could feel the bad feelings coming from him. I wasn't even trying; they just came right at me. Why do people have to have such ugly, nasty feelings?"

"I don't know, Joey. Some people simply enjoy making others feel bad just to make themselves feel better. I do know one thing: you can't let what someone else thinks about you make you feel bad about yourself. You can't let them define who you are."

Joey still looked troubled. Ben decided to try over again.

"Joey, you're not a freak. I can tell you that for a fact. You may be a little different, but everyone is different in some way or another. If you ask me, I think you are different in a good way, believe me. I don't know why you've been given the gift you have, but there must be a reason for it. Just like there must be a reason we were brought together. Maybe there's something larger at work, something we can't see."

"Do you really think so?" Joey asked and brightened a little.

"Yes, I do. As far as the ugly feelings you sense, perhaps there is a way to block them. If you can find a way to climb in my head and talk to me from across the city, then we should be able to find a way to make Freddy keep those ugly feelings to himself."

Joey smiled, and then nodded. "That would be nice."

"But for now, what do you say we go watch them put the roof on the building out back?" Ben said, thinking the distraction would do him good.

"Sure," Joey said, "but I was thinking about what you asked me about finding my dad."

"We don't have to talk about that right now if you don't want to," Ben told him.

"No, it's okay. It's important."

"Okay. What were you thinking?"

"What if I tried the same thing with the room and all?" Joey said.

Ben looked at him quizzically. "Do you think it would work? I knew about the room because of the coma. You and your dad wouldn't have the same connection, would you?

Joey shrugged.

"I guess we could try it and see what happens. What

could it hurt?" Ben said.

Joey closed his eyes and did the same as before, making the living room of his grandparents' home, and then stretching out with his feelings, concentrating on the nasty, hot boiling lava feeling that was his father. It was much more difficult this time. Joey could almost sense the amount of distance between them, but finally found what he was looking for. This time, when he sat in the room, he was alone; the image of his father was not there. "I think I found him. I'm alone here," Joey said. Though he didn't say so, he was grateful for that fact. The sight of his father would've been too much for him to handle. Being inside of his mind was uncomfortable enough. Without realizing it, Joey began to compare the two men—his father, and Ben. Ben exuded confidence, empathy, and courage. His father, doubt, self-loathing, and anger. Both had lost their family, in one sense or another, but how they had reacted to that loss was completely different. Ben blamed himself, whereas his father blamed everyone but himself. Inwardly, Joey secretly feared that he would wake up one day and find out he was like his father. There was no way for him to turn his gift towards himself to find out who he was more like, and even if he could, he didn't think he would.

"Is there anything you can see that can tell you where he is?" Ben asked.

Joey, with his eyes still closed, shook his head.

"Try looking around, I guess," Ben said, grasping at anything that might help them.

Joey concentrated on getting up and moving around inside of the room. Walking past the chair, he realized he could hear something, like an echo or far away voice.

He stopped and listened carefully.

God, it is frigging freezing out here!

"I can hear him talking or thinking... something anyway. It is very faint, but I can hear something about how cold it is," Joey said.

Ben tried to process the information. The cold told him that Joe was almost certainly still in the north somewhere. Joe was headed north when he'd grabbed Joey. Of course, Joe could be almost anywhere. Could be Wisconsin, Maine, or even Canada for all he knew. But something told him he was closer than that, somewhere in the region.

"Is there anything else?"

Joey moved around to the picture window and pulled back the curtain. "The window," Joey said excitedly, "they look out of his eyes. I can see snow, a lake, and road."

"A road. Joey, is there a sign for it?"

"No. It's hard to see because I have to look where he looks. Wait... yes there is a sign for the smaller road. It says Cable Lake Road." Joey paused. "He's going back inside now."

"What do you see in there?" Ben asked.

"It's a small house with one big room. It's messy. He has trash and stuff all over. I'm going to come back. I don't like being here. It feels like I have bugs all over me," Joey said, sounding frightened.

"Okay, come on back," Ben said, and put his hand on Joey's shoulder. "I'm sorry. I shouldn't have made you stay there so long."

Joey opened his eyes. His initial fright was gone. "How was that?" he asked.

"That was great. We have a street name at least. And

you said you could see the lake?"

Joey nodded. "It feels like he's further away than you were when we did it. But it was strong, so it couldn't be far away."

"You think he's still in the area," Ben said, looking down at Joey. "I think you've done enough for today. I'm proud of you."

"I was scared, but I'd do anything to help you and Momma."

"I know, but for now, don't go looking for him unless I'm with you. I don't think he could hurt you or anything. I'd just feel more comfortable if I was with you when you did it, alright?"

Joey nodded. "Okay."

"Come on. We'll go watch them put up that roof. What do you think?"

Joey smiled and nodded again.

Hannah's desk sat next to Megan's in the main office area. Megan had arranged it so she would be Hannah's trainer. The office area sat like a huge H, with the administrative area in the middle, and hallways going up each side, leading to individual offices. The Administrative area was open and had a half dozen desks arranged in two rows. Along the south wall sat the copier and fax machine. The north wall contained a line of bookshelves and filling cabinets. Towards the middle, there was a lounge area with couches sectioned off for visitors, adorned with plastic plants and magazines. Overall, probably six or seven administrative people worked in this area including Megan, and now Hannah.

The morning had gone quickly with Megan introducing Hannah to the office manager, Mrs. Elliott, and the other employees. For lunch, they had gone to Megan's favorite lunchtime restaurant. Hannah had been so excited about the new job that she smiled nearly the whole day.

"So, we're really just general secretarial help?" Hannah asked after they had settled in back at their desks.

"In a sense, I guess you could say that. The top executives have secretaries of their own. Most of us have our own responsibilities to deal with, but the junior execs ask us when they need help, which usually means that you could be doing reports one day, and research the next. I like it because it breaks up the monotony."

"I just hope I'm good enough, so they'll keep me," Hannah said a little nervously.

Megan smiled. "Don't worry. I'll teach you everything you need to know to get by in this place. After a while, you'll get the hang of it."

The cell phone rang in Hannah's purse rang; she pulled it out and answered it quickly. Megan could tell she was talking to Joey, making sure he'd made it to Ben's house after school. It was a very brief conversation. Hannah had only just hung up when Mrs. Elliott came to a halt in front of her desk.

"I know you're new, but personal calls are strictly forbidden during work hours, Mrs. Murphy," Mrs. Elliott said, looking down her nose at her.

"Excuse me, Mrs. Elliot, I think I need to talk to you about that," Hannah said, getting up from her seat.

"There are no exceptions. If you want to talk on your cell phone, hang on—what are you doing?"

Hannah had grabbed Mrs. Elliott and was gently

pulling her into the lounge area. She sat Mrs. Elliot on one of the couches, then sat down with her. Mrs. Elliot glared at Hannah; her lips pursed. Megan followed them, watching the scene, a little dumbfounded by Hannah's uncharacteristic behavior.

"Mrs. Elliott, I don't mean to be so impolite, I just figured it would be easier if we sat down," Hannah said, taking a deep breath. "I only wanted to tell you that I love this job, and I'm so happy that you've taken me on here. I can't tell you how much it has meant to me. I'll also tell you I'd be crushed if I were to lose this job." Hannah's voice turned stern. "But the fact is my ex-husband has already tried to take my son once already —tried to kill someone else I know—and is still on the loose. I must take the phone calls from my son to make sure he's safe. If you cannot allow that, then you'll have to fire me because my son's life is not worth this job, even as much as I want to keep it."

Mrs. Elliott kept a stony, sour look on her face, still glaring at Hannah. Then her features softened. She took Hannah's hands into her own. "You make all the calls you need to. If anybody else gives you grief about it, you have them come see me," Mrs. Elliott told her. Then Mrs. Elliott rose abruptly, as if the matter was settled to her satisfaction. Before she left, she turned to Megan. "I've got to say, Megan, I'm impressed. You could learn a thing or two from her," she said, and walked away.

After a moment, Hannah walked unsteadily back to her desk. Megan's mouth was still open from shock.

"I thought for sure I was fired. I'm so sorry, Megan," Hannah said. "I know you stuck your neck out for me getting this job."

"Don't be sorry. If nothing else, it was worth it to see

Sarah Elliott upstaged for once," Megan said with a wide grin.

With winter finally beginning to break, Joe went outside, stopping at the top porch step. His hand went unconsciously to the hilt of his hunting knife. The sun shone brightly against a clear blue sky; he couldn't have asked for a nicer morning for a walk. He trudged through the remaining slush towards the grocery store. Looking out over the lake, Joe watched the wind blow across the top of the water, making ripples, and gently lapping onto shore. Further down the road, a classic looking, nineteen fifties, black Chevrolet rumbled towards him. It crossed lazily over the centerline and began to stray towards Joe. Joe had only enough time to jump into the ditch to avoid being run down. He picked himself up and looked back over his shoulder. The black automobile swerved back onto the right side of the road and continued down the road as if nothing happened. Joe began cursing while brushing the snow, mud, and grass from his clothes, and then watched as the black Chevy pulled into a driveway not far down the road. Rage coursed through him, and he began to run, full out, towards the house where the car had pulled in. When he got there, he marched up the driveway. A short, gray haired man with thick glasses was standing beside the car. Joe banged the trunk of the old Chevy with his fist.

"What the hell were you doing? Were you trying to kill me, you old geezer?" Joe barked at the little man.

The man looked innocently at him. "Was that you? I'm sorry about that. I'm afraid my eyes aren't what they used to be."

"Didn't ask if you were sorry. You'd best keep your ass off the road if you can't see where you're doing."

"I said I was sorry. I'm afraid that is all I can offer you. If that isn't good enough, then I think it's best if you get off my property!" The old man said, barking back at Joe. He may have been in his seventies, but he wasn't afraid of confrontation. In his youth, Edward Bergman had gotten into his share of fights, mostly because he was shorter than most men and constantly felt the need to prove he was just as good as any other man. With age, he'd found some peace from this curse, but it still got his blood up when someone tried to intimidate him.

Joe grabbed the old man by the neck, pinning him against the car. Suddenly, the old man drove his knee hard into Joe's groin. In an instant, Joe released his grip and dropped to his knees. Mr. Bergman found his wits long enough to run towards the safety of his home. Joe pulled himself to his feet and staggered after him. Mr. Bergman reached the door, but before he could slam it shut, Joe had caught up and slid his arm inside to block it.

"Just go away, you crazy bastard!" The old man shouted.

Joe forced his other arm inside the door and pried it open. Limping slowly and holding his crotch, Joe entered the house. "Oh, we are just getting started. Think you're just gonna kick me in the balls and get away with it? Oh no, you're going to pay for what you did."

Mr. Bergman scrambled to the desk and opened the drawer. Joe grabbed his arm before he could retrieve the black revolver inside.

"What have we got here?" Joe said smoothly, knowing he was in complete control. He maintained a solid grip on the old man but didn't bother pointing the revolver at him. "You weren't planning on shooting me, were you? For shame. That's not a very nice."

"I've got money, anything you want. Just don't hurt me."

"I don't want your money," Joe said with gritted teeth, then slammed him against the wall and held him there. Joe slowly pulled out his hunting knife and showed it to him. "I want to hear you scream." Joe placed the blade against the old man's crotch. Mr. Bergman looked down in total horror.

"No, please... No!" the old man screamed as he felt the knife pierce his body.

Ben stood with the refrigerator door open, gazing intently inside. Joey stood beside him with a bewildered look on his face. Joey was beginning to wonder if Ben believed that if he held the door open long enough, something would eventually materialize inside.

"You know, I really need to get some food for this thing," Ben told him. He closed the refrigerator door. "What do you think? Should we go to the grocery store?"

Without warning, Joey's knees unbuckled, and he fell to the floor in a heap. Ben saw the twisted look of horror and agony on the little boy's face.

"Joey, what's the matter?" Ben asked. Joey's eyes rolled up in his head as he bent to the side and retched dryly. Ben became frantic, shaking Joey by the shoulders. "Oh God. What's the matter, kid?"

After a moment or two, Joey's eyes came back in

focus, and he began to cry. Because he couldn't kneel on his bad knee, Ben sat down on the kitchen floor and held the boy. After several long minutes, Joey's crying stopped, and his breathing slowed too normal.

"Are you okay?" Ben asked him.

Joey nodded, but there was a remnant of the twisted look of anguish on his face.

"Why don't we get you some water? We'll talk about it when you are ready."

Joey nodded again while wiping his eyes with his shirt sleeve.

Joey drank the water down, taking long gasps of air while gulping it down. They sat on the couch and Ben covered Joey with the blanket because the youth was shivering. Ben wasn't sure if it was shock or some sort of sudden sickness affecting the little boy. He seriously considered calling Hannah.

"Please don't call her," Joey said, and took another deep breath trying to calm down. "I'll be okay now."

Ben wasn't certain if Joey had read his mind, or simply guessed.

"Are you sure?" Ben asked.

"Yeah," Joey said and then hesitated, not wanting to go on but knew he must. "It was my dad. He did something awful. He killed a man. Cut him with a knife and there was blood all over—" Joey stopped and took a breath, "I can still hear his screams. It came all of a sudden. I couldn't stop it because it was so fast and so strong."

"Oh, my dear God," Ben said. "I'm sorry Joey, this is my fault. I never should've asked you to look into his mind."

"I wanted to do it," Joey said, "but I didn't expect

this."

"We have to figure out a way to fix this," Ben said. "Tell me again how it happened? You said it came at you all of a sudden?"

"Yeah, kind of like a strong gust of wind."

Ben tried to think, but guilt tried to fog his brain. It was his fault the boy ended up like this and he had to do something to protect Joey from it again. The question was, what? What could he use to protect himself? Then an idea hit him. "Joey, what if you were to make shield of some sort? A mental shield." Ben said, then picked up speed when another thought occurred to him. "Like a huge shield to protect you. Imagine a place that is insulated and safe, and then create it in your mind to protect yourself."

Joey thought about it, and then shook his head. "I have to have some kind of picture in my head to help me," he said. "Maybe if you drew it on paper first so I can see what it looks like?"

"Alright, let's do it," Ben said, sounding encouraged.

Ben led Joey into the kitchen and grabbed his notepad with the mousetrap design on it. Joey caught sight of the drawing as Ben flipped past the page.

"What was that?" Joey asked.

Ben frowned a little; he considered lying, but it wouldn't have been right, especially when Joey had shared his secret with him.

"Promise not to laugh?"

Joey gave him a deeply puzzled look. "Why would I laugh?"

"Okay," Ben said, flipping back to the drawing. "It's supposed to be a time machine. I changed it though. It's going to have an oval cage instead of a flat surface."

Joey surprised him with his reply, "Are you making it so you can go back to see your family?"

Ben shrugged a little. "Yeah, I guess you could say that," he said, and then sighed. "I, um... actually, thought that if I went back, I could keep them from dying in the car accident."

"I don't think you can do that," Joey said, as if it were a fact and not some hypothetical, hair-brain idea.

"Yeah well, I'm going to build it anyway, even if it doesn't work. I just feel the need to finish it."

The boy took a moment to consider what he said while looking over the drawing. "Oh, I think it will work," Joey stated.

"I thought you just said it wouldn't... Oh, never mind. Let's take care of your problem first."

Joey nodded; the subject of the machine seemingly forgotten. Ben began to draw a framework, and then highlighted some of the panels so that it would look like glass, but it lacked depth being dimensionless in appearance.

Joey shook his head. "I don't think I can do that?"

Ben dropped the pencil, sat back, and tried to think. It was important for him to find some way for Joey to protect himself. Another wave of guilt stuck him. "Would it be easier if it was some kind of room, like the living room in your grandparent's house?" Ben asked.

"It might," Joey said brightening a little at the though. "Yeah, I think that would work, if I could see the room drawn out."

Ben rubbed his chin and thought. Another inspiration struck him. He imagined a room with three big windows in front. He began to draw. "We'll make the room a half oval in the front, so you can get a wider view. The windows are made from thick, military grade —" Ben groped for a word that would help Joey use it as a shield, "armored glass. Nothing is getting through it. We add some blinds in case you need to protect yourself from something you don't want to see. They'll drop down automatically whenever you want." Ben stopped for a moment, and then added a control panel with a speaker. "This is in case you want to hear things a little clearer. There's a volume control and microphone," Ben told him. Then, he drew a command chair in the middle of the room for Joey to sit. He finished by adding the rear wall with a door at the center of it.

"See there, the walls are made of titanium, which means they are stronger than steel. You'll be safe inside here."

"What's the door for?" Joey asked, pointing.

"I don't know... um... an emergency escape, I guess," Ben said. He wasn't even certain why he had added it, other than it seemed appropriate. A room needs a door.

Joey smiled at that idea.

"What do you think?" Ben asked.

"I like it, only, could you make it with two chairs? One for me and one for you?"

"Sure, I'd be honored to have a seat in your safe room," Ben said, quickly sketching a second chair to the right of the first.

Joey took the picture, focused on it for a second or two, and then handed it back to Ben.

"Are you sure you don't need more time to look at it?"

Joey shook his head. "No, I got it." Then he closed his eyes. He held Ben's words about armor and titanium in his mind. He wasn't sure what titanium was, but knew it meant strength, and he used that idea to help him. The walls became solid around him, and he was standing in front of the three large windows. They were so much larger than he had expected. The white walls brightened the place considerably. There would be no need for lights. Outside the windows, nothing was visible. This time, it was a comfortable darkness. Joey went to the seat at the center of the room. It gave him the feeling of being on the command deck of some futuristic starship.

"Do you want to try it with me?" Joey asked.

"Ah, sure… I guess I'm up for it," Ben answered, and reluctantly closed his eyes. This time, he was there in an instant, sitting next to Joey in the extra chair. The first thing he noticed where the subtle details Joey had added. The windows were enormous, and the control panel was much more elaborate. Ben thought the room was a fascinating place—considering it was all inside Joey's head.

"This looks like the place, Joey. You can come here anytime you need to get away from your father's emotional… windstorms… I guess you'd call them."

Joey looked to Ben for a moment. "Thank you," he said meekly.

"You're welcome, Joey," Ben said. "Now, what do you say we get out of here and go get some lunch?"

There was a brief knock at the door. Megan walked in followed by Hannah.

"Hello," Megan called out. "Where are you guys?"

Joey came running out of the dining room followed by Ben limping along with his cane. Joey ran to his mother and hugged her.

"Hey, how was your day?" Hannah asked him, kneeling down.

"It was good," Joey said. "We got to watch them put up the roof."

Hannah looked up at Ben. "I want to thank you again for watching him. I know I've told you about a hundred times already."

Ben smiled. "Well, not quite a hundred, yet. How was your first day?"

Megan grinned, and Hannah smiled faintly, almost embarrassed.

"It was interesting," Hannah said.

Ben looked at Megan. "What kind of trouble did you get her into, Megan?"

"I had nothing to do with it. I wish I had. Oh, the look on Sarah Elliott's face—it was priceless," Megan said laughing.

"I don't get it," Ben said.

"Oh, never you mind. We girls get to keep secrets too, you know," Megan said.

"Yeah, I'm sure you do," Ben said. "Do you guys want to stay for dinner?"

Hannah looked at Megan and they both smiled. Ben saw the expressive look that passed between them.

"What did you tell her, Megan?" Ben demanded.

"Ben, I swear, I'd never talk bad about—well—your creative cooking techniques."

"It's not that bad, really," Ben exclaimed.

"Thank you, but no," Hannah said, now grinning along with Megan. "It's nothing personal, Ben. We really need to get going."

"Okay, but you don't know what you are missing," Ben said, and then turned to Joey. "See you tomorrow, kid."

Hannah gave Megan a quick hug and said goodbye before they left. With little deference, Megan threw her purse on the couch and sat down. There was an amused look on her face.

"So, it went well today," Ben said.

"Yeah, Hannah is going to do great. She really is something once you get to know her."

Ben nodded as if agreeing, but it was clear his mind was elsewhere. Megan didn't seem to notice.

"I thought you were going to make us dinner?" Megan said playfully.

"It might be safer if we just ordered out."

Megan smiled at that one, but then the smile fell away quickly. She'd become aware of Ben's preoccupied mood and the lightheartedness she felt earlier disappeared. Her expression turned serious. "Ben, about that night," she said somewhat hesitantly, "I didn't mean for that to happen. I hope you know that." She paused. "I know you're not ready. I mean, we didn't do anything, and there's nothing to feel guilty about, but I kind of pushed you into it." Megan sounded exasperated at trying to explain. "I don't even know what I'm doing—but what I'm trying to say... what I'm trying to tell you..." Megan shook her head out of frustration and then put her hands over her face.

Ben limped over to the couch and sat down beside her. He pulled her hands away from her face and looked her in the eye. "No explanation is necessary. It's all good. I didn't do anything I didn't want to do. There is one thing I don't want. I don't want you to avoid me like you have been. When you're not around, well, let's just say, I'm happier with you in my life. If you want to see Jim, it's none of my business. I'll do my best to remember that and keep my big mouth shut."

Megan sighed and tried to smile. "No, you don't have to keep quiet about it. The truth is I'm not sure what to do about Jim. There's a part of me that still cares about him, but I don't think it's enough. Something inside of me changed when he left. I mean, he's been really sweet and supportive the last few weeks, but I just don't think I could love him the way I did before."

"What are you going to do?"

"I don't know," she said, and covered her face again.

Ben put his arm around her. "You don't have to figure it all out tonight," he said, then grinned and added teasingly, "but it does have to be before the end of the week."

She smiled briefly, laughed, and then hit him on the arm.

"What do you say, should we order Chinese tonight?" he asked.

"Yeah, I'm famished. Some Chinese would be fantastic right about now," she said.

CHAPTER 13

The sun was beginning to dip below the horizon, turning the sky a dull red. Joe gripped the steering wheel tightly. He wanted to stick to the back roads until he was out of state. It was another eight miles to the Indiana state line. From there, he would jump on the interstate and head south toward Indianapolis or Louisville then dump the car. There was no way to know for sure how long it would be before the old man's body was found, but he didn't want to push his luck. If he panicked, he would be caught. At the very least, he would be facing life in prison for murder. Joe shook his head to try and clear his thoughts. He was beginning to sober to the effects of what he had done. The once rational part of his mind abhorred the brutality of his actions.

You gutted that old man like a deer.

Joe frowned. Another voice joined the first.

He had it coming. The old fart tried to run me down. But you know, I really loved making him scream.

At the time, Joe hadn't intended to go as far as he had. Initially, he'd only wanted to scare the old geezer, maybe hurt him a little as a reminder. But the more the old man had screamed, the more it excited him.

Unfortunately, once he was dead, the satisfaction and excitement had disappeared.

I'd really love to see what it would be like to kill someone much slower. Slow enough to where they couldn't scream anymore.

His thoughts turned to Ben Stryker.

It would take a while before Stryker would start screaming, but with enough pain, he would do it. I know he would.

As Joe approached highway 47, he slowed and turned south. Glancing into his rearview mirror, he spotted something that made his heart race. It was the dark blue paint of a State Police car.

Don't panic, he's just following you. There's no way they found that old fart already.

The overhead lights on the police car flashed once then back off again. Joe pulled to the side of the road and the cruiser with him. Joe put his hand on the hilt of the knife, pulled it slowly free of the sheath, and then carefully slid it beneath his thigh. After that, he rolled down the window, put both hands on the steering wheel, and waited. One shot was all he was going to get at this, he had to make it count. Joe held his breath as he listened to the crunch of the trooper's boots on the gravel as he approached. At last, the State Trooper put his hand on top of the car and peered in at Joe.

"Evening, Sir," he said politely. "My, this is a nice car. An Impala, right? Damn nice car. Don't see many of these around anymore," the Trooper said smiling and running his hand along the fender. The officer was a big man in his early thirties and had a round but likeable face. "Looks like you've kept it in perfect condition. What year?" he asked.

"Oh, ah... it's a fifty-nine," Joe answered. He was guessing, and he was probably wrong, but it didn't matter because his brain was already working on the best way of to dispose of Trooper Dumbass once he finished asking his stupid questions about the car. Joe dropped his hand from the steering wheel so it would be closer to the handle of the knife. The way the trooper was leaning over, it would be a quick, easy, upwards thrust. I would make a hell of a mess, but nobody was around, and the man would be dead in a matter of seconds.

"Really? Could've swore it was a fifty-eight. My uncle had a dark blue one just like this, only it was a convertible," the trooper said hesitating. A puzzled look crossed his face but disappeared quickly. "I could be wrong. I imagine the two models were pretty close. Anyway, pulled you over because you forgot your headlights. Figured I would let you know... and get a better look at this beauty at the same time."

"Oh, right, the headlights. I'm sorry, Officer. I swear, don't know where my head is tonight."

"That's alright. Just be careful, would be a shame if someone smashed into this beautiful car of yours by accident. You have a goodnight now," the trooper said, giving Joe a slight, casual salute before walking away. The trooper climbed back into his cruiser, did a U-turn, and headed off in the opposite direction.

Joe pulled the knife out from beneath his leg and slid it back into the sheath. He did it carefully, as if the thing was alive. His adrenaline was pumping, making his hands tremble slightly. Then he eased the car back onto the road, this time making sure to flip on the headlights.

You wanted to kill him, didn't you?

He shook his head in protest.

Maybe it would be better not to come back here. Maybe it's time to relocate to a warmer location—permanently.

"Doesn't sound like a bad idea," he said, his voice sounding a bit shaky. "Not a bad idea at all."

Ben switched on the home computer and sat down. The computer really belonged to Becca; she did a lot of her work on the home computer. At work, he was always on the computer; at home, he didn't have much of a desire to mess with it. In the months since her death, he hadn't even bothered to turn it on.

The computer ran through its startup. The Desk Top picture popped up on the computer screen. Just for a moment, Ben was transported back in time. It was the four of them, his family, their faces crammed together in the frame. It had been Teresa's idea for the picture. All four of them were bent over, butting their heads together, holding the camera under them while taking the picture. They were grinning madly, almost laughing, the purest example of the joy and love experienced by the family he'd once had. Becca liked the picture so much she saved it to the computer.

Ben touched the screen; there was no pain in remembering, not as much anyway. There was only sadness. It was a memory of the life he once had. After a moment, he shook it off and began to search the Internet for a Cable Lake Road in the region. It came back with three matches. One was east, one north, and the last was south-west. Immediately, he eliminated the one to the east near Flint, Michigan. The area Joey described was rural with a lake, and Flint an urban city. The one to the north was in the Upper Peninsula. There was a lake nearby, but it was about a half mile from Cable Lake Road. It didn't seem likely because Joey had seen the lake and the sign together.

The last was in an area near Dowagiac. He clicked on the map location and saw it actually had a handful of lakes in that area. Cable Lake Road ran right through them. It seemed to fit the description Joey had made. The only problem was, it was to the south and to the west, and Joe had been traveling north when he kidnapped Joey. He wondered if Joe would've doubled back. Dowagiac hadn't been his first choice when he began, but now seemed the most likely. It was a little over an hour's drive from where he sat.

With that, Ben picked up the phone and began to dial.

The car slowed as Ben made the turn off of County Road 687 towards Sister Lakes. The little community was considered part of Dowagiac, but only because it was the closest town to it. He'd already called the county police. They said they would check into it, but that hadn't been good enough for him. He wanted to go down there and see for himself. Amy volunteered to watch Joey that afternoon while he borrowed her Ford Taurus to make the trip. Taking the BMW would've been impossible; operating the manual transmission with a bad knee would've been too much for him to handle. In the seat beside him were a dozen flyers with Joe Murphy's picture. Ben planned on passing them out in the hope someone had seen him.

A mile or two down the road, he finally entered the little community. He passed a grocery store, a restaurant, and a bank before turning down Sister Lakes Road, then continuing the half-mile or so to Cable Lake Road. There was a brown cabin on the corner of the two roads that fit the description. He slowed but didn't stop, then turned down Cable Lake Road. Ben had come down here to get a feel of the place, see if it felt right.

It did.

Ben pulled into a driveway further down, turned around, and returned to the intersection at Sister Lakes Road. He studied the brown cabin on the corner. Both the street sign and the lake were visible from the cabin. His first impulse was to get a look inside the cabin but fought the temptation. If this was the place, Joe could be watching him already. Because he was driving Amy's Taurus, his only advantage was that Joe would not recognize the car. After another moment of study, Ben turned back onto Sister Lakes Road and went back to the grocery store he passed earlier.

After parking the car, Ben grabbed his cane and a flyer from the front seat and limped quickly towards the store. He kept glancing about the parking lot, in case Joe Murphy was nearby. If he were living in this area, the grocery store and the restaurant would definitely be places he would frequent. When he reached the grocery store, the automatic door swished opened, and he found an older woman with horn rimmed glasses at the checkout counter. Ben immediately went up to her and extended his hand. "Hi, I'm Ben Stryker. If you're not too busy, I was wondering if I could ask you a few questions."

The woman smiled back at him sweetly and shook his hand. "Of course, I'm Maxine Harris. My husband and I run this place. What can I help you with today?"

she asked.

Ben handed her a flyer. "Have you seen this man?"

She held her hand up to the corner of her glasses while looking over the picture. "Yes, I have," she said frowning. "That's John Norris. He comes in here maybe a couple times a week, usually buying groceries," she hesitated, wanting to be delicate about disclosing his habits, "and other things. Is he a friend of yours?"

Ben shook his head. "No, far from it. He's wanted by the police. I have kind of a personal stake in this matter. The problem is, he's a bit unstable and can be quite violent."

"I had a bad feeling about him when I first saw him. He always gave me the creeps."

"Do you know where he's staying?"

"I know he's staying out on Cable Lake somewhere. Denny would know. He made a couple deliveries to his place," she said, and then turned towards the back of the store. "Denny!"

The door to the walk-in cooler opened and Denny, in his familiar brown cap, appeared. "Did you need something, Mrs. Harris?" he asked as he approached, stripping off a pair of gloves as he did.

"Yes, this is Mr. Stryker. He tells me that John Norris is in some kind of trouble. Wants to know which house he's been staying."

Ben stuck out his hand to Denny. Denny put the gloves on the counter, and they shook. "Actually, his name is Joe Murphy, and I have reason to believe he may have already done something bad," Ben told them.

"You mean around here? Haven't heard of anything, and word travels pretty fast around these parts. People keep a close eye on each other. Anyway, the guy lives down by Cable Lake, the first cabin past Cable Lake Road. Do you want me to show you?"

"Thanks, Denny, but that's not necessary," Ben said, and then turned to Mrs. Harris, "Can you call the police? Tell them what I told you, and tell them to get here, right away."

Mrs. Harris nodded. "Yes, of course. But it will take them a little while to get here. We don't have any police of our own. Have to wait for the county police and they are twenty minutes away."

"That's why I thought I'd go down and keep an eye on the place," Ben said.

"I'll go with you," Denny said.

Ben looked at him for a second; he liked the idea of having help but didn't know if he wanted to endanger someone else.

"Are you sure? He's dangerous."

"I think it would be better if there were two of us in case something does happen—don't you? Plus, it looks as if you could use the help," Denny said, pointing to the cane.

Ben smiled. "Yeah, you're probably right. Besides, we're only going to watch the place."

"Be careful... both of you," Mrs. Harris told them as they left the store. She picked up the phone, dialed, and waited for it to ring. Putting her hand over the receiver, she watched through the window as Ben and Denny got in the car. "Please be careful," she murmured softly, remembering the disturbing look she had seen in Joe's eyes.

At Denny's direction, Ben drove past the cabin and parked further down at a neighboring house that had a view of the cabin. They sat there in silence, staring in the direction of the cabin. Ben decided that if they were going to sit here waiting, they might as well fill the minutes. "Have you lived here long?" Ben asked.

"All my life," was the brief answer given. It seemed the silence was good enough for the young man.

After a few more minutes, Ben tried again. "So, what do you do? I mean, besides work at the store."

Denny chuckled. "I only work there part-time. I'm taking classes at Southwestern."

"Oh, really? I hear they have a good program. What are you studying?"

"Physics mostly," Denny replied. "And philosophy."

"That's an odd combination."

Denny shrugged as if he'd heard it before. "I guess."

"Physics, huh?" Ben said, the subject being something close to mind. "What do you know about the effects of an electro-magnetic field on space/time?"

"Not sure I understand."

"What I mean," Ben said quickly, "is there a way to fold time... and space... by creating an electro-magnetic field?"

There was a moment of thought on Denny's part before he spoke, "The only thing I know of that can manipulate time," he paused deliberately just as Ben had done, "...and space... is gravity." He eyed Ben suspiciously for a moment. "But if you are talking strictly about time, I think there maybe another answer."

"What do you mean?"

"Western Philosophy. You know... I think, therefore I am," Denny replied. "I'm sure you've heard that before. There are some that believe that without consciousness, there is no time. That time and space is consciousness. They say that the past is nothing more than an accumulation of experiences. You asked me if I thought time could be folded by use of an electromagnetic field. Well, if our minds—our consciousness—is nothing more than neurons firing off electricity, then yes, I think it might be possible.

Ben was caught off guard by Denny's eloquence on the matter. It was almost as if he'd transformed during the conversation. In ten minutes, he'd gone from peculiar, long-haired stock boy to a well-spoken, intelligent, young man.

"Wow, you've thought quite a bit about this, haven't you?"

"Yeah, I suppose so," Denny replied almost sadly. After a moment, he asked, "Who did you lose?"

"Not sure I know what you're talking about." He knew full well what Denny was asking but wasn't quite ready to share.

"For me, it was my mom and dad. They died when I was three. Spent my entire life trying to make sense of it. Is that why you're after Mr. Norris? Is he responsible?"

"No, not that part," Ben admitted. "He busted up my knee and put me in the hospital, but no. Joe Murphy threatened some people that I care about. I mean to see he is stopped."

Silence filled the car again as Denny appeared to be distracted. He was staring over his shoulder at the house behind them.

"What's the matter?" Ben asked.

"I'm not sure. It might be nothing. Mr. Bergman's car is gone, and the front door is open," Denny said. "That's not normal for him. He's a little paranoid, likes to lock his door even though he knows damn well we haven't had a robbery around here since…well, since never."

A sick feeling went through Ben. "Denny, stay here!" he said as he opened the car door.

Denny got out anyway. "I think it would be better if we stuck together."

"You may not like what you see," Ben told him.

"We really should stick together."

Ben didn't like it, but once again, the young man seemed determined to accompany him. "Okay. Just be careful."

They approached the cabin cautiously. Denny pushed the door the rest of the way open with his arm. Ben glanced quickly inside; he could find no movement. He nodded to Denny, and they slowly moved inside. The old wooden floor creaked as they took their first steps inside the house. Denny was in the lead but froze in place when he got a good look at what was left of Mr. Bergman. He brushed past Ben as he rushed out of the house with his hand over his mouth. Ben could hear him retching out in the yard.

Ben could only stand there, lost in horror and disbelief at what he was seeing. The body of the old man was pinned to the wall, his arms stretched over his head with what looked like a steak knife stuck through both hands. There was a pool of blood, thick and tacky, like dark red paint on the floor. Ben's stomach suddenly lurched in revulsion, but he fought to control his impulse to be sick. The body of the old man had been mutilated, sliced open from the navel to the sternum. Most of the intestines were either hanging out of the body or lying on the floor in a pile.

"God help us. It's no wonder Joey reacted the way he did," Ben said.

Ben turned and limped back outside to check on Denny. "Are you going to be okay?"

Denny nodded, still bent over on his hands and knees.

"What kind of car did Mr. Bergman drive?" Ben asked.

"It's an older car, one of those huge behemoths Detroit made back in the fifties, you know what I'm talking about? I think it might have been a Chevy, a black one," Denny said, getting to his feet, and wiping his mouth with the back of his hand. There was still a look of shock on his face. "What kind of person would do something like that?"

Ben didn't answer. As far as he knew, there was no answer. He lowered his head. The car was gone, which meant Joe was gone. His one really good chance to catch Joe had slipped away.

"Come on, Denny, let's go back and call the police. A car like that should be easy to spot. Maybe it's still not too late for them to track him down."

Ben looked back at the house, thinking about what he'd seen, and shuddered.

CHAPTER 14

Megan sat, spinning her fork in her plate of fettuccine as Jim talked incessantly about his most current case. The restaurant, Weller's at the Radisson, was generally considered the best in the city. Jim had reserved a prime table and ordered the most expensive wine. Megan was in her best black dress, wearing the pearl necklace and matching earrings Jim had bought her for their last anniversary. She felt uncomfortable in the necklace—a reminder of a ruined past—but Jim had specifically requested she wear them.

Jim continued to talk enthusiastically about his upcoming trial, how he planned to attack the Prosecution's witnesses, and how he had picked the jury he wanted. Megan realized that everything he was saying was an enormous self-promotion. After a while, she got lost in the language of his egotism, and began to see him with fresh eyes. The hardest part for her was knowing he hadn't always been like this. At one time, he'd been a good and honest man capable of real love. She wanted to see that part of him again, the part she had fallen in love with, hoping it was buried beneath the layers of ego that now dominated his personality. But he'd changed. He'd evolved into someone new.

Someone she couldn't recognize anymore.

There was a pause in the noise of his conversation while he cut his veal. Megan tried to use the break to change the subject.

"Work was hell today. Seems like nothing was going right," Megan said, "Luckily, Hannah was there to bail me out."

"I'm sorry, who is Hannah again?" Jim asked, looking up from his plate.

"She's the girl I helped get hired down at the office. You know, she was married to the guy who put Ben in the hospital." Megan felt a little exasperated because she had explained it to him before.

"Oh—right," he said, appearing only mildly interested, and went back to eating.

"Ben came over a few days ago and challenged me to a game of chess. It was the funniest thing—"

Jim cut her off just a bit. "How is Ben?" he asked, looking for her reaction to the question.

"Oh, he's doing better. His leg still gives him trouble, but other than that he's fine," she said brightly.

"Good. That's good," he said flatly, and went back to his veal. However, he clearly wore a troubled look on his face.

The silence between them grew; finally, Megan decided she had had enough. "Okay, what's wrong?"

"Nothing," he stated flatly. The expression on his face said differently.

"Good Lord, Jim, just tell me already. I'm not in the mood for games tonight."

He dropped his fork; it clanged against the dinner China. "Fine, I'll tell you," Jim said, leaning in closer to her and lowering his voice. "I don't like you hanging out with him."

"You mean, Ben? That's funny because he pretty much said the same thing about you," Megan replied.

Jim ignored this. "I've seen how he leers at you. He's only interested in one thing. It's disgusting."

"Really! You know him that well?" Megan said, playing along.

"I know him better than you do, that's obvious. I've seen a side of him that you probably never will, well... not until it's too late, anyway. He likes to use the good guy image to get what he wants. You should hear some of the things I've heard him say." Jim said, then waited a moment to see the effect he was having on her. "Come on, Megan. You might not know it, but he cheated on his wife. He didn't tell you that, did he? Didn't think so. And that's only one that I was told about. The bastard was actually proud he got away with it. Believe me, if he's interested in you, it's only to try and get into your pants," Jim said spitefully.

Megan wasn't sure what upset her the most: The fact that it was a bold-faced lie, or that it was fabricated in an attempt to deflect from Jim's own past. Clearly, it was done Ben look small and contemptible by comparison. Sadly, had Ben wanted to "get into her pants" as Jim suggested, he wouldn't have to try that hard. It was evident Jim felt threatened by Ben, but it wasn't because the look in Ben's eyes that bothered him. It was the way she looked at Ben. It was the way she talked about Ben. Knowing this, Megan did her best to hold her composure. "Unlike you, who has only tried a dozen times to get me to go back to your apartment to have sex," she said, not bothering to lower her voice.

"That's different," Jim hissed. "We were married,

for heaven's sakes. Look, all I'm saying is, I just don't feel comfortable with him hanging around you all the time."

"Are you asking me to choose between you and Ben?"

He considered this. "Well, yes—I guess I am," he said, and reached out and held her hand. "If we're to have any chance of a good, stable, and rewarding relationship, then I think you should seriously consider cutting Ben out of your life," Jim said in his silkiest voice. "I know it won't be easy. I know how much you cherish him, but it really is the best thing for both of us."

Megan pulled her hand from his grip. "You asked me to choose between you and Ben. Alright, I've made my decision. I choose Ben," she said. "The only thing he's wanted so far is my friendship. But I can tell you right now, I'd rather have that, than anything a slimy, low-life snake like you could ever offer." And with that, she got up from the table, grabbed her purse, and walked away without looking back.

Jim watched her disappear. He didn't move, and his expression remained unchanged. He simply sat there, immobile. After a few minutes, he appeared to wake from his trance, raised his arm, and asked for the check. He paid the bill, leaving a generous tip.

Then he reached into his pocket and pulled out a small jewelry box. Inside was the diamond engagement ring he had purchased. He opened the box; it sparkled even in the low light of the restaurant. Very slowly, he closed the box, sat it gently on the table, and left.

Joe slid the plastic card into the slot to open his hotel room. The light flashed green, and he heard the audible click of the lock. Once inside, he slid the gym bag off his shoulder and threw it on the bed. The room itself was spacious. It had a king size bed, a wide Jacuzzi tub, and a balcony that overlooked the Gulf. Out on the balcony, he watched as the waves crashed and rolled on the beach below. The sky was so blue it almost hurt his eyes. After spending most of the winter in Michigan, the self-proclaimed Winter Wonderland, this place was heaven. He didn't care if he ever saw that God-forsaken state ever again.

Back inside, Joe rummaged through the gym bag. Inside were stacks of bills, mostly in fifties and hundreds. He'd emptied the safety deposit box that morning, it came to just about two hundred thousand dollars in cash. There was also a hair trimmer, razor, and shaving cream inside in a little bag. He grabbed it and went into the bathroom. He stood before the mirror, staring at his reflection. The hair over his top lip had begun to thicken into a mustache. He detested it. Even in his winter solitary, he'd taken the time to shave regularly. Beards and mustaches were for freaks and hippies, but he needed the added disguise. He pulled out the trimmer and his hair started to fall to the floor in large clumps as he raced it back and forth across his head, cutting it close on the sides, but leaving a little longer on top giving him something resembling a military style haircut. Afterwards, he stepped back and looked in the mirror. The change in appearance was enough that it would be difficult for someone to recognize him right away.

Joe smiled at the reflection. "How do you like me now?"

His father's voice was back in his head. *You numb-*

nut! You're wanted for murder. Not just an ordinary murder, but a grotesque, brutal murder. Did you actually believe cutting your hair and growing a mustache is going to make that big of a difference? They will find you and—

"Shut up!" Joe said flatly, staring hard at his reflection.

No reply came.

He went back to the gym bag and once again rummaged around inside of it. He pulled out a brown folder he'd stowed away inside the safety deposit box with the money. They were copies of the employee files from the firm. He flipped through the pages.

"Let's see. Who do I want to be? Oh, here's a good one, Clifford James Anderson. What do we have here? Date of birth, place of birth, social security number. Should be enough to get me a new driver's license and a fresh start," he said, and then began to laugh.

Joey sat with his back against the brick wall while Ben was busy bolting a piece of the framework of his machine together inside of his newly constructed building. Ben stopped what he was doing and looked guiltily over at the boy.

"I'm sorry; I know this must be pretty boring for you," Ben said.

"It's okay, I don't mind," Joey said honestly.

"Do you want to help me put it together?"

"Sure. Can I?"

"I don't see why not. Tell you what, I'll hold this while you turn the ratchet," Ben said. Joey seemed delighted to help. Ben showed him how to use the ratchet and pointed to the bolts that needed tightening. He didn't expect the kid to be able to tighten them completely, he could do that later. As Joey applied the ratchet to the first bolt, Ben decided to ask him a question. “How’s your little room worked out for you so far?”

“Don’t know, haven't had to use it,” Joey replied.

“What about your dad?”

Joey shook his head. “He must be too far away.” He finished tightened the bolt, and then looked up at Ben. “We almost had him though, didn't we?”

“Yes, we did,” Ben said frowning. “Wish I’d been a little quicker about it. I’d feel much better with him in jail.” Joey nodded in agreement. Ben limped over and grabbed another piece of the metal frame for the next section.

“I feel bad for Mr. Bergman,” Joey said sadly.

Ben had never mentioned the old man's name.

“Let's hope you never have to go through that again,” Ben said, and truthfully, he never wanted to witness anything like that again, either. There were no new leads on the whereabouts of Joe Murphy. The police had found the black Impala in Louisville. It was obvious he was going south but had no idea were. Hannah had told him that Joe liked going to Tampa for their vacations. It had been a long shot, but Ben had called the Tampa police and asked them to keep a look out for Joe Murphy. He’d even faxed them a picture, even though they had confirmed they had been contacted by the Michigan State Police and were aware of the situation. The story of the grisly murder and Joe’s status as a wanted man was in news for a time. But like most things, it quickly lost traction when the trail had gone cold.

The door to the building swung open. Larry walked in on them.

"I wondered where you two had run off to," Larry said cheerfully. "Hey, Kiddo. I see Ben here has got you doing his manual labor for him."

Joey smiled and nodded. He liked Larry. He'd never used his gift on Larry to find out what he was like on the inside because he already knew what he would find. Larry would forever be one of those people who told you exactly what he was thinking and feeling. But he was genuine and good-natured, and almost always of good humor.

"He's been a big help," Ben said.

Looking over the odd-looking machinery, Larry asked, "So, are you going to tell me what this thing is already?"

"It's a time machine," Joey blurted out, as if it was obvious. Ben looked at him harshly.

"A what?" Larry said, raising his eyebrows.

Joey stared at Ben, understanding that he'd inadvertently disclosed something he shouldn't have. "But you trust him."

Ben tried to smile for Joey. It wasn't easy to do and came out kind of crooked and strained. "Yes, I do. I'd trust him with my life. It's just that this is a little harder to explain."

Larry knelt down beside Joey. "Joey, don't you mind him none. He just likes to keep his secrets, is all," he said, and put his hand on Joey's shoulder.

"I know what you're thinking, Larry," Ben said, holding up his hands.

"You really think so? What, that you're crazy? No. I think you're a man who wants so badly to see his family again he'd try just about anything to do it. And if this project helped you keep your sanity, then I don't see anything wrong with it."

"Thanks, Larry," Ben said, somewhat relieved.

Joey tugged on Ben's shirt. "Aren't you going to ask him to help us?"

With a wry smile, Ben looked to Larry. "Yeah, Larry —would you like to help us build a time machine?" Ben asked sarcastically.

Larry laughed. "Sure, why not? I'd be honored."

"Good, because I was going to need help with the electrical stuff, anyway," Ben added with a chuckle.

An hour later, they were still working on the machine. Ben held the frame while Larry bolted it together. It had become too heavy for Joey, and Ben worried he might get hurt. So Joey stood on the other side, watching them work. Suddenly, a blank look fell over Joey. He staggered backwards, and then fell to the floor. Ben dropped the frame and immediately rushed to the boy. Unprepared for the sudden drop, Larry tried to catch the extra weight before it landed on his foot.

"Hey, hey, hey! What the hell!" Larry yelled. Then he saw Joey on the floor. Ben was shaking him, as if to wake him.

"Joey, can you hear me? Is it your father? Get to the room. Get to your safe room, now," Ben said anxiously.

"What are you talking about, Ben?" Larry asked. "What room?"

Ben ignored Larry for the time being. Joey's eyes were closed. When the boy finally spoke, it was very soft. "It's not that. It's Grandpa, he's dying. I think it's his heart," he whispered.

"Who? You mean, Mr. Pearson?" Ben asked. Joey nodded; his eyes still closed.

Joey could hear Larry and Ben's voices, but they

sounded far away because he was focused on the living room at his grandparents' house. He reached out for his grandfather. It only took an instant; Joey was sitting on the couch and his grandfather standing by the counter, near the kitchen. Joey went to him. George Pearson was in his business suit, the one he wore to the office. Joey also noticed that his grandfather looked much younger than he'd ever remembered seeing him.

"Grandpa?" Joey said in a hurt voice.

"Hello, Joey," his grandfather said, smiling kindly at him. "I'm glad that you could come see me before I go."

"I don't want you to go. Please, Grandpa, don't leave," Joey pleaded.

George Pearson knelt down beside his grandson and put his arms around him. "I have to Joey, it's my time. There's nothing to fear. It's very peaceful."

"I know, it's just—" Joey said, unable to finish. It hurt too much to say aloud.

"You know, I'm going to miss you. You're a wonderful boy with a good heart. Don't ever let anyone ever take that from you," his grandfather said. "I'm going to miss all of you. Hannah, Beverly..." He looked down at Joey. "I need you to be strong, Joey. Difficult times are ahead for you, more difficult than anything you've ever gone through before. I wish you didn't have to, but I cannot stop it."

A brilliant light began spilling out of the kitchen, covering them in warmth. George Pearson got up. He smiled at Joey. "I love you, and I know you will make me proud. Tell your mother and your grandmother that I love them both very much."

George Pearson turned and walked into the light. Then the light was gone. And so was he.

Joey opened his eyes; his face screwed up with pain and grief. “He’s gone, I couldn't stop him,” Joey said, and let out a long, wounded cry.

Ben scooped him up and held him, letting him cry as long and hard as he wanted to.

CHAPTER 15

The gray sky threatened rain; the somber weather matched the mood that morning. Ben stood by the gravesite while the minister spoke. Joey stood close beside him, looking at the mound of dirt and the casket. His heart ached for Joey; Ben knew what he was feeling. At the same time, he was having a difficult time dealing with it. It hadn't been that long ago he'd stood graveside at his own family's funeral.

While the minister droned, Ben flashed back to the day that he stood over the graves of his wife and two daughters. The three caskets: one large and two smaller ones that contained the people he loved the most on this earth. Caskets that had to remain closed, the bodies so badly burned they were unrecognizable. He'd seen the remains of his wife and daughters firsthand. It wasn't something he could ever forget. Overwhelming emotions began wash over him, threatening to overtake him. He wanted to run, to get away from this place. Then, inside his mind, he felt a small and calming voice.

It's gonna be okay. I'm here with you. So is Megan.

Ben turned his head. Joey was looking up at him.

Joey reached up and took his hand. There was sadness, but also stubbornness etched on his face.

Megan, who stood on the other side of him, took Ben's other hand, no doubt the work of Joey.

"I'll be alright now," Ben whispered.

Joey nodded, but the grip on his hand tightened. The minister finished, and Beverly and Hannah moved forward first. Silent tears ran down each of their faces. Hannah had her arm around her mother. Beverly placed a rose on the casket, and then looked to her daughter. Hannah placed her rose next to her mothers. Joey let go of Ben's hand, moved to the casket, and put a rose on top, pausing to look at the casket. After that, he went to his mother's side and took her hand.

With the ceremony concluded, Ben limped back to the car with Megan. They were still holding hands. "I'm going to go talk with Hannah, if you don't mind?" Megan said, softly letting go of his hand.

"Not at all," Ben replied. He stuck the cane in the grass, deep enough to make it stick, and leaned against the car. It wasn't long before Joey appeared. He leaned against the car next to Ben.

"Thank you," Ben said rather humbly.

Joey nodded but didn't say anything.

"I know it must've been an incredibly difficult thing for you to do, helping me when you're grieving so much yourself. You're quite a remarkable young man."

Joey only dropped his head.

"I understand," Ben said, knowing he was not looking for praise at this moment, only solace from the loss of his grandfather. "There's nothing I can say to make it any easier, but I am here for you. I hope you know that. Losing someone you love is one of the hardest things you'll ever have to go through."

How'd you ever get through this? The thought came

from Joey and ran through Ben's mind as clear as if it had been his own. Ben wasn't certain if he'd done it on purpose.

"It isn't easy, but with patience and love, anything is possible."

"Ben?" Joey said almost in a whisper, the hurt in his voice evident.

"Yes, Joey."

"Grandpa said I was in for some hard times."

Ben knelt down and faced Joey. "Whatever happens, I'm here to face it with you. You believe that, don't you?"

"I do, but..." he paused, his face twisted with pain, "I'm not sure how much more I can take," Joey said, holding back his tears.

"I know. There've been times I didn't know myself," Ben said, remembering uttering the almost the exact same words at one point.

Joey straightened up again, taking a couple deep breaths, and putting on a mantel of courage. "I guess I better go take care of my mom," he said, now sounding much older than he actually was.

"Okay, Joey," Ben said. "I'll see you later."

Joey left to go join his mother. Ben watched him, astonished that the little boy could go through so much and pretend to be brave at the same time.

Mr. Walker had walked up beside Ben unnoticed.

"Hello, Ben," Mr. Walker said.

Ben jumped just a bit. "Oh, crap... Sorry! Hello, Mr. Walker," he said.

"Startled you a bit, I take it," Mr. Walker said. "That wasn't my intention."

"No, that's okay. Just kind of deep in thought," Ben said.

Mr. Walker put his hand on Ben's shoulder. "I think we both know why."

Ben wanted to reply but couldn't think of any words. Mr. Walker seemed to understand. "He's a good boy," Mr. Walker said pointing to Joey, knowing Ben had been talking to him.

"Yeah, he sure is," Ben replied.

"Surprising, considering his father. Anyway, I wanted to talk to you about something. I was going to wait, but with George's passing, well, I guess I best not wait any longer."

"I know you and Mr. Pearson were friends for a long time," Ben said. "I'm sorry."

This time, it was Mr. Walker who frowned. "Yes, George and I go back a long way. Back to grade school, if you can believe it. In high school, he pushed me to go to college, then later, got me to go in partners with him in the firm. George always had a steady temperament and level head to balance out my—well, you know—my temper," he said chuckling a bit. "I owe him a lot. I'll miss my friend dearly."

"He was always good to me," Ben said.

"I suppose I should get down to brass tacks, as they say. What I meant to talk to you about was taking over as full partner. You're the only one I'd ever trust with the firm."

"Shouldn't the partnership go to Mrs. Pearson or Hannah?"

"You wouldn't be taking George's place. You'd be taking mine. I'm retiring. As soon as you're ready, I'd like you to take over the firm. Beverly and Hannah have agreed it would be the best thing for everyone. George's partnership will be held in trust until Joey is old enough to take his grandfather's place."

Ben's brow furrowed, it was a big responsibility, and a little intimidating.

"I know what you're thinking, but I have all the trust in the world in you, Ben. The firm will do well because you care about it and the people who work there. That's all that George and I ever tried to do," Mr. Walker said. "There's something else I want you to do. Keep a watchful eye on his family. Beverly, Hannah, and Joey... they may need your protection. Also, make sure Joey gets the education and training he will need to help you run the firm one day. That's if he wants to when he gets older. I'm sure George would've appreciated it."

"Mr. Walker, I don't know what to say."

"The papers are already drawn up. Ben, I just want to add, I'm proud of you and have all the faith in the world in you." Mr. Walker turned and walked slowly back towards his car where his wife was waiting.

Joe parked his red Mazda in the driveway. The car wasn't new, but it had less than 20,000 miles and there wasn't a scratch on it. He'd paid cash and got it for almost five thousand under book value. Bad economic times could be a blessing for those with cash to spend.

He jumped out of the car and went inside the light blue trailer house he'd purchased a week earlier. Another deal he had made due to desperate conditions. It was located in the village of Ozona, northwest of Tampa along the gulf. It wasn't much, but it was at the end of a dead-end street and right off the beach. He had bought the property and the trailer for under forty thousand. The owner had asked for more, but Joe had got him to come down. He also got him to throw in the appliances and furnishings, to include pots, pans, and kitchen wares. All the things he really didn't want to have to go out and purchase himself.

Joe liked the place, with its ocean view and covered deck. Palm trees stood on each end of the trailer giving it a good amount of shade. The only problem that Joe could really find with the place was the fact the air conditioner only worked intermediately, and the paint was starting to peel a bit.

Joe went back outside and stood on the deck. The sky was so clear, only a couple lazy of clouds dare intrude. The crisp, salty breeze refreshed him. He walked out to the oceanfront and watched the waves as they lapped onto the sandy beach. There was a grassy spot near the edge of beach where he sat down. There was something about the ocean. It had a calming effect on him. It was as if the waves washed away all the crap that life had handed him. Since he'd arrived, he'd stopped drinking. And the voices that normally tormented him, especially those of his father, had quieted for the time being.

"I should've done this a long time ago," he said.

The image of the old man he had killed so brutally came to his mind.

It bothered him.

The rational part of his mind tried to make sense of it.

How could you have gotten so out of hand? How could you have done something so inhuman? Joe picked at some of the long strands of grass absently and looked at them.

It won't happen again.

He let the grass fall from his hand while staring at the ocean. *I'm Cliff Anderson. I have a new life. Starting today, I have no past. Today I start my life over.*

Joe smiled at that idea, and then walked casually back toward his new home.

It was dusk and Ben sat alone staring at his machine. The frame was complete, and the glass shielding installed inside the chamber. All that was left was the wiring, and he would need Larry's help to finish that part of it.

The door slowly swung open. Megan stuck her head inside; she spotted him sitting on the cement floor. She didn't say anything, just walked over and sat down beside him. He looked at her and then back to the machine.

"Do you want to know what it is?" Ben asked. "It's a time machine. Isn't that funny? I'm afraid my sister was right. I've invested thousands of dollars to build this contraption, just to keep myself from going crazy."

Megan said nothing. She reached over, took his hand, and held it in both of hers.

Ben continued. "I realized today how much stronger Joey is than I ever was. The kid is incredible. You know, he actually had to help me get through the ceremony."

"I think he gets his strength from you. You may not see it, but somehow, he draws it from you when you're around."

Ben smiled at her. "It would be nice to believe that. I hope it's true," he said. "I feel a little guilty about sitting here feeling sorry for myself when he has had to go through so much today.

"You're allowed to. We both knew the funeral would be difficult for you. Stop being so hard on yourself, okay?"

"Okay."

"Good," Megan said, letting go of his hand and standing up. "Now, let's go inside before we freeze our buns off on this cold floor."

They went back to the house. Ben limped into the kitchen and looked inside the refrigerator while Megan kicked off her shoes and sat on the couch with her legs folded beneath her.

"Doesn't look like there's very much in here," Ben called to her. The one thing he did have was beer. He grabbed two of them.

"You never do," Megan shot back.

"I could make a couple sandwiches, I suppose."

"No need. I ordered a pizza a little bit ago. I figured you'd be getting hungry by now."

Ben limped back in with the beer, opened one and gave it to Megan. Then he opened his own and sat down. "You're a woman after my own heart, Megan," he said with a smirk.

"You bet your ass I am," she said.

Ben hesitated, and then stumbled on with his next question, the one he really wanted to know. "How're things going with—you know—you and Jim. Getting better?"

Megan sighed and shook her head. "No. I broke things off. I finally got the answer from inside of me that I'd been waiting for. All it took was a direct question. A choice," she said, and then took a swig of beer.

"What question?"

Megan shook her head. "Don't think I should tell you. At least not yet. Maybe some other time."

Ben said nothing, but he watched her.

"It was actually quite liberating. To be free of the old

emotions I carried around for him. I guess part of me was afraid of letting go, but once it happened, well, I was relieved."

"I'm glad for you," Ben said.

"Ben?"

"Yes?"

The doorbell rang. Ben reached back and opened the curtain. "The pizza is here. I'll get it," Ben said, getting up and going to the door.

"Did you know how much I love you?" Megan whispered, knowing he couldn't hear her.

CHAPTER 16

Ben sat at his desk with a notepad on one side, and the office inventory and financial statement on the other. He was going back and forth between the two checking numbers. Opening the computer, he clicked on the calculator function and began punching in the numbers. When he was finished, he sat back in his chair and sighed. A stack of old billing statements at the front of his desk were six inches high. He pulled the stack toward him, stood them upright, and tapped them lightly on the desk. Then he put the entire stack under his arm and limped out of the office. He knocked on Mr. Walker's office door and waited for a reply. Secretly, he wished there would be no answer. That way, he could postpone the news at least one more day.

"Come in," he heard Mr. Walker say in a cheerful tone.

Ben went in and found a chair. Mr. Walker stood behind his desk, taking pictures and certificates off the wall, and putting them in a box. He glanced over at Ben but kept at what he was doing.

"What do you think, are you ready to move in?" Mr. Walker asked.

Ben shook his head. "No, thank you. I'm grateful for

the offer, but I think I'll stay in my office for a little while longer. I'm not quite ready for that kind of move just yet."

Mr. Walker shrugged. "That's okay. I figured you would want some time adjusting to it. It isn't a problem."

"There was something else I wanted to talk to you about."

Mr. Walker sat down. "Alright, what is it?" he asked.

"I didn't want to come to you until I knew for sure. I have billing records for the last four years. When Joe Murphy was manager. There are billings for various items, everything from office supplies to copier machines, all of them double billed. The first few years it looks as if he worked small, mostly office supplies and such," Ben took a deep breath, "but last year alone we were double billed for large ticket items in the range of fifty to sixty thousand dollars."

Mr. Walker's expression changed instantly. Ben handed him the billing statements. Mr. Walker flipped through the pages, one by one. "There are two different accounts being sent money for the same item. I take it the second is bogus?" Mr. Walker asked.

"I'm afraid so. He obviously used it to funnel the money. The account is closed, I checked."

"How much? Tell me the truth, how much did he get?"

"As close as I can tell, somewhere in the neighborhood of two hundred and eleven thousand," Ben stated.

Mr. Walker threw the papers on his desk in disgust. "How did I miss this? How could I let that evil little punk get a hold of that much of the firms' money?" He put his head in his hands, looking defeated. It was the only time Ben had ever seen him like this.

"He hid it pretty well. I only caught it by accident," Ben said.

Raising his head, Mr. Walker began to shake it as if to clear his mind. "I think we can count out ever getting that money back. He has probably been using that money while he has been on the run," Mr. Walker said. "What kind of shape is the firm in financially?"

Ben frowned a bit. "It isn't good, but not terrible either. We lost about half our capital, but we can still make payroll. The new accounts have helped."

"I'm sorry to leave the firm in such a condition, Ben," Mr. Walker said. "When I was younger, I loved to play cards. To read people and know when they were bluffing. I always read Joe Murphy to be one that likes to have a sure hand before betting. I thought that the chance at a full partnership in the firm was enticing enough to keep him from trying anything like this. I see now I was wrong. Now the firm is the one that will ultimately pay the price for it."

"I'm sorry, too. I know this place is your legacy and means the world to you," Ben said.

Mr. Walker walked slowly over to Ben.

"It isn't just the company, or the name on the wall. We have an obligation to take care of the people we employ. They count on us to do the right thing and make good decisions, so that they have jobs to come to every day. I fear that my poor judgment in the case of Joseph Murphy has endangered everyone. Unfortunately, the responsibility to make things right now lies with you, Ben. Believe me, it isn't an easy burden to bear."

Ben used his cane to walk back to his office because his knee had been giving him a bit of pain lately. He detested giving such bad news to Mr. Walker. What had him disturbed the most was the way Mr. Walker had presented the idea that he was now responsible for the livelihood of everyone who worked here.

Cliff rapped on his office door, waking Ben from his thoughts. Ben waved him in.

"Hey, Boss," Cliff said.

"Cliff, I've asked you not to call me that. I swear to God, you make me crazy sometimes."

"Okay, okay. Sounds like you're having one of those days," Cliff said, plopping down in the chair across from Ben.

"What do you need?" Ben asked while rifling through the paperwork on his desk.

"Well, that was kind of what I came to ask you," Cliff said in an uncharacteristically serious tone.

Ben glanced up at him. "What is it?"

"I'm having a bit of a problem with my credit report. I'd like to use the fax machine, if you don't mind, to try and iron it out. I know it's not cool doing personal business on company time, but I think one of the ex-wives may be using my name."

"What makes you think that?"

"The credit bureau has me listed with a Florida address."

"What is it, Identity Theft? Someone trying to get into your checking account?"

Cliff shook his head. "Not as far as I can tell. They are just using my name. They have a power bill, cable bill—stuff like that—all in my name. So, it's either an ex-wife, or the credit bureau has me mixed up with someone else. That kind of thing happens all the time from what I understand."

Ben remained silent; there was a faraway expression on his face.

"So, do you mind?" Cliff asked.

"Oh... sorry, Cliff. Um, no, go ahead. Do what you have to."

"Thanks, Ben."

Cliff was halfway down the hallway when Ben called him back.

"Cliff, if you don't mind, what's the name of that place in Florida?"

"Ozone or Ozona, something funky like that. Why?"

"No reason, just curious."

Joe stood at the refrigerator with the door open. He had food, most of it in the form of frozen dinners, but after the long winter, he'd pretty much lost his appeal for anything frozen. Besides, he'd had his fill of microwave food and TV dinners. What really sounded good was a steak. A good old-fashioned porterhouse, or maybe even a thick T-bone. Joe closed the refrigerator and considered it. It was a beautiful day, he could grill-out on the patio. Throw in a potato and some baked beans, it would be perfect.

Back in the bedroom, Joe opened the closet and unlocked the safe he'd purchased at the office supply store. He took out two hundred dollars, hesitated, and then grabbed another hundred. He didn't need that much but liked to have extra on him just in case. He grabbed the keys from the kitchen counter and headed out. Halfway to the car, Joe stopped and looked back down Layette Street. It was a short walk to the grocery store, ten or twelve blocks at the most. He stuffed the keys in his pocket and began to walk. After a short distance, Joe spied a neighbor coming down off his porch. The home was an elegant two-story house. Though not grand in size, it was well maintained, and had a wraparound porch that made it appear larger. Joe had seen the man before, sitting on his porch, watching the street. He wasn't small, at least six feet two, with a protruding gut sticking out over his shorts. He had long brown hair, streaked with gray, which hung in a ponytail down his back. Joe's first impression was that the guy was a biker. As Joe drew closer, it was evident that the man had deliberately come down to talk to him.

"Howdy, Neighbor," the man exclaimed cheerfully while extending his hand. Joe took his hand cautiously and they shook. "I've been meaning to welcome you to the neighborhood, but you seemed like the private type, so I didn't want to bother you. By the way, I'm Jonathan Barker. Of course, most folks around here just call me JB."

"I'm Cliff," Joe said, putting on his best smile. It pleased him that he hadn't stumbled in using his new name.

"Well, it's a pleasure to meet you, Cliff," JB said. "I see you bought Rob Young's place. Poor Rob. His mother got sick, had to move to St. Pete to be with her. You know, he hated to sell the place. You want to come up and have a beer?"

Joe had no interest in the fat man's hospitality but didn't want to offend him either. As much as it irritated him, he realized it would be best to appear somewhat courteous if he was going to live here. “Sure, why not,” he replied.

Joe followed the man up the porch. JB opened the cooler and pulled out a couple of beers. He handed one to Joe before they both sat down.

“Thanks,” Joe said, taking a sip, and then looking curiously at label.

“It’s a Red Stripe. Jamaican beer,” JB told him.

“It's not bad.”

JB laughed. “Yeah, I like it.”

“This is a beautiful place you have here,” Joe said.

“Well, thank you. I grew up here. I left when I was eighteen, and moved back when I retired out of the service. There are some places that will always be home, I guess.”

“You’re retired from the military?”

JB gave a hearty laugh. “Yeah, Air Force. I know I don't look the part, but after some twenty odd years of haircuts, I got a little tired of the idea.” JB sat his beer on the little table between them. “You look as if you would know something of that. What was it, the Marines?”

Joe realized he was talking about his hair. He could’ve lied about it, said he’d been in the service, but seemed like a dangerous route to take. This man knew about military life. He didn’t. Would be easy to catch him in a lie. “Nah, nothing like that. I just like to keep it short,” he said.

The man gave him a nod of understanding. “That’s understandable,” he said. “I suppose I could fill you in on who’s who around the neighborhood.” He pointed to the house across the street. “That there would be Jamie and Michael Saunders house. They're a young couple, good people. The house next to mine,” he pointed to the left, "is Pete McAllister. Now, Pete, he's a mean old bastard. No use even trying to talk to him. And on the other side is Loretta Wallace, wonderful woman. She's a red head, tends to make up her own mind about things. We have been seeing each other for about four years now. Can't quite convince her to marry me yet." JB laughed at his own humor.

Joe manufactured a smile, but inside he felt disgusted by the fat, long-haired hippie, even if he was a veteran.

"So where to do you hail from?" JB asked.

"Lima, Ohio," he said. Joe had already made up a story in case he needed it. Ohio seemed close enough to suffice.

Something flashed in JB's eyes for a second, but he smiled anyway. "Decided to move away from the cold winters, I take it."

"You could say that. My Aunt died a few months ago and left me a nice inheritance. I packed up and moved down here to get away from it all," Joe said smiling.

As they spoke, a woman in her late thirties, a head full of fiery red hair and wearing a white summer dress, bounded up the porch steps. Without a word, she wrapped her arms around JB's neck and kissed him. She hovered over him for a second to get his reaction.

"Well, good afternoon to you too, Darlin," JB said. She only smiled, putting her hands behind her back as if waiting for him in some fashion. "Cliff, this here is Loretta, if you hadn't guessed already."

"Nice to meet you," Loretta said politely without really looking at him. She appeared to have no interest in Joe whatsoever.

"It's nice to meet you, too," Joe said. He finished his

beer and started to get up. “I really should be going. Thanks for the beer and everything. I hope we can sit and talk again sometime.”

“Yeah, sure… anytime, Cliff. You have yourself a wonderful afternoon, you hear.”

JB watched as Joe walked away, his brow furrowed in thought. Loretta sat in the chair Joe had previously occupied.

“What's the matter, Jay-bee?” Loretta asked, stretching out his initials in her typical southern accent.

He hesitated and pushed his lips together in a crooked frown. “I’ll tell you, Loretta, but don’t be spreading my words around or anything. You promise?”

“Oh, Jay-bee, I won’t go saying anything.”

“I know. It’s just that we have to live in the same neighborhood with him. Wouldn’t do if he got wind of what I’m telling you.”

“Will you just tell me already?” she said, sounding a little irritated.

“I asked him where he was from. He told me Lima, Ohio.”

“What's wrong with that? You got something against Lima, Ohio?”

“No, Darlin. It’s just that he said it, with an 'e'— 'Lee-ma'. The thing is, I was stationed at Wright-Pat near Dayton for a time, and folks around those parts are kind of particular about how you say it, because it’s pronounced with a big 'I' sound, like 'Lime—a'. It’s easy enough of a slip to make, but not from somebody who lived there. He doesn't come from Ohio, that much I know. And if he's willing to lie about that, makes you wonder what else he's hiding."

Loretta narrowed her eyes at JB and sighed deliberately. "Oh, stop worrying about him. I'm sure it's nothing. Now, come inside with me, otherwise I'll go home."

"You've got me convinced," JB said, getting up from his chair. Loretta grabbed his hand and led him to the door. JB swatted her on the butt with his other hand as she went by. She yelped and let go of his hand while covering her backside with her hands.

"Jay-bee, you'll get yours for that," she said with a stern but playful tone before going inside. He hung back for a second.

He thought about what Loretta had said about it being nothing. "I hope so, Darlin. I sure do hope so," JB said somberly. He glanced down the street after the tall man and shook his head. There was something seriously wrong, and he knew it. His intuition was usually pretty good, and right now, it was nearly screaming at him.

"Will you get in here?" JB heard Loretta call out to him.

"Yeah, yeah, just hold on a second, Darlin."

JB shook his head again. It was damn bothersome, but it would have to wait, whatever it was. With one last look down the street, he turned and went inside.

Ben sat at his computer, staring at the screen. The thing Cliff told him about the credit report was bothering him. He entered Ozone, Florida on the search engine. There were no cities or towns in Florida by that name.

Ben sat back again, trying to figure out why it was so

important to him. He took a deep breath, sat up again and typed in Ozona this time. This time he had a hit, a small town on the west side of Florida. He clicked to enlarge the map; Ozona appeared to be part of Palm Harbor, Florida. He zoomed out again to get a wider view of the area. The city of Ozona lay just north of Tampa Bay. Suddenly, something clicked inside of his brain. He suddenly realized why it had bothered him. Hannah had mentioned that they vacationed in Tampa every few years. Joe probably used the time to transfer the money he'd stolen and put it in a Tampa bank. Ben was certain Joe would keep it all in cash. At least that's what he would do. If Joe went there to get the money, and then decided to stay. And had access to personnel records from the firm...

Ben picked up the intercom and dialed Cliff's office; there was no answer. He limped down the hallway, finally locating Cliff in the copy room, working the fax machine.

"There you are," Ben said limping in.

Cliff gave him a funny look. "Of course. You said I could use the fax machine. What's wrong?"

"What was the address given on the credit report? You know, the one in Florida?"

Cliff scanned the report for the address. "It's 152 Layette Street, Ozona, Florida. You gonna tell me what's going on, Ben?"

"I think it might be Joe Murphy. I think he's using your name, taken up residence there. Ten will get you twenty, he stole information from your personnel records. The reason he isn't getting credit in your name is because he doesn't want to draw attention to himself. Besides, he has the money he stole from here."

"What money?"

Ben realized he opened a subject he hadn't intended to, but he trusted Cliff. There was no reason to hide the truth from him now. "Don't say anything, but it appears Joe Murphy embezzled a pretty large sum of money from the firm."

"Should've figured that ass-munch to do something like that. He tried to run the place like it was his own private candy store. What are you gonna to do?"

"I'm gonna call the Florida police, make sure they arrest him. I just pray they understand how dangerous he is."

"What if you're wrong?" Cliff asked.

Ben thought about it for a second, and then shook his head. "I know I'm right, I can feel it," Ben said anxiously. "But if I am wrong, and it's just some guy with the same name as you, well, no harm done. It can't hurt anything just to make sure."

"Okay, I'm with you," Cliff told him. "Let's go make a few calls and get things rolling. I can't stand the thought of that prick using my name."

JB lay curled up with Loretta beside him. She was sleeping soundly by this point. Shortly, there came a loud knock at the front door. JB swore silently and tried to get out of the bed without waking Loretta. She turned and grabbed his hand before he got away completely.

"Where you going?" she mumbled sleepily.

"Someone's at the door," he said, and kissed her on the forehead. "I'll be back in a minute."

Without hesitation, she let go of his hand, rolled over, and went back to sleep. JB threw on his clothes and went downstairs. "That woman needs to get some regular hours," JB said, shaking his head as he reached the door. When he opened it, he found a police officer waiting patiently for him.

"Officer Munoz, how can I help you?"

"Come off it, JB, you've known me since I was a kid running down this same street," the officer replied.

"I know, Bob, but figured you were here on official business and all," JB said, and went out onto the porch. He closed the door quietly behind him. "Sorry. Loretta is sleeping upstairs right now, and I don't want to wake her."

"You still haven't gotten her to marry you, huh?"

JB shook his head. "No, after her last marriage ended, she vowed never to do it again. You know, it really takes an idiot to screw up a beautiful woman like that." JB paused for a moment. "I don't imagine that's what you came here to ask me."

The officer shook his head. "Do you know the guy who bought Rob's old place?"

"Yeah, I talked to him only an hour or so ago. Says his name is Cliff, but I wouldn't hold my breath waiting for the truth on that."

"Why do you say that?"

"Well, he flat out lied about being from Ohio. Plus, I get a bad feeling from him."

Officer Munoz turned and looked in the direction of the trailer, and then pulled a wanted poster from his pocket and unfolded it. He gave it to JB. "Is this the guy?"

JB studied the poster for a second. A worried look crossed his face when he handed it back. He had seen what it had said at the top of the poster. Wanted for Murder.

"It's him alright. He's cut his hair, grew a mustache,

but it's him. I could swear to it."

Joe walked casually towards home, holding a bag of groceries in one arm, and a six-pack of Red Stripe in the other. He was halfway down the street when he saw the black police cruiser parked in front of JB's house. He began to walk cautiously, slowing his pace. Gradually, he moved off the sidewalk and behind a tree, setting the groceries and the beer down at the foot of the tree. His mind began to spin.

Either JB has gotten himself into a little trouble, or the cop is there to talk to him about me. He's a busy body and the cops would know that.

Joe crept silently along the yard until he was within hearing distance. He could clearly see JB and the police officer on the porch talking but couldn't quite hear what they were saying. Joe watched as the cop turned and looked in the direction of his trailer house, then pulled something out of his pocket and handed it to JB.

That, I am guessing, is a picture of you, and our fat little hippie friend is about to sell you out.

Joe moved away from the house, and exited out the backyard, leaving the groceries behind. He jumped a fence, ran through another yard, and then began to race toward Main Street for the city bus stop. After that, he would need to get a car somehow. He figured he had about twenty minutes or so to get out of town before the police figured out, he wasn't coming back.

His father's voice spoke mockingly inside of his head.

Dumbass! Screwed up again, didn't you? They figured out that you're using an alias of someone you knew, someone you worked with. What a moron. Always said you were too stupid to do anything right. When they catch you —and they will catch you—you'll pay for what you did, oh, yeah. You are going to pay!

Joe was running at this point in an all-out sprint. Up till now, he'd never truly considered the ramifications of his actions. He knew prison was a possibility, but it seemed unreal to him. Now, he pictured the disgrace of being caught, handcuffed, and stuffed into the back of a cop car. Worse, being thrown into a dirty prison cell along with the perverts, freaks, and reprobates that belonged there. He would spend the rest of his days inside a room with four walls, constantly in a state of revulsion, disgust, and dread over what they might try and do to him.

Fear began to fill his brain. He didn't deserve that kind of fate.

"It's not my fault," he said almost out of breath. "None of this is my fault!"

CHAPTER 17

"Are you done yet?" Ben asked again.

"No!" Larry said hotly, his hands stuck deep inside the fuse box. The control panel and the fuse box were located behind a brick partition separating itself from the machine. There was a door and single large window in the partition that looked out onto the machine. "For the last time, I'll let you know when I'm done."

Ben laughed. To him, there was nothing better than aggravating Larry when he was in a mood. He limped over and picked up the digital clock he had bought and hung it on the wall facing his machine. Ben figured that he would need a point of reference if the machine actually did work. The digital clock had large red numbers with the date clearly displayed below; he needed something he could see clearly. He just hoped the powerful magnetism of the machine didn't screw it up.

"Joe Murphy got away, then?" Larry asked, still working inside of the fuse box.

"Yeah, the police found the trailer and the car he'd bought, but evidently, he walked away and never returned. They also found a bag of groceries nearby. It's thought he spotted the police and ran for it. They're still looking for him, but once again, it looks as if he's vanished."

"Do you think he'll come back here?"

"Don't know. They said they recovered a lot of the firm's money from the safe inside his house. There's a distinct possibility he's running low on cash," Ben said. "Sometimes I wonder if it might've been better to let him stay down there. Now that he's on the run, God knows what he will do. Hannah wasn't too happy when she heard the news. I think she was counting on them locking him up. I can't say as I blame her."

"Let me ask you something," Larry said, grunting while his hand still stuck inside of the fuse box. It looked like he was having difficulty connecting one of the wires. "How'd you get them to make the parts for this thing without anyone asking too many questions?"

"I used four different fabrication shops to build the parts. None of them knew what the others were doing."

Larry pulled his hand out of the panel. Ben looked at him with his eyebrows raised. "It's done. I just have to turn the power on. Are you happy now?" Larry said.

"Yes, I am," Ben replied sarcastically, and then paused. "Thanks, Larry."

Larry flipped the main breaker, and then went to the control panel. "Okay, looks as if everything is working properly," Larry said. "The timer and the temperature controls are set. You should be all set to go."

Ben limped over, climbed inside the chamber, and sat down.

"Looks like you are inside of a coke bottle," Larry said, referring to the heavy glass panels, almost green in color, which covered the interior of the chamber.

"Time in a bottle," Ben whispered.

"What did you say?"

"Nothing," Ben said. He climbed out of the chamber.

"What do you want to do now?" Larry asked.

Ben shrugged. "You think we should test it first?"

"Would probably be a good idea. It's your machine, Ben, you tell me."

Ben hesitated. "Well, first we have to get all the tools and stuff out of here. This thing should generate quite a magnetic field, so we really don't want any metal around it. Then we will set it for—what—ten revolutions?" Ben asked.

Larry shrugged and nodded half-heartedly.

Ben nodded back at him mockingly. "You aren't being much help, Larry."

"If you think *I'm* taking responsibility for this thing, you're nuts."

Ben grinned, and then laughed. "Thanks a lot, Buddy. Okay, I'll do it."

They packed up the tools and took them outside. When they came back, Ben switched on the control and set the counter for ten. Then he set the temperature control for seventy-two degrees. Excessive heat would be another problem they would have to deal with. With a deep breath, he put his hand on the power switch. "Now we find out if the cooling system we put in here works," Ben said. Larry's contracting company had installed an industrial sized cooling system for this project.

Ben hit the switch and the magnet began to give off a low hum. The arm came to life, swinging around once, then twice; a strange sort of power could be felt surging through the place. It went around three and four times. A light blue haze began to encompass the entire chamber. Ben glanced down at the temperature; it was holding at sixty-seven degrees, same as it was when they started.

After five and six times around, the blue haze clearly encompassed the sphere. It frightened and fascinated Ben in turns.

It completed the last four turns, then slowed to a stop and shut down.

“Did you see that?” Larry asked him.

Ben stood there with his mouth open.

“Ben!” Larry yelled this time, trying to get his attention.

“I hear you, no need to shout,” Ben replied in a surprisingly calm tone.

“You can't tell me that wasn't weird,” Larry said.

“Okay, I won't tell you.”

“Quit joking, Ben. What in God's name was that?”

Trying to get past his astonishment, Ben tried to act as if all was expected. “Alright, what do we know?” he said, as if it was possible to be somewhat scientific about what they’d witnessed. “It didn’t heat up like we expected. As far as I could tell it presented no magnetic qualities whatsoever. And it had a strange blue—”

Larry cut him off. “I could care less. Whatever that thing was doing, it wasn't natural.”

“You're scared of this thing, aren't you?”

“You bet your ass I am,”

“Why?”

“Because it doesn’t feel right. You can’t tell me you couldn't feel the same thing?”

“No, it didn't feel wrong. Just… I don’t know.” Ben didn't know how to finish. Objectivity wasn’t big on his list right now. All he wanted was to go. He ached to get in and see what happened, no matter what the consequences. And not because he felt like a daredevil, but because he could almost *feel* something on the other side of that blue haze.

"You aren't seriously thinking of taking a joy ride in that thing after what we just saw, are you?"

Ben looked a little astonished at the question. "Why wouldn't I? I'm not the one freaked out by a little bit of blue light. So, it feels a bit weird. So what? Maybe it's supposed to do that? The damn thing is a time machine, Larry. A time machine! Something strange is bound to happen, don't you think?"

Larry began to point his finger at his friend. "I never would've helped you with this thing if I knew this was going to happen," he said, looking completely flustered. "Just promise me you won't try anything until we know a little more about it."

"What exactly are we going to learn that's going to make you feel better?" Ben asked.

Larry narrowed his eyes, and then closed his mouth.

"Everything will be alright," Ben said, putting his hand on Larry's shoulder. "Trust me on this, it will be fine."

Larry looked up at the machine. "I'm glad you think so."

Joey lay on his bed, doing his math homework. They were working on fractions in class and some of the questions he was working on had been on the board earlier that day. He closed his eyes and focused; he could see the blackboard clearly in his mind. He didn't consider it cheating, not when it was already inside his head. Suddenly, a glowing blue light blocked the picture of the blackboard. Slowly, the bright blue light dimmed, and he was in Ben's outhouse building. He could see Ben and Larry at the machine, a shimmering blue light emanating from it. From inside that light, Joey could hear voices, small and far away. He felt certain one of them belonged to his grandfather. It was beautiful, fascinating, and scary all at the same time. Then, in an instant, it was gone.

He sat back in his bed, forgetting the homework for now. Ben and Larry had finished working on the machine. Something about the entire ordeal left a question in his mind. His gift and the machine Ben's backyard. Was there a connection between the two? He felt strongly there was but had no way of knowing how they were connected.

Joey pushed the question aside for the moment. There was no use pondering something in which he had no answers.

It was the darkest evening Joe could ever remember, but he kept walking. The country road he found himself on was void of traffic at this hour. He looked back every minute or so, knowing he really didn't need to. If someone were to come along, he would see the headlights beforehand. He guessed he must've walked at least ten miles, or maybe it just seemed that way. He'd gotten a couple rides, the last had stranded him on this desolate road in the middle of nowhere. If the local police were to drive past and decide to investigate, it would be all over.

As he walked, he felt the road rising up from the

rest of the land around it. Looking down into the ditch, he realized why. It was entirely swampland below, probably filled with alligators. Behind him, he saw the reflection of headlights coming off the road. He stuck out his thumb and waited. The car slowed and then stopped. The driver rolled down the passenger window. Behind the wheel of the sky-blue Toyota Corolla was a young man with ginger hair. Joe suppressed a laugh; in a way, the shape of the boy's nose and eyes kind of resembled that of a large red headed mouse.

"Need a ride?" The young man asked.

No, I'm out here for my health. Thought I'd take a walk in the middle of the night, Joe thought. *I stuck out my thumb because I was lonely.*

"Yeah, thanks. I was beginning to think no one would come along," Joe said.

"Where you headed?" the redheaded, mouse-boy asked as Joe climbed in.

"Nashville. But if you're going anywhere north, that would be fine."

"Well, can't take you to Nashville, but I might be able to get you a little closer. I'm heading to Birmingham. I can get take you that far."

"Are you from Birmingham?" Joe asked.

"Yep, I was just visiting my sister in Orlando."

Joe started to calculate things in his head. "So, if you were to go missing, it might take them a while to realize you were gone," Joe stated, and looked back over his shoulder to see if any other cars were coming.

"What are you talking about?" The boy asked.

In a sudden lurch, Joe grabbed the mousy-looking boy by the neck. The young man tried desperately to wrench Joe's hands away from his throat, but Joe doubled his grip. Then Joe felt something in the boy's throat crunch and realized he had crushed the kid's windpipe. Joe released his grip and watched as the young man thrashed around, kind of slapping with one hand while holding the other over his throat, making sharp little gasping noises. Soon his eyes were bulging. Joe sat there, watching as if it were a kind of theatrical performance. Out of desperation, the boy opened his car door. Joe jumped out of the vehicle just as the red-haired boy fell to the pavement and stopped his struggling.

Joe picked up the rag doll that was once mousy boy, carried him down to the ditch, and threw him into the swamp. The dense undergrowth hid the body pretty well.

"Alligators will find you before anyone else does," Joe said, wiping his hands on his pants. After taking one last survey of the deserted roadway, he climbed the embankment and drove off.

Joey woke up, unable to breathe. It was as if there was a hand was on his throat, choking off his air. Quickly, he closed his eyes and went into the room inside his mind. He could breathe again. Joey took a deep breath to let the air back into his lungs. The giant windows displayed a red headed young man with a pair of hands around his neck. Hands which he knew belonged to his father.

"Close—close—close!" he shouted. The blinds crashed down all at once. Joey threw himself on the floor and pulled his knees up into his chest. He waited another five or ten minutes before finally opening his eyes. The knowledge that his father had just killed again hung over him like a shadow. He tried to go back to sleep, but the haunting look of the red-haired boy wouldn't leave him. After a while, he got up and shuffled into his mother's room. Moving to the side of the bed, he stared at her; she was sound asleep. A quick sob escaped him, but his mother remained unmoved, the sound gone unheard. Finally, he climbed into her bed, putting his arm around his mother, and holding tight.

CHAPTER 18

Ben opened the front door and threw the mail on the table by the door. He went into the kitchen, opened the refrigerator, and looked inside; it was empty again. Ben shook his head in disgust.

"One of these days, I'm actually going to buy some food for that thing."

As he crossed into the living room, he suddenly got the oddest sensation, as if he was being watched. He began to search the living room, vaguely looking about, without satisfaction. He went upstairs next, going into each of the rooms in turn, and finding nothing out of the ordinary.

Inside his mind, Ben could hear his own thoughts turn in a funny way. He distinctly heard "Hello! Can you hear me?" Then it dawned on him. Joey must be trying to contact him.

Ben sat in his recliner and closed his eyes, but there was nothing there. "Joey?" he said aloud with his eyes still closed.

Nothing happened.

He got up, went into the bathroom, and flipped on the lights. He put his hands on the sink and looked in the mirror; his reflection merely stared blankly back at him. Ben heard a brief knock at the front door. A moment later the door opened.

"Anybody home?" Larry called out.

"Be right there," Ben shouted. He was still feeling a bit baffled about what was going on inside of his own head. The strange paranoia was still present. He flipped off the bathroom light and went into the living room. Larry was standing near the doorway, looking nervous.

"Did you still want to do that tonight?" Larry asked.

"Yeah, sure," Ben replied distractedly.

"What's the matter?"

"I don't know. For the last few minutes, I've had the strangest feeling. I don't know what it is, but it's like I'm being watched or something."

"Is it Joe Murphy? You think he's hanging around the neighborhood?" Larry went to the window and pulled back the curtain.

"No, I don't think so. I mean, it isn't like that. "Oh hell, I don't know," Ben said.

"It's the machine," Larry said. "You're having second thoughts about it, and it's making you paranoid."

"I'm not having second thoughts. And I'm not paranoid." The last part was a lie, but he wasn't going to admit it.

"Still, maybe we should cancel," Larry said hopefully.

"You'd like that wouldn't you?"

"It was worth a try."

"Would you rather I just did it alone?"

Larry hesitated, but then shook his head. "No, I'll help you, even if I don't like the damn thing."

Suddenly, the sensation of being watched was gone, and Ben felt a little more at ease, though he didn't mention any of it to Larry.

"Tell you what, I bet you a hundred dollars nothing happens when I get in it," Ben said.

"You can keep your hundred dollars. I just don't want anything creepy to happen."

"Like what?"

"I don't know, and I'm not really fond of finding out."

There came another brief knock at the front door, and it swung open once again.

"Does everyone just walk into my house these days?" Ben said, acting as if he was offended when he saw it was Megan.

"Oh, shut up, it's just me. Hi, Larry," Megan said. Megan gave Larry a quick hug and then looked at Ben. "I came over to see what you were doing for dinner."

"I hadn't thought that far ahead," Ben said.

"In other words, you haven't got anything in the house, and hadn't quite figured out what you were going to order. Just not pizza. Don't know how you can live on pizza all the time."

Ben chuckled. "Yeah, you know me too well. Actually, we were about to do a test on the machine. That is, if Larry hasn't completely lost his nerve."

"Sounds interesting. Mind if I watch?" Megan asked.

"I don't see why not? Just take off any jewelry or anything metal. It may not be a problem, but better to be safe than sorry," Ben said.

Megan took off her necklace and earrings and laid them on the desk and followed Larry out. Ben hesitated for a moment and looked down at the wedding band on his left hand. The thing had remained on his hand up until now. Taking it off would feel like he was leaving Becca behind. Maybe it was the right thing to do. The ring was a reminder. Even if things worked out, if the machine he'd built actually worked, in this life, this reality, it felt wrong to continue holding onto a symbol of dedication when he had such deep feelings for someone else.

Megan.

Only at this moment did he fully grasp just how much he loved her, to allow himself to admit it to his own heart. He opened the desk drawer, hesitated for a second, and then put the ring inside.

Larry stood at the controls while Megan helped Ben into the chamber. Ben sat down and tried to get comfortable.

"Start it up when the clock hits the top of the hour," Ben called out.

"Just ten revolutions, like before, right?" Larry asked.

"Yep, just to see what happens," Ben said while gripping the arms of the chair for courage.

Thirty seconds remained. Larry set the controls and held his hand over the switch. Ben had a delay built into the panel he could have used, but he wanted someone here to see what would happen while he was in the machine. Of course, if he got burnt to a crisp, he would need someone to call an ambulance. That is, if there was anything left of him.

The digital clock went from 5:59:59 to 6:00:00, and Larry flipped the switch. Ben heard hum as the machine started up. The swing arm went around, and Ben began to see quick images flash inside his mind, like an old-style movie projector, running in reverse. It was the three of them in the building before he got into the chamber, then of them walking across the backyard, then of him putting the ring in the desk. Suddenly, the images stopped, and he was standing in front of the refrigerator with the door open.

"One of these days, I'm actually going to buy some food for that thing," he heard himself say.

He tried to move his arms and legs, but nothing happened. It felt as if he were a passenger in his own body—a body that was now going into the living room. He could see and hear everything that was going on, but that was it.

His past self began to look around the couch and then headed upstairs.

Holy cow, it was me. I'm doing this. That's why I was so paranoid earlier.

Ben wondered if there was any way to contact his past self.

"Hello! Can you hear me?" he shouted, and then remembering hearing that clearly in his mind earlier.

Like before, Ben sat down, closed his eyes, and tried to talk to Joey. After that, he went into the bathroom and looked into the mirror.

It works, just not the way I thought it would. Jeez, this is weird.

The ensuing knock on the door was expected. He watched as the previous conversation with Larry was reenacted in front of him. Then he felt an odd sensation as he slipped back to the present and found the firmness of the seat beneath him. As the swing arm made its last pass and came to a stop, he heard a high-pitched scream.

It was Megan, and she was screaming his name.

Ben climbed awkwardly out of the chamber. Megan ran over to him, grabbed him, and put him in a full bear hug. Then she pulled back and looked him over, from head to toe, as if inspecting him.

"You aren't hurt? Are you alright?" she asked, almost in a panic.

"I'm fine," Ben said, "Why, what happened?"

"There was this strange kind of electricity, and I swear, it looked as if you were being electrocuted. There were sparks and lightning jumping all over the place. It was all around you," Megan said, and began crying. Ben pulled her into his arms and held her tight.

"It's alright now. Whatever it was, it wasn't electricity. I'm fine, Megan, really."

Ben kept his arms around her and looked up at Larry. He had an 'I told you so' look on his face.

"So, I didn't disappear when it happened," Ben asked.

Megan sniffled and shook her head.

"No, you were in the chair the whole time," Larry said, "and it scared the living-daylights out of the both of us."

"But I went back, Larry. I did. Remember when I told you it felt like someone was watching me? It was me, only inside my own head. I guess the only way to go back in time is through our consciousness. The body doesn't go back, just your mind."

"You're kidding, right?" Larry asked. Megan cut them both off.

"Please, don't do that again. There's something not right with it, I can feel it. Please Ben, don't ever do that again!" Megan pleaded.

Again, Ben looked to Larry.

"Don't look at me. You know how I feel about that thing," Larry said. "By the way, you owe me a hundred bucks."

CHAPTER 19

Megan slept soundly, curled up next to Ben in his own bed. The incident with the machine had disturbed her quite a bit. Ben had convinced her to lie down, but she had asked him to stay until she fell asleep. He wasn't tired, but if he moved Megan would surely wake. Plus, it felt good to have her there next to him.

Ben looked around the room; Megan had helped him pack up this room and the girl's rooms a month ago. He had kept the personal things he wanted, the rest they had donated to charity. It felt like kind of a harsh thing to do, but necessary. Megan suggested that he pack it all away and put it in a storage unit, but he knew that Becca would've wanted it this way. It wasn't long after that he'd started sleeping in the bedroom again. The house was becoming his. The ghosts of the past had finally retreated. It didn't hurt anymore.

He began to mull over what had happened with the machine earlier in the day. Astonishment was the least of it. Had he not been there, he would've been on the verge of total disbelief.

Megan and Larry both do not like that machine. Is there something that feels fundamentally wrong with going back in time? Whatever it is, why don't I feel it? Aside from that, the way it is now, even if I were to go back in time—to before the accident—I can't do anything to stop it. My voice is heard, but would that really be enough to get my past self to listen? He doesn't know about the time machine and wouldn't know where the strange thoughts are coming from.

Ben began to focus on the morning he had slept in. The morning Becca and the girls died.

Why do I still have a feeling of guilt over this? It hangs over me even now. If I go back, I might have a chance to give them a warning and stop them from going.

Megan stirred. She rested her arm across his chest. Ben looked at her longingly.

God, she really is beautiful. I don't know what I would do without her.

He suddenly yearned to kiss her. Ben leaned in to steal a kiss while she slept, but something made him stop. He backed off and stared up at the ceiling. Then he felt Megan's hand as she placed it on the side of his face. She was gazing intently at him. They moved at the same time and engaged in a long passionate kiss. They broke apart for a moment. Neither of them spoke except with their eyes. Ben removed his shirt off and threw it on the floor. She looked at him hesitantly.

"If this is what you want, Megan, I want it just as much," he said.

She smiled widely, pulled off her top, and tossed it aside. Then she moved forward, kissing him quickly, trying to take off the rest of her clothes while Ben was busy struggling with his pants.

Joe lay on the bed, propped up, with his hands

behind his head. He'd rented a room at a little roadside motel outside of Lexington, Kentucky. The television was showing the national news. The story of his narrow escape in Florida hadn't led but was within the first ten minutes. His buddy, JB, had even gotten a brief interview. Joe imagined the fat hippy was enjoying his fifteen minutes of fame. Luckily, the people who ran the motel didn't appear to be the type to follow the news.

He reached over to the nightstand and grabbed the bottle of tequila. The room had cheap wood paneling and the windows were covered by a filmy layer of filth. The place retained a stale, moldy, odor that Joe despised. But the place was cheap and accepted cash.

What are you gonna do now, Joe?

He grabbed the remote and flipped through the channels, trying to find something else to focus on.

You've killed two men now. The police are after you, and you have nowhere to run. Eventually, you're going to run out of money, and they will find you.

That thought was enough for him to take a long drink from the bottle of tequila. The alcohol was doing its job, but his mind insisted on wrestling over his situation.

"Son-of-bitches should've just left me alone. I was happy where I was."

I'm gonna make them pay. Make them all pay. I owe the Misses. My darling, Hannah. She deserves to die. She has it coming, as well as the kid. I ought to skin the little brat right in front of her. A little payback for making me look like a fool back at that fire station.

Joe laughed out loud at the idea. He sat up, pulling the large hunting knife from its sheath.

"Oh, I can just see the look on her face when I hand

her his skin. Watch her scream in agony. My baby, you killed my baby!" Joe said, mocking her would be shriek. "She'd probably beg me to kill her after that."

He gripped the bottle again and took a drink, some of it running down his chin. He wiped his mouth with the back of his hand. "And then there's Stryker. Of course, we wouldn't have an audience to watch him die. Maybe I should record it so I can watch it over and over again," he said and broke into a wild cackle of laughter.

Another voice inside his mind joined in.

What are you going to do after that? Where are you going to go?

Joe drained the last of the tequila and threw the bottle on the floor.

There is no after.

Ben pulled the blanket over the two of them. Megan was snuggled next to him; she had her head on Ben's shoulder with her leg draped over him. Ben gently rubbed her shoulder and back, enjoying the feel of her soft, fragrant, skin.

"Do you want me to get you anything?" he asked.

Megan shook her head. She placed her hand on his chest, and then said softly, "You're going to get in that thing again, aren't you?"

Ben didn't answer her.

"I know you are," she whispered, "despite my objections, aren't you?" She sat up and looked him in the eye. "I hope you know I didn't plan on sleeping with you. I'm not trying to manipulate you or anything. I was genuinely frightened for you. I still am. Not of any physical danger. Well, not entirely, that thing scares me to death. But there are other reasons. Do you understand?"

"Megan, you don't have to be afraid," Ben said dismissively. He hadn't meant it to sound that way, but immediately realized that it was a mistake.

"No, don't you dare," she said, a fury beginning to rise up inside of her. "Don't pretend I don't know what you're thinking. You want to climb back in that thing and change the past. You think you can stop that accident."

"What do you want me to tell you?"

"I want you to tell me that you aren't going to do it!" she said firmly.

"I can't do that," Ben said flatly. "If I even have the remotest chance to save Becca and the girls, I have to try."

"It's wrong, Ben," she said. "Can't you see that?"

"I know you say that, but I don't feel it. There's nothing in my guts, or anything else, that tells me that I shouldn't do this."

"Okay, Smartass, tell me this. What if it works? What happens to us if you go back and save them?"

Ben's mouth fell open. He hadn't thought that far ahead.

"I guess you know the answer to that, don't you. Everything we shared together will be gone forever. Erased, as if it never happened," she said.

"Megan..." he said, wanting to explain.

"Damn it, Ben! I've fallen in love with you. That's right, I love you! The problem is, you'll always have this between us. You'll always use Becky to keep me out until you do this." Megan climbed out of bed and began to get dressed.

"You love me?"

"Yes, Moron, I do!" she shouted spitefully and threw a pillow at him. "So, go on. Go back. Save them," she said, slowing down and then sitting down at the end of the bed. Her tone softened. "I can't hate you for that. A part of me wants them back just as badly as you do. But I guess I'm a little selfish because I need you here with me, too."

"There's no proof I can actually save them."

"There's no proof you can't, either. And I know you, Ben. You won't be happy until you try." She took a deep breath. "Something tells me I shouldn't have been with you until I had all of you, until you were able to love me as much as I love you. But sometimes I can't stop what my heart wants."

Megan went over, held his face, and kissed him softly. There was a long moment when they only stared into each other's eyes. "Goodbye, Ben. Please be careful," she said sadly and left. After a few moments, Ben heard the front door shut.

"I love you, too," he whispered.

CHAPTER 20

Morning had come and Ben stood by the machine, running his hand over the cool metal framework. It had been a several hours since Megan left. He'd already checked her driveway. The car was gone. Everything she said swirled around inside his brain; the confusion was enough to drive him mad. Megan was right about one thing, if he went back, if he saved Becca and the girls, everything would change. Even as hard as it had been, the time he'd spent with Megan, the feelings he had for her now, were powerful, and nearly impossible to give up. He'd be sacrificing that for them.

He limped over to the control panel and looked things over. Using the first trial as a standard, he calculated that it would take some thirteen thousand revolutions and nearly three hours to complete. Looking up, he saw that the clock read 10:20 in the morning.

"Damn it, what am I supposed to do?" he shouted at the walls. It echoed through the little brick building. He sat down on the hard concrete floor and hung his head. Hesitantly, he pulled the cell phone out of his pocket and dialed Megan's number. It went straight to her voicemail. She didn't want to talk to him. Ben stuffed the phone back in his pocket.

A terrible dread ran through him. It reminded him of the morning the police had arrived at his door, giving him the news that changed his life forever.

If only I had told Megan that I loved her and gave up this quest.

Another thought mirrored the first at the same time.

If only I had gotten up and stopped them from going.

Ben gazed at the machine sitting in the middle of the room. When he started this whole mess, he'd never actually dreamed it'd work. It had been nothing more than a coping mechanism, something that got him moving forward, doing something instead of grieving for his family. He wanted to build something, construct something so he felt productive and alive again. Instead, he found he'd built something even more significant with Megan. He wasn't lying when he said he loved her, even if it was after she'd left.

Unfortunately, Megan was right about something else. If he had the chance to save them, he had to do it. No matter the odds, no matter cost, he had to try. He would never be able to live with himself, or Megan, if he didn't try.

"Like it or not, I built this contraption," he said.

As if that were enough to make up his mind, Ben pushed himself back to his feet and went to the control panel. He set the delay timer for sixty seconds, and then hit the power switch. Moving quickly, he limped over to the machine and climbed into the chamber.

"Here we go," he said, just as the machine powered up.

Hannah held the jeans up to Joey's waist, measuring them for fit. She set that pair down, picked up another pair, and went through the same routine again.

"I swear Joey, you're growing too fast. I just bought you pants this winter," she said, still holding onto the pair she had in her hands and picking up another.

Joey looked up at his mother and sighed. She was busy flipping through the stack of jeans on the store shelf. They'd been clothes shopping for a couple hours now. He really didn't need new pants, or anything else for that matter, but she loved to buy him clothes when she was feeling good about herself. His mother had rebounded after the death of her father. She had her work to occupy her mind, and that helped minimize the stress that would've otherwise plagued her. She appeared determined that they should be happy despite the fact Joe had not yet been captured. Joey was so glad for her that he didn't complain about their extended shopping trip. He did wonder how much longer they were going to be at it.

"I think we'll get you the two pair of jeans and these three shirts," she said, and noticed he was doing his best to be patient. "I'm sorry, Honey. You must be bored to death with this. I'll tell you what, I want to stop at one more store and then we'll go by Dairy Queen and get some ice cream, alright?"

Joey broke into a large grin and nodded enthusiastically.

"You really are a good kid," Hannah said. "I don't know how I ever got so lucky to have you as my own."

Joey sat in the back seat with his ice cream. He stopped for a moment, looked at the ice cream cone, and wondered if there was anything in this world better than chocolate ice cream.

His mother glanced at him through the rear-view mirror. "Something wrong with your ice cream?" she asked.

Joey shook his head. "No. I was just wondering what makes chocolate taste so good."

Hannah laughed. The laughter was short lived as the car began lunging and sputtering. She turned on the flashers and pulled to the side of the road. The engine roared loudly, rattled a bit, and then gave one last gasp before stalling.

"Oh, for heaven's sakes," Hannah said, trying the ignition. The engine tried to turn but wouldn't start. She gripped the steering wheel and swore a little more loudly than she intended. Joey giggled when he heard it.

Hannah turned and gave Joey an embarrassed smile. "Did you hear that?"

Joey nodded while continuing to grin.

"Sorry about that. Well, it looks like the car has given up on us. Are you up for walk?"

Joey nodded again.

"We're not that far from home. It won't be too bad," she told him.

"It's okay, Momma, I don't mind walking."

Hannah unbuckled Joey from his seat and set him on the sidewalk, then grabbed the shopping bag from the car and closed the door. Joey stood waiting, still holding onto his ice cream, trying to finish the last of it before it melted.

"I hate leaving the car here like this, but what else can I do? When we get home, I'll call the garage and have it towed," Hannah said, and then held out her hand for Joey to take. She burst out laughing at the sight of her son. Chocolate ice cream covered her son's face, hands, and shirt.

Joey held out a chocolate covered hand to his mother.

"No way, Buddy," she said, still laughing. "C'mon, you can walk beside me."

The blue Toyota rolled down Main Street of Sturgis, Michigan. Joe had grown up in Sturgis. He passed The Strand, the local movie theater, and it was like seeing an old friend. Growing up in this town, going to the movies had been one of his few escapes.

Since his mother's death, Joe avoided coming back to this town, even though it was not far from Kalamazoo. He never really had any friends to speak of here, and never felt any real affection for the town. The only gratitude he had was for his former high school football coach. The man had taught him to use his aggressive nature to become a better football player which allowed him to get a football scholarship later on.

Joe drove to the north side of town and parked on Prospect Street, a block from his father's home. This town, this neighborhood, flooded him with memories of his childhood. Most of them were hurtful, filled with awkward humiliation, abuse, and degradation; his father's shadow was behind every one of them.

He scanned the streets and homes to make sure no

one was watching. As he walked, Joe pulled the hood of the sweatshirt over his head to hide his face. When he got closer to the family home, he cut through the neighbor's yard and into his father's backyard. He moved quietly to the rear of the house and tried the lock on the back door. As he expected, it was unlocked. Joe tried to slow his breathing and calm himself before going in.

Have to be careful, the crazy son-of-a-bitch has a gun.

It was the gun he wanted. Killing the old man was just a bonus. If it had been possible, he would've avoided confronting his father. Patrick Murphy was a dominant figure in his mind. It frightened him to think about the power the man held over him. But he'd pretty much determined that he needed the gun if his other plans were going to work. He'd just have to do it very quickly, and maybe, just maybe, it would silence the damn voice inside his head as well.

It's just after noon. He should be watching his program.

Joe put the hunting knife inside the front pocket of his sweatshirt, his hand gripped firmly on the handle, and then opened the back door.

Ben was beginning to feel almost seasick from all of the images flipping through his mind. At first, they moved somewhat slowly. He saw himself walking out to the machine, then when he had his coffee that morning, and then an image of Megan and him when they'd first kissed. Now, they were moving so fast, they were mere blur of shapes and colors passing before him.

All at once they stopped. To him, it felt like a car slamming on it brakes. It took him a second to regain his bearings. Looking out, Ben could see his hands on the grill with a scrapper and wire brush. It was a warm spring day, and the sun was so bright it nearly hurt the eyes. Ben knew something was wrong because he was scraping the grill a little more forcefully than was necessary. His hands began to bang the grill with the scraper which had no effect except to make noise.

The patio door opened, and Becca stepped out.

"Okay, Ben, I get it. You're upset," she said while deliberately setting her hands on her hips. "Now will you cut it out?"

"I don't know what you are talking about. I'm just cleaning the grill—*as instructed!*" Ben said in a patronizing tone.

"I only asked you to clean the grill because our guests will be arriving soon. Look, I know you're angry because you wanted a quiet day to do nothing—"

Ben cut her off. "It wasn't so I could 'do nothing.' I wanted a quiet day to spend with my family, maybe go to the movies or... I don't know... anything. I work all week and like to relax on the weekend. I told you Wednesday I didn't want to do this cookout, but you went ahead and planned it anyway."

"And I told you I was sorry I didn't consult with you beforehand, but I'd already invited our guests by the time you said something. Silly me, I didn't think it'd hurt to have some friends over for a cookout. God forbid I make plans that cut into your watching baseball or football or whatever else it is now."

"Damn it! That's not the reason I was against this little party of yours, and you know it!" Ben said nearly shouting by now. He threw the scrapper at the grill; it clanged off the front of it and dropped to the ground.

"Just forget it. We'll have your damn party, and you can have your social hour, and then you can just leave me the hell alone."

Watching this, Ben could tell Becca was fuming, but she said nothing. She folded her arms in front of her. He expected an explosion, but instead, she turned and went back inside. The future part of his consciousness watched the entire incident in disbelief. The argument had been completely forgotten. It was Saturday—the day before the accident. There must've been a miscalculation. The machine sent him back too far. He tried to remember—did they make up before she left the next morning? He thought yes but didn't know for sure. That time was all a blur to him now.

Ben started yelling at his past self. *Hey, Stupid! Go in there and tell her you are sorry.*

After a minute or two, he finally did get up and go inside the house, pausing to close the patio door behind him. Teresa ran up to him and hugged him.

"Hi, Sweetheart. What are you doing?" Ben asked her.

She looked at him funny, as if it wasn't evident. "I'm hugging you."

Ben smiled. "Well, thank you for the hug. I really needed that."

"I know. Mom is really mad at you," Teresa said, her big blue eyes on him.

"She's really mad, huh?"

Teresa nodded. "Yep!"

"Do you think I should go talk to her?"

Teresa tilted her head a little, and then shook it. "No, you better wait a while. You know how Mom is."

"I guess I do," Ben said, grinning at his daughter.

Teresa ran off back towards the stairs.

Ben waited a few more minutes before going into the kitchen. To make it less evident why he was there, he went to the refrigerator and grabbed a beer. Becca was standing at the sink with her back to him, her hands moving in the soapy water, washing dishes. She knew he was there but didn't turn around. Ben stared at the back of her for a moment, started to say something, and then began to walk away.

"I'm sorry, Ben," Becca said. Her back was still turned to him. There was a little bit of a strain to her voice when she said it.

"Me, too. I really shouldn't have made such a fuss over something so stupid," Ben said, setting his beer down on the table, then walking over and putting his hands on her waist. After a moment, Ben realized she was crying. He turned her so she was facing him, and then embraced her.

"Oh, Becca, don't do that. Jeez, I'm sorry. Can you forgive me for being such a stubborn jackass?"

She returned his embrace, her wet hands on his back. "I really do love you," she said. "And I realize it wasn't fair of me to throw all of this at you when you didn't want it."

"And I love you, Becca, always will. It wasn't the party, or you not telling me about it first that made me angry. I just woke up this morning tired and anxious. I used it as an excuse to get mad. I don't really know how to explain it to you. There are times when I feel like I want to just be alone for a while and recharge. It has nothing to do with watching sports or anything else. Sometimes I just feel a little overwhelmed, and don't know how to deal with it."

Becca looked at him with her eyes still a little red. "What if I were to promise you one whole day of nothing but solitude? Tomorrow morning I'll take the girls and go visit my parents. Mom hasn't been feeling well, and it'd be good to go over and help out. How does that sound? You can sleep in and everything?" she said, trying to smile for him.

"It sounds like heaven. Thank you," he said. "I'll help you get the stuff around for the party and promise to be in a better mood from here on out. Scouts honor," he said, holding up two fingers.

Becca gave him a small laugh and kissed him. "Alright, but I know for a fact, you're no Boy Scout."

The future Ben, locked in this room of consciousness, began yelling. He wanted to use the arms to start pounding on something, but he had no control over them. *NO, NO, NO! Don't let her go on that visit. You idiot, you want time ALONE? You are about to get more of it than you ever imagined.*

CHAPTER 21

Ben watched as the past unfolded around him. The clock on the kitchen wall read 2:15. He figured he had been in a guest in this place for about two hours. His body, the part of him from the past, stood at the kitchen counter, busy mixing the hamburger with the onions and the ranch mix as he always did when making his famous ranch burgers. His wife allowed him to refer to them as famous only because, in her opinion, nothing else he attempted to cook was eatable. While he was doing that, Becca busied herself with making the deviled eggs.

The doorbell rang at the front door. Both Ben and Becca looked at each other, but neither of them moved.

"Come in!" Ben hollered at the door when it became obvious to him Becca wasn't going to go.

"Just go see who it is, will you?"

Ben looked at his hands. They were covered in raw hamburger meat. Through the kitchen doorway, he saw Tia run to the front door and open it.

"Hello," Tia said brightly.

"Hi'ya, Princess," Larry said, calling her by the nickname he always used. "Where's your dad?"

"He's in the kitchen with Mom. Hello, Mrs. Snider,"

Tia said. Amy was carrying a casserole, obviously still hot, because she used potholders.

"My, Tia, don't you look pretty today," Amy told her.

Tia used her hands to smooth the frilly blue dress her mother had put her in that morning. "Thank you. It's brand new. Don't you think it's the prettiest dress ever?"

"I do, Princess," said Larry, "the prettiest ever."

Tia smiled brightly. It was evident she was excited about the party.

Larry followed Amy into the kitchen. Amy began talking with Becca while Larry watched Ben mix the hamburger.

"That looks like a lot of fun," Larry quipped.

"Oh yeah, it is," Ben said. "Do you want to try it?"

"No, no, I'm trying to quit," Larry shot back. "You got a beer for me?"

"In the fridge. Grab one for me, too, please," Ben said, wiping the meat from his hands, and then going over to the sink to wash them. Amy was standing next to the sink, still talking with Becca. Ben bumped her hip to move her. "Excuse me," he said, running the water to wash his hands.

"Ben, I was trying to talk here," Amy said, sounding thoroughly annoyed.

"Sounds like you still are."

"Oh, you're a brat," Amy said, hitting him on the arm, but not hard enough to hurt.

Ben dried his hands on the dishtowel, grabbed the hamburger and hotdogs, and put them on a tray. Larry followed him through the dining room towards the backyard. They got as far as the patio door when the doorbell rang again. Ben looked at Larry.

"You gonna get that?" Larry asked, raising his eyebrows.

"I was kind of hoping you'd do it for me," Ben said knowing Larry was just being a pain. "Oh, forget it. Here, take this, and I'll get the door. I'll be back in a minute."

"Yeah, I guess I could do that much," Larry said, taking the tray from Ben.

When Ben reached the front door, he found Jim and Megan waiting.

"Hey, come on in. Becca is in the kitchen," Ben said to Megan. Tia and Teresa both came running down the stairs to greet Megan.

"Hello," Megan said to them, "I wondered if you two were going to come down and give your Aunt Megan a hug."

"We were playing," Teresa told her.

"What were you playing?"

"Just dolls," Teresa said a bit smugly. "I'm a little too old for that, but Tia likes to play dolls, so I did it for her."

"You do too like to play dolls," Tia told her, looking a little hurt.

"Only with my favorite sister though," Teresa said, seeing the hurt in her sister's eyes.

"But I'm your only sister," Tia said, "aren't I?"

"Yes, she is," Ben told her, laughing a bit.

"Let's go see what your mother is up to, okay?" Megan said to the girls, taking their hands, and walking off towards the kitchen, leaving Ben and Jim standing there.

"Want a beer?" Ben asked.

"Um… sure. Why not," Jim replied.

They got the beer and went out into the backyard.

Larry had already started the grill for Ben.

"Should we throw the burgers on?" Larry asked.

Ben shrugged. "Don't know. Haven't gotten clearance from the boss yet," he said. Jim went around Ben and shook Larry's hand. It was not a warm greeting. They didn't hate each other, but they weren't exactly friends, either.

As they awaited instructions from the wives, Ben and Larry drank beer and began to talk at length about the upcoming college football season. Not a big sports fan, Jim frowned a lot and remained silent. Not wanting to be rude, Ben tried to change the subject to include Jim.

"How's the law practice going, Jim?"

"It's going great," Jim replied enthusiastically. "I got a call from Richard Bernhard, the Chairman of Clark Pharmaceuticals. His son, Richard—who's only nineteen—was arrested for DUI. Of course, he wants me to represent his son. It's a beautiful thing, because the mayor's office wants the whole thing to disappear because of the pressure he is getting from..."

Ben found himself tuning out. He did his best to appear engaged, but it got to the point where he felt genuinely sorry he'd even asked. If there was one thing Jim could do, it was talk about Jim. Ben gave Larry a quick sideways glance, who just rolled his eyes. They were relieved when Jim finally began to wrap up his story.

"Anyway, I told them my services are not cheap, and then I gave them a number. Bernhard didn't even blink. Didn't blink. Can you believe it?"

"Wow. Sounds like you are making quite a bit of money," Ben said.

"Yeah, I'm getting to the point I'm not sure how to spend all of it," Jim said, now grinning with self-satisfaction. "The best part is all of the money and notoriety attracts all kinds of women. You wouldn't believe—"

Larry cut in. "You aren't cheating on Megan, are you?"

Jim's grin all but disappeared. "Oh… well, no. I wouldn't do that."

"Good, because she doesn't deserve it," Larry said curtly.

The patio door opened, and Becca came out with Megan.

"You guys got the grill going yet?" Becca asked and gave Ben a quick peck on the cheek. Megan stood next to her husband, but there appeared to be a bit of awkwardness between them.

A slight frown pulled at the corners of Megan mouth.

Still trapped in the conscience of his past self, Ben saw Megan clearly as she was.

You really were unhappy, weren't you, Megan.

"No, I was waiting for the signal from you," Ben said to his wife.

"I suppose you can go ahead and start. Just about everyone has arrived. Bob and Sandy are here, so is Joe and his wife. Have you seen their son, Joey? He's such a cute boy. I think Tia and him went off to play."

"So, who are we missing?" Ben asked.

"Just Cliff and his girlfriend. What is her name, anyway?"

Ben shook his head. "I'm not sure… what week is it?"

"Oh, Ben, be nice. It's not his fault, he just hasn't found the right one yet is all," Becca told him, hugging his arm tightly.

"It's not from a lack of trying," Ben smirked.

Ben threw the hamburgers on the grill while the women disappeared inside. Jim appeared uncomfortable around Larry and announced he was also going inside. Joe Murphy came out, passing Jim as he went in.

"It was nice of you to invite us to your cookout," Joe said stiffly.

"You're welcome," Ben said, busying himself with arranging the hamburgers on the grill. He hadn't invited them, Becca had. He wouldn't have admitted it to Becca, but it was one of the reasons he'd gotten so sore about putting on this shindig. It was bad enough he had to spend his office hours with the man. The idea of spending any part of his weekend with the overbearing prick was too much.

"I was told they gave you the Dugan Aviation account," Joe said.

Ben looked at him, knowing Joe wasn't saying it to be congratulatory. "Yeah, Mr. Walker handed it to me on Friday."

"Must be nice to be hand-picked for the job. Funny thing, they didn't bother to ask my opinion."

"The reason they gave it to me is because I'm the only one who has worked on the deluge system they need for the hanger. I did the work up for the fire suppression system at the airbase in Battle Creek," Ben said in a calm tone.

"I just get a little tired of you going behind my back, is all."

Ben expected this. "I didn't go behind your back. They gave it to me. If you have a problem with the way they do things, then I suggest you go talk to Mr. Walker and Mr. Pearson," Ben said firmly, pointing the spatula at him.

Joe's eyes narrowed, but he said nothing.

"Come on, Joe. Let's not talk about work, alright?" Ben said, trying to break the contentious mood; the last thing he wanted was an incident. "Just grab a beer and try and have a good time"

Joe appeared to be thinking, but then gave Ben a smile, disingenuous as it was, and nodded. "That's probably a good idea," he replied. He hesitated for a moment, as if to add something, but slowly turned and went back into the house instead.

If I had known what a psycho you were, I would have shot you right there.

"That guy gives me the creeps," Larry said.

"I know. Me, too," Ben said while flipping the burgers and adding the hotdogs to the grill.

Larry finished his beer and pointed to the bottle. "Want another one?" he asked Ben.

"No, I'm good."

A moment later, Tia came out of the house with Joey in tow. She led him to her father. In one hand, she carried a doll.

"Hi, Daddy," she said brightly as ever.

"Well, hello, Ladybug. Who have you got there?" he asked his daughter.

"This is Joey."

"Hello, Joey," Ben said, holding out his hand to shake Joey's hand.

"Hello, Sir," he said politely.

"We're going to play Time Machine," Tia said.

"Time Machine?" Ben asked. "How do you play that?"

"We're going to build a machine to send dolly back in time," she said holding up her doll to him.

That's the doll I used in the first model. Is she trying to tell me she knows about me? Jeez, how could I have forgotten this?

"Okay, you guys have fun," Ben said.

Tia took Joey by the hand and led him away. Joey took one last look back at Ben as if he wanted to ask something, but Tia pulled him away.

Megan appeared moments later. She was alone. "Are they done yet?" she asked.

"Almost," Ben said. He noticed her distracted look. "Tell me, how've you been?"

"Good… really good," she replied. "Jim's practice has been doing really good, and, um… things are good…" Her words trailed off into silence.

"I didn't ask about Jim. I was wondering how you were doing."

Megan tried bravely to smile. "I'm fine," she said glancing over at the house, and then back to Ben. "We've had our problems, but you know how it is. Everyone has problems. It's just a part of being married."

"Yeah, I can definitely relate," Ben said heartily, thinking of the argument had with his wife earlier.

The future Ben looked at Megan, and his heart ached. He truly loved her but realized that this wasn't the Megan that he loved. Both of them had become different people; the two people standing there by the grill had yet to go through the hard times, had yet to be changed and hardened by the events to come. They were broken people that used pieces of each other to fix each other. The Ben standing there now loved Becca. It wasn't that he didn't love Becca, but something inside of him had changed forever. Suddenly, all he wanted was to go back to his time to be with his Megan.

I have to finish what I started.

Then, a blinding darkness enveloped him, and felt as if he were moving, sliding in some manner, down a steep hillside, away from the past. The sensation suddenly stopped, and Ben felt the arms of the chair inside the chamber of his machine. Slowly, he opened his eyes. The swing arm was making its last pass as the chamber lowered back down, the pegs on each side catching the cradle and coming to a rest.

Ben looked at the digital clock on the wall. It read one-thirty-four; he'd been gone for over three hours.

CHAPTER 22

Joe moved quietly through the kitchen. He could hear the theme to The Price is Right blaring from the next room. He stepped to the edge of the living room and peeked in; his father sat in his favorite green chair, preoccupied with the game show. The chair was pulled up to the old, nineteen-inch, television. His father's eyesight was slowly getting worse, and he didn't like to wear glasses. Over the years, the chair had moved closer and closer to the television. Joe stepped lightly into the living room; the floorboard creaked, and Patrick Murphy turned his head.

"Who's there?"

"It's just me, Papa," Joe said, moving into full view of his father.

Patrick squinted trying to get a better look.

"Joseph? Is that you, Boy?"

"Yes, Papa," Joe answered. He stood in front of the television set for his father to see him. Joe realized that his father's white hair had gotten noticeably thinner. The man that once towered over him now looked hunched and frail.

"I heard about some of your doings lately," his father said sharply, "Is it true? You beat Hannah and tried to kidnap little Joey?"

Joe simply nodded at his father.

"What a dumbass. If I told you once, I told you a hundred times, Hannah was the best thing to happen to you, and you screwed it up, didn't you? I'll tell you this now, if you'd harmed one hair on my grandson's head, I would've hunted you down and killed you myself. I hear tell you put someone in the hospital. Nearly killed the man. What's going on inside of—"

"Shut up, old man," Joe said with gritted teeth.

"Or what, you gutless turd? Are you going to try to beat on me, too? God knows, everybody already knows what a coward you are."

Joe moved swiftly, pulling the knife from his pocket, and plunging it into his father's chest. He held the knife there for a moment before slowly pulling it out again. There was a look of shock on the old man's face as he looked down at the bloodstained shirt. His mouth opened and closed silently. With grim determination, Joe stabbed him again, and again, and again. Patrick Murphy's white T-shirt became crimson.

"You will never, ever, talk to me that way again, Old Man!" Joe shouted, out of breath, and then sat down hard on the wood floor. He stared at the body of his father for a several minutes, his breathing finally becoming normal. He knew his father would never move again, but there was something haunting about his appearance. He had an accusing look on his face. The image burned into Joe's mind.

"Now who's the dumbass?" Joe said smugly, but the sight of his father still disturbed him. He grabbed a blanket from the couch and threw it over the body. But even after covering him, Joe couldn't move. His eyes were locked on the brown blanket draped over what was once his father. Something deep inside his mind finally clicked and he began to move. Inside his father's nightstand, he found the 45 caliber Glock he wanted. He ejected the clip to see if it was loaded. It was.

"One down, three to go," he said flatly, pushing the clip back inside and hearing it click.

Joey finished spreading the peanut butter on a slice of bread when the first waves of his father's violent emotions hit him. The butter knife clanged to the floor as he immediately closed his eyes and went into his safe room.

"Close, close, close," he said quickly, trying to avoid witnessing another vicious scene that would surely play out before him. The blinds slammed shut and he huddled on the floor beside his chair. Secretly, he wished Ben was here with him. The thought of contacting Ben crossed his mind, but something warned him it was not a good idea right now—not with his father in a murderous rage. Joey climbed in his chair and conceded that he would have to ride this one out by himself. After a minute or two, Joey heard something else.

"Joey, what is the matter?"

It was his mother's voice.

She must have found him standing in the kitchen with his eyes closed and probably looking quite catatonic.

"Joey, talk to me. What's wrong?" She was beginning to sound desperate. Joey had a decision to make, and he had to do it quickly.

"Open," he said, and braced himself for the worst. When the blinds did open, the only thing he saw was a gaunt figure in a chair, covered by a brown blanket. There was something familiar about the room, someplace he'd been before, but he couldn't place it. Joey opened his eyes. Hannah was kneeling in front of him, shaking his shoulders and crying. When she saw that his eyes were open, she grabbed him and pulled him into a hug.

"Oh, Honey, you frightened me so badly. What was wrong? What were you doing?"

"It's okay, Momma. I was just thinking," Joey said, trying to lie.

Hannah looked at him, studying him. She knew her son well enough to know when he wasn't telling the truth. "Come with me," she said, leading him into the living room. "I know you're lying. I also know you wouldn't do that unless you had a really good reason. But if you don't tell me what's going on, how am I supposed to help you?"

Joey thought about how she might take knowing the truth. He was afraid that it would change how she felt about him.

"If I tell you, will you still love me the same?" Joey asked.

She broke into a large grin. "Yes, of course. There's nothing you could ever tell me that would change how much I love you."

Joey sighed. Telling her still would not be an easy thing to do. "I can… kind of… feel things that most people can't," Joey started.

"What kind of things?"

"Like, what kind of person they are or what they are

feeling."

"You can?"

Joey nodded. "And I can put myself in other people's minds. Like when Ben was in the hospital and was asleep, I helped him find his way out."

"I don't know what to say," Hannah said.

"Right now, you are scared. It feels like prickly heat. You're scared for me, scared that something's wrong with my mind," Joey hesitated for a moment, "worried that I have something wrong with my mind like my father."

Now Joey really was scared. He never should have told her. He could endure the violent scenes and emotions put out by his father, could endure any kind of heartache, but to lose his mother's affection would be too much for him to take.

Hannah gave him a startled look but recovered quickly.

"You're right, Joey. I'm sorry, that did pass through my mind. Tell me something else... why were you standing there with your eyes closed. Were you in a trance or something?"

Joey shook his head. "It was because of dad. When he does bad things, the bad feelings he has come at me, and I have to hide."

"Where do you go to hide?"

"Ben helped me make a room—a safe room—inside my mind, where I can get away from it."

"So, it's happened before?"

Joey nodded. "I can show you the room if you like."

"You can?" she said, sounding curious and a little apprehensive at the same time.

"Close your eyes."

Hannah closed her eyes, and like Ben before her, she was amazed at what she saw. They were standing in the middle of his room. She looked down at her son and tried to smile, even though it was an uneasy experience for her.

"You made this room?"

"Ben thought of it. He drew it on a piece of paper for me. I sort of copied it."

"What are the windows for?"

"I can see out of someone's eyes through them."

"And Ben Stryker helped you with all of this," she said. "I always wondered why you two were thick as thieves." She paused. "How long have you had this... thing?"

Joey shrugged. "Since last summer, I think."

"Why didn't you tell me before?"

"I was afraid of what you'd think. Plus, you had enough trouble already without worrying about me."

Hannah opened her eyes and so did Joey. She hugged him tightly before saying anything.

"You're the only worry I've ever had. And even at that, I wouldn't trade that in for anything in this world, because I love you."

"I love you too, Momma."

She looked at him seriously and said, "So now, the next time you have to go to your safe room, I'll know, and can help you if I can."

Joey nodded and it was evident he was relieved. "Okay," he said, finally smiling.

"Let's not tell your grandmother about this just yet. I think she might have a little trouble understanding, and it just might frighten her a bit."

Ben climbed out of the chamber and went to the door. He looked back at the machine. A lot of confusing thoughts were going on inside of his head.

"I could use a drink," he said. The walk back to the house became painful as his leg began to ache something fierce. Sitting in the same crouched position for three hours had aggravated his knee. He went inside and lay down on the couch. His body may have been relaxed, by his mind continued to churn. There came a halfhearted knock at the door, and it opened a crack.

"Ben? You home?" It was Larry.

"Yeah, come on in," Ben said, not bothering to get up.

Larry came in, moving almost tentatively as if he were unsure of Ben's state of mind. It was evident he was concerned by what happened between him and Megan. He sat down across from Ben in the recliner. "So, hey… how's it going? I came by earlier and got no answer," Larry said.

"Yeah, I was busy," Ben said, nodding his head towards the backyard.

This was not the response Larry was expecting and it showed on his face. "Not that damn machine again. Christ on a pogo-stick, how could you get back in that thing after the way Megan freaked out? Seriously, how could you even go near it?"

"I had, too," Ben said. He glanced over at Larry. "We stayed the night together last night."

"Wait a minute. You mean you and Megan?"

"She told me she loved me, and then ran out the door."

"Why?"

“Because she knew I was going to get back into that thing, and it would take away everything we have together.”

“Well, go get her, drag her back here. Obviously, the thing didn’t work, otherwise we wouldn’t be sitting here talking about it,” Larry said.

“I can’t, not yet. I still have one more trip to make. When I went back, I overshot by one day.”

“Saturday,” Larry said solemnly, “the day of the cookout.”

“You remember that?”

“Sure. It was the last time we were all together. Something like that is apt to stick to my brain. Now that I think of it, there was something else. At one point, you told me you’d had a creepy feeling as if someone was watching you, almost the same way you described it before.”

“When did I tell you that?” Ben asked.

“As I recall, it was after we had eaten. About the time Hannah, Joey, and that psycho left because you thought he might’ve had something to do with it.”

“Well, it definitely wasn’t Joe,” Ben said. “He hesitated before introducing the subject really occupying his thoughts. “Did you know that Becca and I had a fight that morning? I acted like a total ass. I still can’t believe I did it. I was angry because she’d made plans for that cookout when all I wanted was to be alone that weekend. That’s why she left with the girls left that next morning. She promised to give me time alone.”

“Oh hell, Ben, you guys got into plenty of fights. Some worse than that, because by the end of the night you two were really cozy. It’s easy to forget the fighting and bickering because the only thing you want to remember is the good times. There's nothing wrong with that. It's only human."

"You don't understand. It's my fault. If I hadn't acted like a child, they would still be alive."

"You don't know that. A hundred things, in a hundred different ways could've caused their deaths. What do you think, you can foresee every circumstance, every decision that might keep someone from dying? It was an accident, whether it happened because you wanted a little time to yourself, or because they were going to the supermarket to buy groceries."

"I know, I know," Ben said, aggravated by Larry's logic. "But it's obvious that I felt so guilty, I totally blocked it out."

"Well, at least now you can understand it," Larry said. "If I thought it would make you feel better, I'd tell you to keep your guilt. But you know as well as I do, you never intended for it to happen."

With a heavy sigh, Ben continued on with his next point. "I also realized something else," he said. "I'm not the same person I was then. I still love Becca, but it has changed. I love Megan now, and the only thing I really want is to be with her."

"Then why in God's name do you insist on going back?"

"Because I have a shot at stopping that accident. How can I walk away from that? How could I ever live with myself if I didn't at least try?"

"Sounds like you've already made up your mind," Larry told him. "I think you're an idiot for doing it, but I'll help you if you want."

Ben smiled at his friend. "Thanks, Larry."

CHAPTER 23

At her parent's home in Kalamazoo, Megan sat at the kitchen table with her mother, a hot cup of tea in front of her. She had gone there to get away and think. Her parents lived on the north side of town, only fifteen minutes away, but she didn't visit as often as she really thought she should. It wasn't because she didn't love them. It was just difficult at times because her mother tended to treat her like a child at times. Megan had spent most of the afternoon with them in a silent, somber-like state, unwilling to share details of her sullen mood. Only after several hours did she find herself prepared to talk to her mother about her situation with Ben. She had left out the details as it would be difficult to explain Ben's machine. Even with everything she'd witnessed, she wasn't completely sure if she believed it.

"What are you going to do, Dear?" her mother asked.

"I don't know," Megan answered softly. She picked up her tea but got it only halfway to her mouth before setting it back down again. She hung her head and sighed.

"Do you love him?"

Megan nodded, not looking up. The frown on her face deepened.

"Then go get him. Life is too short to be waiting for love. If you've found it, you have to hold on to it."

"I can't," Megan said, her eyes apparently fixated on the pattern on the tablecloth. "It's... well... it's complicated. Let's just say, he may not be emotionally available yet."

"No, I don't understand. Does he love you?"

"I think so," Megan said.

"So, you haven't asked him, then?"

Megan shook her head.

"And why not?" her mother asked.

"I'm afraid of what the answer might be."

"Well, I don't know how you can decide when you haven't even found out for sure what his feelings are. Seems a little silly to give up before you even get started, don't you think?"

Megan nodded again, trying to smile. "Yeah, you're probably right, I should talk to him, but for now I want to stay here, think things through. I feel like part of me is kind of screwed up. I want to think clearly for once."

"You know you are always welcome to stay," her mother said, patting her hand. "But I will tell you this much, when it comes to love, you can never think clearly. I would've thought you'd learned that by now."

"How long with this take?" Larry asked, standing at the controls.

"About three hours," Ben said, limping painfully over to the chamber. His knee continued to give him trouble and was only going to be worse by the time he was done.

"Three hours. You're kidding, right?"

"Nope, the last one took that long. We're only cutting this trip down by about half a day," Ben said, "but if things work out right, we'll never know."

"What do you mean?"

"Well, the past will change. We might be doing something else by this point in the future. Does that make sense?" Ben asked.

"No," Larry replied irritably. "Oh hell, what does it matter?"

Ben sat down in the chamber. His knee ached so badly it was making it difficult for him to think. "Okay, I'm ready when you are," Ben said grimacing.

"Are you all right, Ben?"

"Yeah, it's just my knee. It doesn't want to sit in this thing again."

"I wouldn't either," Larry grumbled.

"What was that?"

"Nothing, nothing," Larry said quickly. "I'm starting it up. Good luck!" The motor began to hum, and the swing arm took off. The surge of power and the distinctive blue haze Larry disliked so much began to encompass the machine. Small arcs of electricity began jumping all around the chamber. The haze got so thick it was difficult for him to see Ben inside the chamber. Within minutes, Larry's head began to ache, and he felt lightheaded. When his guts began to churn as he ran from the building. He only just made it outside when he gave up his lunch.

"God, I really hate that friggin thing," he said, holding his stomach.

Like before, the past flashed before him. When it finally stopped, Ben found himself looking out at a wall of darkness. He could no longer feel the pain in his knee, but he had a hard time understanding why the darkness prevailed in this place in the past. He wanted to move or see, something to give him some kind of control. Then, listening closely he heard a noise. It was breathing.

His breathing.

I'm asleep, that's why I can't see anything.

It was a little aggravating from his standpoint because he had no idea when or where he was. There was no way to gather any kind of information, other than how loud his breathing actually was. Then he heard a voice, soft and sweet voice. One he knew well. The eyes opened just a bit, like a brilliantly lit portal to the outside. Then he saw Becca through those hazy, half-opened eyes.

"Good morning, Sleepyhead," Becca said.

"Hi, Beautiful," Ben mumbled drowsily.

"I just came up to tell you that we were on our way... and to tell you how much I love you," she said, and then kissed him.

"Love you, too."

She ran her fingers gently through his hair. "Enjoy your day off. We'll see you tonight," she said before she left.

Get up! Get your ass up! Don't let them leave the house. If you ever want to see them again you had better GET UP!

Ben rolled over and stuck a pillow over his head.

That's not going to help you idiot, I'm inside of your head! Now, GET UP AND STOP THEM!

Ben pulled the pillow off of his head and threw it across the room. "Shut up, I just want to get some sleep."

AAAAAGGGGGHHHH! GET UP! GET UP! GET UP!

Out in the drive, he could hear the minivan start up.

Becca and the girls are in danger! If you do not stop

them, they are GOING TO DIE!

This got his attention.

"Why are they in danger?" he asked.

Car accident! They are going to die in a car accident on Sprinkle Road. The gas station out by the highway. A Semi hauling gasoline is going to pull out in front of them. If you don't leave now, THEY WILL NEVER COME BACK!

With a start, Ben threw back the covers and jumped from the bed; that was enough to convince him to get moving. Without bothering to get dressed, he ran down the stairs in his pajamas, grabbed the keys, and ran out the door. The engine on his BMW roared to life. He backed out of the drive and raced down Forest drive at breakneck speed.

You have to get to Sprinkle Road and cut them off.

"I know, I know. I'm trying," he said. With a short pause he asked, "Who are you? How do you know these things?"

I'm you. And no, you're not crazy. I know that's what you're thinking. Just trust me when I say I tell you something bad is going to happen unless you stop them now.

Without slowing, Ben turned out onto the main road. The BMW skidded sideways and narrowly missed the oncoming traffic. When it straightened out again, Ben pushed the car even harder, sprinting through traffic.

She will probably take Centre Street to Sprinkle.

Ben must have been listening closely to his voice now because he said, "What do you mean probably? You mean you don't know?"

I know where the accident is going to be, not how she gets there.

Sprinkle Road was just ahead, but traffic was stopped, waiting for the light to change. Ben cut through a gas station on the corner. The BMW dashed past the gas pumps, missing two cars and a skinny teenager walking back to his vehicle before coming out onto Sprinkle Road. Ben resumed his terrific speed as he scanned the traffic ahead of him, trying to spot the green Pontiac minivan that held his family.

"Tell me we're going to make it in time," he said.

I just don't know!

"Damn it, tell me we're going to make in time to stop them!"

A half mile up the road, Ben finally spotted the green minivan. He could also see the sign for the Speedway ahead in the distance. The BMW darted past two other vehicles, switching lanes at the same time before finally pulling alongside the green minivan. He could see Becca and the girls inside. He tried to honk the horn, but his hand disappeared through the steering wheel as if he were a ghost. Next the car began to dissolve around him. It was still moving forward, but the vehicle appeared to be coming apart in long strings of particles. Time began to slow, everything moving in almost a kind of freeze frame, segment by segment. He could not catch them. The minivan remained ahead of him. The gas station was less than a hundred yards away.

The top of the BMW fell away in a blur. Ben stood up in the driver's seat and began to scream while waving his arms in the air. Both cars were heading straight for the semi-truck. Ben could feel the last of the car disappear. He was moving through the air as if he were flying. His former body was only a shadow of a presence. The last thing he heard was a loud screeching of tires on pavement and felt the white-hot fire of an explosion.

Suddenly, the air became filled with a thick, acrid smell of smoke. It was coming out of nowhere, as if invading the memory of the past. Then, as if jerked away, Ben felt himself sliding once again as he was pulled into darkness, back towards the future, but even faster than before. The heady smell of smoke remained as his consciousness resettled in the present. His machine was in ruins. The chamber sat tilted on the floor. One of the supports had completely broken off. The swing arm had become twisted and was embedded into the framework. A small flame burned from the motor, and white smoke was rolling out of the control panel.

Ben climbed out of the chamber, stepping around the heavy chunks of broken glass, and began to survey the damage; something had gone seriously wrong. He couldn't understand why had the machine had torn itself apart. He attempted to wave the smoke away. "Larry, are you still in here!" he shouted. Ben conducted a quick search, but Larry wasn't to be found. He cut the power to the building and pushed the door open to let the smoke escape.

"Larry!"

Without receiving an answer, Ben made his way back towards the house. He made it as far as the patio door when Larry came running around the side of the house.

"I heard you yelling. What happened?" Larry asked.

"I'm not sure," Ben said. "Something went wrong. I couldn't stop them."

"Why? What happened?"

"I don't know. I remember going back into the past, but I wouldn't wake up. Then, I fell into the nightmare I used to have. You remember, don't you? The one where I wake up and go after them, make it down the road, almost caught up, and instead become engulfed in the explosion along with them. But then I wake up and the cops are at my door. How can that be? Why would I go back and fall into a dream of going after them?"

"Probably because you did," Larry said.

"What do you mean?"

"Maybe what you used to think of as a dream was really something that actually happened. Ben… did you ever consider that maybe you weren't made to stop them. Maybe time don't like to be messed with."

Suddenly, everything made sense. Time had a way of protecting itself—wasn't that what Becca tried to tell him. The only thing he'd accomplished was to get a glimpse into the past, to come to terms with it. Maybe that was all he really wanted all along.

Ben hung his head. "Time has a way of protecting itself," he said.

"What?" Larry asked.

"Something Becca tried to tell me," Ben said. "I was never going to save them."

Ben sat down hard on the ground, his knee throbbing, but he didn't really feel it. He pointed at the building. Larry appeared confused.

"What happened in there?" Larry asked as he noticed the smoke.

"I think I know," Ben said. "If Becca and the girls hadn't died in the car accident, I never would've built the machine. My life would've gone on as normal. I never would've thought of changing the past, much less building that damn thing. As soon as I tried to change the past, it swept me back here. I turned what I did into a dream, and the machine tore itself apart because I tried to go against the natural flow of time."

Larry sat down on the ground next to him. Ben simply stared at the building.

"When I was in that coma, Becca came to me. Don't think I ever mentioned it to you. I'm not even sure how much of it was real, but she told me something then, and I'm only just remembering it now. She told me that time didn't like to be messed with... that it has a way of taking care of things. She also said that sometimes, happiness comes from sorrow. I didn't know it at the time, but she was talking about me and Megan."

They both sat in silence for a minute or two longer.

"Do you know where I can find her?" Ben finally asked.

Larry shook his head. "No, but I'd be willing to bet that same hundred dollars you owe me she went to her folks. You might try there first."

"How many Jacksons do you think there are in Kalamazoo?" Ben asked.

"Couldn't say, but I've got the feeling you're about to find out."

CHAPTER 24

Joe cruised slowly past the Pearson house. He wasn't planning on making any kind of move during daylight hours, but he wanted to scope out the place, see if anyone was home. He had no idea if Hannah and Joey were still living there; she may have moved into a place of her own by now. That looked like a distinct possibility because her car wasn't in the driveway.

He pounded the steering wheel with his fist.

"Damn! I'll have to come back when it gets a little darker. If nothing else, I should be able to get George and Beverly to tell me where they are. They probably won't like the method I use to convince them to give me the information, but that's not my fault."

The voice of his murdered father crept back into his mind.

Do you really think you can do anything without screwing it up. You're such a miserable little—

"Shut up old man, you're dead!" he shouted, pounding his fist even harder on the steering wheel.

Oh, but I'm always here, Son. I'll be with you until the very end—which may not be very much longer. You'll screw things up again. To tell the truth, I'm counting on it.

He could almost hear the old man laughing at him.

"I hope you're burning in hell, old man," Joe said, but his voice was strained with emotion. "You were supposed to go away when I killed you. You were supposed to leave me alone." He waited for a reply, but none came. In need of sleep, Joe pulled into a nearby Burger King and parked the car. He climbed into the back seat and stretched out. The smell of fast food made his stomach growl, but he didn't want to eat. He closed his eyes and tried to get some sleep until it got dark. It was difficult to do, because inside his mind he could still hear the laughter of his murdered father haunting him.

Ben sat with the phone book open in front of him. After nearly an hour worth of phone calls, he was beginning to get discouraged, and he was only a little over halfway through the listings. The fact that the number could be unlisted was something he tried not to think about.

He picked up the phone and dialed the next number.

A woman answered after several rings.

"Hello, my name is Ben Stryker. I'm looking for Megan Jackson. I have reason to believe she is staying with her parents. I was hoping this was the right number to find her," he said. After numerous calls, Ben had pretty much memorized the introduction.

"I have a daughter named Megan," was the reply. "Are you the Ben she has been telling me about?"

"I suppose I am."

"I am Judith, her mother. Do you mean to tell me that you have been going through the phone book trying to find her?"

"Ah—yeah, I know that might seem a little stalker-ish, but it's very important that I talk to her. Is she there? Could I speak with her?"

"Nonsense, I think it's sweet that you would do that. She is here, but I want to know something first. Do you love her?"

"Um... that's something I thought I should discuss with Megan."

"If you want to talk to her, then I suggest you answer my question," Judith stated flatly.

Ben hesitated, but only for a moment. "Yes, I do, very much so."

"Good, then you can come over here and tell her yourself. The address is 2191 Gull Road. Do you know how to get here?"

"I think so. It's on the north side of town, right?"

"Yes, the house is near Northside Hospital on the corner of Market Street. I suggest you get here soon, Ben. I look forward to finally meeting you," she said, and immediately hung up.

Ben grabbed his keys and hobbled quickly from the house, leaving the front door wide open. He jumped in the car and took off down the street.

Larry and Amy witnessed the entire scene from their garage. Larry put his arms around his wife.

"He really is an idiot," Larry said.

"He's an idiot in love, that's all," Amy told him.

"I guess I'm an idiot, too, then."

"You better be," Amy shot back, smiling, and then kissed her husband. "Now, go close the front door for him, will you?"

"Why can't you do it?"

"Because I asked you too," she replied quickly.

"You're just as capable of doing it as I am."

"I have to finish cooking dinner. Now, please go close that door or you'll be making your own dinner tonight," Amy told him severe frustration showing in her voice.

Larry smiled. "Yes, Dear."

"You did that just to irritate me didn't you?" she asked as he walked away.

"Yep," Larry said, "it's my job."

Joey sat on the couch, watching a movie. He tried to focus on the movie instead of the nagging feeling he had in the pit of his stomach. It had followed him most of the day and he wasn't certain what was making him feel that way. There was an edge to it, as if danger was nearby. His instincts told him it was his father, but when he went into his safe room to search for his father's mind, he found nothing but darkness outside of the windows of his father's eyes.

Hannah came in and sat down next to her son.

"I like this movie," she said.

Joey nodded. "Uh huh... me, too," he said.

"Do you want me to make some popcorn?"

"I'm not hungry. My tummy has been doing flip-flops."

"Are you feeling all right? You're not sick, are you?" Hannah put her hand to his forehead. "You're not running a temperature." She dropped her hand and hesitated for a moment, looking at Joey. "It isn't anything else, is it?"

"You mean Dad?" Joey asked, and then shook his head. "No, that's what I thought, too."

A relieved look came across Hannah's face. "Well,

maybe the ice cream upset your stomach," she said. "I'll get you some medicine for it, okay?"

"Okay, Momma," he replied mildly. He didn't believe it was the ice cream, but it was as good as an explanation as any. "Where's Grandma?" he asked as his mother searched the medicine cabinet for a bottle of Pepto Bismal.

"She went to the church to help with the food bank. She called and said she would be home about nine."

Joey settled back into the movie. He had tried to contact Ben earlier in the day and got nothing. It was unusual, almost as if Ben had disappeared from the face of the earth. He decided if the feeling got any worse, he would try again.

Megan went into the living room where her mother and father were busy watching the evening news. She leaned over her father and gave him a quick hug and a kiss on the cheek.

"Bye, Daddy," she said. Her father grunted noncommittally, his eyes still on the television set.

"Where are you going?" her mother asked.

Megan let out a deep breath. "Home. I think it's time for me to go back."

"You can't," Judith told her. "Not yet, anyway."

Megan raised her eyebrows. "And why not?"

"Well… I think you should stay just a little longer, that's all. It's getting late… maybe you should stay the night."

"What's going on, Mother?" Megan asked suspiciously. "What are you up to?"

"Nothing, really," her mother replied quickly, and

then slowed her tone. "I suppose I should mention that your young man called here looking for you. I may have suggested he come here to talk to you."

"Mom, how could you?"

The doorbell rang; Megan glared at her mother.

"You did this. Go tell him I don't want to talk to him right now," Megan said, pointing to the door.

"No, Meg Dear, you have to face him. It's no good putting things off. You might as well do it tonight."

"Fine," Megan said, furious with her mother for starting the conspiracy… and with Ben for agreeing to it. She gathered her thoughts before opening the door. She found Ben on the bottom step, a sheepish grin on his face. With an angry push, Megan slammed the door shut behind her.

"Hi Megan," Ben said, trying to find her eyes. She avoided his gaze altogether.

"I don't think it is a good idea that we talk just yet," she said.

"I'm in love with you," he blurted out.

She stared at him, bewildered. "What?"

"I love you!" he said a little more firmly this time. "And I want to spend the rest of my life with you. That's if you don't mind."

She shook her head. "No, Ben, you don't. I will not…" she couldn't find words, her emotions twisted up in knots.

"Be hurt again," Ben finished for her.

"No. I won't be your second choice, Ben. Becca will always be first in your heart. I'll be the person you settled for."

Ben frowned. "I guess it would be easy to think that."

"It's the truth," Megan said stubbornly.

Ben watched as her blonde hair blew slightly with the evening breeze and her blue eyes became shiny, close to tears. She tried to hold them back, turning her head so he couldn't see. He held his hand out to her.

"Walk with me, okay? Just walk," he said.

"Why?"

"You don't have to, just come with me because you trust me."

"That isn't fair."

"I know, but I don't always play fair. I guess that is something you will have to learn about me."

Reluctantly, Megan reached out and took his hand. Ben led her along the sidewalk; a steady silence remained between them.

"I went back," Ben said. "I'm guessing you already know that."

Megan nodded; the breeze was again blowing her hair back from her face. "What happened?"

"I discovered that I'm not the same person I was. Neither are you."

"You couldn't change things?"

"Nope… and I never could. The past, it seems, is pretty well set."

"What about Becca? I know you still love her."

"There's a part of me that always will."

"What am I supposed to do with that?" Megan asked firmly, as if confirming what she had maintained all along.

"Like I said, we are different people now. Things are forever changed. There was one important thing I learned by going back. Becca was my past. You are my future. The whole time I was there, I could think only of getting back to you," Ben told her.

"How are we ever going to make this work, Ben?" Megan asked, her face showing the twisted agony she was feeling. Darkness had come and the streetlight flickered on overhead; Megan's face was highlighted against the light.

"How?" Ben shook his head. "That, I don't know. But I will tell you this—I love you just as much as I ever loved Becca, maybe more. There was a time I never thought I would be able to feel anything ever again, thought my heart had died along with her. You know that. But we found each other at the most desperate point of our lives. I don't know what the future holds, but I'm done with holding onto the past. I want to the future to be ours, Megan, not because I'm settling for you, or because I'm afraid of being alone, but because you're the only one I want." Ben paused, again trying to find her eyes. "I've never been one to talk of true love. Some people spent their entire lives searching for it. I've been lucky enough to find it... twice... in a lifetime."

"Damn it, Ben," Megan said, still trying to be angry, but losing the battle to do so. She sighed. "I do love you, Ben Stryker." She rested her head on his chest, and he surrounded her with his arms. Megan looked up at him and they kissed, holding each other tightly.

CHAPTER 25

Joe parked across the street from the Pearson's residence. No one had come or gone in the last two hours, and it was making him a little edgy. The house wasn't dark; the kitchen light remained, but he'd been around his in-laws long enough to know it was frequently left on. What he didn't like was the fact that Hannah's car was absent. Joe balled his fists in frustration and punched the inside of the door four times in rapid succession, resulting in bruised and bleeding knuckles. Time was running out on him. The police would surely be searching for the stolen car by now, and he had nowhere left to run. His father was right, the endgame was coming soon, but he refused to allow Hannah to escape his justice. She owed him, and she would pay—and so would the boy.

A moment later, a white sedan pulled into the drive. The headlights reflected off of the garage and red brake lights glowed brightly again the darkness before going off. Joe quickly jumped out of his car and crept up to the side of the house. When he saw Beverly get out of the car, he looked around to make sure she was alone. Approaching from behind, Joe grabbed her and squeezed her into a bear hug. Beverly gasped and tried to scream out for help, but Joe shoved his hand over her mouth and pulled her into the darkness.

"Where'd they go—Hannah and Joey—where are they?" he asked.

Beverly's eyes were filled with fear, but they cut involuntarily towards the house; he instantly knew that they were inside. From that point, her usefulness to him ceased. Joe put both hands around her neck, thinking of the way mousy boy had died. He wanted Beverly to suffer the same way. Joe dug both of his thumbs deep into her throat, but instead, he heard the bones in her neck snap and her body went limp.

He'd broken her neck.

Joe swore quietly to himself, unhappy with how quickly she'd died. He dragged her body to the back of the house and threw it into the flowerbed.

"You always did like flowers, didn't you, Mom," he said sarcastically, and chuckled at his own humor. He edged his way back to the side door and turned the door handle. Then he quietly bumped the door open with his shoulder to open it.

"They better be in here. Otherwise, I'm going to be bent," Joe said, and then slipped inside.

Ben and Megan strolled, hand-in-hand, back to the house. The warmth of her hand in his matched in every way, the warmth of his heart at this moment. His limp was slight. The pain had subsided and was all but forgotten in the midst of everything. If there had been a way to freeze this moment in time, he would do so, and play it over and over again. There had been one thing he had learned from all of this was, you only get to keep these moments for a brief time before you move on to the next. Life was like a river, flowing and moving. There was no way to know what was to come around the next bend, so it was important to recognize and live in every moment, because they would not come again.

Megan smiled, giving Ben a knowing smirk, and squeezed his hand gently. "You mean to tell me you called every Jackson in Kalamazoo trying to find me?" she asked.

"Not all of them—but damn near. I was on the phone for nearly an hour before I finally got your mother. And then she kind of took over, told me to get my ass over here to get you. Not exactly in those words, though."

She grabbed hold of his arm and held it as they walked. "Well, I'm glad you did."

"From the sounds of it you wouldn't have talked to me anyway. I guess I owe her one."

"Yeah, she's a sneaky one, isn't she? I always told myself that when I had a daughter—" Megan stopped suddenly. Ben knew why.

"Megan, I was serious when I said I wanted to spend the rest of my life with you," he said, then grasped both of her hands and looked deep into her blue eyes. "I'm not saying you have to answer me right away, but I want to marry you. I want us to have a family—maybe even try for you the daughter you've always wanted. You can think about it if you want. I know it's a lot to throw at you all in one day."

Her face lit up. "Do you honestly believe I would need to think about it? Seriously, after everything we've been through?" She grinned slyly, as if to toy with him a bit. "I suppose… if you really have your heart set on it… then yes, Ben, I will marry you," she said, kissing him again.

Ben held her off the ground as they did so.

"You know, for a moment, I was afraid you might say no," he said.

"Not on your life."

They stood outside the house, leaning against his car, still kissing. Megan pulled back just a bit; her arms folded around his neck. Ben held her around the waist, their bodies pressed together. "I want you, Ben Stryker," she said in a silky voice.

"Don't you think your parents would be a little disturbed by the sight?"

"Not here, Dummy!" she said giggling.

Ben suddenly dropped his smile. A blank stare replaced it.

"What's the matter?" Megan asked.

"It's Joey, he's in trouble. Oh, Good Lord, it's Joe. He's there, at their house. He intends to kill them." Ben grabbed the handle of the car. Megan pulled him back.

"How do you know that?" she asked.

"There's no time to explain," Ben said in a rush. "Call the police. Tell them Joe Murphy is at the Pearson home and they're all in danger."

"I'm coming with you. I didn't get you back just to lose you to that psycho. We'll call the police on my cell phone."

"I can't convince you to stay here?"

"No!"

"You're not going inside, no matter what," Ben said, as he got in the car. Megan got in on the passenger side and they took off, tires squealing.

Joey sat watching the ending of the movie with his mother. The credits began rolling on the screen just as his nerves suddenly ratcheted up another notch. He decided to try again and see if he could find his father. He closed his eyes and went into his room. Joey's breath caught when he realized what he was looking at was the side of their house. His father was right outside, standing beneath the kitchen window.

Joey opened his eyes. "Momma, we have to get out of here now! Dad is outside the house. I can see him!"

Hannah had a brief look of fear and dismay, but it changed quickly to one of determination.

"Joey, we can't leave. He'd catch us before we could get away. We're gonna have to hide."

Hannah took Joey's hand and led him into the kitchen. She opened one of the lower kitchen cabinets under the counter and looked inside; it had plenty of room for Joey to squeeze into. As a child, she'd hidden in this same cabinet when she wanted to be alone. No one had ever discovered her secret place, and she prayed it would protect her son the same way.

"Get in here and stay. Don't make a sound. If you hear me shout for you to make a run for it, you're to immediately go to the neighbor's house and call the police. Do you understand?"

Joey nodded.

"Otherwise, I don't get out of that cabinet, no matter what." She paused, gazing keenly at her son. "I love you, Joey. I hope you never forget that," she said softly, then quickly inserted Joey inside the cabinet.

"Momma, I don't want you to get hurt. He wants to kill you," Joey said pleadingly from his crouched position inside the hiding place.

"I don't want to die either, Honey. I'm going to do my best to get him before he gets me, and just maybe finish this once and for all."

Hannah closed the cabinet door and went into the living room. She didn't really have a plan. Hiding Joey had been her first priority, now she wanted something to kill that bastard with. Her father had kept a rifle in closet upstairs for deer hunting but sold it a few years back when his tromping through the woods got to be too much. Just then, the back door opened, and she could see Joe peering in. When he saw Hannah, he began to grin madly. "Hi, Honey!" he said in a spritely tone. "What? Aren't you happy to see me?"

Hannah didn't bother with a reply; instead, she took off across the living room and ran into the downstairs bathroom. Once inside, she closed and locked the door.

She could hear Joe calling out to her.

"Where are you, Babe? What, no hug and kiss for your dear husband? Such a shame, I brought something for you. But I can almost guarantee, you aren't going to like it—not one bit," he said with an increasingly menacing tone.

Hannah searched the bathroom for something she could use as a weapon.

Why didn't I grab a knife when I was in the damn kitchen.

She glanced into the mirror on the medicine cabinet and got an idea. Quickly, she grabbed a towel from the rack and hung it over the medicine cabinet. Then, with a quick blow, she used her elbow to smash the top corner of the mirror. Pulling back the towel, she found a shattered piece of mirror about ten inches long with the end narrowed to a point. Using her fingers along the edge, she pried it free of the frame, and then wrapped the towel around the end of it for a grip. It was not lost on her that she would only have one shot at this, and that her life, as well as Joey's, probably depended on it. She moved forward and silently unlocked the bathroom door. She stood poised with the mirror shard in one hand and the doorknob in the other, waiting to feel it turn.

"Come out come out, wherever you are," Joe said, taunting her again.

Hannah held her breath, hearing his voice, knowing he was close.

The doorknob turned just slightly in her hand. Hannah, knowing the deathly moment had arrived, gritted her teeth, yanked the door open, and rammed the broken piece of mirror into Joe's midsection. The mirror shard penetrated his body, breaking off just beneath his ribcage. Joe fell back, but managed to fire the gun twice, hitting Hannah once in the arm and once in the chest. The gunshots threw Hannah backwards. She landed against the bathtub, lying on the floor in a half-sitting position.

Joe fired two more shots at her out of anger, both missing her. He looked down and saw the embedded glass protruding from his flesh. Every time he took a breath it felt as if it was digging deeper into his flesh.

"Stupid Bitch, look what you did to me!" Joe shouted. He ripped open his shirt and looked down at the injury; the shard had splintered into several pieces, and he was bleeding profusely from the open wound. He tried to pull the largest piece from the wound; the pain began to make him ill as bright colored blood ran down his side, staining his pants. He gave up on that and grabbed a hand towel from the shelf to cover the wound.

He moved closer to Hannah and stood over her, his teeth locked as he glared at her.

"Where's Joey? Where's the little brat?" he demanded.

Hannah stared vaguely at him and shook her head the best she could, letting him know she wouldn't tell. Her eyes were beginning to look glassy and her breathing labored.

"I know you've hidden the little window-licker around here somewhere. Where is he?" Joe grabbed her hair and put his face close to hers. Hannah spat in his face. He wiped it with his sleeve. "That isn't very lady like." He stuck his finger in the wound on her arm, pressing hard. Hannah squirmed in pain. "Where is he?" Joe asked again.

Hannah shifted her eyes upwards, as if looking upstairs.

Following her eyes, he began to smile. People could be predictable when enticed by pain. "You're hiding him upstairs? Probably put him in the closet." Joe showed her the hunting knife. "Hannah, Dear, I just wanted you to know that the last thing you ever see in this life will be your precious son being carved up like a turkey on Thanksgiving. I just want you to hold on long enough to see that, okay, Honey? Do you think you can you do that?" he said, then returned the knife to the sheath and ran upstairs.

Joey sat in the kitchen cabinet in complete darkness. He closed his eyes and tried with all his might to contact Ben again.

Please, please, Ben! We are in trouble. My dad is here, and he wants to kill us. Get here as quickly as you can.

He could hear Ben's thoughts come back to him.

I'm coming, Joey. Just hold on.

Too frightened to even breathe, Joey listened as his father taunted his mother. A few minutes had gone by before he heard the scuffle and the shots. Joey's arm and chest burned with pain; he understood what it meant. Joey put his hand on the cabinet door, wanting desperately to go to his mother, but fought off the urge to do so. His eyes welled up with tears. She was dying and he had to remain in this dark space. It was the hardest thing he'd ever had to do.

Soon, Joey heard footsteps racing up the staircase to the second floor. He fought through his emotions and tried to think. They needed time until Ben could arrive with the police, and at the same time hope his mother could hold on that long. He closed his eyes and went into his safe room, looking out through the windows of his father's eyes. Joe was searching his bedroom, going through the closet. Joey got an idea; he wasn't sure it would work because he had never tried it before. Joey went to the microphone and turned up the volume. Then he did his best to duplicate his own image and projected it beneath the bed.

"I'm under here!" Joey shouted into the microphone.

When Joe turned, he received a flicker of an image of the kid under the bed. He rushed to the bed and swept his arm beneath it. He got nothing but air. Bending over increased the bleeding, the towel over his wound had become bright red. He grunted from the pain but got down on both knees to check under the bed. There was nothing there.

"Where are you, damn snot-nosed brat?"

Joey projected his image in his mother's bedroom across the hall.

"I'm in here," Joey said into the microphone.

Joe turned again and saw Joey in the other room, now waving at him from the bed. He got back to his feet and dashed into that other room, grabbing at the boy and landing on top of the bed. His son had disappeared once again.

"I don't know how you're doing it, but you'd better stop screwing around, Joey," Joe said, and then tried to soften his voice. "I just want to talk to you."

Joey moved his image into the hallway next. Joe took careful aim and fired three shots at the mirage; the bullets passed right through him. The Joey he saw grinned and ran down the hallway away from him.

By this time, Joe's head was swimming. He looked down at the towel; it was saturated with blood. The haunting voice of his father's had been right; he was not leaving this place tonight. Hannah had made sure of that.

Joe gritted his teeth and spat. If he was going to die so was that brat. He stumbled to the bottom of the stairway just in time to hear a voice that he'd not expected.

He'd never been so happy to hear that particular voice as he was right now.

Ben crept through the kitchen with Megan close behind. They could hear the television playing in the living room. Ben spotted a knife rack on the counter; he removed a knife and held it out in front of him. They'd contacted the police on the way over, but Ben, having only been to the house one time before, could only give them a general description of the location. The dispatcher told them that the police would be on the way and for them not to go into the house. Ben had disregarded that, determined to do his best to fend off Joe. In his thinking, Joe hadn't used a gun in any of his attacks so far, so it was unlikely he had acquired one now, especially with him being on the run. But a knife, that was different. Joe was almost certain to have a knife on him.

"Joey… Hannah!" Ben called out.

Ben and Megan moved into the living room. Ben shut off the television set. There was the slight chance that Hannah and Joey had escaped when Joe arrived. Turning on the spot, Ben saw that the bathroom door was open, and the light was on. He drew a deep breath when he spotted the bottom of Hannah's feet on the floor inside.

"Hannah!" Ben exclaimed and started for the bathroom. Just as he did, a shadow from the stairway moved and came into full view. It was Joe. He stood at the bottom step with the gun pointed at Ben. Ben stopped in his tracks, and then began slowly backing away.

"Well, hello, Ben," Joe said grinning savagely. "Why don't you be a pal and throw that knife into the kitchen, will you?"

Ben glanced down at the knife. He hated the idea of giving up the only weapon he had, but right now there wasn't much he could do. He pitched the knife into the kitchen and watched as it slid across the linoleum. "The police are on the way, Joe. They'll have this place surrounded in no time unless you leave now," Ben told him.

"Oh, I'm not going anywhere. My running days are through," Joe said, pulling the towel away from his wound, showing it to Ben. Joe tossed the blood-soaked towel to the floor. "My dear wife made sure of that. I just thought of something, we finally have something in common—both of us are widowers," he said chuckling, and then started coughing. The gun dipped just a little when he did. Ben took a step forward, but Joe held the gun up again. "I'd hoped to kill the little brat, too, but he has evaded me pretty well so far. He's hiding upstairs somewhere. I did end up with a great consolation prize. Never in my wildest dreams did I think you'd show up here tonight."

"Why would you want to hurt Joey?" Ben asked indignantly. "He's your son, for crying-out-loud."

"I have my reasons, but seeing how he has escaped my wrath," Joe said, while crossing over to the kitchen counter that separated the two rooms, "I guess you're the lucky one."

"I was pretty impressed with the way you siphoned off so much money from the firm without anyone noticing. I only found it by accident."

Joe laughed, and then began coughing again. His lips were stained red with blood. He leaned against the counter. His face had a drained look and his legs appeared shaky.

Ben continued on, “What did you do, transfer all that money in a separate bank account down in Florida?”

Joe shook his head faintly. “It was in a safety deposit box. It was my own little nest egg. The money they owed me for the humiliation I endured the first few years of working for the firm.”

“How did you get— “

“Enough!” Joe shouted. His eyes narrowed as his gaze went to Megan. “What are you doing here? You’re the neighbor, right? Married to that loudmouth lawyer,” he said. Then it dawned on him. He looked back and forth between the both of them. “Oh, this is priceless. Ben Stryker, messing with the neighbor’s wife. Is that it?”

Ben backed up, trying to get in front of Megan. “This is between the two of us, Joe. She has nothing to do with it.”

Joe gave him a hacking laugh. “I’m only interested in one thing…” he said sternly as he raised the Glock and fired a single shot at Megan, “…and that’s making you suffer.”

Astounded, Ben watched as she fell. He got down on his good knee and held her head and shoulders in his arms. Blood stained the blouse above her heart. In the distance, the sound of the police sirens could be heard. It wasn't long before the flashing red and blue lights appeared through the window.

“Sorry we don’t have more time, Ben. I really would’ve loved to have drawn this out a little more, but it’s time for you to die,” Joe said, pointing the gun at him. Ben closed his eyes and braced himself. But all he heard was a click.

The gun was empty.

When Ben opened his eyes, he saw Joey kneeling on the counter behind Joe; he was holding something in his hands.

"Hi, Dad," Joey said with a severe tone.

Joe turned, not registering the fact that the boy was holding Ben's kitchen knife.

"So, there you are," Joe said weakly, his eyes sullen, his face white as a sheet. The gun slipped from his hand and fell to the floor. Joe casually glanced at the knife pointed at his chest and then held out his arms as if daring his son. "Go ahead, Joey. I don't blame you." Joe smiled a gruesome smile; there was blood showing on his teeth and around his mouth.

"I don't want to," Joey admitted. His voice shook with fear. "But I will if I have to."

"Oh, you want to," his father said cruelly. "I killed that bitch you called mother, isn't that enough? I know damn well you want to. Don't lie to me, Junior. We are just alike."

"We are nothing alike," Joey replied coolly. "Besides, I know something you don't."

"What is that?"

"You're already dead."

"Not yet," Joe said. Fumbling, Joe reached for his hunting knife but lost the handle. It tumbled to the floor. His eyes now appeared drowsy as he looked down at the knife. To him, it appeared a million miles away. He staggered one, and then two, steps. His legs gave out and he fell hard to his knees. It seemed like an eternity before his large frame finally leaned over and toppled to the floor, dead.

Joey dropped the knife, jumped down, and immediately ran to the bathroom. He sat down beside his mother and held her hand.

"Momma, can you hear me?"

Hannah opened her eyes, but they were heavy and unfocused. She saw Joey and a slight smile came over her face, as if gratified to have held out long enough to know her son had survived.

Then her eyes closed again.

"No, Momma, No!" Joey yelled.

Joey closed his eyes and went into her mind. Again, it was the living room, the same room located only a few feet away from him right now. The bright light was there already, shining through the kitchen. Hannah was already beginning to walk into it.

Joey grabbed her hand, trying to pull her back. "No, you can't go, Momma. You can't!"

Silhouetted by the light, Hannah looked back at him. "I'm sorry, Honey. I know it's hard for you to believe, but things will be alright. I will miss you more than you know. You are an incredible son and an incredible person, even so young. You are so loving, so giving. I couldn't be prouder of you. Now I must ask you to be strong and go on without me. We are only given one thing in this life, and that is time. I'm just glad that I got to be your mother and that I got to spend some of that time with you."

Hannah moved closer to the light. Joey held on to her with everything he had.

"No, Momma. Please don't go. Please, please, Momma!"

"Goodbye, Joey. I love you!"

She slipped from his grip and disappeared into the light. Joey lay on the floor, heartbroken and crying.

Ben propped Megan in his lap and held her. Her eyes were shut, and her breathing appeared shallow. "Megan, talk to me," he said urgently. When he got no immediate response, he turned his eyes skyward. "Please God, don't take her from me," he prayed.

"You really do love me, don't you?" she said, her eyes open now.

Ben smiled and let out a brief laugh, partly out of relief. "Yes, yes, I do! And I'd prefer that you hung around a while."

Megan grimaced a little and then tried to smile back at him. "I'll see what I can do; after all, you already promised to marry me and everything. Can't let you out of it that easily."

The police rushed into the house with their guns drawn. Ben pointed to the body lying on the floor and explained what happened.

Megan shifted uncomfortably and looked to Ben. "Ben, go check on Hannah and Joey," she said. "I'll be okay."

Ben waved a police officer to his side. "Take care of her. I'll be right back," he said getting up slowly. The police officer appeared a little uncomfortable with the request but said nothing. He took Megan's hand as if to comfort her. When Ben arrived at the bathroom door, he took pause at the scene. Hannah's eyes were closed, and her skin was a pale, ashy color. Ben picked up her wrist and found she was cold to the touch. He checked for a pulse and found none. Joey was seated on the floor beside her with his legs crossed. His eyes were closed and his hand still clutching his mother's.

"Joey." Ben shook the boy. "Can you hear me?" There was no response. He was breathing, but it appeared as if he was deep in a trance.

"Joey!" he shouted.

The paramedics pushed past him to get to Hannah. Ben used the opportunity to pick up Joey and move him out of the bathroom.

"Joey, if you can hear me, please wake up," Ben said softly into his ear. "I know it's hard to do, but please, open your eyes and come back to me."

There was no way to know if Joey could hear him or not. It didn't matter because the little boy was not coming back.

CHAPTER 26

Joey sat in his safe room with the blinds down. He'd pulled his knees up to his chest and his arms wrapped around them, staring blankly ahead. Everything he had in the other world was gone. He stayed here because he didn't have the will or the strength to go back.

Suddenly, the back door opened, flooding the room with light. A little girl stepped into the room. She walked delicately around the chair and faced Joey. If it hadn't been for the blue dress she wore, it might have taken him a little longer to recognize her.

"Hi, Joey," Tia said. Her eyes were bright, almost as if that same brilliant light she had emerged from was a part of her. Joey could tell that she was trying to hold onto her physical form in order to speak to him now.

"How'd you get here?"

"Who do you think has been helping you all this time?"

"That was you?"

Tia nodded. "Not just me. My Mom and sister helped."

"How?" Joey didn't even know how to begin to ask how she had done it. She already appeared to understand his question.

"It's not an easy to explain. Our spirits live on in both the past and the present, but we are not allowed into this world. When Daddy made that thing in the backyard, it opened a kind of crack or doorway we could go through," she paused, almost sadly, "only the door will soon be closed."

"Can I see my Momma one more time, please? Will you go get her?"

Tia bit her lip and shook her head. "I can't. The reason I came here was to get you to go back. It's not good for you to stay here."

"I don't want to. There's nothing left for me there."

"There is something there for you. My Daddy wants you there—and Aunt Megan, too." Tia moved closer to him and put her hand on his. Joey felt a weird surge of power emanating from her touch; it was both strange and exciting, like being plugged into some strange cosmic outlet. "I know how hard it's going to be without your Momma. I still miss my Daddy sometimes," she said, "but things change, they always do."

The mention of his mother, combined with Tia's touch, sent a momentary sense of her being through him. He realized they were connected, they were all connected—Tia, her mother, his mother, his grandfather—they were all linked together somehow. His mother would know he was here, would be able to see and hear him. Joey sensed her, but could not see, couldn't touch, couldn't communicate with her. She was lost to him in that spirit world. Joey yanked his hand away as eyes welled up with tears. He shook his head and put his head into his hands, trying not to cry.

"Joey, if you don't leave, you'll be trapped here," Tia pleaded.

"I don't care!" he shouted angrily.

Tia frowned and began moving back toward the door. She looked back at him one last time. "When you leave here, you'll no longer have the gift I loaned you. It was a terrible thing for you sometimes, I know. I'm sorry about that. It was the only way I could help you."

Joey became even angrier when he heard this. "Why didn't you use it to help me save my mother then?" he screamed at her.

"We wanted that just as much as you did, but things don't always work out the way we want. She gave her life to save you. It was a choice she made gladly. Don't throw it away."

Tia moved back towards the door and the brilliant light shining through it.

"Goodbye, Joey," she said sadly, and moved into the light. The door closed, and he was alone once again.

Ben stood beside Megan's hospital bed and held her hand. The doctor had sedated her, and she was sleeping soundly. The bullet had passed below the left clavicle. The doctor had considered her lucky. Had the bullet had struck her another six inches lower, she very well could've been killed.

Ben ran his hand along her arm in long, soft strokes, feeling the softness of her skin. The door opened, Larry and Amy entered.

"How is she?" Amy asked.

"The doctor says she's going to be alright," Ben said. "She wouldn't even be in here if I'd made her stay in the car."

"Yeah, and you would be dead. And it would be

Megan standing at the funeral home right now," Larry said quickly.

Ben glanced up at him, knowing it was the truth. If Joe hadn't used that last bullet on Megan, Joe would've shot him instead. Ben had been standing only feet from Joe, and even as bad off as Joe had been, there was no doubt the bullet would have been fatal.

"Still—" Ben muttered.

"Don't tell me that would've been better. If you were to ask Megan, you know damn well she would tell you she would suffer through this rather than lose you," Larry said.

"Do you always have to be right?"

"No, just when it's important," Larry shot back. "By the way, how's little Joey doing?"

Ben shook his head, "No change. The doctor says there is nothing wrong with him physically, he's just gone away."

"I can't say as I blame him," Amy said. "He lost his entire family at the hands of his father. I think I would be comatose myself if that happened to me."

"That's not even half of it," Ben said.

"What do you mean?" she asked. Ben looked at Larry for a second.

"Nothing," Ben said, unwilling to share Joey's secret. "He's just had a lot to deal with."

"Well, I'm going to go down and visit him for a little bit," Amy said. "He's such a sweet boy. I just wish there was something I could do. What room is he in?"

"Room 324, on the south side," Ben told her.

"I'll go with you," Larry said. "See you later, Ben."

As they turned to go, Larry took his wife's hand. A silent look passed between them. Amy smiled at her husband, and they left.

Several hours passed and Ben remained at Megan side. Finally, she shifted slightly under the covers and slowly opened her eyes.

"Hi, Beautiful," Ben told her.

Megan smiled. Her voice was soft. "Do you remember when you said that to me the morning after Christmas?"

Ben nodded. "I didn't think you heard me."

"I did. I think that's when I first fell in love with you."

Ben grinned. "And I'm so happy that you did." He leaned forward and kissed her.

Megan moved her arm to put it around his neck but grimaced with pain. She dropped that arm immediately. "Ouch! I don't think I'll be using that for a while," she said, then lifted her other hand to put it on the side of his rough and unshaven face.

"I'm so sorry you ended up in here, Megan. God, if anything would've happened to you."

"Don't be sorry, Ben. I'm going to be okay. Let's just be thankful we're still alive," she said, and then asked him what she already suspected. "What about Hannah?"

Ben shook his head. There was a long pause. "Joe killed her mother, Beverly, too. They found her body out back."

Tears began to spill from Megan's eyes.

"And Joey?" she asked.

"He's alive, but he's in shock or something. I think he's locked himself up inside of his own mind, kind of protecting himself. I just don't know what to do for him," Ben said quietly.

"I thought you two had a special way of

communicating."

"We do, but it was Joey that could do it, not me," Ben said.

"Maybe he just needs some time."

Ben nodded half-heartedly. "Maybe."

Megan nodded as well, and then something in her look let him know she changed her mind. "Oh, Ben. Just go to him. See if you can, you know, get to him."

"I don't think it'll work, Megan. Joey—"

"Just try, alright," she said abruptly. "He'd do the same for you, wouldn't he?"

"Yes, yes, he would. Joey would've probably already been down there," Ben said chuckling.

Ben stood beside Joey's bed. The little boy lay peacefully with his arms at his sides. It looked as if he were sleeping.

"Joey, can you hear me?"

There was still nothing, not that he expected it to be that easy. Ben took a deep breath and closed his eyes this time. He tried to remember exactly how the little safe room they had made looked and felt. Then he did his best to see the over-large windows, to the feel of the chair. After several minutes, he opened his eyes again. "This is ridiculous," he said and began to walk away. He got halfway across the room before looking back at Joey; he knew Joey wouldn't have given up so easily.

"Okay, Ben, you can do this. Joey is counting on you."

He closed his eyes again and tried to think of the room again. This time it began to grow clearer in his mind, but there was no substance to it; it was just an image. He opened his eyes again and gripped the rail on the hospital bed. "Joey, you have got to help me here," he pleaded. "How do I get to you?"

Another memory came to mind. He was standing graveside at George Pearson's funeral and Joey was speaking to his mind, giving him courage. Ben closed his eyes and focused on that feeling. Suddenly, he found himself walking in darkness, his feet silent as they hit the ground. His hand was out in front of him. He was being pulled along by someone or something, but he couldn't quite make out who or what it was. A doorway opened and his vision became flooded with light. As he went inside, the room became clearer in his mind, and a chair became solid beneath him. Ben found Joey sitting next to him.

"How did you get here?" Joey asked him. His voice was flat, holding no emotion.

"It wasn't easy, I can tell you that."

Joey slumped down into his chair, folding his arms in front of him.

"You don't look very happy to see me," Ben said.

"What do you want?" Joey asked without looking at him.

"I came to get you."

"I'm not going," Joey stated.

"C'mon, Joey. You can't stay here."

Joey glared at him stubbornly, his jaw locked and his bottom lip sternly protruding.

"Okay—yes. You could stay here," Ben conceded, "but I want you to come back with me. I won't lie to you, it'd probably be a whole lot easier for you to just give up and stay here. It's hard to go on when you've lost the people that are dearest to you, I know. If I had one of these rooms when Becca and the girls died, I never would've left it, either. I'd probably be in a bed just down the hall from you right now."

Joey unfolded his arms and looked skeptically at Ben. "I can't do it. I can't go back. It hurts too much."

"It'll be tough, I'll grant you that. And it will probably get harder before it gets easier. There will be days when it will be damn near impossible for you to get out of bed. There will be times when your memories are going to haunt you—try to hurt you. Later, you'll start to feel as if you're finally climbing out of the darkness, only to be knocked back down again. Then, the day comes when you get back on your feet, and the pain is all but gone, and a part of you will want to feel guilty about it because it feels like you are leaving them behind. The thing is, it does get better, and I'll be there with you Joey, every step of the way."

Joey appeared to be thinking about it; Ben didn't push him.

"I don't know where I'll live, where I'll stay," Joey said finally.

"You'll stay with me. Well, with us. With me and Megan."

"Are you sure you want me to live with you?"

"Yes. There's nothing I would want more, but the decision is yours."

"And Megan... she won't mind?"

Ben smiled. "No, she won't mind. She's just as worried about you as I am. As a matter of fact, she was the one who told me to come down here and help you out of this. To be honest, I'm not even sure how I pulled this off.... unless... you?"

Joey shook his head. "No, it wasn't me," he said, pausing, "but I think I know who it was."

Ben gave him a quizzical look. "Who?"

He knew of only one person that had the power to make it happen. The girl in the blue dress. "I'll tell you another time," Joey said.

"Well, what do you think?"

"I'll do it. I don't want to, but—" Joey bowed his head and whispered, "—I know my mom would want me to," he said, and then looked to Ben. "Do you ever stop missing them so much?"

"You never stop missing them," Ben said. "But it gets easier once you let them be a part of your heart and carry them with you that way. Unfortunately, there's only one way to do that, and that's with time. So, do you want to give it a shot? Be a part of my family?"

Joey nodded. It wasn't enthusiastic, but Ben was willing to take what he could get. They got up and Ben held Joey's hand. Ben was about to open his eyes when he heard Joey again.

"It's not working," Joey said, closing his eyes then opening them again several times.

"What isn't working?"

"Going back—I can't go back. I'm stuck here."

Ben was confused. "Why? What's the matter?"

"I don't know. It's usually pretty easy to do. Now, no matter what I do, all I see are these walls."

Ben turned and looked at the door at the back of the room.

"What about the door? We made it to escape, remember?"

"What if it doesn't work?"

"Then we'll figure something else out," Ben said. "I'm not leaving here without you."

They went to the door. Ben reached out for the door

handle. Joey pulled on his hand to stop as Joey paused to look around at the room one last time.

"Once I leave, I'll never be able to come back," Joey said.

"Is that really a bad thing? I mean, do you really need it anymore?"

"I know, but..." Joey knew he would no longer have the gift once he left. As dark and painful as it had been, there had been times he enjoyed the kind of insight and power it gave him. He gave a sigh of sadness and of relief at the same time. "Okay, I'm ready," he said.

Ben opened the door; as they expected, it was deep and dark.

"Keep holding on to my hand, Joey, don't let go," Ben said, remembering when it was Joey who led them out the first time. They walked through the door together.

When Joey opened his eyes, he found Ben looking down at him. "It's good to have you back, Kid," Ben told him.

Joey tried to smile, but it faltered quickly. "You said it gets harder before it gets easier."

"It does. Not gonna lie to you about that," Ben said, "but time has a way of healing. And as someone very dear once told me, happiness sometimes comes from sorrow. You just have to wait for it."

The End

www.ingramcontent.com/pod-product-compliance
Lightning Source LLC
Chambersburg PA
CBHW060349260626
47160CB00006B/2255

* 9 7 8 1 6 0 3 0 7 2 8 0 9 *